The Ruby Ring

The Ruby Ring

a novel

DIANE HAEGER

THREE RIVERS PRESS · NEW YORK

Reader's Guide copyright © 2005 by Three Rivers Press, an imprint of the
Crown Publishing Group, a division of Random House, Inc.

This is a work of fiction. Names, characters, places, and incidents either are
the product of the author's imagination or are used fictitiously.

Published in the United States by Three Rivers Press, an imprint of the
Crown Publishing Group, a division of Random House, Inc.,
New York.
www.crownpublishing.com

THREE RIVERS PRESS and the Tugboat design are registered
trademarks of Random House, Inc.

Library of Congress Cataloging-in-Publication Data
Haeger, Diane.
The ruby ring : a novel / Diane Haeger.—1st ed.
1. Luti, Margherita, 16th cent.—Fiction. 2. Raphael, 1483–1520—
Relations with women—Fiction. 3. Raphael, 1483–1520—Death and
burial—Fiction. 4. Artists' models—Fiction. 5. Rome (Italy)—Fiction.
6. Convents—Fiction. I. Title.
PS3558.A32125R83 2005
813'.54—dc22
2004016396

ISBN 1–4000–5173–8

Printed in the United States of America

Design by Karen Minster

10   9   8   7   6   5   4   3   2   1

First Edition

To Rebecca Seltzner,
for your encouragement,
support, and love.

Acknowledgments

WHILE THIS IS A WORK OF FICTION, THE STORY IS BASED on the actual discovery of a ruby ring that lay hidden for over five hundred years beneath a thin layer of paint on Raphael's very sensual painting *La Fornarina* ("The Baker's Daughter"). The mystery was ignited in 2002 during a cleaning and X-ray at the Palazzo Barberini in Rome. By whose hand the ring was hidden, and the full reason for concealing it, may never be known. This novel explores one possible scenario.

As with all works incorporating the imagination, some of the dates, character ages, and full Italian names have been altered, and the span of time between some events has been condensed for the sake of continuity. Tying together the ring's discovery with notions and suppositions that history has left are the sixteenth-century writings of Giorgio Vasari, the nineteenth-century research of Rodolfo Lanciani, and also the later work of Vincenzo Golzio. I am also grateful to the work of Konrad Oberhuber concerning the subject of Raphael and Margherita.

I owe a personal debt of gratitude to Professor Susana Salessi for her patient guidance with the nuances of the Italian language, as well as with the translation of the Renaissance sonnets; to Antonio Cintio, Massimo Avitabile, and Danilo Patané, for arranging things in Rome so seamlessly; to my incredible agent, Irene Goodman, and my editor, Rachel Beard Kahan, for her truly extraordinary care with this book; and finally to Ken, Elizabeth, and Alex, who followed me eagerly in search of the long-forgotten pathway through the lives of Raphael and Margherita because it is what you do. Your devotion and support remain my inspiration.

The way my heart sees you, your beauty is clear.

But my very faithful paintbrush cannot compare it.

My love for you weakens all else.

FROM THE SONNET WRITTEN ON A SKETCH
BY RAPHAEL

The
Ruby
Ring

PROLOGUE

Rome, 1520

SHROUDED IN A CLOAK AND HOOD OF MIDNIGHT-BLUE velvet, Margherita stood silently amid the deep and mournful sound of tolling bells. They resonated across the cold, vaulted office chamber—a call to matins at the convent of Sant'Apollonia. Folds of luxurious fabric rippled around her, edged with swirls of gold thread, cascading like a rich, blue waterfall, and concealing a body as beautiful as it was notorious.

Her face was nearly obscured as she stood, stone still, on the uneven gray slate floor inside the sparse room with soaring white-washed walls, and adorned with a large crucifix. Only her eyes were visible to the two elderly nuns, both dressed in flowing muslin habits of pale gray, with stiff white collars and black wimples. Both peered up at her from behind a wide oak desk.

But Margherita's eyes, deeply brown and flecked with gold, spoke volumes.

They were the eyes that Rome had seen re-created in a dozen different likenesses. Paintings and frescoes. Portraits, innocent and seductive. Most scandalously, the image of the Madonna. That such a grand *mastro* had dared to paint his own mistress, in that way!

She made no sound. Words had been beyond her since the moment of his death. Now there was nothing but the great hollowness that had taken possession of her, even as the well-dressed young man beside her argued on Margherita's behalf.

"I am sorry, Signor Romano, what you ask is now impossible. We cannot take her."

"But *Mastro* Raphael requested it a fortnight ago! I brought the request to you myself!"

"I am afraid I have been reminded that it is not our custom to take so infamous a woman into our sisterhood for the expressed purpose of protecting her. Not when she will not willingly repent her past."

"Her coming here after his passing was agreed to! Nothing was said about her open repentance as a condition!"

The abbess drew in a rheumy breath then coughed behind a veined hand as she leaned to her side, listening to the nun beside her. A moment later she calmly said, "There has been an objection."

"Pray, who could object to what has already been arranged?"

"Cardinal Bibbiena came to see me yesterday."

Margherita heard the name without surprise. Memories, moments in time, circled in her mind like black crows. *So Your Grace has your revenge at last.*

"You understand, of course, why he is opposed to this," Giulio Romano argued on.

"I do. Yet it changes nothing. The cardinal is a very wealthy and powerful man."

"One who made Signor Raphael the richer."

"But as you so wisely observed, Signor Raphael now is dead. And even *she* cannot be protected forever from the scandal they created."

As the two stoic nuns exchanged another glance, Giulio drew from his own dark cloak, edged in silver thread, a black velvet pouch full of gold florins. He had spent the last ten years of his life anticipating the needs of the great master, and he was driven to honor him in death with that same loyalty. With a flourish, he tossed the pouch onto the desk between the two old women.

"One hundred gold florins. And if that does not suffice, there shall be more. The *mastro* meant to see Signorina Luti safe here now that he has—"

He did not speak the jarring word himself, and Margherita knew that had been for her benefit. Giulio, with his tawny, smooth-skinned face and gentle smile, had been so good and loyal, such a talented painter in his own right. And now greatness lay before him as it once had for Raphael. That fact was bittersweet, no matter how much she cared for Giulio.

At twenty-six, Margherita felt older and more jaded than the two ancient women who now sat in judgment of her. This was her life now, and the love of that life, the focus of her existence for the last six years, was lying cold and alone in a marble coffin, at the tragically young age of thirty-seven.

She closed her eyes for a moment as Giulio did her further bidding. The truth was, she did not care what became of her now. She could spend the rest of her days in the convent of Sant' Apollonia, or she could return home to become a spectacle back in her family's bakery, if they would even take her. And yet it should not have come to this. He had so much more to accomplish, so much more to paint. Someone else now would be named architect for the new Saint Peter's, and the great Raphael would one day be nothing more than a footnote in Vatican history—if Bibbiena had his way.

"Five hundred gold florins to the convent."

The nun's counteroffer in a voice holding no emotion, shook Margherita and she looked back down at the spindly, aged woman with her parchment-pale face and sunken dark eyes. Margherita would be safe here, yes. But this place was also to be her punishment.

"The florins . . . *and* the ring."

Margherita felt herself go cold. She had not seen the blow coming. Instinctively, she curled her hand into a fist as if to protect the jewel she wore.

Amid the stunned silence Giulio's honest eyes were eventually upon her, and they urged agreement. He was only doing as the *mastro* had bid him, the wide gray green eyes silently pleaded.

In her mind, she saw the painting still on Raphael's personal easel, so newly completed—an image of Margherita herself seductively smiling, happy, with their whole lives before them. He had painted her alluring, in only an exotic turban wound through her glossy hair, a sensual strip of shimmering gauze across her naked body, and a band on her arm bearing his name, Raphael Urbinas, as a sign of his love and possession. It had been a declaration that she was, and always would be, his . . . and, as if to punctuate that claim, there, too, was her betrothal ring painted boldly on her finger.

Please give her more florins instead! she longed to cry out. *Give her anything but this ring!* For who alive now in this world but she knew what it symbolized?

"Three hundred florins and the ring. That is my final offer," said the nun, her face pale and flat, void of expression or color.

Glancing down, Margherita saw the nun's old, veined fingers curled like a claw around the turn of the desk. And she saw the simple gold band on the woman's left hand. So that was to be her penance. A symbol of undying love between a man and woman, her priceless ruby, was to be exchanged on her hand for the plain band of the bride of Christ. The irony of that did not escape her.

It was at last agreed upon and Margherita became nothing more than a silent witness to the arrangement of her future. Only then did she and Giulio walk somberly out and stop beside the convent gate, the walls around them covered in a sadly faded fresco. There, they bid one another a final farewell beneath a stone arch leading out into the street. As Raphael's most trusted assistant held her tightly against his chest in an afternoon sun that shimmered a fiery opalescent orange, Margherita felt the familiar sting of tears. His strength reminded her of Raphael.

"I shall see your private painting into good hands," he whispered against her cheek.

"It does not matter. Nothing does anymore."

"Come now. You are still a young and beautiful woman."

"A woman forever marked."

"Nonsense." He smiled unconvincingly at her, and she thought then how Giulio had always worn his heart on his sleeve. "Remain here for a time, until things calm down a little. A year, perhaps two. Then you shall be free to make a new life."

But Raphael had forever changed each of them and, for an instant, their shared grief was a balm. She looked up into Giulio's kind, calming expression.

"What will you do with it?" She had meant Raphael's final, sensual portrait of her—the one that bore all of their secrets. The one meant as a wedding gift to her.

"When the time comes, I shall see it into safe hands. But, for your sake, not as it was." He had altered the portrait to protect her. As much as she understood it, that fact brought her great pain. He lowered his gaze and tone. "Cardinal Bibbiena still despises the two of you for what he believes you cost his niece. I must see to it that your enemies have been mollified when it is time for you to emerge from this place."

She kissed his cheek, but her own face was without expression as she felt the ring with her thumb for a few desperate moments longer, still secure on the finger onto which Raphael himself had slipped it. "Many thanks, *mi amico,* but I shall not be coming out of this place. We both know that."

"I will be back to see you in a few days once you are settled. We shall speak of it then."

"Do not come, Giulio."

"But the *mastro* would want—"

She stilled his words with the tip of her finger, and the small ruby ring glinted in the last light of what was now a fiery red Roman sun. "It will only hurt us both more if you do, and remind us of times that no longer are, nor can ever be again."

He looked away from her and out into the Piazza Sant'Apollonia, as they stood clinging to one another one final time. "He was always a great artist—*you* made him a better man," Giulio murmured, his voice breaking.

"And you were the friend with whom he shared everything," Margherita said in return. "He trusted you."

"And I shall never betray that trust."

"Now, you must go before someone sees you here with me. You have such a brilliant career of your own ahead of you."

"Only your protection matters to me."

Her smile was bittersweet. "He loved you, as well," she said softly. "He would want you to thrive and prosper now. Was that not what all of your years and work together was about? Honor him by making *that* matter to you most of all."

Wrapping her arms around herself, she watched him walk away from her then, and out into the crowded street. Her eyes followed him until he was lost amid the shoppers, horse carts, and tall, crumbling buildings of the Piazza Sant'Apollonia. Turning slowly, she walked back through the convent gates, preparing to surrender the last dear thing she had in all the world. She could no longer bear to remember the scandalous life she had lived . . . or think of what might become of the precious ruby ring, and why a simple baker's daughter from Trastevere had come, for a moment in time, to wear so priceless and exquisite a thing.

Part One

OCTOBER
1514

An old story,
but the glory of
it is forever.

Virgil

❧ 1 ❧

IT WAS A COLD AND DARKLY CLOUDED AFTERNOON AS
Margherita made her way down the narrow, cobbled streets of the
neighborhood called Trastevere, shielded by a tangle of shoppers,
merchants, stray dogs, oxcarts, and gangs of children. The air
smelled of horses, sheep, and drying laundry that flapped between
buildings above her. Before her father could ask her to draw the
dozen fresh loaves of *baccio* from the blazing bread ovens she had
slipped out the open door of the bakery, carrying the dozing toddler on her hip. It was the only way to get a moment's peace.

Cloaked in a midnight-blue wool cape and a simple green
cloth dress, she had vanished the moment all of the waiting cus-
tomers had been served. Surely Letitia could assist Father a bit
more for a change. It might actually benefit her sister, she thought
with a rueful little smile, to do something other than complain
about life's unfairness, and the lack of leisure time, when she continued to insist upon producing children in such rapid succession.

Walking briskly away from the Via Santa Dorotea, Margherita
passed a toothless woman, her face a patchwork of wrinkles, and a
garland of garlic wrapped around her neck, as she sat before a
shop bearing cows' heads and pigs' feet hanging from bloody
strands of rope. Above the shop on the narrow, shadowy street
were large windows barred with heavy iron grates. The massive
wooden doors between street-front shops were studded and
bolted in iron as well. Even in this weather she was glad to be outside, glad it would rain soon. Her mother, God rest her soul, had

said that the rain always washed away the predictable and brought with it possibilities, and she, too, liked to believe that.

Putting a sleeve across her nose, she moved away from the gutter where a blue-black sludge and rancid piles of horse dung had gathered tainting the air. She passed the busy fish market, and the vendors calling out their prices, amid the pungent smell of the day's catch. Such a tangle of odors, and so much activity. Nearby was an apothecary shop, a grocer, and, beyond that, a grand stone stable block for the nearby villa of the powerful banker Agostino Chigi. Her sister's husband, Donato, worked there as a stableman.

She held her cherub-faced little nephew, Matteo, who adored her especially, close to her chest beneath her cloak as she walked with brisk purpose onto the Via della Lungara toward the wildly opulent Chigi Villa. *To dream is to live,* her sainted mother had also taught her from the time she was old enough to understand the words. And dreams were the only way out of a predictable existence. Here, away from Trastevere and the bakery, she could make herself believe she was almost equal to the women of means who moved around her. Here, she too was simply a woman, with a child, out on a day's errand. Free to breathe, and to imagine. The baby's presence would keep men, and their unwelcome attentions, at bay.

Moving nearer, her heart began to race with anticipation, as it always did, as the majestic manor on the banks of the flowing Tiber came into view. *Dio!* she thought, feeling the warm rush of freedom's pleasure as she quickened her pace, avoiding more pools of sludge, and pockets of litter and dung, along the path. She felt her smile broaden with the little boy asleep in her arms, the hem of her simple dress and cloak whispering across the cobbled stones, at last once again in the shadow of the grand, classically frescoed Palazzo Chigi.

And the fantasy was always the same. What must it be like, to live amid this great, regal stuccoed giant, with its many elegant mysteries? To actually know that sort of magnificent existence beyond the slender pilasters, terra-cotta frieze; past its walls of rough-hewn, honey-colored stone, with silk dresses, servants, and meals on platters of Tuscan silver. When she was feeling brave like this, and a little in need of her mother's dreams, she would steal herself here to catch just a glimpse of the fantastically grand stone villa beyond the daunting iron gates. Seeing it was, she thought, to glimpse a bit of heaven.

Margherita could actually imagine that life of nobility that her sister mocked. She would be like a princess, one who lived in something like this villa of the great Chigi family. When she was alone at night, brushing out her hair, and free to give into her thoughts, she allowed herself to imagine servants readying her bed, laying out her jewels and gown for the following day. There would be silken sheets, rose petals cast upon them, and a coverlet full of goose down . . . a banquet of sole with pine nuts, of rich Etruscan wine, and a table just for sweets . . .

Checking Matteo, she glanced down and saw her rough hands. Baking flour rimmed her small, round nails, as it did her father's. She cringed, confronted again with a reality no magic could sweep away. Margherita felt the dream steal, like a frightened child, back into the corner of her heart. It was where she kept it safely locked away, with all of the other memories of her mother, who had died when she was young. It was the place she forgot to go more and more now, between the mending and cooking, and the work at the bakery that needed doing. Those were a child's dreams. She had a woman's life now—and that life was firmly rooted beyond the ancient Porta Settimiana, in Trastevere.

"You there! *Signora!*" The menacing baritone voice startled her and she glanced to see a green-and-gold liveried guard, glinting sword drawn, glowering at her. "Move along! You've no business here!"

Margherita swallowed hard, feeling a sudden odd spark of haughty indignation flare up through the initial burst of panic at the authority in his tone. It was an unexpected sensation, and she tipped up her chin.

"I believe you do not know that, *signor guardia.*"

The guard, in formal puffed trunk hose, vest, and puffed toque, looked at her appraisingly. A moment later, he began cruelly to chuckle. "Indeed I do know it, *signora*," he condescendingly declared. "If not by your garments, then certainly by the expression of pure inferiority on your pretty, young face."

Well-dressed passersby gaped at her, some of them whispering behind raised hands, one man even chuckling to himself.

Angry at the sleight, something suddenly caused her to reply. "*Allora,* is this not a public street, *signor guardia,* where I may look at whatever I wish?"

"The street is public, the residence you ogle is private."

"I stand only on the street, bothering no one."

"Like a bug landing on a sweet cake."

"Are you always so charming?"

His response was a snarl. "True spirit, *signora,* falls flat in one without the means to sustain it. It takes no more than a glance to see that this neighborhood is well beyond the likes of you, and that there is no good reason on earth for you to loiter here, and so I tell you again to pass!"

"You know nothing of me. You yourself are but a servant to those beyond *your* scope. And, by the way, brute force," she haughtily countered, "falls just as flat as spirit—in one without the *mind* to see it through!"

"I shall not ask again," he growled. "Move along, I say, back to whatever rabbit warren you come from!"

Someone behind her laughed mockingly then and Margherita felt the heat of embarrassment redden her cheeks. The moment was over, but spirit, for Margherita Luti, the baker's daughter, was a harder thing to press away forever.

RAPHAEL STOOD FIRMLY, arms crossed over his chest, in a velvet doublet of deep scarlet, with full gold sleeves. His face, beneath umber-colored, neatly tamed waves of shoulder-length hair, was tight with frustration. It was not a classically handsome face, but sensually intense. His cheekbones were high, his chin was small, and his eyes were like clear black glass. Through the long, unshuttered window of the richly paneled workshop, his *studio,* with its soaring ceiling and heavy beams, a stream of buttery sunlight crossed the woman. She sat perfectly still on a stone pedestal before the master and his assistant. *"Per l'amor di Dio,"* he groaned, then turned from her.

Beside him, still occupied with his own task, a young apprentice in a dark-blue working robe, belted with frayed rope, stood at a long plank table grinding colors into a wooden bowl. Another stood, tying miniver paintbrushes, while still another sharpened drawing pencils. Swirling throughout the workshop was the pungent odor of oil paint and linseed oil, and all around was the relentless hum of ceaseless activity. Worktables were littered with pallets, empty pewter tankards, half-eaten plates of food, and unlit candles in puddles of dry wax from the evening before — the unruly environment of a group of men focused only on excesses of work.

Raphael nodded to the tall, ruddy-faced bear of a man, with a distinguished shock of gray hair, punctuating his order with an absent wave of the hand. It was a silent directive to pay the girl for her trouble and see her home. It was the second time this week alone that he had dismissed a model. Giovanni da Udine, the assistant who had been with him the longest, let an audible sigh as his heavy lidded eyes rolled to a close. The search would go on.

Raphael ran a hand over his face. He had known instantly she was not right. To Giovanni, an artist far more literal than himself, the faces of these girls were only acceptable circles, ovals, and other linear or geometric shapes. A study of composition forced the assistant to see forms as highlights and shadows, tones and halftones to be added to or rejected from the work. To the master of this workshop, the *mastro,* however, the criteria could not be more different. She — this girl — was not right. Not for a Madonna.

There was nothing extraordinary in her eyes.

When he turned from the girl she was gone from his mind. Raphael Sanzio was behind schedule on many projects more pressing than this, and even the very lenient Pope Leo X had begun to show frustration. Too many accepted commissions, from too many places, Raphael thought now, and no matter how many apprentices he was given, the works were still his to complete.

The rest of the large workshop, facing out onto the murky and foul-smelling waters of the Tiber, was stacked with half-finished works. Altarpieces, portraits, banners, and chests shared the room with apprentices and assistants, in their paint-stained aprons, all of them painting, mixing, carrying, or moving something. There were Carrara marble pieces strewn about, heads and hands of wax, and pieces of wood prepared for painting. In a corner nearby was a large, intricate panel of the Assumption.

Standing before a huge hunting tapestry on an iron rod, another assistant was now doing the skilled work of applying sheets of beaten gold onto the panel. On the other side of the room, nearest the large, walk-in stone fireplace, sat an ancient-looking, withered old man with a thatch of unruly white hair. He modeled for a gaunt-faced assistant, also covered in a paint-stained working robe, who added to a black chalk sketch he had begun earlier. Raphael studied the man's sunken eyes, protruding lower lip, and plunging nose, all of which suggested determination and weariness with life. They were elements he could use on the face of Noah in *God Appears to Noah,* for one of the ceiling bays in a new *stanza* — a grand room, at the Vatican Palace which he was designing for the Holy Father. He made a mental note to speak later with Giovanni about it.

Beside the old man, another senior assistant stood at an easel adding a vivid shade of crimson oil paint to intensify the heavy cloak in a new papal portrait, while still another was just beginning a panel by applying the first layer of underpaint. Everywhere there were works of art in various states of completion. The sketched figure of a Madonna with no definable face dominated the workshop on a tall, narrow panel propped on a large easel. It was to be part of a grand, gabled altarpiece bearing the Apostles in solemn guardianship, destined for the church of San Sisto. And now it was to be delayed yet again.

As the girl stood and took the handful of coins, Giovanni turned back to Raphael. "But what will you do if you do not settle for this one, *mastro*? You have promised Cardinal Bibbiena the altarpiece by month's end, and you have yet to find the model!"

"Then we can do nothing more than keep searching, can we?"

In point of fact, the commission for the new Madonna had been granted to Raphael four years earlier, by the previous pontiff, Julius II. It was to be a gift to the Benedictines in Piacenza as a token of that city's voluntary annexation by the papal states. With all of the other work given to Raphael by Julius's successor, Leo X, this old project had claimed little of his attention. But there was to be a celebration in Piacenza and the new pontiff wished to present the painting then. It was whispered that Cardinal Bibbiena, a personal friend and secretary to the new pope, was using the incomplete panel as a way to undermine Raphael's standing at the Vatican. The reason involved his own niece, Maria, to whom Raphael was betrothed, yet who he had thus far successfully avoided marrying.

Bibbiena was growing impatient and angry, and the unfinished commission gave him an excuse to nip at Raphael's heels.

"*Dio mio*," da Udine could not keep himself from groaning. "But this one really did fit the form perfectly."

"I do not care if you believe she fits. Use her at Chigi's house for one of the lunettes in the *Galatea* room if you like. She is simply not a Madonna!"

"Respectfully, *mastro*, could you not have made any of these women we have brought you into one?"

Raphael turned to him. His dark eyes were set deeply with commitment. Yet they were eyes that saw life in a different way; with consciousness of form, a strong graphic sense and luminous penetration of detail. How could he make anyone else understand that he must be inspired by a face—driven to re-create it as the very image of the mother of Jesus Christ? It was not that he did not care. This theme had come to symbolize, for him, his own mother holding him as a child. A mother he had lost tragically, when he was just a boy. To Raphael, painting various Madonna images had always been a way to bring her back to life—a mother he idealized far more than he remembered her, but a mother whose loss had forever changed his life.

Raphael had painted a dozen Madonnas since leaving Urbino. Beneath the tutelage of his own first master, Perugino, the Madonna had become his most resonant theme. He had based them all at first on the models, and the faces, chosen by Leonardo da Vinci, under whom he had studied in Florence. But Raphael was no longer a pupil. Now, at the age of thirty-one, he, too, was considered a master—a *mastro*. And the idealized face of his youth, the one he had repeated in Madonna after Madonna, would no longer satisfy his goals for the work.

Here in Rome, at the personal behest of the pontiff himself, the stakes were much higher than in Urbino or Florence. The highest commissions of the new papacy had been bestowed upon him. Michelangelo, once his greatest rival, had fled to Florence, prevented from even completing the tomb of Julius II. Raphael was the one to gain contracts for several drawings, called "cartoons," to be used in grand tapestries for Michelangelo's newly completed Sistine Chapel. He had also promised the pope his full personal attention on the dark and dramatic sequence, *The Mass of Bolsena,* being frescoed over a window arch, that would ornament the second, grand papal *stanza.*

In addition, Alfonso d'Este, duke of Ferrara, was waiting impatiently for a *Triumph of Bacchus* he had ordered for his family castle. Bibbiena had his *stufetta,* a very grand bathing room, in his Vatican Palace apartments, the concept drawings for which were only half complete, and the fervent call by King Louis of France for *St. Michael* and *The Holy Family* had gone thus far unanswered. Raphael also had numerous portraits awaiting his brush, the loggias at the Vatican, more frescoes at the Chigi palace, and such minor projects as drawings for engravings and designs for mantelpieces. Amid this wild torrent of work, Raphael had been given yet another lofty honor which he had no idea how to find time to complete. He had personally been recommended by a dying Bramante to succeed him as the architect of Saint Peter's, in spite of the fact that he had no architectural experience at all. Raphael's patience was low and his energy waning. So much work and too little sleep had made him irritable. No matter to whom he delegated the painstaking details, he was still keenly aware that all of the commissions, and the assistants were entirely dependent upon his creative authority and ultimately upon him.

In all of the notoriety and wealth, Raphael Sanzio had lost sight of what had brought him to artistry in the first place. Most days, there was little or no heated passion toward creation, as there had been at first. But the assistants did not know that. No one was allowed to get that close.

"So tell me this, Giovanni," he asked, coolly tossing a velvet cape over his shoulders. "Did the Lord God *settle* when choosing his Virgin?"

To that, of course, da Udine was wise enough to know there could be no retort. In need of air, and the rhythm of simpler times, Raphael left the workshop alone, forgoing a groom or horse. He pressed away the entourage of assistants who always traveled with him throughout the city, and instead walked blissfully alone out into the cobbled stone street.

It was a threateningly dark midday, rain clouds having moved in from the north, quickly covering most of the azure sky as he headed toward the Vatican. Deep, heavy bells tolled at the church of Santa Cecilia. For a moment, as a breeze off the Tiber lashed at him, he felt almost like the child he had been in Urbino, tugging at his father's cloak. With that, a stronger memory came back to him. It hit him fully then, and he felt it all again. He saw himself, a small boy, begging to leave his father's workshop on a threatening day like this one, but long ago. He had wanted to be safely at home, away from the smell of paint and turpentine that now defined his own life. Irony twisted bitterly in him when he thought how his own workshop was more home to him than any other place in Rome.

His father, Lorenzo Sanzio, had been a court painter at the ducal palace in Urbino. Raphael felt the heavy pull of old sadness recalling the man who had given him his love of painting, but had found little of his own fame or fortune. The same beloved man who had died in his arms when he was a boy of only eleven. The door now opened, another memory came at him.

"Seize what you can from this life, Raffaello mio . . . You have a great talent, far greater than my own, it is certain . . . I have given you all that I can. I am dying. But now you must go on, you must seek your own great destiny."

"Per favore, *let me stay*, padre mio! *I have nothing without you!"*

"No, my son, what you have is what you see when you take a paintbrush into your hand. Depend on no one or nothing but that. Make me proud, Raffaello . . . do justice to your mother's memory and her love by depending upon only that . . . "

And so he had. Raphael squinted through a last pale shaft of noonday light that shot through a heavy cloud, and caught the reflection of tears in his eyes. They had both left him much too soon. Neither of his parents had seen the success he had made of his life, nor seen any of his most acclaimed works. The modest boy from Urbino had painted works like *The Marriage of the Virgin* that hung now in Milan, the portrait of Pope Julius, so lifelike that people had gasped upon seeing it, and his own version of a pietà, after Michelangelo, painted for a church in Colonna. Fulfilling his father's wish had consumed the last twenty years of his life. Only now, at the age of thirty-one, wildly successful and wealthier than he could ever have dreamed, did he realize fully how completely unfulfilled all of it had left him.

TRASTEVERE, the densely inhabited area of houses and *bottegas* between the river and the slope of lush Il Gianicolo, was a meager working-class neighborhood. The Romans there were a world apart from the wealthy and powerful figures like Signor

Chigi who filled the pontiff's coffers with enough gold florins to aggressively pursue the arts. But Raphael liked the modest area for its raw energy and sense of place. Against the advice of Cardinal Bibbiena, he had intentionally set his workshop there.

The path he took now from the Via Gianicolo toward the Vatican was the longest one. He walked through the small and ordered Piazza San Pietro, hemmed in by buildings wrought of mellow, peeling stucco, the area devoid of grass or trees. Here were shades of orange, cinnamon, and gold cast upon buildings that stood too closely together, creating a dank tunnel of cobbled stones and faded stucco, cooing pigeons on rooftops, and echoed voices.

Above him, women hung from windows, held out laundry, and called to one another in a rhythmic echo of domestic chatter. On the street level were shops—an ironmonger, a weaver, and a few doors down the workshop of a musical instrument maker— and above them were the modest dwellings of those who ran them. He passed a trash-strewn alleyway where two scrawny dogs scavenged near a drunken man lying in a heap. The smell from piles of garbage was vile.

He passed them all, as a cart pulled by two dray horses, loaded with baskets of olives, clattering loudly over the cobbled stones. Yet he saw nothing. Raphael needed time alone to do battle with a fatigue that was consuming his spirit. He missed the old work that had filled him with youthful enthusiasm. Madonnas. The Florentine portraits. Wide-eyed boys. Apple-cheeked babies. Old women, their faces etched with years. The images of those who mattered to this world.

A few raindrops fell, warning of the approaching storm.

Raphael clasped his cold hands and closed his eyes. Images of his parents moved across his mind again. Elements of his home in Urbino. Smells, sights. Echoes of childhood laughter he no longer felt, but still heard. His life now was too serious for laughter. Too full of commitment for revelry.

Giovanni had been right. The girl he had presented today had been acceptable. Good bone structure, warm dark eyes. In truth, he was not at all certain what had held him back from filling in the parts of her he did not see. He simply expected too much. The new Madonna he needed to paint was really the least of his commissions but, by delaying, he had made it more important than it needed to be. And in this hot game of rivalry with every other artisan in Rome and Florence, he could not afford to incur the pope's disappointment.

"*Dio mio,* give me strength to do it all," he murmured to himself. He walked through an ever-darkening Roman afternoon toward the Vatican and the papal room where his assistants were now at work on a detail on the ceiling, *Moses Before the Burning Bush.* He had been there earlier in the morning to add to the final sketch of Saint Peter in the particular corner in which they had worked the rest of the day. He trusted Giovanni and Gianfrancesco Penni implicitly, and yet he was the *mastro*—the one upon whose reputation all rested.

He made his way through the light rain, away from the Porta Settimiana, the entrance to Trastevere, away from the spider's web of narrow streets, and avoided the straight and orderly Via della Lungaretta in favor of a country idyll in the heart of the city, the wooded hill called Il Gianicolo. Raphael picked up his pace now and moved toward the sloping green incline and a shady arch of plane trees before him. It was not a quicker path to the Vatican, simply a more peaceful one.

He felt himself breathe more easily as he reached the top of the hill and passed beneath a rich canopy of bristling evergreens. Before him was a sweeping view of the ancient wonders of the city, including the Pantheon, which sat majestically in the distance. Raphael was late already, but for a moment it seemed not to matter as he slowed his pace along the gravel walkway, bordered with delicate purple bluebells and a shimmer of perfume from the wild jasmine bushes. The pope wished to be given a personal accounting of the work going on in his room, with its odd-shaped ceiling, four truncated pie shapes, in which the artwork needed to fit exactly. After that, there was the work at Chigi's villa to assess—

the mythological fresco, a scene of Perseus and Medusa, being added to the fresco there.

Raphael drew in a heavy breath of the deeply scented surroundings. He lingered for a moment near a lush jacaranda tree. High above the rooftops and domes, above the little classical statues set between the trees, a dark flock of birds crossed the Roman sky. He felt his heart slow. This lush hill, the escape here, was the closest thing he had to a personal bit of life. Of course there were the women, courtesans, other men's wives, and the ever-present whores who threw themselves boldly at any famed artist. Yet they were nothing but a momentary indulgence—a distraction.

He thought of Maria Bibbiena again, the woman to whom he was betrothed, and he cringed. With sallow skin, sunken dark eyes, Maria was quiet and consumptive. But she was fascinated by the painter from Urbino. Shortly after arriving in Rome, her uncle, the powerful Cardinal Bibbiena, had offered her to Raphael as a prize. And thus he found himself now in a situation from which there was no escape.

In a foolish moment, full of more ambition than wisdom, he had accepted the cardinal's offer. Seeing quickly the repercussions of a moment's wild decision, he had tried promptly to break the agreement. And he had been trying ever since. But the cardinal was tied as closely to Pope Leo as if they were brothers. Offend one, he quickly saw, and he offended the other. So delay had become his sole defense. An impolite tactic that had, thus far, lasted four years.

He kept walking as the grand domes and towers of the city became nothing more than gray shadows across the Roman vista behind him. But he liked the rain, the vital sense of nature bearing down upon him. He felt alive beneath its increasingly heavy force. Alive and *almost* free.

Raphael passed a marble bust of Socrates, a hand extended upward toward the heavens, the other bearing a heavy book. There were strollers coming down the hill toward him, men in their nether hose, velvet caps, and cloaks, women in full, wide gowns and decorated hoods. As he glanced up, a female figure walking alone behind them drew near. She wore a midnight-blue cloak, hood up over her head, and she was shielding a child she held beneath the weighty reach of fabric.

The child was a small boy, whose eyes, like hers, were magnificent, a deep and fathomless brown, turned out upon the world, yet wary of it. But it was her gaze that drew him unexpectedly, beneath fabric that framed her face. The face was a perfect oval, her skin as flawless as the child's. In spite of her youth there was an unexpected gentle grace in her eyes that could only have come from the pressures of a difficult life. His body blocked her path. She stopped. His throat closed. He did not recall ever being made speechless in the sudden presence of a beautiful woman. But the rightness of her made it so.

"Gesù," he heard himself murmur quite against his will.

She was still looking at him, the hood of her wet cloak framing her face in the way a veil would. She moved backward a single step, not afraid, but as though she sensed something impending. She fixed a radiant gaze on him with what Raphael found was a painful intensity. Her smooth face, with its enormous, expressive brown eyes and creamy olive skin, stunned him.

She was, this woman, this stranger, he knew instantly, the Madonna.

"Perdona," she said, softly trying to move past, but she spoke in a voice that resonated cool confidence. Her voice was full and slightly husky, belying a hidden sensuality. It was not what he expected, given the extraordinary delicate grace in her eyes, and that alone rocked him.

He stepped backward, thinking in that instant of absolutely nothing he could say to stop her.

"Signora, I—"

The two words across his lips, which came out as a rasp of sound, were a surprise to him. As the rain fell, she lifted her face and looked at him again. In this odd light—gray, yet with a streak of sunlight through the heavy clouds—her face held a unique glow. Hers was an alluring beauty that bore no expectation, as though she had no idea how striking she truly was. In the world in which he now lived, full of privileged and eager women, that such a thing could even be was astonishing.

He was completely disarmed, and she had uttered but a single word.

"I must paint you," he said, hearing the declaration pass his lips in a tone of desperation.

He saw her frown slightly. There was a moment's consideration. "Pray, excuse me. I am late in returning home."

He tried to think, to breathe, but he found himself unable to do either. "I . . . I am Raphael Sanzio," he blurted, not with the confidence he had intended, but with the sudden abandon of a much younger, and less-experienced, man. "Would you allow me at least to make a sketch of you? I would be willing to pay you quite handsomely for it!"

She looked up at him again. The silvery sun hit the bit of her hair above her forehead, and he saw that it had the exact color and sheen of sable.

"Do you mock me, sir?"

"I mock you not, *signora*."

"Would not the true Raffaello have a grand collection of companions or, at the least, a magnificent horse on which to ride? I doubt the great artist would walk a pathway alone as the common rest of us."

Raphael glanced around. He willed himself to slow the delivery of his words, so as not to frighten her away.

"Perhaps it is so," he said in a measured tone that he struggled to find. So she was possessed of a natural sort of spirit as well. The astonishment intensified. "And yet the man they call *mastro* might also take this quicker route alone if he were in need of a moment's reflection from all the pressures placed upon him."

Her smile was a fleeting gesture. "If that is true, *signore,* then I am a contessa."

He moved a step nearer to her, desperate for her to feel the same sweeping power of the inevitability that he felt. "If you told me you were such, I would be obliged to believe you."

Someone called out to him then, shattering the moment. As she clutched the wide-eyed boy to her chest, Raphael turned and saw his youngest assistant, Giulio Romano, out of breath and running down the hill toward him.

"*Buon giorno* to you—Signor Sanzio," he heard her say with just the slightest hint of mocking. It was clear that she had not believed a single word. When he turned back to her, she had already stepped away from him and was moving toward a crowd of other strollers heading back down into Rome. Raphael went after her and had nearly caught up with her when he felt a hand clamp down on his shoulder. He spun around angrily, preparing to cast off the youth's hand as though he were an assailant.

"*Dio!*" Giulio panted. "His Holiness is nearly out of patience with you! He has held his schedule all morning! I came to find you before any more damage could be done!"

Raphael glanced back down the hill but the girl, his Madonna, had disappeared into the growing crowd. For an instant, he thought of going after her, but his priority must be the Holy Father.

"You must go the other way! I will go to the pope but you must find the young woman with the blue cloak, carrying a child! Find out where she lives! She must not be allowed to get away!"

The young man smiled, knowing the *mastro*'s penchant for beautiful women, having seen the many who had crossed the doorstep of the workshop. Giulio Romano nodded to Raphael and dashed down the hill, moving quickly toward the daunting shadows, the walls of weathered stone, and the many magnificent ruins of ancient Rome.

PRESSING BACK the odd sensation of the man's gaze on Il Gianicolo, Margherita walked beneath the swinging sign above the door, and back into the family's small bakery on the Via Santa Dorotea. She kissed her father's fat, stubbled cheek as he stood wiping his hands on a soiled apron, tied at his stout middle. Francesco Luti was rough and pagan, a little bullfrog of a man, with wide-set green eyes flecked with brown, a thick neck, and a large mouth. His shirt collar was stained with a brown ring of perspiration and he stood, wide-legged, on a floor covered with a thin patina of flour. He smelled of the familiar fragrance of flour and sweat. It was the only fragrance that had ever been about him, Margherita thought. She drew back the hood of the blue velvet cloak, and gently set Matteo at her feet. The child clung to her leg for a moment, then crawled away.

The bakery was cramped and stifling from the blazing bread ovens behind the muslin curtain. Everywhere there were wicker baskets brimming with fresh bread and rolls. Dense sweet nut bread, airy round loaves stuffed with wine-soaked raisins, strips of sweet knotted bread called *sfrappole,* and *pizzelles,* the little light wafers the baker gave out to children who he favored. The walls of the small shop once had been a delicate cerulean blue when it had housed a cobbler's shop. But that was from another lifetime, before the heat of a bakery, flour, and time had faded it almost beyond recognition, and caused the paint behind the baskets to peel away steadily from the plaster walls. Out beyond a rounded door was a small back garden with a few meager vegetables growing through dirt and weeds, and a line of white laundry moving with the rhythm of a now cool and, once again, rainless breeze.

"And where have *you* been, my girl with the penchant for wandering?" he gruffly asked his younger daughter. "I expect you to help me with the *baccio* and yet out you go with the child and your sister is here, sick with dread!"

"*Dio, Padre,* Letitia is always sick with something." She smiled and drew a warm *pizzelle* from the wooden tabletop. Francesco Luti slapped his daughter's hand, as if to prevent her from taking it, but it was a playful lifelong gesture, the grand way in which the *famiglia* Luti displayed affection. It was, in fact, the only way. Emotion, Francesco Luti ordained, was a sign of weakness. No good could come of an open heart, he had warned his daughters. What he meant, Margherita knew, was that he had married their mother for love, and he had paid the heavy price of missing that love after her premature death.

Margherita kissed her father's cheek again in a whimsical way that always diffused his anger and, touching the boy on top of his head, moved into the back room as she removed the damp cloak. She went behind a muslin curtain to where her sister, Letitia, stood mixing water into a large earthen bowl of flour for their father's next batch of bread dough.

"I told him you would return," Letitia said blandly, without looking up, "yet still he worries."

Letitia Perazzi cared little that Margherita had been off with her son. Matteo was her fourth son in a few short years, and a break from the whining, constantly nursing toddler was welcome. For this blissful morning, her three-year-old, Luca, had slept in the baby's oak cradle near her, and the older two boys, Pietro and Jacopo, today had gone to help their father, Donato, at the Chigi stables.

Mucking out horse droppings and oiling grand saddles was not a life of nobility, Letitia's husband said, but an honest living nonetheless, and as close to greatness as he ever would get. He put food on their table and helped Francesco to keep a roof above their home and the bakery. And that, for him, was enough.

"*Prego,* Margherita! Do you have a reason, better than the last time, why you were out and not here stoking the fire for the afternoon loaves!"

Margherita traced a casual finger along the rough-hewn table, parting the thin dusting of flour there. "What would you think if I told you I met the great Raffaello today and he wished to paint me?"

"So you mock your *padre* who still puts clothes on your back, and food in your belly? In spite of the fact that at your age you should be married?" her father snapped.

Letitia chuckled at that and pulled down the muslin bodice of her dress to reveal the wide pink nipple of a swelling breast, onto which the little cherub in her arms quickly latched with rosebud lips. "Oh really, *Padre mio,* can you not see Margherita's attempt to put even the slightest hint of a smile on that sour face of yours? Both of you have so little joy in your lives these days."

"What has joy to do with life, Letitia, can you tell me that, eh? Only something to betray your soul when you give into it, if you ask me!"

As he looked back and forth between his two grown daughters, the quiet was broken by the smacking sound of the suckling child. Each of his daughters bore elements of their father, and their lost mother as well. Margherita's features were more delicate, but her coloring was of Luti, shades of olive, and her skin smooth. Letitia was fair as new milk with crow-black hair gathered up and worn tight like a crown at the back of her head. She wore a coarse beige dress, a white apron around her waist, and rough leather shoes in the manner of a baker's wife. Margherita wore her mother's clothes. They were finer things, memories of her dreams wrapped in fabric and laces. Their size had been the same exactly. At times, late at night, when he had drunk too much trebbiano wine, Francesco would cry that his daughter tortured him by bringing him visions of the past. But Margherita, a daughter lonely for a mother's love and dreams, reveled in that small connection left to her.

"I did not actually believe it was him. Imagine! Well dressed or not, to pass himself off to anyone as the great artist," Margherita casually explained. "And so I left."

"This man was well dressed?" Francesco stroked his short, square chin with two flour-caked fingers "What if it were him? *Per l'amor di Dio!* Did he . . . this man . . . this stranger to you . . . did he perchance offer to pay you for your trouble?"

"He said he would pay to draw me, *sì.*"

His round green eyes bulged with incredulity. "Did you at least tell him where to find you? Perhaps, if we saw some proof that—"

"When a messenger came for him, I disappeared before he could proposition me further."

Beyond the little baking room, a bell tinkled over the door of the shop announcing a customer. Francesco glanced briefly toward the muslin curtain dividing the two spaces, then back at his daughters.

"And what if it really were the great Raffaello? What on earth did you turn away from?"

Margherita's lips parted as she gazed in amazement at her father. Her young life was flour and water, and the predictability of days as a baker's unmarried daughter. Then marriage, equally as expected, to Donato's younger brother, Antonio, when she gave up hope of anything else.

"*Padre mio,* worry not. The man I met, while grandly clothed, was alone. No good could come from my playing his foolish game. What would the great painter who walks among princes, dukes—and even our Holy Father—want with a common baker's daughter anyway?"

❧ 2 ❧

AS HE MADE HIS WAY UP THE WIDE STONE STEPS OF THE Loggia della Benedizione and through the ornate Vatican gate archway, Raphael's head swam with the image of the mysterious girl he had seen so briefly—especially her extraordinary eyes. They were the eyes of a Madonna.

A wagon loaded with beef carcasses heading for the papal kitchens trundled past him along the path, then disappeared as two guards closed another gate behind it. Raphael did not notice the movement or the pages, or even the clergy in their starched vestments who passed him as he strode up the first wide flight of stone steps, and then the second, toward the *stanza* in which his assistants had been working, and where he had been told the Holy Father would graciously receive him.

As the heels of his decorated leather boots clicked on the inlaid mosaic floor, Raphael did his best to chase the girl's face from his mind. He needed to create a tolerable expression of humility instead of the flushed excitement he was feeling now. Not two days earlier, the pontiff had admonished him personally on the vices of women and their danger to a man with such a powerful gift from God.

"You waste yourself on lust, Raffaello *mio*," he had sternly warned, pointing a fat, jeweled finger. "Better to join the priesthood, to keep yourself chaste, if you will not take Bibbiena's niece as your wife!"

Raphael thought of the pope with his own sin—gluttony— and pressed back a smile. Neither the pontiff, nor his cardinals, cared anything for Raphael, the man. Each cared only for the projects that would reflect their own greatness—and they were willing to see them to completion by any means.

He was so deep in thought that when he came to the last corridor he did not notice at first that his way was coldly barred. Two stone-faced papal guards now stood before him in puffed crimson-and-gold striped uniforms, and steel helmets with red plumes. Today their halberds were raised to bar him when generally he was given free passage in the vast papal wing, the decoration of which had been largely his doing.

"What is this? I am expected," he said with a sharp note of indignation, his voice echoing through the ornate vastness.

"You are late. In your absence, His Holiness agreed to receive another," said the guard whom he knew best. The tone had been low and revealing. Raphael knew it was a warning of something he would not like. "Now *you* are to be made to wait."

"Who it is, Bernardo?"

The guard leaned forward slightly, the plume waving on his steel helmet. "Signor Buonarroti."

"Michelangelo has returned to Rome? I thought he had stormed off to Florence months ago when our new Holy Father refused him a commission!"

"Apparently he has returned."

It had taken very little time, in the previous papal reign, for the two great artists with very different temperaments to become rivals. Secretly, Raphael, younger by over twenty-eight years, regretted that turn of events. Michelangelo Buonarroti was a true genius. The first time he had seen the artist's sculpture of the pietà it had brought him to tears, as it did nearly everyone who saw it. Nothing finer, Raphael believed, had ever been wrought on this earth by human hands. And, in fact, they had worked together, a corridor away from one another—Raphael on the pope's *stanza,* and Michelangelo on his Sistine ceiling. But it was not long before others, who wished to fuel the flames of their budding rivalry, began accusing Raphael of copying the style and color of Michelangelo's characters, and any sense of camaraderie was lost to them forever.

Michelangelo was a sullen and temperamental sort who not only resented Raphael's way with women, but the ease with which he apparently found more wealthy and powerful benefactors than he could accept. When the Medici pope, Leo X, had been elected a year ago, Raphael was offered the first, and best, commissions from him. To Michelangelo, who had been a great personal friend to the previous pontiff, nothing of value was offered. Eight months ago, he had left Rome. Now, apparently, with Raphael overburdened, overworked, and behind schedule, he had returned.

Raphael found himself waiting alone on a cold stone bench outside the *stanza* that he had personally designed, and where his own crew of assistants was still painting. He glanced down the long vaulted corridor, delicately frescoed with intricate images from the Bible. Raphael's smooth Umbrian complexion had mottled red when the tall painted oak door finally opened. Michelangelo, in white nether hose, a black velvet doublet, a cape, and a toque, swept out before him, then paused.

He had aged, Raphael was startled to see. Michelangelo's hair now was shot with gray, and his deep ebony eyes had dimmed and sunken deeply into a gaunt and withered face, all punctuated by a smashed little nose that had been badly broken years earlier. Raphael stood as they greeted one another coolly, yet with the familiarity of those who possess a deep history. "I might have known you would be here, Signor Sanzio."

"It is more than I can say for you—Signor Buonarroti."

Michelangelo grinned cautiously at that. His unmoving eyes were weary. "Ever the quick one, eh, Raffaello *mio*? Life and work are always such a game to you."

"My life, perhaps. But you, of all men, should know how seriously I take my commissions."

"It is that which separates us, Raphael. To me it is love of the work that moves me. To you, it is love of all that the commission brings you."

"That is not all that separates us," Raphael said angrily. "I, for example, would never have left Rome only because of a change in patronage. That certainly is being moved by something other than the work!"

Michelangelo lowered his gaze. "Well, Raffaello, I will say this: You and I are really nothing at all alike. That is absolutely certain."

Looking at the aging artist before him, slightly stooped, his long hands, through which so much talent flowed, now veined and gnarled, Raphael felt an unexpected stab of sympathy. Such utter brilliance in one man. A talent bestowed by God, like his own. There were so few on this earth who spoke their language, who understood the passion and the frustration of living so closely to one's art. How then had they ever become such bitter rivals?

"Will you remain in Rome?" Raphael found himself asking.

"I came to the city only to personally beseech the Holy Father for news on the progress of funding for Pope Julius's tomb."

"You are still going to do that?" Raphael was surprised. In spite of the friendship between Michelangelo and the previous pontiff, it seemed unwise to badger an unsympathetic successor about a monument to immortalize his predecessor.

"It shall remain my life's primary goal," said Michelangelo with unshakable commitment, "to build a lasting monument to a Holy Father like no other."

In the quiet depth of the massive hall, with only the stone-faced guards around them, Raphael shrugged. He did not entirely believe it. There had been rumblings for days that with the pontiff's impatience had come a quiet search for new artists to continue the grand commissions—help for Pope Leo to realize his own legacy.

"I wish you good fortune with it then," said Raphael, nodding deeply.

"And I you, Raffaello *mio*. If you can get out of the way of yourself, I expect you shall find your true place in history. But you have always been your own worst enemy, you know."

"And *your* greatest nemesis."

"It is true that if I am able to defeat you in the eyes of the Holy Father, winning back the lion's share of papal commissions, I shall do it in a heartbeat, so beware."

What Michelangelo meant was that he would try to do it with the help of his unscrupulous protégé, Sebastiano Luciani. Now *that* was a name that caused the hair on the back of Raphael's neck to stand on end. Sebastiano was a young painter who envied Raphael almost as much as his master did. Sebastiano certainly had talent on his side. But his unchecked ambition was against him.

They had been pitted against one another once before at the grand villa of the wealthy banker, the pope's great friend and benefactor, Agostino Chigi. When Raphael received a commission for a large, decorative panel depicting the sea nymph, Galatea, for an expansive salon that faced the Tiber, it was Sebastiano Luciani who received a companion commission to paint a large panel of his own directly beside it. Once the two panels were complete, Chigi released Sebastiano from further commissions, and hired Raphael exclusively to work in the villa and to ornament his family's two private chapels. It was the beginning of open warfare.

"I shall consider myself warned," said Raphael.

The rivals nodded to one another as though their dialogue had been the most civil of exchanges, and with that Michelangelo swept past him. But not before he left Raphael with a sense of foreboding. His critics were correct, he feared, as he was motioned into the pope's chamber. As Michelangelo predicted, he might well find only himself to blame for his own undoing.

"HOLY FATHER," Raphael knelt and kissed the ring on the bulging finger of the Medici pope, enthroned on a crimson-draped dais and garbed in stiff and elegant white silk. A skullcap was perched at the back of his balding head and across his shoulders was an ermine-trimmed cape of crimson-colored velvet. Around the pontiff a collection of cassock-clad cardinals, bishops, secretaries, and emissaries gathered. They stood both in protection and judgment while, across the room, a boy sat on a tufted cassock, lightly strumming a lute for the pontiff's pleasure. Behind him, another stood holding a silver tray piled with marzipan, pastries of pine nuts and sugar, Eastern sweetmeats, and other delectables topped with little clouds of whipped cream.

This was the second major room Raphael had been commissioned to decorate in the Vatican. Begun for Pope Julius II, this *stanza*, expansive and grand, with great high ceilings, was the private receiving room in which the pontiff welcomed dignitaries. But the grandeur of these commissions, and the urgency to see them completed, signaled something far more than a love of art. Since these men of the Church could not have children—at least not ones they could openly acknowledge—these exquisite works, done especially for each of them, would give them an immortality nothing else could. It was their only legacy, and the scheme for many was to manipulate however — and whoever—necessary to see that legacy made reality.

Still incomplete, the walls of this second room were steadily being covered with intricate, evocative, and passionately colorful scenes from different chapters in the history of the Church. Raphael and his team of assistants had grandly depicted the *Expulsion of Heliodorus,* the *Mass of Bolsena,* and, in their final panel, now half finished, the *Repulse of Attila,* in which an image of Pope Leo himself was to be immortalized. It was intentional, Raphael knew, as he was ushered into this room, that the scaffolding and drapery sheeting in the unfinished area had been cleared away.

"I bid Your Holiness, forgive my delay. But at last I have found the perfect Madonna for your panel for the church at San Sisto."

The pope lifted a jeweled hand and swatted at the air. He was unimpressed. The Madonna had been commissioned by his predecessor, Julius II, and Pope Leo had other works—his own ideas—that had come to concern him far more.

Breathing heavily, the pontiff ran a hand down the rotund expanse of his white damask cassock as he, too, gazed up at one of the ceiling images, that of *God Appearing to Noah.* His face was full and pasty, his lips like a pink rosebud stuffed into the folds above his chin. But the eyes, limpid blue, bore a kindness that had won Raphael's personal allegiance quickly. A moment later, he sank back into the gold and jewel-encrusted throne, covered over in crimson silk.

"So tell me, Raffaello." He stroked his chin, then reached for a rich, sugary pastry from the glistening silver tray poised beside him. "What are *your* thoughts on our increasingly tenuous position with France now that the new young, and very ambitious, François is poised to be crowned king? Certainly you know even now, before the death of the old king, he is attempting to form an alliance with Spain in order to gain strength against Henry in England. He would like us allied with him in that."

Raphael was surprised, and taken off guard—the desired effect, he assumed. *Politics?* he thought. *What on earth has that to do with me?* "I would not dare to offer an opinion on something so important," he cautiously replied.

"Nonsense. You are among our inner circle here," Pope Leo

nodded, doubling his chin. "And from time to time all of my most intimate members have been called upon to offer keen insight in matters to which I have become too close."

"Your Holiness knows I am but a simple artist, unqualified to advise someone so great and learned as yourself on matters of state."

"Ah, but your art betrays you, my son." He smiled patiently. "Nobility has always come through your paintbrush, as in the grand motif of church history you have brought to life here in our midst." The pope glanced around them, as if to punctuate his point. "I therefore desire not advice on the matter, but rather your own noble observations."

Raphael knew, as did everyone within the papal sphere, that Pope Leo wished to remain neutral in the political firestorm for power brewing between France's young heir, Emperor Maximilian, and Henry VIII in England. Not yet king, nevertheless François was endeavoring to form a pact with Spain to obtain Milan and Genoa by matrimonial alliance. He also knew how vexed the pontiff was over what to do in the matter. Pope Leo was a peaceful man, and his prime concern was the independence of the Holy See, and the freedom of Italy.

Knowing this, with the greatest care, Raphael said, "Then, if I am to be tested in this way, Holy Father, I would say that one is prudent to sail with two compasses. Negotiation on all sides for as long as possible seems the most judicious course in any difficulty if peace is the objective."

"Very well said indeed, my son." The pope's rosebud lips lengthened into a more pleased smile. "The truth of the matter," he conceded a moment later, leaning forward, as if in confidence, "is that this small test was prompted not by me but by Bibbiena."

That surprised Raphael. Bernardo Dovizi da Bibbiena had been his first ally at the Vatican, even before Leo ascended to the papacy, and before Raphael had become betrothed to the cardinal's niece. It was, in fact, Bibbiena's loggia that had inspired the new pope to commission one of his own, decorated by Raphael, based on the unearthed palace of Nero, called the Domus Aurea.

"His Grace, the cardinal, wonders if perhaps the reason you have yet to marry Maria, after so lengthy a period of betrothal, is because you are not the man of the world you presented yourself to be. And that if you are not qualified to marry his niece, the power and access bestowed upon you here has been in error."

I have not married Maria Bibbiena because I do not love her, nor can I ever. Knowing that, I can only hurt her, and she does deserve better than a man who sees opportunity in every other woman he meets, and generally partakes of it . . .

"I am saddened to hear that after living among you like this for so many months, my actions alone have not been proof enough of the man I am," Raphael said instead, his mind filling quickly with images of the thin, pale, and consumptive niece who rarely smiled or spoke.

"You know you have become like a son to me, Raffaello, and care though I do for Bernardo, I cannot bear to think that he might be correct in this, that his Maria is . . . well, that she is too far above you."

So the sudden examination of current events was apparently the pope's convoluted way of coming to the true heart of the matter. To, as it were, frighten him into submission. Nor was it a coincidence that he had been summoned to this particular room that, by his hand, remained incomplete for a full year. Or that his greatest rival had been received here first.

So that was what this was about. Not only a censure, and to remind him of his place, but a visual warning of just who would swiftly be there to take over the *stanza* projects — if he failed to put himself back on track.

There were some truths on both sides, and Raphael was determined to have confidence enough to see that through. "I have come to realize that to go through with marriage to Signorina Bibbiena would be the gravest of errors for us both."

Still the pope was calm. "But did you not, of your own accord, promise yourself to that very young lady of his family whom His Grace offered to you in marriage?"

It seemed a lifetime ago now, and he, someone else entirely. "These past years, Signorina Bibbiena and I have only grown apart, Holy Father."

"We speak of a marriage, Raffaello *mio,* not some frivolous random matter of the heart! Is it not business for those of the world like ourselves? Bibbiena, who brought you before me, has been good to you, and you have benefited greatly from your association with him and his niece, not to mention, dare we say, with your Holy Father." He then lowered his watery, bulging-eyed gaze powerfully on Raphael. "No other artist in all the world is on the brink of marrying so high as you are!"

"But, tell me, Holy Father, as payment, do I owe the cardinal my soul?"

It surprised Raphael that the pope gave him a fat, wet-lipped smile. "Your freedom, my boy. Only just that."

"I cannot give him that!"

"*Santissima Maria!* What is it that you *do* wish?"

"To be free of my promise to marry Maria."

"And that is the one thing, dear Raffaello *mio,* that is not mine to give you. Nor, for the sake of good Bibbiena's honor, would I if I could." A moment later, in the echo of a strained silence, he said, "Michelangelo Buonarroti has just left us."

"We exchanged our greetings as he departed."

The pontiff brought his gaze back to Raphael. His full face held a sheen of perspiration, but there was something more in the bulging blue eyes and contrite smile. There had been something underlying in the comment, and the addition of his greatest rival to the conversation. "Did you ask Michelangelo if he had come to Rome to steal your commissions from you?"

Raphael lifted a brow. He felt his jaw tighten. He waited, one beat then two, cautiously choosing the words, and the tone in which he spoke them. Their normally easy manner with one another had swiftly changed. "Did he come to Rome for that, Your Holiness?"

"If he did not tell you, then perhaps it would be best for you to be left to wonder for a while, as it seems a good means of returning you to the focus of your work, and to remembering from where it originates."

Raphael shrank back a half step, surprised at the frankness of the pontiff whose custom it was to be jovial and affectionate with him. "Holy Father, has my work displeased you in some way?"

"Only your lack of it, Raffaello *mio*. Of the outstanding commissions you hold, I am distressed to see that only the drawings of the *stufetta* for Bibbiena are near completion. And I trust you shall understand my intemperance in being disregarded so that you may begin another Madonna, no matter how magnificent the model. It does tend to chafe at a pontiff waiting for his own official portrait to be complete."

"At your suggestion only, Holy Father, I have searched for the model these months to complete the commission. I have also had my work at the Chigi funeral chapel, and now, as well, Signor Chigi is pleased enough with my past work to have enlarged his latest request. He has now included a mosaic ceiling to his family's private chapel. And forgive me for saying that everything seems to have the same deadline of yesterday!"

"Much of it is work, in the initial stages at least, for your many assistants, *non?*"

"The execution, perhaps, Your Holiness, but the concept and structure rest solely with me."

"Perhaps a new perspective . . . another artist with a bit of youthful vigor to lend you a hand?"

Raphael kept on with his caution. He saw quickly where this was going. "Has Your Holiness someone in mind?"

He scratched his shining chin and the jewels on his fingers glinted in the light. "Michelangelo tells me that his good friend Sebastiano Luciani would be willing to consult on this room."

The pope was a patient and generous man but he was also a

Medici, not given to fully revealing his allegiances to any one in particular. Raphael felt trapped suddenly by that, by his own waning ambition, and by something unexplainable that was drawing him away from the torrent of work before him. He leaned forward and clasped his hands.

"Before I do anything more, this room shall be complete for your more formal audience after Mass on Sunday, if I must work without sleep to make it so. I will need no more assistance on it than that which I already have. And"—he held his arm out flamboyantly, charmingly—"as a crowning glory, a symbol of my indebtedness to you for your patronage—and your most gracious indulgence of me—I shall bring Your Holiness the first sketches for the most glorious, innovative Madonna you can imagine, within a fortnight, and they as well shall be my personal gift to you!"

"This chamber complete?" he pointed, each breath heavy, labored. "*Finally*, by Sunday?"

"Sunday it shall be."

The pontiff seemed genuinely pleased with Raphael's groveling, and with his promises. A more sedate smile now lengthened his small, thick lips. It broke the tension that had sprung so suddenly between them. "Well, I am *most* anxious to see it."

He put a hand on Raphael's shoulder in a fatherly gesture. The square emerald ring on his last finger sparkled in the light through the long wall of leaded-glass windows. "And what of the women, Raffaello *mio*? Do I have your word that you will cease with your distraction there, at least until some of the outstanding commissions are complete?"

His sharp Medici nostrils flared almost imperceptibly, but Raphael took the warning within the question. Perhaps it was true that Michelangelo had returned to Rome only to inquire after the Julius tomb. Or perhaps it was to advance Sebastiano's claim. But either way, Raphael must take no chances with the lives and welfare of dozens of assistants who depended upon him, and on the good graces of their pontiff.

"You have my word," Raphael agreed. And the promise was

not all that difficult, drawn as he was, not by the thought of
women, but of one woman—the mysterious girl on Il Gianicolo—and his hope that by now Giulio had found out who she
was, and where she lived.

ONCE RAPHAEL had taken his leave, a tall, exceedingly elegant
man with a thick black beard emerged from the collection of cardinals and clerics at the pope's side. He was clothed in a pumpkin-
colored silk tunic and hose, beneath a luxurious fur-trimmed cape
of forest-green velvet. A heavy bronze medallion hung from his
neck. On either side of the pontiff, yet another crimson-clad cardinal now stood. *Like great ecclesiastical bookends,* thought the wealthy
banker, Agostino Chigi. But Giovanni de' Medici had been his
friend before he had taken the title Leo X, and Chigi owed a debt
to that stroke of good fortune. He must never forget by whose
grace he held a place at the pontiff's very grand Vatican table, or at
his musical parties, and opulent hunting events—those were the
places where real policy was made. Chigi had given himself great
wealth. Pope Leo had given him the power to use it.

"I say let us enjoy the papacy since God has given it to us,"
Pope Leo frequently said. Having been elected pope barely eight
months before, he planned to make the most of his life's appointment. And so he did enjoy it, from food, to music, to an explo-
ration of the most glorious arts. Made a cardinal at age thirteen
by the far-reaching powers of his infamous family, he had survived the first papal election, called the first scrutiny, by receiving
only a single vote. His supporters bade their time and advised
him well. Despite some concern that so youthful a pontiff might
not be up to the burden, at the age of thirty-eight, Medici, nevertheless, became Leo X.

Chigi, was a big man on a bull-like frame with a crown of
dark, thick rings of hair. He bowed reverently, and kissed the ring
on Leo's plump finger in accordance with the custom. The pope's
hand smelled, not of the many pastries he consumed, but of
chicken grease from an earlier meal, Chigi noticed, as repulsed as

ever. Giovanni de' Medici did everything in a grand way. He ate much, drank overly, and enjoyed life to excess, in spite of an inconvenient call to reflection and prayer.

"You heard everything, I presume?"

"Certainly far more than expected, Your Holiness," Chigi replied in a well-schooled voice, dripping sincerity like honey wine. "I had no idea our dear Raphael was so behind schedule on his commissions for everyone else as well."

Pope Leo stood, stepped down from the dais, and took Chigi's arm. They moved slowly together then out of the richly decorated room and into the corridor in time with the pope's sluggish, shuffling step.

"And it will certainly continue unchanged if he goes forward with more of his Madonnas. I had expected him to be finished with the frescoes for my family chapel at least by All Saints' Day, since we missed the summer. And of course, Your Holiness awaits the completion of your audience chamber there, which craves the utmost of his personal attention before all else," Chigi recovered with a deeply deferential nod. "Not to mention your formal portrait, which he has yet even to begin."

One of the papal secretaries, a balding, slightly stoop-shouldered man named Bembo, dabbed the pontiff's glistening forehead with a white silk kerchief, edged in Venetian lace, as they walked. "He trusts you, does he not?"

"I believe it is so, Your Holiness, for it was I who brought him to Rome in the first place."

Pope Leo imperiously stroked his chin with two of the fat fingertips. *"Molto bene.* Then we shall direct him to proceed with the works for you before all others."

"It must not be! Your Holiness is first in all things!"

He held up a firm hand. "Patience, Agostino *mio.* It is the greatest of the virtues. Having Raffaello tied closely to you shall serve greatly to enhance your hold over him. And a trusting friend is one who speaks freely. A more approachable friend to him shall suit me. Only someone who has the benefit of his intimacy will know when it is his appetites, and his women, who stand alarmingly in the way of his production. We needs be apprised continually of where the center of his heart truly lies. For without Raffaello's full attention, he shall never be able to give us the volume of work we desire."

"So we silently guide him to our own purposes then, just as a monkey on a leash. Is that not so, Holy Father?"

"Precisely so," agreed the pope.

"WELL? HAVE YOU FOUND HER?"

Later that afternoon, Raphael met Giulio Romano at the rounded door of his busy workshop, the huge space he maintained on the Piazza Sant'Apollonia. He held on to the sturdy brass door pull, his eyes wide with anticipation, as though he were the boy he had been once, long ago, in Urbino.

Giulio removed his cloak and walked with Raphael back to the paint-spattered worktable where he had been putting the setting resin onto a new portrait. Strewn across the table's work surface were dozens of pen studies, layered with wash and traces of black chalk. Others on small bits of paper had been done in different mediums: black chalk over stylus or silverpoint done on gray, prepared paper. Pens, stubs of blue, black and red chalk and paintbrushes, their handles stained with a melange of colors, lay around them.

"I found her."

"Has she agreed to come? Will she allow me to sketch her for the Madonna?"

"I am afraid the girl would not see me."

"*Porca miseria!*"

"She sent her father out to tell me that she was uninterested in being propositioned by any artisan."

Raphael flung down his wet brush, thick blue resin splattering the worktable and his own shoes. *"Proposition?* She speaks like a Campo de' Fiori tart! I did no such thing, Giulio!" He raked the straight hair back from his forehead, feeling strangely undone. "Did you not make clear who I am? Or all that I wish from her?"

"Forgive me, but she was most firmly set against any involvement. For what it is worth, you have taught me well, *mastro.* I saw her peeking out from behind a curtain as we spoke, and I do understand what you see in her." He spread a consoling arm across Raphael's shoulder. Giulio continued with a boyish smile. "That face of hers, *mastro,* the eyes most especially, are extraordinary, and if you will pardon me, the words of the man and not the artist, her body seems quite mattressable indeed!" It was uncharacteristically crude, and not in keeping with this boy.

Raphael closed his eyes. Giulio was young and unpracticed in so many things. To work here, among these men, that would need to change, he reminded himself. It was an entirely different perspective, youth.

In spite of her beauty, bedding the girl was not an option. To Raphael she was the Madonna—mother of Christ. One did not consider crossing the emotional chasm that would sully that vision and likely scar the very work he sought to create. Besides, she was nothing at all like the women who lured him and seduced him. But there was no use explaining that to his young, untried apprentice, who did his best to exist in a world of salty-tongued, harsh-tempered artists, far older and more worldly than he. Especially when the young woman had so far refused his offer. And this wild, impetuous thing that had taken hold of him was something he could not allow, nor accept. He was, after all, *Raffaello*—painter to popes and kings. He could not—would not—be undone by a common woman!

Raphael drew in a breath and felt dizzy, but he resisted the sensation. "Then I simply must go to her myself and explain the situation," he said carefully. "What is the address?"

"Twenty-one Via Santa Dorotea. Very near here. Just over the Ponte Sisto, actually."

"And her husband? Did he seem an impediment?"

"I saw only the father, who was most anxious that she should reconsider."

"Then it is the father I must entreat to reason with her." And then, almost as an afterthought, he asked, "Did you not ask her name?"

"She is called Margherita, *mastro*."

Raphael felt a strange smile tug at his lips as if it suited her. "*The pearl* . . . Well, she certainly is that—luminescent . . . rare. And her family name?"

"Luti. She is Margherita Luti."

"I know the name not. Ah, well. No matter. She is still my new Madonna, and I shall do what it takes to convince her of it." She should be honored to be asked, he thought smugly. His work graced many of the great churches and villas of Rome, Florence, and beyond. He had the ear of dukes, princes, and the Holy Father himself. Could she truly turn away from an opportunity such as that? Tomorrow morning he would present himself in the impressive manner she expected, then, of course, he would convince her, and that would be that.

RAPHAEL LEFT his house early the next morning. Dressed grandly in a slashed yellow doublet, scarlet hose, and scarlet velvet cap, a folio of drawing paper and sketches beneath his arm, he moved alone soundlessly along the wide Via dei Coronari. Amid the first slivers of pale pink sunlight, he pulled his cloak up around his shoulders to ward away the cold. A heavy dew had fallen during the night, and the wet streets and narrow alleyways around him floated in a kind of opalescent haze. It was too early for many to have arisen except an ambitious painter with more work than time. He made his way even before the shutters opened and servants began their own early morning task of tossing buckets of soiled water, slop jars, and the contents of chamber pots from open windows.

Raphael had wanted at first to go to her alone, but apparently she had expected him to travel nobly, with an entourage. So to get what he wished, he would give her what *she* wished. Before him was the image of those deep, expressive eyes — eyes belonging to a young woman about whom he knew nothing, other than that he must paint her. And he must convince her husband that it would be worth their while.

Walking with purpose, in long, bold strides, Raphael passed an old stone wall studded with brass rings to tie up horses. Beyond was a butcher's shop, as yet unopened for the fast-approaching business day. He came out onto an open piazza. There, a team of his assistants — Giulio Romano, the older and more stoic Giovanni da Udine, and the potbellied, rosy-faced Gianfrancesco Penni, with his unruly red-gold curls — all garbed nearly as expensively as the *mastro,* waited for him. Together, the four well-dressed, important-looking men walked onto the next street and into the wisps of fog that moved around them all like great, illusive fingers of smoke — until Raphael came to a sudden stop.

At 21 Via Santa Dorotea, they all stood before a slope-roofed, salmon-colored facade, with a little brick-colored door and a wooden sign printed with the word *Panetteria* swinging gently on two wide brass hooks above it. Giulio had not told him that his new Madonna model was a baker's daughter. She had seemed to him too delicate, too elegant, for such a common existence. Nevertheless, Raphael drew back the weathered shop door, took a step down onto the rough stone floor, and stood amid a collection of early morning patrons and baskets of fragrant bread.

"Is it a loaf of the fruit bread you are after?" asked the short, squat man with the green, wide-set eyes who held back the muslin curtain with a meaty hand. Behind the man, Raphael could see sacks of flour propped against the wall, and he could smell the rich, sweet scent of rising bread dough. "If you are, I've just told everyone else they'll not be ready before—"

The man, lightly caked in flour from neck to toe, but for the sheen of perspiration covering his beefy round face, stopped in midsentence. Raphael saw his lower jaw slacken as he focused on the four elegantly dressed companions, far too grand for this neighborhood bakery. Still, Raphael lowered himself into an elegant and courtly bow, tipping his scarlet cap as he rose again and stepped forward. Everyone else inside turned as well, and the chatter fell to an abrupt and noticeable hush.

Beyond the smudged panes on the bakery window a crowd had gathered. "I am Raphael Sanzio, and I wish to speak to the husband of the girl called Margherita."

"Much to my great sorrow, Margherita has yet no husband. But I am her father, Francesco Luti," he explained, his chest puffed up a little with hopeful pride as he wiped his floury hands on the apron tied tightly below his paunch. "I understand you wish my daughter to model for you."

"*Sì*, I do wish it very much."

"*Per favore*," said Francesco with a sweeping hand, indicating the small back room. "Will you not come inside, Signor Sanzio, where it will be more private for us to speak?"

Raphael followed Margherita's father into the small, stifling kitchen, with its heavy oak beams, the room dominated by two fiery bread ovens and a scarred, flour-coated oak table. Francesco Luti drew out a chair and offered it to the man known as royalty by everyone in Rome.

There was something in being here Raphael thought, some echo of his long forgotten childhood that struck him. The rich, sweet scent of baking bread brought it quickly back for him. His own father had been a painter at a ducal palace, yes, yet their life had been quite humble. As a boy, there had been trips to the butcher, the wine merchant, and the baker after the duke had gone to his own opulent table. Even in his fine silk doublet and elegant hose, he suddenly found, at this moment, that the world of his childhood did not seem so very far away.

"So she is unmarried," Raphael repeated casually, remembering the man he had become.

"It is so."

"I assumed by the small child she carried that—"

"Her sister's youngest son, Signor Sanzio."

Raphael saw a glitter in Luti's eye, as though his mind, and his coin pouch, were working faster than his mouth. "My daughter, Letitia, is blessed with four strong sons. Of course I wish the same for my Margherita, but at times, what the mind knows the spirit refuses—"

"You would do well to hold your tongue further, *Padre mio,*" came a soft, slightly husky female voice from behind them. "I am certain the great Raffaello does not desire to be bothered with the inner workings of our family."

Seeing her standing in the door arch, with a narrow stairway behind her, Raphael rose, smoothing out the front of his doublet with both hands like an uncertain youth. For a moment, as before, he could not find the quick-witted banter she would expect. What the devil was it that made him feel so uncertain before her? Only women he was driven to bed had ever, even momentarily, had this same upper hand.

Margherita stood looking mistrustfully at him. Her sable-brown hair, in this light, parted in the center and drawn away from her face, was glistening, the shades more vivid than he remembered. It would take days, he thought, to mix the precise paints to achieve the highlights there. Her neck was graceful, slim, and creamy olive. Because of her cloak, he had not noticed its indescribably delicate turn. She appeared even more rich and complex than the young woman he had first seen yesterday. But that spark of determination and spirit in her eyes was still his greatest draw.

"On the contrary," Raphael managed to say. "I find great insight in your father's words."

She moved forward. "And, pray, *signore,* how is that?"

"I hope it will explain why you have refused the offer from my assistant."

"And why I shall refuse you myself. I am a decent woman, Signor Sanzio. I know my place in this world. I am meant to make an honest life."

He bit back the coming of a bemused smile as he glanced at his assistants, who were smiling with him. "And what has modeling to do with that?"

"Is it not unseemly, and illegal, to position a woman's body in a manner for study by a stranger who intends to survey every surface of one's face and form?"

She exchanged a sharp glance with her father, whose lower jaw had fallen open in disbelief at her brazenness. "Margherita!" Francesco interceded, his voice rumbling with anger even as he managed a humble bow before their important guest.

"Would you ask that question, I wonder, of Isabella of Aragon? Or perhaps our Holy Father himself, both of whom have previously sat willingly for me?" He settled his eyes directly upon her. "There is modeling, Signorina Luti, and then there is portraiture."

"*Per favore!* Signor Sanzio, I implore you! Forgive my daughter!"

"Forgive *me?*" Margherita gasped.

"I am afraid she has too much of her mother's haughty spirit for her own good! Believe me, it was a trait I cherished in my daughter for the nostalgia it brought—until today, that is!"

"Tell me, Signor Sanzio." Margherita took a step forward, hands clasped behind her back, her chin lifted, not with rudeness, but rather an unexpected confidence. "Was it your expectation that merely by your coming here yourself, cloaked in velvet and silver, and surrounded with your equally finely dressed minions, that I would be more easily convinced to change my mind?"

The way she had phrased it, the circumstance seemed instantly tawdry.

"I would not have guessed that a girl—" He stopped himself in midsentence. That tactic was not going to help things with her. But it was too late.

"What was it, *signore*? You would not have guessed that a simple girl from Trastevere could keep pace with someone so grand and worldly as you?"

He moved to deny it, but the truth was that this was exactly what he had meant. Women had always been without consequence in his life. There was no struggle in obtaining them for what purpose he wished. That was not the case now, very suddenly, in this most unlikely situation. While he barely knew Margherita, she already angered him, confounded him, and entirely bewitched him, all at the same instant.

When he did not readily respond to her question, she said, "Make no mistake, *signore*. Because I assumed a great *mastro* would move with an entourage does not mean I would be swayed by its appearance at my door."

Giovanni da Udine, in wine-colored velvet, was tall, broad-shouldered, and exceedingly elegant, with a shock of silvery hair that gave him a distinguished air. Despite that veneer, he stifled a snicker behind his jeweled hand. Raphael heard it and shot him an immediate look of reproach. A dozen retorts vaulted through his mind, but he realized then, in the awkward silence, that she was worthy of none of them.

It was getting late, and Raphael had the metal point study of an allegorical Mars to heighten with white chalk for the other Chigi chapel, and a few pencil studies to outline so that his assistants would know what he desired them to paint. Then there was the application of the last layer of plaster on the final Vatican fresco to oversee. There was also a problem with the expression on the pope's face, as he sat in profile astride his horse, in the *Repulse of Attila,* which he must deal with himself, and it must be accomplished before midday.

He still very much wanted Signorina Luti, but he could not paint her—he could not capture that essence of a Madonna, if her sitting for him was a chore for her. He reached down and drew from his cloak a pouch of gold florins. Gently, he set it on the empty table between the three of them, the coins making a little clinking sound as they settled in the bag.

"We must take our leave. But in the meantime, I have left a first installment on what my studio will pay you to allow me to make several pencil sketches, culminating in a full-color panel of you dressed as the Madonna for my commission by the late Pope Julius II that shall hang in the great Chapel at San Sisto in Piacenza."

Francesco Luti gave a sound somewhere between a moan and a wail, then made the sign of the cross. *"Santissima Maria!"*

"You may pray to the saints, Signor Luti, but as you wait for their reply you would do well to reason strongly with your daughter. This is an existing commission, and I am *not* at liberty to wait forever." Raphael nodded courteously. *"Buon giorno* to you both."

"Mastro Sanzio, one question if you please."

The throaty alto voice was Margherita's. Raphael pivoted back.

In the light of early morning, when Rome was still pink and opalescent, her face looked radiant, and he thought then, for the first time, that he had fooled himself. She was actually remarkably sensual and, *sì* . . . appealing, in a way that now piqued all of his senses, not only the initial creative ones.

"May I ask why you have chosen me?"

"Why does anyone make a choice of something, *signorina?*" he said in a flippant tone that was part style, and part self-defense. "There is an element of instinct, and another of fate. With my painting, one is always tied so tightly with the other that I have learned only to honor it, and not to question why. Once again," he nodded. *"Buon giorno* to you."

"I DO NOT understand you!" Francesco Luti wailed. He slapped his forehead with the palm of his flour-caked hand, as he cast his eyes dramatically heavenward. "Had I not been here to see it for myself, I would have thought it a cruel jest! Now I *know* without doubt that you have taken full leave of your senses! Where has this come from? This is not you! Thanks to your mother's dreams for you, you have put Antonio off, waiting all of your life for something extraordinary like this to happen, and now that it has—"

Her mother, so beautiful, and so full of dreams, had told her many stories as a child, like that of the famous and married emperor, Nero, and his love for Poppaea, a girl beneath his station. Their romance had brought a cloud of scandal to Rome. There was always great excitement in her mother's whispered voice, as she told how Poppaea had become Nero's great love—and finally his wife.

And so it can happen to any clever, beautiful girl, Marina Luti had whispered to her youngest daughter—the one who listened the most intently—as she tucked her beneath the bedcovers and pressed a kiss onto her forehead. *And one wise enough to believe in the beauty of her dreams!*

But her mother was dead now, her dreams gone to dust. And Margherita was here, still living in the real world.

"Perhaps you do not know me so well as you think," Margherita declared, remembering the tragic end of the love story of Nero and Poppaea.

He pivoted away. "Och! It is too much!"

"And what of your family, Margherita, eh, what of us?" Letitia intervened, preparing to mount a full attack. "Could we not all benefit from the florins Signor Sanzio has promised you? To help Father stop working so hard? Perhaps he would be able to hire an assistant to give his swollen ankles a rest."

There had always been a rivalry between the two sisters. Letitia had been the first to marry, but Margherita was the more beautiful. And so, in her way, Letitia had always sought to undermine her sister's dreams, encouraging her to marry Donato's younger brother, Antonio, and to strive for no better than what she had. It was a future their father had sanctioned—and to which Margherita had grudgingly agreed.

"Do not lay it all at my feet, Letitia!" she argued.

"Is that not precisely where it lies?"

"My daughter is a fool!" said Francesco gruffly as he shuffled back to his daughters.

"Perhaps I am, *Padre mio*. But I will not be taken for granted— not by anyone!"

"Then you would do well to make your peace with life as a saddle boy's wife! For that is surely the best fate has to offer Antonio!"

"You have always wanted me to marry him!"

"That was *before* I knew there might be another choice! Oh, I bid you, look beyond your nose, Margherita! There is a whole wide world out there, and none of us has ever had the chance to see any of it beyond the Via Santa Dorotea!"

"Is it my duty to go as if I were no better than the hound at the great painter's heels? I know what you and Letitia want, both of you fawning over his grand clothes and his elegant friends. But the price for your ambition, *Padre mio,* is too high for me to pay!"

His small eyes narrowed and his face darkened with rage. "Where did a baker's daughter from Trastevere learn to believe she was so high and mighty that she could walk away from a purse full of gold florins?"

"From the woman *you* married, *Padre mio.*"

"Is this chance not precisely what she desired for you?"

"Not with a man of his reputation! My mother married you against the wishes and advice of nearly everyone she knew. She trusted her own mind *and* her heart. Is that not the story you have always told us? She waited not for opportunity—but love!"

Francesco Luti shook his head and let a heavy sigh as his eyes filled with sudden tears. "God rest her precious soul, it was the truth. And God help us all . . . you are just like her."

NEAR MIDNIGHT, when the workshop was cool and empty, and all of the assistants and apprentices were gone, Raphael stood alone at his easel with a wet portrait panel centered before him.

Beside it on the worktable, draped with a paint-splattered sheet, was a large, untouched jug of wine, a wooden bucket full of dirty paint water, and cups stuffed with brushes. Pausing to study the image, he then filled his boar-bristle brush with a mixture of taupe and salmon pink paint, and skillfully applied it, causing a flesh and veined hand to burst forth.

The massive room was lit by two large oil lamps with smoking flames that cast their dancing shadows onto the wall behind him. Raphael felt a shiver of excitement—a kind of caged energy that coursed through him. *Dio,* it was good to work like this, he thought, good to connect with the panel, to feel the paint, to take the acrid smell of it into his lungs, to bring from nothing a representation of that which almighty God had created! *As I once did . . . as I sometimes believe I have forgotten how, for having to be "Raffaello" . . .*

Only in this act of quiet solitude, with the easy companionship of his well-used paintbrush, did Raphael feel fully the sensation that had possessed him as a boy, as he had watched his own father paint at the Urbino chapel—as he had first held his own brush. It had been a long road from that simple act of glorious communion—the commissions, the power plays, the clothes, the dancing lessons, the fencing lessons, the elocution lessons, the daily need to flatter and ingratiate himself to people. But that was his world now, and most days he was glad of it. Until a moment like this, in the still, dark hours, surrounded and taken up by wet paint and supple brushes. It made him remember the simple boy from the countryside, with only talent and dreams. And he was still that boy beneath all these trappings and pressures of courtly success—a little lost and awed by what he had become, and the unyielding pressure to maintain it.

Raphael studied the face he had created: Baldassare Castiglione, the great courtier and writer who had befriended him in Florence. He would be pleased. The likeness in oil was uncanny. His face would be as immortal as the elegant words he laid down in his book, which Raphael had been told he meant to call *The Courtier.*

It was that grand scholar, in fact, who had awakened in Raphael his love of learning. Not formally schooled as a child, Raphael had begun by borrowing Homer's *Iliad* from the sage old man who insisted he be called Baldassare, even by an inexperienced youth. After that literary suggestion had come the more humorous works of Aristophanes and Virgil. Raphael had rapidly devoured those as well, asking questions on the occasions they met, and listening to the wise, kindly elder statesman explain about the other great masterpieces he should come to know: the works of Socrates, Plato's *Republic,* and particularly Aristotle's writings concerning the soul. Raphael wanted to understand and to see things the way the brilliant minds did. He wanted that knowledge to move through him and out onto his panels and frescoes. His friendship with Castiglione had awakened something in him that had not been put down since. The evidence of that was his own steadily growing library on the Via dei Coronari. Like his workshop at night, the library of leather-bound volumes was a sanctuary, a place to be surrounded and possessed by something far grander than himself.

Raphael looked at the old man's kind face—the dark turban and cloak that drew the viewer to his eyes and small, subtle mouth. Raphael smiled sadly, greatly missing his sage counsel. *If he were here now, he would tell me I have taken on too much,* Raphael thought. *Unlike my father, he would tell me I am too possessed by the things outside myself to hear the things within. Sì, he would say exactly that. And he would be right.*

The fire in the coal brazier beside his easel had gone to glowing embers long ago. It was time to go home, but he could not move. From somewhere he had not been for a long time, the energy surged. It clawed at him. The desire. The need. With it came a flare of that old, relentless ambition. *Create!* it urged. *Paint!*

All through the night, Raphael remained inside the small, private room in his workshop. Now, having brought his easel here, and having bolted the door, he stood alone, dripping with oil paint, hands darkened with chalk, and blinded by an urge not to delegate or discuss, but to work.

And when the flurry ended near dawn, when he was spent and exhausted, what he saw spread around himself on the floor was a sea of parchment as thick as a layer of new snow, and each sheaf was decorated with hands, eyes, arms. As he glanced around, only then did he realize that the images were all parts of her.

Why was Margherita Luti so set against him? And, more than that, with so many other pressing commissions to trouble him, why did it matter?

You have never cared this much about obtaining a model before, he heard the echo of Giovanni da Udine's declaration before he had gone home earlier. And Giovanni was right. The young Florentine woman he had used for the many earlier Madonnas, so blond and serene, had let him sketch her face, study her eyes, nose, and lips, been paid for the trouble, then left his life compliantly.

Was it merely Margherita's refusal that had confounded him? Surely not. In spite of a measured attraction to her, he now grudgingly reminded himself, Margherita still was nothing like the lusty Roman women whom he seduced with impressive regularity. Why then was he absolutely compelled to convince her to enter his world? Certainly she was the Madonna. That face, the delicacy of her bones, the luminescence of her skin, her haunting eyes, and the unmistakable pride born by the mother of Christ.

But she had refused him. Twice.

In a rage of fatigue and frustration, as a pale pink dawn filtered in through the leaded-glass windows, Raphael began to shred the parchment into small bits. He was destroying what he had only just been driven to spend the night creating.

MARGHERITA SAT ALONE ON HER OAK-FRAMED BED IN A small, spartan room above the bakery. Beneath the coarse, gray blanket, knees curled to her chest, she gazed beyond the window at the starry night sky. The room would be stifling, even in autumn, were the shutters beside her bed not partially opened to draw in the breeze. On the other side of the wall, Letitia and Donato's bedchamber was shared with their two smallest sons. The older boys slept in the attic loft of the odd-shaped little house. Living so near a couple long married, Margherita had learned much about the private world of a husband and wife. Those sounds, with their primal rhythms, had ignited the fears she now had of a life with Donato's brother, Antonio.

She could not help but think of the two of them like that, softly laughing, murmuring, pleasuring one another, in a private, unhurried way that did not involve inconvenient barriers. Antonio had shown her something else, a world of secretive cloaks, and the pungent smell of horse stalls where he had, twice before, stolen her away for a sensual kiss. Since they were children, Donato's younger brother had vowed he would marry her. And there was safety in that life. Safety and an end to dreams.

Until today.

So, her family truly wished for her to pose for the great Raffaello? And there would be more gold coins to come. If she would only leave Trastevere, risk the unknown, and sit for his painting. A baker's income was meager. A stableman's even less. But there was something unseemly about a woman earning the money a family required. Would not the wives of the neighborhood whisper about her? And would they not be right to believe that the family had lowered themselves by allowing her to sit before the probing eyes of another man in exchange for money? "What has she done for the great *mastro*?" they would doubtless titter. What liberties had he taken? As Signor Sanzio stood downstairs, so elegantly clad in velvet and satin, jewels on his fingers, rich embroidery on his doublet, with half the neighborhood peering in through the windows, she had imagined how it would be, and she had despised him.

But mixed with those thoughts was the memory of his hands. He had such elegant hands, with long, tapered fingers, she had thought, through which magic flowed.

Hands that could make her immortal.

The thought had only confused her more.

The great Raphael Sanzio wishing to paint me! . . . And what more does he wish in return, giving such an honor? A small voice inside her posed the question with jarring clarity. And therein lay the real dilemma. What did the famous and powerful Raffaello truly want with a baker's daughter from Trastevere? His wild reputation with women was nearly as well known as his work. He was a master. An icon. He could have anything—and anyone—he wished. She was only a simple girl with a simple future. One day when he was finished with his painting, he would send her back here, to this place and this life. And she would never be the same.

Margherita wanted more for her life, as her mother had wanted it. But she had, at last, accepted the notion of a future with Antonio because the dreams had begun to fade along with the memory of her mother. For his part, her father had always sanctioned their informal courtship, envisioning no greater fate for his younger child. It had been that way since her mother's death ten years before after a violent fall from a horse. Margherita had been almost nine. Antonio, nearly eleven, had been more mature in the face of loss, having buried his own father the year before. They had walked down to the Tiber, where the water's edge met the mossy bank. That was where a little lost girl with feet too small for her hand-me-down shoes had come to rely on a boy who lived only two houses away.

A stray memory crawled out from the back of her mind then—one that had not come to her in a very long time. She was that child again, sitting in this very bed, Antonio beside her, a tall and worldly ten-year-old, his arm around her heaving shoulder, holding her as she wept.

"Margherita, you must go to the church!"

"She cannot be dead! She is my mother! God cannot be so cruel!"

"She is still here with you," Antonio had murmured kindly. "She is watching you from heaven. And it would make her awfully sad to see you still crying."

She had lifted her tearstained face to him then and sniffled. "But there was no one like her, Antonio! She believed in me, she took care of me! She promised me that my life would be different! Now I have only my father and his bakery! He will be too busy to care for me now."

"*I* will always take care of you, Margherita," he had said earnestly as he took her hand and helped her stand.

"Do you promise?"

"For the rest of our lives, we will share everything. *Promesso...*" When she managed the faintest smile, he said, "Now will you go to the church to listen to the Mass said for her? The others are already there."

Margherita sniffled again. "Will you come with me?"

"I will come with you . . . and sit beside you . . . and, one day, I will even marry you."

The childhood image crawled back into her memory as swiftly as it had emerged, safer there. Protected. It felt to Margherita that she had belonged to Antonio for her whole life. She had kept him as one does a favored childhood blanket, for the comforting predictability of it. Now the wildly famous painter represented something far more magnificent. Something rich, exciting, and unknown. If she did this, saw things beyond Trastevere, there would be no returning for her heart, not back to the ordinary world that now existed around her. It would be like a Pandora's box, the contents of which, once revealed, could never be put away. And the idea of that frightened her terribly.

And it drove her back to imagining her future in Trastevere.

Antonio Perazzi, Donato's errant younger brother, was a saddle boy and apprentice stirrup-maker, for now. But he was one with the promise of a brighter future. Last year, he had accepted a job assisting his brother at the stables of the Palazzo Chigi. It was only a matter of time, he boasted, until his true talent was discovered. Then he would be promoted to the position of full stableman, one who might actually squire the great and powerful

Signor Chigi, or one of his mistresses, between the villa and the Vatican, where they were frequent guests.

Hearing light footfalls on the patch of roof beside her window, Margherita sprung from beneath her bedcovers. She cast them back, drew open the window shutters fully, and, in a haze of shock, helped Antonio inside her small, sparely furnished bedchamber. Suddenly, as if her thoughts alone had called him, he stood before her in the shadows, wearing a forest green tunic with leather at the hem, buff-colored wool hose, slashed leather boots with cuffs, and a small leather hat, his hands placed pointedly on slim hips. The unmistakable gritty odor of horseflesh swirled around his smooth, beardless face and tousled, honey-colored hair.

"This is madness! What are you doing here?" she asked on an incredulous whisper. "You'll be discovered!"

"I made certain I was not seen. But I must know! How did the great Raphael of Urbino not only meet you, but find *you* suitable enough to pose for one of his paintings?"

"Donato told you."

"Of course. My brother tells me all."

"We met on Il Gianicolo yesterday," she said with hesitation, as if revealing something private. "Naturally, at first, I did not believe him. But when he had his apprentice follow me home, his hands stained with chalk dust, his hose spotted with paint—"

Antonio stopped. His steel-blue eyes widened. Suddenly he slapped a palm against his forehead. Then he took her shoulders in his hands bracingly. "You must do it!"

"Do what?"

"You *must* pose for the *mastro!*"

She looked away. "I don't know what I will do."

"You must consider only your good fortune, *cara*. Fortune smiles only on those willing to seize it boldly!"

Disregarding the platitude, and an odd sense of warning that began to snake its way up inside of her, she said instead, "Did you not tell me my greatest fortune was in finding *you*?"

Seizing her shoulders with commanding fingertips now, Antonio drew her against him as he first had when they were much younger, found her lips, and began to kiss her with a wild hunger that entirely disarmed her defenses. "Do this for us, *cara*," he murmured. "To help our beginning. *Per favore!* Say you will at least reconsider his proposal."

Margherita felt the insistent pressure of his taut body and felt herself yielding to the power of it. "I will consider it."

"Va bene." He moved his lips to kiss her cheek, then smiled. A moment later, he was poised once again beside the open window, and turned around, as if with an afterthought. A cool breeze blew the thin muslin curtains in around him. "The gold florins that the great Raffaello left with you," he said, and his eyes were twinkling mischievously. "It would be most helpful to give one to my mother, if you have one to share." His steel-blue eyes were made a deeper blue shining in the moonlight. "I cannot be certain, of course, but I should think it would go a long way to convincing her that you are committed totally, at last, to seeing her as your mother-in-law."

"I cannot possibly go downstairs now. My father would hear me!"

"Then bring it tomorrow to the stables on your way to the *mastro*'s studio? You know you must see him again. To apologize."

"Since you asked me, I shall consider it."

Antonio's eyes glittered. "Consider nothing but that, and you shall please me greatly."

IN THE SHADOW of his passionate kiss, the sweet taste of his mouth, and the turmoil of adolescence remembered that had been rekindled within her there came a soft rapping on her closed bedroom door. Before Margherita could respond, the handle was turned and Donato, Letitia's husband, stood in the doorway. "Are you asleep?" he asked. "I thought I heard something in here."

"I am awake," she called in reply.

Donato was the brother she had never had. They had grown up together, all four of them, in the narrow streets and alleyways of Trastevere, a short walk just beyond the ancient Porta Settimiana to Agostino Chigi's opulent waterside palace.

Donato sank onto the edge of the bed beside her. The familiar odor of leather and horse sweat was comforting. She smiled looking at him as they sat in the circle of light cast from her flickering lamp. Tall and lean, with sleek, dark hair to his shoulders, a flat, Tuscan nose, and ruddy skin, he was so good, she thought—steady and firm. It seemed to her that he was kindness itself. And he was one of the reasons she cared for Antonio.

"Letitia told me what happened today," Donato said gently. "Are you all right?"

"It is all so unbelievable." She cast a glance back at the unshuttered window where, only a moment before, Antonio had stood, taking her back to a time better forgotten.

"And yet you have refused the chance to discover whether it might not actually be real?"

"What could someone like that possibly want with someone like me, Donato?" She leaned forward, drew up her knees again beneath the blanket, and wrapped her arms around them.

"You are a lovely girl, *cara*. Is it so impossible to believe that a great *mastro* might not see that in you?"

"He paints kings and princes, and the works in the Vatican, home of the Holy Father himself! We sell bread, Donato! How could the great Raffaello possibly see beyond that? And if he does, and I allow it, what shall become of me afterward?"

"Then the whole world shall be before you. Your life shall become the stuff of legends!"

"And your brother? What shall become of *him*? We have always had something of an agreement."

"Antonio shall be just fine, *cara mia*. Don't worry about that." Seeing the hesitation on her soft face, he took her hand gently. "Poor Margherita *mia*. I wish you could see yourself as others do.

As *I* have always seen you." A smile played across his lips. It made his dark eyes dance in the light that the moon cast across the two of them through the window. He leaned nearer, clutching her hand more tightly. "I know of a woman, a lady's maid in the Chigi villa. Someone I met through my brother." He seemed suddenly uncomfortable but continued nonetheless. "I showed her a courtesy once with regard to Antonio. She says she owes me a favor. Tomorrow morning at dawn, come with me to the stables. There just might be something I can do to change your opinion, and your mind, concerning the weight you give my brother versus your interest in Raffaello."

She smiled as well, feeling so safe and happy in Donato's company. There was nothing she would not do for him.

THE MORNING AIR was crisply cold, and a thick fog rolled around their ankles and around their heavy cloaks. Passing an oxcart heavily laden with baskets full of vegetables on the way to market, Margherita and Donato stepped out of Trastevere. Each step brought them closer toward the elaborate, three-story Chigi stables.

The important facade was an architectural work of art itself, where Signor Chigi had actually held parties to boast of the building's unique splendor. It was an imposing, square, sandy stone building ornamented with intricate cornices, and sleek pilasters, and a rounded, stone-trimmed gate. In the courtyard beyond the large carved door, and hidden from the street, was a splashing fountain designed in the manner of a waterfall, the ribbons of water falling into a circle of marble goddess statues.

She waited quietly with Donato amid lush fig and plane trees, and rich emerald vines of ivy overhanging the high walls of weathered stone. Margherita was unable to still her racing heart. She could barely believe the opulent world she had entered, so oddly close to their modest bakery.

A beautiful young woman crossed the courtyard to meet them.

"Buon giorno," she whispered to Donato in a tone that seemed to imply something. Margherita saw that she was older and startlingly elegant, with her wide gold-green eyes, and honey-colored hair smooth and long beneath a soft cap stitched with silver thread. Her sweeping dress, of claret-colored silk, with gold and silver embroidery, had tight sleeves and a very tight bodice, enough to highlight a willowy, elegant form beneath.

There would be only a moment or two, she explained. They dare not risk more. Early or not, one of the other servants or a page might discover them. Then she and Donato both would likely lose their positions with the Chigi family. The woman led them silently from the courtyard. Margherita followed behind them, feeling as if she were not so much walking as floating. Something drew her forward past the juniper trees, magnificent statues, and Grecian urns. They went through a small side door and into the palazzo itself. Margherita's heart raced so that she almost could not catch her breath. Never in her life had she done anything so impetuous, and been rewarded with the sight of such grandeur!

The hallway they entered was low, shadowy, and silent. Margherita clutched Donato's hand tightly to keep from making any sound. They rounded a corner and abruptly entered a large, magnificently frescoed room, facing out to the large formal gardens and the snaking Tiber beyond. Margherita stepped back, stifling a little gasp with the back of her hand. Grand and imposing, the frescoes rose up before her. One in particular drew her gaze. It was the image of a magnificent woman, her hair flying out behind her as she rode in a chariot drawn by two dolphins. Around her were small boys with Cupid's bows and arrows aimed directly at the heart of the beautiful sea nymph. All of it seemed to jump out of the work and into her emotions. Such beauty and grace, yet such power and authority! It was the mythological figure Galatea, but the effect of her being painted in pale, soothing colors, her hair loose and flowing, was to make her seem a kind of everywoman. Raphael had envisioned her, not grandly, but humanly. A sudden rush of admiration shook her, and Margherita was breathless. She had no idea Raphael might be so sensitive, or perceptive.

"They say she is modeled on one of Signor Chigi's mistresses, Imperia," the girl informed them in a careful whisper. "And I can tell you that the artist has made her exactly how she is in life—her face is exactly as I saw her only yesterday. Though she is in less favor now that he has had another child with his other mistress, Francesca." The girl glanced around then. "That is all the time we dare take in here. But the debt for what happened—is that now paid?"

"Fully," Donato returned quietly.

She nodded silently and led them out of the magnificent chamber, the hem of her fine silk dress whispering along the polished marble floor of the passageway before them, like the edge of a claret-colored cloud.

"I cannot believe you had seen something so magnificent as this before and not told any of us at home," Margherita whispered as they walked alone back toward the stables.

"I had not seen it before."

"And yet you knew it was here?"

"It was described to me."

"But who would tell a stableman about a place like that? People like us would never be invited there by anyone but another servant—"

Yet as she asked, the answer was before her, reflected in Donato's kind eyes. She saw who had found favor with the pretty servant girl above his station, and who had seen these frescoes with her before today. The same one who, by so doing, had betrayed the friend from Trastevere he had claimed to love all his life. Margherita felt her blood go cold. She was dizzy as the image of Antonio in the arms of this worldly servant girl flashed before her. She had known there were others, but to see one of them, and to have her be so elegant and beautiful . . . Bitterness at a betrayal she had not expected hit her squarely, then twisted like a dagger. Unable to control her tears, she tried to wipe them away with the back of her hand as Donato brought her against his chest.

"He is my brother and I love him. But I am in agreement with your father," Donato murmured, smoothing her hair. "Do not give up the possibility of something extraordinary in your life for a man who can never be all that you deserve."

So much was swirling in her head, and she could not help but wonder what might lay beyond life here in Trastevere.

A CANDLE FLAME flickered in the library of Raphael's narrow three-story house on the Via dei Coronari. It was a sanctuary of gilded wood paneling, heavy Portuguese painted furniture, and silver candlesticks. The overwhelming fragrance that met him when he returned home so late tonight, and every other night, was of linseed oil and richly fragrant stew warming, just beyond, in the kitchen. The newly completed panels he kept there beckoned him more than a dish of sweet cooked veal. Supper was provided by a full-faced girl, with pretty light-gray eyes. She did his marketing, prepared his meals, laid out his wine cup and plate, then pulled in the long shutters before she left him alone to dine in solitude.

In addition to Elena di Francesco Guazzi, who cooked what he liked and kept order in his house, Raphael possessed two of his own liveried attendants, as well as several fine horses that were housed and cared for at the Chigi stables. He also employed a fencing master, a dancing instructor to keep him current with the latest nuance added to the pavane, and a personal valet. But only the valet, a silent, sloe-eyed boy named Ludovico, dwelled in the house with him. Ludovico laid out clean clothes for the *mastro* in the morning, assisted him in dressing, then shaved the stubble of beard that he often was too busy to realize had grown.

By day, Raphael belonged to his benefactors. He painted for them, ate with them, joked with them, flattered them, and strove to please them. But here, on the Via dei Coronari, he craved privacy. Even the women who passed through his life, he did not like to bring here—mainly preferring the brothels around the Bocca della Verità, in the little labyrinth of lanes there called the Bordelletto. Here, he needed some bit of the boy remembered, instead of the artistic commodity he had become.

Use the cerulean blue for that, but only a touch, Raffaello. It will make the eyes more limpid. More believable . . .

Feeling his father's presence with him suddenly, he allowed the memory in just a little further. The great full, dark beard. Long, tapered fingers, the nail beds stained with color. Eyes that were bold and dark, possessed by work. And always, the odor of sweat and paint swirling wildy around him.

But can I not go out with the other boys, Padre mio? They have asked so often. What if they no longer ask and I wind up with no friends at all?

One day everyone shall be your friend, my son! You are an artist, Raphael! That is your future, your destiny! I have seen your work—I know well the talent there. Waste it not on trifles, and you shall be a mastro far greater than I could ever dream of being!

But will I not be a man with a happy life as well? I have no friends. We have no friends . . .

Your life will be your art! And art will be your life, as it is my own. Only that.

But what if I want more? What if I want what you had with my mother?

Love is not for you, Raffaello mio. Matters of the heart would only stymie your talent . . . impede what you are meant to become, as it did me. But the rest—the adoration, the piles of gold, . . . and sì, the women—that all shall follow. Expect to claim the greatness that lays even now at your fingertips, Raphael! Expect it, and seize it boldly, as if it has only ever belonged to you!

Loving my mother was—a mistake? Raphael could still hear his own boyish voice ask, and his own words echo back hauntingly. Profound. Painful. Loving her and having me was a mistake? That was what he was meant to ask, but even at the age of fourteen, he knew he would not have been able to bear the reply.

If your mother had not found me, Raffaello, there is no telling where this world might have taken me, and what sort of artistic commissions I might have been offered by now, far beyond the court of Urbino . . .

The bitter memory of a man whose life was punctuated by regret . . . At that point in the recollection, Raphael sank wearily into a stiff armchair of upholstered red velvet fringed in gold, set before his carved wood desk. Other than the day they buried him, it was his most vivid—and the most painful—memory of his father. The call to greatness the phrase that had spoken the loudest—had defined Raphael from that impressionable day forward.

It had also shaped the relationships he had sought—and those he had avoided.

His hand was calloused, his body, his arm, and his fingers were numb and aching from a day of sketches, painting, and frescoes. The chair in which he sat faced a massive desk inlaid with mother-of-pearl and supported by four lions in black wood. Beneath it was a rich Persian carpet softening a dark, polished floor. Raphael was alone here amid the candle lamps, and the echoing silence around him—for the first time in many days—was compelling.

. . . And the eyes, Raffaello, done so vividly as you can do them, ah! Now that is what shall always make your paintings unforgettable! The eyes must be unforgettable! Paint your women as you feel them, and you shall need no other lover!

A stray cat that he fed jumped up onto the surface of his writing table then and stretched beside an uneaten chunk of bread and a slice of Prosciutto di Parma, chasing away the last of his memories. He swatted the cat away absently, but the straggly tabby only returned. *This is what I deserve,* he thought, *for having been soft with this mangy little creature when it had first come to my door.* Softly, lovingly, he stroked the cat's back then and it began to purr.

"Ah, if the world could only see the sad limit of real affection for the vaunted Raffaello," he murmured, smiling ruefully to himself.

Moonlight came in past the iron grille and through the tall, half-shuttered window beside his desk, and Raphael turned to gaze out. It came to him then as it often did when he was alone: What if he were to die a young man? Now . . . without ever having loved? Without having known the sort of passion and commitment about which he painted every day of his life? It was a fear he could not recall being without. After the death of his mother, the fear had intensified. No matter how famous, how important, or how necessary life seemed to make one, everyone was expendable.

Pressing the thought away, he once again picked up the sketching chalk and tried to recall the shape of her eyes. What he had before him was not exact. He could not *see* the girl in the image he had created. He tossed down the nub of chalk and thrust back his chair. Outside, between the tall, narrow buildings, the sound of horses' hooves echoed on the cobbled stone and broke the night silence.

Why would she still not allow him to paint her? When royalty was clambering after him to immortalize their images, what on earth did she fear? He had so little time left before the pope thought better of the commission altogether, and she was perfect for the Madonna. He stood then and paced the length of his room, with its broad windows of painted leaded glass, rich paneling overlaid with gold leaf, and heavily carved furniture. He ran a hand behind his neck and poured himself a goblet of Chianti from a jeweled decanter given to him personally by Cardinal Bibbiena. Staring at the decanter, opulent beyond measure, set with rubies and pearls, he wondered for the first time what this vessel that had sat here for nearly two years, silently serving him, was actually worth. He had taken so little time to consider it before because riches meant little. He could only imagine what a girl like Margherita Luti would think of it—or what it might buy for her family.

Alone with the silence and his thoughts, Raphael glanced down at his desk and a bronze medallion of Hercules given to him in Florence by Leonardo da Vinci. The medallion represented determination, the kind, elderly artist had told him. It would bring him good fortune. Beside it was an unopened letter from the secretary to the noble and beautiful Isabella d'Este, who still sought him to paint her portrait. Since Raphael had come to

Rome, it had been all about the work. The process, and his success. Nothing more. And it was the first time he had realized that
there was nothing more in his life than that.

A north wind had blown away the clouds, and the stars in the
evening sky were already bright, glimmering beside an iridescent
half moon. He drank the heady red wine and poured another.
Raphael thought for a moment of actually sending for, and bringing here, one of the women—more out of habit than desire. But
he was too taken up with finding a way to get this Trastevere girl
to model for him.

Absently, he glanced at a table beside his desk, littered with
old chalk and charcoal sketches, studies of anonymous arms, hands,
and torsos he had used for some of his earlier Madonnas. Fanned
out atop the rich oak table, he caught sight of one of his favorite
studies—the Madonna holding her child in one hand and an
open book in the other. But it was her face, the expression there,
which he believed he had captured exactly—the pain of knowing,
mixed with resolution, and its ultimate sadness. If only Margherita
could see these—see *this*—to understand the sort of pure work he
was after.

And then the idea came to him.

His face lit, along with his mood. Of course. Why had he not
thought of it before?

EARLY THE NEXT MORNING, Raphael returned to his workshop on the Piazza Sant'Apollonia. Absently, he cast his cloak of
rich aubergine velvet and gold fringe onto the workbench near
the door. Moving across the wood plank flooring into the huge,
high-ceilinged workshop, Raphael was immediately pulled into
the feverish pitch—the rhythm of work already going on around
him. Across the room, with its creaking floor, and painted open
ceiling beams, were two separate models sitting motionless as two
of his assistants sketched them for figures in the next phase
of the Vatican fresco. The old man from yesterday, sitting for
Giuseppe's red chalk sketch, then a young boy whose nearly

perfect face Giulio Romano was carefully highlighting with white chalk for the character of Perseus in a new fresco Raphael was proposing to Chigi.

A younger apprentice was mixing a precise shade of umber to add to the skin tone on a portrait on Gianfrancesco Penni's grand oak easel. Around them were large paint-splattered cloths, wooden buckets full of murky water and paintbrushes, jugs of wine, and trowels for spreading the colored fresco plaster. There were piles of used, and reused, sketching paper spread throughout the workshop amid tubs of various colored drawing chalk.

The assistants to the *mastro* wore loose white muslin shirts, belted in worn leather, the sleeves pushed up over their elbows. Giovanni da Udine wore a dark leather apron over his muslin shirt, as did Giulio Romano. Everything around them was coated in daubs and splatters of paint, or great, dark smudges of chalk.

Amid the constant movement and low hum of activity, Raphael moved to his own worktable beside the window with a sweeping view of the rooftops of Rome, and its many cupolas. He also had a small private room near the door where he dealt with his accounts and correspondence, but when he worked, he preferred to be among his men. He opened his folio and riffled through to the chalk drawing he had begun to make of Margherita while her image was still fresh in his mind. The eyes met him first—piercing, determined, yet achingly fragile in what lay beneath. He ran his fingertips over the eyes he had drawn. Perfect, he thought. But the mouth was wrong. It was too full, the lower lip out of proportion enough to change the essence of her. He rubbed a slightly moist cloth over the lower area of the face and began the mouth again, his mind swirling with images of their tense, fruitless second meeting. She *was* the Madonna. She had to be. It was as fated, he knew, as his destiny as an artist.

He raked his hands back through his hair and gazed down at the image. He had offered her all that he could. But something was holding her back. Something over which even the great Raphael of Urbino had no control. It was, lately, a theme of his life, he chuckled ruefully to himself. The more things he tried to harness, the more they slipped from his reach. The work was like that, a blinding and varied host of commissions with which even he, and a collection of vibrant, powerful assistants and apprentices, could barely keep pace because, at the heart of it, he would always compare himself with his great mentor, Leonardo da Vinci.

And even with his great rival, Michelangelo—for whom work *was* life.

He glanced down again at the red chalk drawing and felt an unexpected shiver. It was beyond him, and for now, so was she.

Raphael closed the folio, stepped back, and glanced around his workshop until his eyes rested upon Giulio, who, at eighteen, was his youngest senior assistant. So full of raw, natural talent, he thought, yet plagued by a hesitation he had not yet been allowed to understand. Raphael went to his table and stood over Giulio's shoulder as he sketched the flawlessly featured boy whose light curls were like soft locks of gold curled softly near his face. Raphael wondered where Giulio had found so perfect a youth, one whose bare chest was hairless, sculptured and smooth as alabaster. The master watched his assistant work, filling in the contours of the cheek with a perfectly blended bowl of flesh-toned paint one of the young students had mixed for him.

Raphael looked back and forth from the model to the sketch, and noticed it then—the bright red slash across Giulio's smooth, beardless cheek. The area was raised and gone purple, and the small place where the flesh had been broken was at its center.

"*Caro?* What happened?" Raphael said softly as he worked on.

Giulio did not answer at first but continued to work intensely, daubing at the image with the tip of his charcoal pencil stub. "It is only a scratch," he finally acknowledged, still not turning away from the sketch. "Do not be concerned. It is nowhere near the eyes I need to work."

The comment, and the sentiment behind it, were jarring to Raphael. These were men with whom he worked and worried—

with whom he broke bread and drank wine. They became a family. Giulio Romano was no exception.

"Leave this," he instructed, taking the chalk from Giulio's hand and laying it gently on the cluttered table between them. "You may rest," Raphael called to the model, who very swiftly rose from the hard stool, covered his own tautly muscular body with a muslin drape, and walked barefoot to the fire across the room to warm himself.

"What has happened? Who has done this to you?" he asked gently. "Was it your father again?"

"It is truly nothing, *mastro mio*. Only a scratch. You must not concern yourself with such trifles."

"You are my friend, Giulio, my good friend. *You* concern me. And your mind and hand are every bit as gifted as mine. I have only had more practice and time."

As Raphael spoke gently, Giulio seemed to soften. "It was a street fight only. Truly it was. After I had drunk far too much good trebbiano last night, I was unwise with my words, and this ugly plum on my face will remind me of that for a good while to come."

Raphael wanted to believe him. The panel and its oil paints, the communion of the hand and brush, created a unique kind of brotherhood into which few were admitted. But there was something else that had bound them like family. A conversation, a confidence shared on a different occasion, months ago, when Giulio had seemed more trusting. *My father, he sometimes takes out the strains of his day, the disappointments of his life, on me. He hates that I wish to be an artist. He believes I should desire a future more certain for myself. He wishes a life for me . . . things, I have never wished for myself."*

Words spoken between them months ago surfaced now and swam circles in his mind like the fish in the pools at Santa Croce. This had been more than a street fight, he knew without doubt. It was more than something minor to be passed off.

When the golden-haired boy returned to model once again for Giulio, Raphael left them, but he did so with a heart that was suddenly heavy, because of the things Giulio would not say. And as much a friend as Giulio Romano had in Raphael Sanzio, there was a door between them. One that remained, at least for now, unopened.

❧ 5 ❧

"MARGHERITA!" LETITIA WAILED FROM INSIDE THE BAK-ery, her high, grating voice rolling out into the small back garden. "Something has arrived for you!"

In the late afternoon, Margherita stood outside drawing in dried clothing from a rope. The pieces gently fluttered, like col-ored waves in the breeze, rippling against a stone wall that was draped in vines heavy with fat purple grapes. The sky was bright and cloudless, and on the wall dividing their garden from the next, a ring of doves perched, fat and white, cooing as Margherita pulled the last bit of clothing from the line. She wiped her hands on the apron at her waist and came inside.

"What is it?"

Letitia and Francesco Luti sat together at the kitchen table, just beyond the weathered green garden door. Each of them had a full cup of dark wine before them, and the baby once again lay at Leti-tia's uncovered breast. On the table they used for mixing the bread dough, covered still with a thin layer of flour, was a sheaf of paper, wound and then tied with a thick scarlet ribbon. Margherita stud-ied it warily as it lay beside the rust-red clay jug of wine.

"It came from *Mastro* Raphael's studio. His young apprentice, the one from the other day, just delivered it himself," Francesco explained. He sat slumped in the scarred wood chair, legs spread, a large hand surrounding the old wooden wine cup. His voice was rasping and heavy.

"Well? Are you not going to open it?"

She backed away from it. "You do it, *Padre mio*."

"*A Dío,* Margherita! I doubt it is anything dangerous! He is, after all, trying to win you over." Letitia took a long swallow of the wine as a cool evening breeze blew in through the door and surrounded them.

"That is just what I am afraid of."

"Not win you *that* way, heaven portend!" Their father scoffed. "He wishes to win your cooperation as a model! A girl like you would not likely interest so grand a man in a personal sense!"

"Well, if you do not open it, I shall have to!" Letitia demanded, reaching across and slipping the ribbon off the end of the parchment.

The paper unfolded before the three of them, revealing a sketch of a Madonna and child, done in black chalk with silverpoint and traces of white heightening in the eyes. The Madonna's gaze was cast away from the viewer contemplatively as the Christ child played with a small ball she held for him, and her other hand rested gently upon a small open book. Letitia's small gasp was the only sound as they looked at the crosshatch lines of her gown, the gently tapered fingers, and the expression on her slim, lovely face, whoever she was.

"It is breathtaking," Letitia finally murmured, fingers splayed across her lips.

"If he is trying to impress you, it should have worked," Francesco declared.

"I think it is more that he is trying to show me I need not fear him."

"I suspect there is little to fear in being represented as the greatest of all virgins," Letitia quipped, running her fingertips gently over the image of the baby as she held her own in her arms. "Especially since she always has her clothes on!"

"Perhaps I have misjudged Signor Sanzio," Margherita admitted.

"Perhaps?" her father rasped with incredulity. "He is *declaring* to you in this that you need not fear him!"

"His work *is* startling," Letitia murmured. "It looks as if this girl might actually come right off the page!"

"More than that, she makes me want to weep," Margherita said with uncharacteristic emotion quaking in her voice. "She knows what the future holds for her child. You can see it in her gaze, the sadness . . . She wishes to keep him for as long as she possibly can." Margherita looked up. There were tears in her sister's eyes. Their father, too, was stunned.

"If what Donato showed you this morning did not sway you, this certainly must," Francesco determined. "It is a chance at immortality through *Mastro* Raffaello's paintbrush. God Almighty put you in his path, and you must not turn from that. You must go to him, you must tell him, Margherita, that you have changed your mind!"

"*Sì.* Of course you are right."

"Take Donato if you like," Letitia offered as she laid the now dozing toddler into the wooden cradle beside the table. "It would be wise to have a chaperone in any case. A girl alone going to an artist's studio, no matter what the reason, will not help your reputation. Everyone there must see you as a serious portrait model, not one of those girls who models for artists without their clothing."

"Then we are in agreement," Francesco announced after another long swallow of the wine, which dribbled down onto his stubbled chin. An ambitious glitter lit his tired eyes. "As soon as Donato returns from his work at the stables he will accompany you to see *Mastro* Raphael. You will thank him for showing you the sketch, return it, and then you will tell him that you have changed your mind."

SHE STOOD before him at the opened, heavy workshop door, holding out the rolled sketch, her arms draped in the sleeves of an unadorned pale-blue dress, once her mother's best dress, with its slight touch of faded elegance—her feet beneath covered in scuffed strap shoes. Her hair was parted in the center, and the smooth length of it was held by a small blue cap, her mother's also, ornamented with just a few simple beads. Donato stood beside her in modest attire—burgundy hose, tunic, painted leather belt, and white shirt beneath. This was his finest attire as well.

"Signor Sanzio," Donato bowed deeply. "It is indeed the greatest of honors. I am Donato Perazzi, husband of Margherita's sister."

"A pleasure," said Raphael with a nod, but his eyes were instantly upon Margherita as the artists behind him fell into a sudden hush.

"I have come to return this," she said evenly, her deep brown eyes flecked with gold, wide and honest. She was dressed plainly, he saw, but Raphael, who had been called over by one of the apprentices as she stood at the workshop door, saw the dignity in the utter simplicity of what she wore.

"The drawing was for you."

"But your work, the perfection of it, is something you must not—"

"It was only a study for an earlier Madonna. It was my hope to show you what caliber of painting I hoped you would sit for."

"That was my thought upon seeing it. The caliber of your work." The smallest tinge of a smile edged up the corners of her mouth.

"Signorina, I have waited nearly two years to fulfill this commission. I have painted many Madonnas before, so many for churches and chapels that now I can scarcely remember them all. But with this one, something has stopped me. I could not commit to an image, a face for her—that is, until the day I met you." He lowered his gaze. "Signorina Luti, honestly, I would have done anything to convince you."

"I believe you have done that."

"Thanks be to God," Donato quietly murmured, glancing heavenward.

But Raphael was silent, seeing only her—her direct manner and her simplicity.

"As long as you have come all this way," he said suddenly, conscious of his manners. "Would you and Signor Perazzi like to have a look around?"

He knew it would be obvious that he was trying to impress her with a tour of his grand workshop, with its draperies, male models, easels, and drying portraits painted on large wooden panels. But if it helped to keep her here with him awhile longer, he was pleased to do it. All of the hand flourishes, the clever quips, and the show of wit that so amused the wealthy and powerful of Rome would not work with Margherita Luti.

Silently, Margherita followed him around to the various artist tables, shadowed by her sister's silent, awestruck husband. She saw all of the various works in progress, and dozens of studies for earlier Madonnas.

"And where do *you* work?"

"That is my table," he replied, pointing to a paint-stained table, cluttered with brushes and two palettes, amid all of his assistants. A large empty easel was set beside it.

"You did not expect that?" he asked, with a hint of pleasure that for a change it was he who had surprised her.

"I suppose I expected something more . . . more—"

"Something more *grand?*"

Her face flushed crimson. She took a moment to respond. "I might have expected a *mastro,* so critical to the very fabric of Rome as yourself, to require more private space in which to . . . *concentrate.*"

"Camaraderie, not privacy, is the heart of this studio. Here, my assistants learn from me. And, just as importantly, I learn from *them.* These are my companions in life, as well as in art."

"And will they gain your reputation along with your talent?" she unkindly asked.

For a moment he did not smile, nor say anything. Then, very suddenly, he tipped back his head and let a huge, happy laugh. "Signorina, you certainly are a challenge to understand," he said through his laughter.

"I was just going to say the same of you—Signor Sanzio."

"Please come," he bid her, placing a hand gently at the small of her back, and leading her toward his own workspace.

As they walked, Raphael was aware of the furtive glances of the other artists and apprentices upon her, and even a low, muffled snicker from the shirtless old man with a long white beard who was posing, seated on a Roman column. Margherita was being told she was not the first girl to be shown around the great artist's studio, nor was she likely to be the last.

"Do these men know the reason I am here?" she asked with discomfort.

It took a moment, as he seated her on his model's stool beside the easel. He glanced around like an afterthought when her question settled in upon him. "My men know me well, Signorina Luti."

"And should I not fear precisely that?"

"They know you are the new Madonna model, and what value I placed on finding you. Your coming here today, after your previous refusal, holds divinity in itself. They know how exceedingly pleased I am that you have changed your mind."

"Only for the Madonna, Signor Raphael."

"*Sì,*" he said without smiling. "Only just that."

MARGHERITA REMAINED at the workshop for over an hour, with Donato protectively seated nearby, allowing Raphael to make several rapid red chalk sketches of her face and neck. In each he altered something just slightly—the tilt of her head, the focus of her eyes, the set of her mouth. For one of the sketches, it was only a shift in the direction of her gaze he sought. But what he felt was her watching him with rapt fascination, his powerful hand, the bit of hair there below the knuckles, and the long, tapered fingers that commanded the chalk, alternately caressing and gripping it to force an image up from a blank slip of paper. It was an odd kind of intimacy, her gazing at him like this, and Raphael felt the power in it.

Finally, when he had finished, and the sun had paled from a rusty crimson to shadowy gray through the tall, half-open window shutters, Raphael led her to the door and summoned

Donato, who had been waiting beside the fireplace, watching the unique encounter. Raphael chose his next words cautiously. It had amazed him that she had come here at all, and he must tread softly with that now.

"Will you return tomorrow at this time to let me make a few further sketches for the painting?"

"It cannot be tomorrow, Signor Sanzio. That is the day we make the *schiacciata*. It is our most important day. We always sell twice as many loaves of our fruit bread."

Raphael drew a palm full of gold coins from a pocket in his doublet and held them out to her. They glistened like jewels in the shaft of light through the window behind them. "Will this be enough to find someone else to assist in the baking?"

She did not reach out to take them; rather, she tipped her head and silently studied him for a moment. The inbred grace there, and just a hint of her enormous pride, set him once again handily off balance. "Is it always about buying what—and who— you wish, signore?"

"Money is not an evil, Signorina Luti."

She flicked her hand at the coins still looking squarely at him. "Nor is it always the objective."

She was right, of course. He knew it instantly, and he felt small for having been so quick with the offer. There was a goodness about her that surprised him again and again. It certainly set him off his game—the one he had played with women for as long as he could remember. With her, like it or not, he was in control of nothing. "I only meant that with this, you could have someone else assist your father so that we might continue our work together."

"It is my family's business, and *my* work, Signor Sanzio. The task to which I shall return once you have completed your Madonna. It is my duty to help in the preparation of the *schiacciata*, a portion of which we deliver to the poor at church. I cannot leave my father to someone who knows nothing of our business for a handful of coins."

He took a measured breath, feeling Giovanni da Udine's judgmental, disbelieving stare from across the room. "Very well then. When *can* you return?"

She thought for a moment, and was silent. "It would be possible on Saturday."

On Saturdays, it had long been his custom to dine midday with Chigi. It was a gathering the pope himself often attended. In Raphael's circle, things were all intricately woven together. It would be unwise to decline the standing occasion. There would naturally be inquiries if he did not attend, especially considering his past penchant for the ladies.

Margherita must not be seen as any part of that.

"Can you arrive on the hour of three?" It would give him enough time to break bread with Chigi and the Holy Father, then dash back to his workshop without compromising either commitment.

"If you desire it."

"Indeed. I desire it greatly."

Something moved him to take her hand and draw it to his lips at their parting, but he resisted the urge with all of his strength. She would misunderstand the sentiment. After she had nodded to him and left, Giovanni da Udine looked at Raphael, arms crossed over his barrel chest. The burly assistant, with his wavy shock of prematurely silver hair, shook his head, biting back a smile. "If I had not seen for myself, I would never have believed it!"

"I fear you are too easily struck, *caro*," Raphael replied with believable nonchalance. He moved back to his easel and the preliminary sketch of Margherita that remained there.

But Giovanni da Udine followed him, looking at the exquisite face gazing back at them in chalk lines and shadows. "And everyone here knows *you* are too easily seduced by a pretty girl."

"I have told you before, Giovanni *mio,* it is not like that with her."

"You do not find her attractive?" da Udine bruskly goaded.

"She is exquisite."

"Not good enough for you?"

"Probably *too* good for me, Giovanni."

"Her grace is dissuasive then?"

"As is her caution." Raphael removed the image from the easel and laid it on the worktable next to him, not wanting those eyes to unnerve him any more when he was working so hard at denial.

Giovanni laughed. "Really, *mastro.* I have known you for a long time, and I have never known such a small thing as perception to stand in your way."

He tipped his head and cast a glance back at the door through which Margherita had only just passed, the cleanly scrubbed fragrance of her hair still heightening the air around them all. "Ah, but then neither of us has known this particular *signorina* before. Have we?" asked Raphael.

JUST AFTER DARK that evening, when everything was alive with the rich golden glow of candles and oil lamps, Raphael walked into the magnificent Chigi stable building, and up the flight of stone stairs. Not exclusively stables, it was a grand building that housed a collection of fine horses on the ground level and elegant rooms above it. The walls were lined with tapestries and pastel-shaded frescoes. The floors were ornamented by Persian carpets. He had been summoned here to present what drawings and concepts he had formulated thus far for a new fresco with the given theme of the marriage of Cupid and Psyche. Raphael moved up the twisted stone staircase, past the ever-present scaffolding that his own workmen had left.

In a grand salon at the end of the corridor, he found Agostino, his friend and mentor. As velvet-clad servants swirled around him, Chigi himself lay on a velvet-covered lounge. His second mistress, Imperia, her breasts exposed, seductively massaged scented oil into his bare feet. This flaxen-haired beauty, Raphael knew, was living here. Across the street, in the villa itself, was Francesca Andreozza, the mistress who had just borne his third child, and the woman most actively vying, by her fertility, for the vaunted title of Signora Chigi.

Agostino lounged on his side, propped on his elbow, all beard
and dark chest hair, gazing up at two of Raphael's apprentices as
they applied bright orange painted plaster to the drapery portion
of Perseus Beheading Medusa. The room was grand beyond measure for the second floor of a stable. There were art treasures all
around. Raphael always wondered if his benefactor fully appreciated the rich Bible stories and elegant mythological frescoes coming to life before him, or the irony of placing them here, where he
housed a courtesan.

"Ah, Raffaello *mio! Come va?* So have you come with drawings
for me?"

"I hope they are as you wished," he said, forcing a humble tone.
While he respected and admired Chigi, there had always been
something he could not quite put his finger on, something that
made him wary. Perhaps it was the reality that were it not for
Raphael's singular talent, which he desired to harness, there would
have been nothing at all to align their two very different worlds.
Certainly he was indebted for the great banker's patronage; Raphael
was simply mindful of the greater things that separated them.

Chigi took a sugarcoated grape from Imperia, then groaned
out loud as he swallowed it. With a Cheshire smile beneath his
smoke-gray eyes, he said, "I often ask myself if there is anything
finer in all the world than feasting with all of the senses at once?"

Raphael imagined that Chigi did not so much require a
response as a smile of complicity while he drew the girl down to
him. He kissed her sensually, fondling her bare breasts, not caring
that there was an audience around him, or perhaps heightened by
it. A moment later, he motioned the girl away with a broad, non-
chalant sweep of his hand. Raphael averted his eyes as Chigi sat
up, his nude torso exposed, then wrapped himself in the long silk
sheet, looking not unlike an ancient Roman in a finely spun toga.

"I was thinking of adding more cherubs," Raphael said, ignoring Imperia, as Chigi unrolled the drawings and began to study
them. "Brilliant," the banker smiled. "The drawings are perfect,"

he said, as he draped a fraternal arm across Raphael's shoulder. "But will this, exactly as it is, actually ever grace my loggia?"

What he meant was, will it be finished?

"I hope I have not disappointed you so far."

"You have not," Chigi smiled. It was a vain yet winning smile from a man who was tall to the point of majestic, with a wavy shock of crow-black hair and prominent Roman nose. "But can you make this project your first priority?"

"Unfortunately, His Holiness requires the same distinction."

"Ah, *bene*." Chigi shrugged. "Then there are two things you must remember. First, that no one comes before the Holy Father. Second, that I introduced you to him in the first place."

He grinned so slyly that it forced Raphael to chuckle. His first benefactor in Rome had been Cardinal Bibbiena. But there was something vastly endearing about Agostino Chigi's arrogance. He certainly had not gotten to where he was without those qualities, thought Raphael admiringly.

"But seriously, *caro*. Is there anything you need just now? More assistants to speed things along?" He was so charming when he was feigning magnanimity, Raphael thought with a little half smile.

"An experienced assistant would be nice," Raphael agreed. "But one who needs to be trained, no matter how talented, would be like adding a larger rock for Sisyphus to push up his hill."

The two men moved together toward an open gallery. Below them lay the formal gardens, and before them a vast table was set with white linen, sweet wine, and every sort of cake and exotic fruit.

"Then tell me, what *do* you need, Raffaello?"

"Time I do not have to finish the Madonna for His Holiness."

Agostino chuckled, and Raphael was instantly sorry for the admission. "Another Madonna, is it, when so many other projects beckon? Have you not, to your credit, painted dozens of Madonnas already?"

"It was commissioned, promised, and begun."

"And with so much more important work to complete, you feel compelled to do *this* now?"

"I believe I have finally found the model to help me see it to completion."

"Do let me guess. You met her last night drinking mulled wine down in the Campo de' Fiori with that insatiable apprentice of yours . . . what is his name? Da Udine?"

"In truth, I met her in the broad light of day on Il Gianicolo. Certainly light enough to assess that her eyes are extraordinary and—"

"And how kissable were her lips beneath?"

Raphael shook his head and smiled ruefully. In the middle of Sodom and Gomorrah, he was trying to describe Madonnas. "Her mouth interests me only in how it is to be painted."

Chigi chuckled and braced a hand on Raphael's shoulder. "You like my Imperia, do you not? Now, *her* lips are desirable!"

"Indeed, she is lovely."

"Then take her to your bed this evening as a little gift from me. Or, if you like, take her here, in her own bed. Evidence of how pleased I am with your work, *and* your friendship."

"The offer is a generous one, Agostino, and I bid you thanks."

"You know that she is fond of you."

"And I am fond of her. But a backlog of work will keep me occupied all the rest of this night, I am afraid," he wisely replied, and unrolled another of the drawings before Agostino could repeat the offer.

"Well," he shrugged. "This *is* a new turn for you. I do not believe you have ever refused a woman. Especially one of mine!"

"His Holiness has asked me to avoid those sorts of diversions, and I am doing my best to honor his wish."

"That is commendable, if not entirely practical for a lusty man like you, *caro!*"

Raphael glanced down at his own drawings, refusing to take the bait. "Well, the practical side of me would very much appreciate knowing what you think of this one."

Agostino tipped his head, seeing that the debate was over. Finally, he, too, looked down at the drawings for his newest fresco.

It seemed to Raphael that since Chigi had chosen a marriage theme for the new design, perhaps he did mean to marry the mother of his children, after all. At least he had gambled on it by portraying the bride and groom as Francesca and Agostino, surrounded by a throng of family and friends. Gianfrancesco Penni would do the detail work of flowers and tiny cherubs, and Giulio Romano, of course, would help him with the lion's share of the actual characters.

"Does my vision of the story please you then?" he asked as Chigi silently studied each area of the long, narrow drawings that would grace the wall of the loggia where it met the ceiling. "Or are there changes you would desire?"

After a long silence, Agostino looked back at Raphael. His gray eyes were very wide. "Can you actually achieve this, with all of the detail, in a year's time?"

"Realistically, it will take a bit more than that with all of the work you have already ordered at your family chapel."

"Very well. One must not hurry perfection, after all." He was smiling. "Nor must a man deny basic needs, Raphael, lest he be drawn in a dangerous direction. Consider, will you, my offer of Imperia? She shall give you what you need, as any proper courtesan should, yet distract you not from the important work." He anchored his hands on his hips, leveling his gaze. "And for the rare breed of men like you Raffaello *mio*, the work is the only thing of true consequence. It is life, is it not?"

Smiling, yet without reply, Raphael turned his attention back to the fresco and scaffolding, where several of his own assistants labored. "Before I leave you for the evening, tell me, Agostino, is the palette of colors they are currently applying to your liking?"

"If they are colors conceived by you, Raffaello *mio*, they are gifts from God I shall not refuse," he replied, meaning every syllable—at least of that. But the warning, and the sleight, so cryptically delivered, still hung heavily between them. Raphael was not to become distracted by a woman. At least not one particular woman who might ever become an obsession. Raphael belonged to the powerful of Rome. And they, by any means, would keep him that way.

"We shall see you on Saturday, as always?"

Raphael moved toward the door. Margherita Luti, he still suspected, would be dismayed by the hypocrisy of the world in which he thrived. But this was the world he had created for himself, and which had made him a very rich man. It was the life he had thought he desired.

"As always, Signor Chigi," he replied. Raphael's private thoughts, for the moment at least, remained his own. He had too much at stake to do otherwise.

AS RAPHAEL SAT HUNCHED ON A WOODEN STOOL AT HIS worktable, finishing an ink-over-stylus drawing, his fingertips blackened by ink, he could not keep his mind from what had happened earlier in the week. Perspiration beaded on his brow as he gazed down at the Conversion of Saint Paul, another work commissioned by the pope. But it was Giulio Romano, and the nasty gash on his face, that troubled him most profoundly.

Around Raphael the workshop vibrated with the hum of activity. Male models of different sizes and ages sat in varying stages of undress, their bodies twisted, bent, and shaped into forms that would fit subjects in the ever-increasing list of commissions. It took Raphael, his three principal assistants, several junior assistants, and a host of apprentices just to keep their heads above water—and to keep Il Sodoma, Sebastiano, and Michelangelo from nipping at his heels.

Raphael ran a hand through his smooth, brown hair and slumped back, letting a sigh of frustration. He felt protective of Giulio. In spite of his enormous talent at sketching, as well as paint and fresco work, he was yet a boy of eighteen. Vulnerable, tentative about his place in the world. Raphael knew that Giulio Romano, careful as any other serious artist of his hands—the critical tools of his trade—would never have been foolish enough to have engaged in a common brawl.

No, this involved Aldo Romano again, Raphael felt certain of it. He had met Giulio's father four years ago, when he had agreed to take on the son. Aldo Romano was a coarse and greedy man, small and bald. Giulio was tall, young, and smooth-skinned, his manner refined, steeped in youthful energy and innocence—the striking physical antithesis of his father. There had always been something different about Giulio. It was a gentleness that went beyond the fact of his youth.

Raphael thought of the countless nights he had spent in the brothels of the Quartiere dell' Ortaccio, accompanied happily by his senior assistants, Gianfrancesco Penni and Giovanni da Udine. But never Giulio. Even now, here among men upon whom the pressures were as great as the need for diversion, a father's influence reined supreme. That had to be it. Why else did Giulio always refuse their company, and their masculine pursuits?

He cast down his pen and washed a hand across his face. He was too tired to deal with more problems, but Giulio was his responsibility, and his friend, and Raphael felt the weight of that. He went to the easel where Giulio was working, applying a rich shade of umber to cover Raphael's underlying guideline sketch of the prophet Isaiah.

"Let us take a walk," Raphael casually declared.

Giulio glanced up in surprise. It was not like the *mastro* to be diverted during the tumultuously busy workday, especially lately. Giulio's inquisitive fox-brown eyes were quickly wide with concern. Losing a position as important as his would be devastating to the young boy from the dark Bocca della Verità quarter of Rome.

"Have I done something to displease you, *mastro?*"

Raphael smiled. "I just require a bit of fresh air, and I would welcome the company."

Giulio put his paintbrush into a tall cup with a collection of other brushes, then wiped his hands on a cloth. Reluctantly, he turned preparing to do as he was bid. Outside the workshop on the Piazza Sant'Apollonia, facing the small walled convent that took in wayward girls, the autumn air bristled with a crisp northerly breeze as they strolled past it. Both of them were warmed by rich cloaks, Raphael's of black velvet with silver thread, Giulio's much simpler, of burgundy velvet with a black silk tie at his neck.

They walked past windows adorned brightly with boxes of clematis, honeysuckle, and weedy geraniums, and then past a grand house with an open loggia. They turned onto a narrow alleyway, past a swarm of dirty-faced children in threadbare clothing who were playing kickball. From a pocket in his cape, Raphael drew forth a handful of coins and tossed them out to them. He always gave whatever he carried to urchin children when he encountered them, but moved on quickly after that, as if moving away from his own motherless youth before it could confront him.

"I would like you to consider staying with me for a while, at my home," he said without ceremony as they passed through a small square with its ancient central well and darkened arcades.

Giulio looked up in surprise. "*Live* with you?"

Ahead now, the next quaint little alley was stuffed with an endless web of houses and *bottegas,* one selling brightly colored majolica; beside it was the shop of a glove maker. Raphael stopped, pretending to consider the gloves on display.

"I have that huge house, designed to impress, and yet all I ever do in the little time I have within it is ramble around listening to the echo of my own footsteps."

"What of your groomsman and the house girl? Are they not companionable enough?"

"My man, Ludovico, lives in my upper rooms and makes himself scarce unless I need to dress or undress. And Signorina di Francesco Guazzi does not remain at my house at all. She cooks and manages the place for me, then returns to her family in the Borgo Pio."

"It is just that I have seen so many sketches of the girl in your folio, I assumed—"

"You assumed she was my mistress."

"*Sì*. She certainly is lovely enough."

"That is true. And for a few scudi additional now and then she has been amenable to modeling for me. But I have not taken Elena to my bed," he lied smoothly.

And it was not entirely a lie, as his grand indiscretion had not occurred anywhere near a bed. But he lied now to protect Elena's honor.

Elena di Francesco Guazzi's family once had sound wealth, prominence in Rome, and a strong friendship with the family of Cardinal Bibbiena. But lavish spending by Elena's father had reduced their circumstances, created scandal, and brought about his suicide.

Unable, for propriety's sake, to employ a young unmarried woman in his own home, the cardinal prevailed upon Raphael, by then betrothed to his niece. Raphael would understand the need for absolute discretion, the cardinal was certain. The task given to Elena would be unimportant. Saving the family from complete ruin by means of a respectable wage was the only goal.

Raphael was still uncertain about why he had allowed the indiscretion, which had occurred almost a year ago. They had never spoken about it afterward. Elena had modeled for him several times and there had never been so much as a spark between them. But that one evening he had crossed the line, partly out of boredom, and partly, he knew, from the biting loneliness he felt in his grand house, with only his thoughts and his self-doubts to keep him company into the night.

Yet whatever excuse he made, he hated himself for that vile sort of weakness. He was a scoundrel—a lonely one, but a scoundrel nonetheless.

He would have given her more in compensation if she would have accepted it. Having to face her every day in light of that was not only penance, Raphael repeatedly told himself, but a reminder of the price to be paid for indiscretion. He might always get what he desired. But there were consequences to everything . . .

Even for the great Raffaello.

"Come stay with me and keep me company, *caro*."

Giulio smiled. The bruise above his eye had turned a gruesome bluish yellow. "But my family, *mastro*—"

"Someone told me long ago that family and love do not serve as an advantage, Giulio *mio*, particularly in an artist's life," Raphael said philosophically, remembering his father's words. "And sadly, it is true. It can be difficult for some to understand the existence we lead—what we paint, or why."

"Some like my father."

"I had considered him. I believe it would be better for you to be away from his influence."

There was a silence then between them as they continued to walk, Raphael's hands clasped behind his back, as he nodded good-naturedly to the awestruck people of the neighborhood who saw the great artist in their midst. Men tipped their soft cloth hats reverently to him and women smiled and giggled in shock behind raised hands.

"I appreciate your offer, *mastro*. It is generosity beyond compare."

"Indeed it is." Raphael rolled his eyes humorously, hoping to diffuse Giulio's discomfort.

A stoop-shouldered old woman in gray cloth came before them then and held out a slightly wilted wild daisy to Raphael. He smiled, then bowing to her as though she were a duchess at the court of Urbino. He took the flower and watched her withered face light, before they continued on.

"It is not to do with painting," Giulio said at last. "but with my father."

"*Sì*."

"He says I am confused. That I am drawn to wayward things, and he must relieve me of that evil by his own hand. That it is the only way, he says, to ensure that I will become a real man."

"And what do *you* believe?"

Giulio sighed and shook his head. "I wish I knew, *mastro*."

"It is difficult in the studio, *non?* The male form is indeed magnificent, faced as we are so continually with unclothed flesh, being forced to consider, day after day, every nuance, every muscle of the male body, and you a young virile man yourself."

Giulio looked at Raphael, his full, youthful lips parted. "It is not like that. I do not desire what I paint or draw, *mastro*," he declared, color rising into his full cheeks. "Certainly not in the sinful way your friend Il Sodoma does!"

Giovanni Bazzi, the brilliant artist of the fresco in Agostino's upstairs bedroom at the villa, had been a good friend to Raphael. He was a clever dinner companion and a talented artist. He was also, as Giulio's father would have said, a sodomite. He had blithely accepted the sobriquet Il Sodoma, content that his talent, a winning smile, and highly placed friends would protect him from any real sort of danger or scorn concerning his proclivities.

"But your father does not believe that," said Raphael.

"My father believes what he wishes, and only that. Men, he says, are not to see other men unclothed. My father accuses me of being like Bazzi because of what I draw and paint. For his interest in boys, my father says, his official name throughout Rome now is Il Sodoma, and you will be next!"

"And Bazzi wears it like a badge of honor." Raphael laughed and put his arm across Giulio's back as they walked. "It defines him, he says. But that is not me, and it certainly does not define *you*."

"No."

"You are old enough to live a man's life, Giulio. Stay with me awhile. Take some time to consider your future—what it is that *will* come to define you. And learn from the rest of us, the desires and the outlets . . . in short, the lives of artists."

"What of my father? Will he not reproach you, considering what he already believes of me?"

"You leave your father to me." Raphael smiled engagingly.

"I shall not forget this, *mastro mio*. Ever. How will I ever repay your confidence in me?"

"Only continue on painting in the manner in which you have begun. Keep learning along with the rest of us, and that shall be more than payment enough for me."

7

RAPHAEL DID NOT WISH TO BE IN THE SHABBY QUARtiere dell' Ortaccio, with its darkly painted walls and creaking beds. No matter how grandly ornamented the houses, or how richly painted the women, this district of Rome, on low-lying land, too near the Tiber, was squalid. When the river level rose, the accumulation of sewage for miles was vile and stinking. But women of easy virtue were the only other indulgence Raphael could any longer allow. There was the mind-numbing amount of work, and the pressure, then afterward mindless release at places like this. He had no time for a proper mistress, and Agostino was right—he was wealthy, successful, passionate, and incorrigible.

Raphael knew how many feathers he had ruffled in Rome and Florence, but he no longer cared. He was two men: the libertine who they gossiped about, and the one no one knew, who was lonely and weary of the world.

Surrounded by a group of artists, he entered the brothel clad in a dashing smoke-gray velvet cloak with silver thread and a matching cap with a long purple plume. Raphael held up a jeweled hand, and the other guests all turned to see him. The bawdy laughter faded and he could hear their excited whispers that *Raffaello* had entered the room.

"Wine for everyone!" he declared with a broad gesture and a smile he did not feel.

One of the prostitutes took his cloak and another his cap, and the nicest velvet-covered chair was quickly offered at one of the busy gaming tables. But lust, not card games or dice, was what had brought him here this night. After draining one large goblet of wine, then a second, and exchanging a bit of polite banter with the awestruck gamblers, Raphael chose a girl with long, dark hair and wide but unexpressive eyes. It was better, he thought, that she made no impression on him beyond the size of her breasts, which burst forth above a blue lace bodice.

Once upstairs, alone with the fleshy, nameless girl, with her clouds of coarse and inky hair, the impending act was beyond his control. He was hard, achingly so, and the breasts beneath his tapered artist's fingers were ripe and pliant. Yet driving into her, it was not her face he saw, but another—a fact which surprised him. Fascinating, desirable . . . unattainable . . . *Margherita* . . .

God save him, but he should not want the Luti girl this way— he should not desire her carnally. She was surely a virgin. An innocent. But only now, with those forbidden images of her face in his mind, did he finally feel the release begin to build. The sensation came swiftly then, and at last he groaned and was pouring into her in a draining rush.

A moment later, his breath slowing, Raphael lay motionless in the tiny garret room, beside the lolling, plump girl, who smelled of wine and other men. His naked torso glistened with perspiration, his tight, muscular body was pleasurably spent. Music, laughter, and the pungent odor of wine and candle smoke snaked up through the unshuttered window beside them. On the painted table beside them lay his glistening coins. Payment. Gianfrancesco Penni was in the next room and Giovanni da Udine was slouched over a gaming table downstairs. It was late and, in search of revelry and distraction from the burdens of unending work, they had all drunk far too much wine, and he had given in to a vice he had promised the pope he would avoid.

Yet now, rather than relaxed and replete, Raphael swiftly felt an unfamiliar sting of guilty regret. Silently, he rose and strode naked across the creaking wooden plank floor to the pile of his clothes on a single chair, and he began to dress. The girl rose without a word, and dressed again in the erotically low-cut blue gown. Then she drew up the coins and tucked them safely into her tightly laced bodice.

Perfunctorily, Raphael pressed a kiss onto her cheek and smiled wearily.

"I will see you again soon?" she asked.

"I suspect not."

She studied him for a moment, then smiled. "Are you in love?"

"Nothing so romantic as that, I am afraid. My work is the only real mistress I have time to desire." He smiled. "And she demands too much of me these days to spend myself here."

"Yet you forgot about that tonight!"

"And for forgetting, I shall pay a heavy price tomorrow when I must be in seven different places at one time."

Her laugh was rich and bawdy. There was a wide gap between her front teeth he had not noticed before. That was odd. As an artist, he usually noticed everything. "In case you should change your mind, Signor Raphael, my price for you, in spite of your success, shall remain the same. You are a pleasure to see, and an even grander pleasure to bed."

He opened the door and turned back to her with a jaunty little grin. "I shall try to remember that." But of course he would not. Strangely, he knew that it would be a very long time, if ever, until he desired a place, or a woman, like this again.

WHEN HE RETURNED HOME, the sun had only just risen, its fragile glow a pale pink across the horizon, casting the buildings of the Via de Coronari in rosy morning silhouette. Yet Giulio was already out of bed. Raphael's assistant was sitting contemplatively beside the great soot-stained kitchen hearth, a big black iron kettle suspended from a hook inside of it. His simple morning meal was uneaten on the table before him. Out past the windows that faced the street, they could hear the birds and the first horse of the day clop past across the cobbled stones. Raphael patted Giulio's shoulder, then slumped into the chair across from him. "It is too early yet for Elena. But she will be here soon enough."

"I could sleep no longer, so I fetched something to eat for myself. I hope you don't mind."

"My house is your house, *caro*. You may do as you wish here."

Giulio smiled and took a bite of bread. There was a moment of silence between them before he said, "So you finally sketched the girl yesterday."

"*Sì*, and I am pleased with the result. But I shall want your opinion on the positioning of the other figures in the work I have planned."

"And were you fortunate enough to sketch the comely baker's daughter late into last night as well?"

Raphael lightly cuffed Giulio's head, and smiled. He was tired and sorely in need of a bath, but he would always be brotherly with his assistant. "You know very well I was out wenching and drinking with Giovanni and Gianfrancesco all evening. You might enjoy it yourself, if you would give it a try."

Giulio looked into his mug of mulled wine, his expression swiftly changing. "It is not for me, that side of life."

"A man's needs are his needs, Giulio *mío*. Perhaps if you tried—"

"I have tried."

They looked away from each other, unspoken thoughts hanging between them as pale pink light filtered in through the three arched kitchen windows. Raphael had always thought it unmanly not to desire women. Naturally, if one did not require it, the comparison to sodomites was unavoidable. In Raphael's own life, he had never considered that there might be other reasons.

The heavy kitchen door swung open then with a little squeal, and a young woman came across the threshold carrying a wicker basket full of bread, cheese, and fish. A mélange of aromas came with her. "*Buon giorno*, Signor Sanzio," she said softly, setting down her basket and removing her cloak.

Elena di Francesco Guazzi was almost twenty, but her small, plump body, light-gray eyes, and the smattering of freckles dusting the bridge of her nose gave her the appearance of one younger, and more vulnerable. Her straight, pale hair was held away from her face by a white cloth cap, and a shy, tentative smile bloomed above her little receding chin. Giulio stood politely as she turned to greet him.

"Elena, this is my assistant, the most brilliant and talented Giulio Romano, whose work shall one day exceed mine in its greatness. He shall be staying here with me for a time. You are to treat him as you would treat me."

She nodded properly, then smiled. "It is a pleasure to meet you, Signor Romano. Whatever you require I shall do my best to find for you."

"I would not trouble you by asking," Giulio stammered nervously. "I am fine on my own."

"It is never trouble that brings me here each morning. Signor Raphael has given my family and me a good life in circumstances far reduced from what they once were. I am honored to see to the needs of his assistant as well."

Elena was engaging and sweet, Raphael thought. He was pleased to see, by Giulio's expression, that he agreed. He admired her for her ability to set everyone at ease, even someone as confused and inexperienced as Giulio was just now about women. It would be good for her to be here, to help settle him into a calmer existence that could only enhance his work at the studio.

"Elena," Raphael said, breaking the gaze between Giulio and her. "I am sorely in need of a bath. Would you see to heating the water? And fetch Ludovico from upstairs? I require a fresh costume laid out before I depart this morning."

"At once, *signore*." She turned to collect a large iron pot. Then, as an afterthought, she pivoted back. "I am pleased you are here, Signor Romano. The *mastro* could do with a bit of good company in this grand old house. It has been a long time since he has brought anyone home who mattered to him at all."

Stung, yet knowing he had deserved the veiled sleight, Raphael paused for only a moment to glance over at her. Then he swiftly left the kitchen.

❧ 8 ❧

WHEN SATURDAY FINALLY ARRIVED, RAPHAEL WAS DIS-
tracted. His decision about the sort of clothes he should wear
when he saw Margherita again had made him late for his weekly
supper. She would likely see the manipulation in something too
plain. Something too elegant, on the other hand, would only
alienate her. He felt like an uncertain boy again, and entirely on
edge, even before he entered the vast dining loggia at Chigi's villa,
ornamented by his own magnificent *Triumph of Galatea,* and the
overwhelming hulk of Sebastiano's *Polyphemus* beside it.

Attired in a moderately grand gray brocade tunic, with a
slashed red silk shirt and hose beneath, Raphael moved easily into
the crowd of invited Roman dignitaries, and was shown to his
place. At the head of a table laid grandly with silver dishes sat
Pope Leo in a large carved throne, draped in crimson, flanked by
his cousin, Cardinal Giulio de' Medici, and his brother, Giuliano,
Duke of Nemours. Fanning out around him, like leaves on a tree,
were several Spanish bishops and prelates. Raphael conversed
politely with the duke's courtesan, beside whom he had been
seated, but his mind relentlessly returned to his own workshop
and Margherita Luti.

She was really such a simple girl, certainly one unimpressed
with his life or his art. Modeling to her was not the honor it had
been to his other models, or even to Maria Bibbiena, who had
modeled for him once, in the early part of their courtship. To
Margherita Luti, it was purely business. Money for her father's
bakery, and nothing more.

Could it be her disinterest that intrigued him?

In any case, he argued with himself, even if he did find her
appealing in a sensually earthy, common way, anything personal
between them was out of the question. Even from the little he
knew of her, Margherita was not the sort to bed with him. And if

that were not enough, Raphael Sanzio was a man promised to another.

As if his thought of another woman had summoned her, Maria Bibbiena turned her head on her slim, aristocratic neck, and smiled her uneven smile. Immediately, she stood and began to move toward him on the arm of her powerful uncle, the crimson-clad Cardinal Bibbiena, in his cassock and skullcap. Maria was even thinner than the last time Raphael had seen her, her young face made gaunt and old now from illness and worry. She was an alarmingly frail girl, with wide owlish eyes and a tentativeness about her.

Against his better judgment, he had given in and used Maria Bibbiena as a Madonna model two years ago. Her pleading with him to repeat the honor, and thus increase the intimate time they spent together, had been unrelenting since. Looking at her, the hope in her eyes, his heart lurched, then sank, as it always did.

She came upon him clad in a gown of robins' egg blue damask embroidered in pearls, with long bell sleeves. He stood politely, kissed her cheek, and embraced her. He then bowed reverently to the cardinal. Though his thin, straight hair was a darker shade than his niece's, the cardinal had the same gaunt Bibbiena face, the same unsettling owlish eyes, long hooked nose, and hollow cheeks.

"Your Grace is looking exceedingly well," Raphael lied.

"And *you* are looking successful as ever. Pray, tell us where have you been keeping yourself?" the cardinal asked.

While you were not in the company of my niece was what he meant.

"Yet more commissions have come into my studio, Your Grace, and even with a collection of skilled artists about me, it is a daily struggle to keep up with it all. You have heard, I trust, of my recent appointments as architect of Saint Peter's, and also as the pope's commissary of Roman antiquities?"

"I have heard that, *sì*. But many things in life, Raffaello *mío*, require effort and attention. Not only your work. You would do well not to let one go in favor of another."

Maria was looking directly at him. But the hope on her face, rather than the anger she should have felt from his indifference, rocked Raphael. Maria, quite simply, adored him, when he felt only affection and pity for her.

"Your Grace always provides me with much food for thought."

"Consider well, my boy." He lowered his gaze in warning. "Especially that which affects the house of Bibbiena."

Raphael nodded courteously. He walked a fine line with this man who held the ear of the pope and who had the power to cancel many of his commissions.

"I thank Your Grace, as always, for your wise words."

Bibbiena smiled a dry, thin-lipped smile. "*Buono.* Now, walk awhile with your betrothed before you sit with the others to dine, and inquire after *her* world."

It was a command, not a request, so Raphael led Maria into the long, vaulted hall, which he was now commissioned to paint. A gentle breeze off the Tiber rushed in at them through the series of open glass doors.

Maria linked her bony arm through his as they strolled, and he could feel her smile without actually looking over at her. He had no idea how he could extricate himself from their engagement if he meant to retain his many lucrative commissions, or even his life. No one crossed Cardinal Bibbiena without dire consequences.

"I have missed you," she softly declared as they walked, her soft voice straining with open affection for him.

"Surely you know by now that my days are not my own."

"I know it well. But so long as your time belongs not to another woman, I am content to wait."

They stopped at a window with a stone seat and a painted embrasure. Raphael motioned for Maria to sit, then he sank beside her and took up her hands. "This existence can not be good enough for you. You are a fine woman who deserves a man who can be devoted only to you."

She ran a finger along the line of his jaw and smiled. "It is enough, *amore mio,* that I am devoted to you."

"But how can that be?" he blurted out.

"When we marry finally this shall all have been worth it."

Frustration mounted within him. "But I am not prepared to marry anyone at this time, nor do I know when I might be! I have always warned you that my work is a jealous lover, Maria, requiring all of me!"

The cardinal's niece covered his hand with her own cold, heavily jeweled fingers—the extent, thus far, of the intimacy between them. He was unpleasantly reminded of how thin and brittle her small body was. "Work may be your only lover, Raphael, so long as I become your only wife. My uncle and the Holy Father are counting on that."

He needed a cup of wine. No. There was not enough wine in all the world . . . .

Raphael stood and faced her wearily. Maria remained calmly seated, her watery eyes cast up adoringly at him, her heavily embroidered skirt fanned out around her legs like the petals on a lush spring flower.

"You have not answered my question, you know. The one I posed in this very corridor the last time we were together in it."

When would he call her to model for another of his Madonnas? Raphael sighed at the inevitability of it as he gallantly helped her back to her feet. For a moment, he felt real compassion for her, a young woman willing to throw away her entire life for a man who could never love her.

"As I have told you, I am swimming in commissions, Maria. I am barely keeping myself afloat. Forgive me, but I cannot consider such a generous offer as yours just now."

Her spine stiffened. "His Holiness has told my uncle that you have found time to paint one particular Madonna without my assistance."

So that was what this was all about.

Raphael led her slowly back toward the loggia, where the guests were beginning, amid conversation and laughter, to dine.

"It was a standing commission, Maria, one I am relieved is nearing fulfillment at last."

"And you find this new woman superior to me?"

"Not superior," he hedged. "Just more appropriate for the concept."

They were seated at the table now, and Raphael could not help but feel relief. What, he wondered, would Maria Bibbiena think if she knew he planned to leave this meal early enough to meet this other model? And, moreover, what would her uncle do?

"Tell me only that you shall paint me again," she pressed, grabbing his wrist with surprising firmness.

Do not force me to lie to you, he was thinking. *You deserve better than that.*

"I would be honored, of course, to have you model for me again when the project calls for a model with your style and particular beauty."

He could not tell her the truth. Cruelty had never been an option. He only hoped that in the end, time would wear away Maria's hope of a future between the two of them, as well as relieve her uncle of his patience with delay.

Right now, time seemed his only hope.

Just then, with a great showy flourish, and in a swirl of burgundy velvet, edged in silver thread and striped hose, Il Sodoma entered the room through the tall, frescoed arch. It was a dramatic entrance, meant to be appreciated. He had a style and a presence Raphael long had admired, mainly for the attention it deflected from a reputation that otherwise might have been his downfall.

Il Sodoma's frescoes at the monastery of Monte Oliveto Maggiore were breathtaking. Raphael had traveled there especially to view them. His delicate and graceful pietà, *Saint Sebastian,* and his *Road to Calvary* had fascinated Raphael, and their common artistic language had begun a friendship. But talent alone in a city of gossipmongers and ambitious power players was not enough. Bazzi had always expertly deflected the more serious consequences of his amorous adventures. His grand fresco upstairs, gracing Agostino's personal bedroom wall, was a masterpiece.

"Ah, Raffaello *mio!*" Bazzi exclaimed in an earthy baritone. His lips were full and feminine beneath a neatly trimmed swirl of umber-colored mustache. Large feather plumes adorned his hat. "You are the very picture of health and success!"

"As are you." Raphael smiled and embraced his old friend.

"But if the rumors of a new Madonna are true, you shall once again have me at a distinct disadvantage."

"You have always held your own with me, Bazzi," Raphael chuckled.

"And *you* flatter me, Raphael."

"*You* make too much of my success, compared with your own."

"There is no comparison, Raffaello, especially not in the divine eyes of our beneficent Holy Father."

"Times can change," Raphael volleyed, remembering Michelangelo's meteoric rise under Julius II, and his subsequent fall from the pinnacle of papal grace in the eyes of Leo X.

"So, apparently, has your model for the Madonna."

He sat in an empty chair beside Raphael, and filled his cup in almost a single fluid movement. "I hear you have found a new virgin."

A true courtier, Raphael merely smiled and nodded.

"So the rumor is true."

"I shall only say that she shall make irrelevant every other Madonna I have ever painted."

"You're in *love* with her?" Bazzi gasped, as though the thought was repugnant to him.

"Don't be absurd," Raphael countered, adding a soft chuckle for effect. "She is only a girl."

"Yet a girl who has changed your vision of Madonnas!" Bazzi persisted slyly.

Raphael was relieved when de' Rossi, a doe-eyed cardinal with a low, straight fringe of bangs on his forehead, leaned toward him across the table and rescued him from Il Sodoma's clutches. Yet still the damage had been done. In spite of a kind heart, sweeping talent, and an enormously engaging style, Bazzi was the biggest gossip in Rome.

❧ 9 ❧

WHEN RAPHAEL ARRIVED BACK AT HIS WORKSHOP, Margherita was waiting for him. As it was late on a Saturday, the other artists had gone and the door had been closed. Although it was unlocked, she had chosen not to enter on her own. Instead, Margherita waited in the outside corridor, as serene as ever. Her hair was parted in the center and pulled away from her smooth face, but otherwise it was unadorned. Her round, dark eyes eclipsed all else. It was a moment before Raphael realized that her brother-in-law, Donato, had once again escorted her. Margherita saw the recognition and then a momentary flicker of what looked like disappointment cross his face just before he opened the door fully and nodded for her to enter.

Margherita moved inside first, her green wool skirt sweeping past them, along with the faint fragrance of chamomile from her freshly washed hair. She was surprised at the vast silence that had descended on the cavernous workshop without the hum of activity, posing models, and many busy assistants. Raphael took her cloak silently, and Donato's gray wool cape, and set them on a model's stool. After he lit a fire in the hearth, he came back and focused intensely on her. "I am so pleased that you have come."

"Did I not tell you I would?"

Raphael tipped his head, and paused for a moment. "People have told me a great many things in this life, Signorina Luti."

"I shall only ever say what I mean, Signor Sanzio."

His lips lifted in a smile. "Well, then. That shall indeed be refreshing."

"It is pleasing to know that something about me shall make a fresh impression on you other than my appearance."

"Oh, you have made an impression on me in many ways, *signorina*. Do not doubt that." He quirked another charming smile that she dared, just for a moment, to find appealing before reminding herself that this was purely business, and would only ever be.

"Shall we begin?" he asked, removing his expensively beaded cape and moving toward the growing fire. Donato sank silently onto a stool nearby, and Margherita watched Raphael then don a black paint-stained smock, rub his hands together in preparation, and let out a heavy, cleansing breath. His smile faded. She saw the artist reemerging. He had such intensity, and she was drawn to it. Realizing it surprised and frightened her.

Raphael seated her on a stool in front of the fire, the gold-and-crimson firelight dappling their faces. He moved her head from one side to the other, then tipped up her chin. Margherita clenched her hands at her sides so that he would not notice her discomfort. Being here was awkward enough, but having him study every nuance of her face and body was actually a bit disturbing. Margherita tried desperately not to let it show. She tried to be the confident model he believed her to be as she watched him move and flex and strain to pull an image from the paper. She saw and felt the unmistakable sensuality in it.

Apparently satisfied at last, Raphael turned to spread out the previous sketches of her onto his own worktable, and studied them for body, neck, and head position. It was so difficult not to move as the time wore on. Margherita was unaccustomed to the long periods of remaining still, and she was not at all certain she enjoyed it, even with the look in his eyes.

At this point he knew only some of the ways he would make her unique, he told her. This Madonna would be standing, of that he was certain. She would be barefoot, and she would look directly at the observer with all of the grace and dignity that he had seen on Il Gianicolo that first day. This would be his most human representation ever.

After an uncomfortably long period of silence in which Margherita fought not to shift the position of her face or the tilt of her head, Raphael turned to her again, and held out a hand to draw her back to her feet. Margherita felt a shiver of panic at the sudden desire in his eyes. It was all still so strange for a modest, working-class girl, this utter intensity—the complete concentration concerning her face and body—and she fought hard to control her fear of it.

Next, he pulled the stool away and positioned her with her arms at her sides, though at a slight angle away from her dress, as if they were floating upward. Then he did something that surprised them both. She knew it by the way their eyes met for only an instant, and his were the first to cut away. Without a word, Raphael knelt, removed her black cloth shoes, and placed them neatly beside the stool. She was actually glad Donato was here, as the sensation of having Raphael Sanzio touch her bare skin slowly and tenderly, almost caress them, felt shockingly sensual. Yet she had begun to feel a new, odd thrill in this lack of familiarity. Something foreign, and dangerous.

"Signor Perazzi, *per favore,* do help yourself to a glass of trebbiano," Raphael called out in an uneven tone, cutting into what felt to Margherita like thick, nearly unbreathable air. "There is a silver decanter on the shelf behind you."

"And shall I pour one for you?"

"Thank you, but no. I am unable to drink wine when I work. It clouds my perception," Raphael explained, beginning another chalk sketch now that he had declared that the full concept for the painting had come to him. Margherita felt his eyes boldly upon her once again, and the same shiver of fear raced through her. Everything about this place, this moment, was unfamiliar to her, and that, most of all, frightened her into silent compliance. "Hold your hands just a bit farther from your body, and face your palms outward," Raphael instructed with the slightest catch to his voice. "*Sì,* that is it . . . *sì* . . . perfection."

RAPHAEL WORKED feverishly for almost an hour with the chalk, his feeling of inspiration like a wave engulfing him so that there was nothing else but the heady sensation of creativity— and Margherita. His eyes moved back and forth from her to his paper in a swift rhythm as his hand moved over the sheet. "And your eyes, keep them on me . . . *sì* . . . your chin up slightly. *Perfetto.*"

Dio, she was utterly breathtaking. The opalescent light behind her through the slatted shutters was like a halo, and the green velvet curtains on either side of her became an unintended framing device that he actually considered using. Raphael worked on through the powerful undercurrent of attraction that refused to be ignored. The curtains . . . *sì* . . . a loose veil flowing from the top of her head . . . more ideas rushed into his mind almost faster than he could take note of them.

"Eyes up again, on me . . . Just a bit more!"

It was the most unnerving sensation. As she looked at him, she seemed to be peering directly into his soul. Raphael felt his always certain fingers tremble slightly as he gripped the chalk. What on earth was that? He had sketched a thousand faces in his life, dozens of bare breasts and thighs, voluptuous women who had lay naked before him, and even when he was physically drawn to a woman who posed for him, it never once had shaken his concentration.

Raphael washed a hand across his face, shifted uneasily from one foot to the other, and continued. Moving away from the image of her face, he began to outline the folds of her dress, the way the fabric highlighted her waist, then clung to her legs. It was November and yet the room was suddenly stifling, and he felt perspiration drip from his brow.

He worked on her bare feet next, small and perfectly shaped, deciding how he wished to see them positioned for the work. The Madonna would be floating majestically on a heavenly cloud, so they must not seem too firmly planted on the ground. She was a human representation, after all, he reminded himself, yet ultimately a Madonna. Her feet and toes were so perfect, small and delicately shaped, and, jarringly, an image pressed back into his mind, a salacious memory—a dark room, raucous noise below . . . the feel of a girl's bare feet wrapped across his back . . . *raw desire* . . .

He cast his chalk down beside the paper. It snapped in two, startling her. "That is enough for now. You may relax, *signorina*."

"May I see it?" Margherita tentatively asked.

She seemed to expect something dark and forbidden. He bit back a smile.

"Signor Perazzi, *per favore,* I believe I will actually have a glass of that wine now if you would be good enough to pour."

Donato glanced up from the stool in surprise. He had been looking through a small black leather-bound book he had found on the shelf. "You actually read this sort of thing?"

Raphael could see that it was his copy of an architectural treatise by Vitruvius. "I find I must, as it helps me with the themes I am called to paint," he said, hearing that he sounded somehow apologetic. The truth was that an artist's duty, even more than a courtier's, was to be as well versed in the broad themes of classical thought, architecture, and religion as was humanly possible. But he did not say that.

"I have been reading it this entire time and I don't understand a word of it."

"It does take patience. I quite agree with that," Raphael smiled kindly. "It is said that Vitruvius's Latin is so difficult to understand that those who spoke Latin thought he was writing in Greek, and the Greeks thought it was Latin. The drawings, at least, are exquisite."

"They are indeed," he said, leafing once again through the pages.

"Would you like to borrow the book?"

Donato's expression was apologetic. "I am afraid, Signor Sanzio, that I would only be looking at the pictures."

"Then perhaps one day both of you will allow me to read the descriptions *to* you."

"Perhaps."

As Donato poured him a cup of wine, Raphael watched Margherita move slowly toward the table and the new sketch. Rarely did he allow a model to see his work, especially a work in progress. He watched her look at the chalk image of herself, next to which he had lightly drawn the faceless shape of another woman, planned as Saint Barbara. On her left, the shape and heavy cloak of a man kneeling devoutly at her feet was meant to become the third-century pope Sixtus II.

Raphael watched two fingers move to touch her own lips as she gazed at the sketch. "It is magnificent," she said in a soft voice.

"It is only a beginning," he replied casually as he came back across the room to stand beside her. Raphael took a second swallow of wine, then a third, as he watched her fan out the earlier sketches beneath this new one. "I often take details from several other sketches and incorporate them into the finished work. A hand gesture from one, a gaze, perhaps, from another."

Donato brought Margherita a cup of wine then, and the three of them stood looking at the various representations he had already created of her.

"This *is* lovely," Donato remarked of the last one, a sketch of Margherita's face, her head tipped to the side on her graceful neck and her gaze directed straight and serene at the observer. "You have captured her entirely."

"It was my first drawing of the *signorina* from the last time you were here."

"First or not, the eyes—"

"*Sì*, they are extraordinary."

"And they are Margherita's precisely!"

"*Grazie bene*," Raphael nodded gallantly, forbidding himself to reveal that he had looked at that same sketch, and particularly at her eyes, a hundred times since he had seen her last. No, he would never admit that. He barely allowed himself the thought.

"I fear it is getting late," he reluctantly declared, knowing that he still had Giulio's concept drawings of the Coronation of Charlemagne for the pope's next *stanza* to review, and plans later to meet Gianfrancesco and Giovanni for another evening of gambling, drinking, and very likely whoring as well.

"Have you finished with me then?" Margherita asked as she

set down her glass of wine. He could see that she had not drunk a drop.

Ordinarily, this was all he ever used a model for: the preliminary portrait sketches, and then perhaps one last time during the final painting to adjust eye color and skin tone. But suddenly for Raphael, that was unthinkable. He had fought too hard just to get her here. For what he intended to pay her family, he deserved to get as many studies out of her as he needed in order to capture the Madonna.

At least that was what he had told himself.

"For today, sì. I have enough to begin the actual painting. But once I have laid it out—" He wanted to sound as if he were just considering this. "Then it will be critical to have her return for coloring, confirmation of expression, those elements, primarily."

"Very well," Donato agreed, without consulting Margherita. "We wish you to achieve what it is you desire."

What I desire suddenly has less to do with painting her than it had at first, Raphael was thinking.

"When will we be able to see the painting?" she asked.

"It may take some time, and we well may need to meet again more than once, before it is suitable for you to judge it. I have been, you see, taken up with the painting of another image, of late, and shall be again."

He watched her eyes closely for a response. "A Madonna?"

"Oh no," he smiled at her, betraying himself not at all. "Nothing like that. This portrait is of a very different sort." Donato's eyes shifted from Raphael's to Margherita as Raphael said, "There is something I would like to show you. Would you come with me?"

Margherita looked at Donato for his approval. "With my brother-in-law?"

Raphael gave her a gallant look. "By all means."

He told them nothing more, but as they neared the gates of the Vatican Palace, Margherita's heart began to beat wildly, straining against the ties of her dress. Raphael, the great artistic *mastro,* was going to lead them into the very seat of power and influence in Rome, and they were going to do it with as much ease as if they actually belonged there. First, an inside glimpse of the Chigi Villa, she thought with a little burst of excitement, and now this! She and Donato exchanged a glance of disbelief as the papal guards, in their striped uniforms and steel helmets, nodded respectfully to their guide. He led them easily through the Porta Viridaria, named for the gardens kept behind the palace, through crowds of people clambering at the tall gates, then past the gates themselves.

They did not, however, go toward the great papal buildings, or toward the massive construction area of Saint Peter's, but down a small dirt path, bordered by neatly manicured hedgerows, and dotted with classical urns and statuary, just beyond the ancient wall that connected the palace with Castel Sant'Angelo. She resisted the urge to ask him where they were going. He seemed to want to make a game of it. Margherita walked happily beside Raphael, taking in the lovely rosebushes, leafy oaks, cypress trees, and antique Roman sculptures. Ahead was the papal menagerie, with cages holding a cheetah, a lion, and parrots, at which they gasped in amazement—and then the most massive beast she had ever seen in her life was before them.

"*Madre mia!*" she cried, hands flying to her face as they approached.

"*Dio!* What is it?" Donato asked, equally alarmed at the giant, gray animal standing in a pen full of straw.

"A gift to the Holy Father from the king of Portugal. It is called an elephant—and *he* is called Hanno. The other subject I am painting!"

"Hanno?" Margherita asked shakily as Raphael extended his hand slowly over the waist-high barrier and began to stroke the animal's long, gray trunk, which arched up in what seemed like approval.

"It certainly is an odd-looking creature!" Donato chuckled, shrinking back a step with Margherita, as Raphael took a small handful of hay lying in a trough and offered it to Hanno. "What manner of beast is it?"

"He is actually very gentle. He would not dream of harming you. Only crowds frighten him, if the Holy Father sees fit to trot him out for a more public showing. That is the only time I have ever seen him disquieted."

"Just the same . . . " said Donato warily.

Raphael exchanged a glance with Margherita. "I believe he is lonely here," he mused. "So far from his home . . . from his family . . . "

"His family?" Donato laughed. "A massive beast . . . with relatives?"

"And why is that so difficult to believe? All creatures have others of their kind to whom they cleave, make families, and with which they live. I am told elephants are very sociable and family-oriented beasts. That has been taken from Hanno."

Margherita looked at him again, then at the elephant. She drew in a steadying breath, moved alongside Raphael, then slowly extended her hand. "It's so rough!" she laughed as she felt the thick gray skin. As if on cue, Hanno responded to Margherita's gentle touch by folding his knees, kneeling to the ground before her, and inclining his head, as if he were greeting her directly.

"Goodness!" she giggled nervously.

"He likes you," Raphael smiled.

"How do you know?"

"I come here nearly every day to visit him, and I have never seen Hanno kneel in greeting to anyone—except the Holy Father."

"Not even you?"

"Not even me."

Margherita knelt as well, and reached out her hand to Hanno, just above his trunk and she began to stroke him again. "I find it so sad. To think of him taken from his wild home somewhere, and brought here to be stared at, poked at . . . laughed at." Hanno lightly wound his trunk around her forearm just then, in a manner that felt to Margherita much like a caress. She laughed softly again. "I believe he understands! He really is extraordinary!"

Raphael was smiling at her broadly with what she thought was pride. "I knew the two of you would get on well."

"*Sì*, I believe Hanno does fancy me. I sense that he does, anyway." She was still stroking the elephant's rough, dry skin and did so until suddenly it did not feel so foreign to her any longer. "Try it, Donato!" she smiled at her sister's husband. "It really is not so bad. He is rather gentle."

"Oh, no! I believe I will leave *that* for you two brave souls!"

"I would not mind coming here to see him again sometime," Margherita said, gazing with a warm smile at the animal who still knelt before her.

"And I would be honored to escort you," Raphael replied.

After a time, they strolled together away from the menagerie, up the rise of the hill and through the lush grounds, protected, yet in the center of the bustling city. The branches above them made a broad leafy canvas of shade as they walked.

Donato hung back and eventually sank onto a stone bench as though the walking had wearied him. But they did not notice. Raphael was explaining yet another of his many tasks to Margherita, this being his work as commissary of antiquities where work excavating at the Domus Aurea was well under way.

"The magnificent building was conceived and built by Emperor Nero, then destroyed, buried, and hidden from the rest of the world by an envious successor—Trajan, if I am not mistaken."

Raphael's eyes lit with surprise as he regarded her. "Well. I *am* impressed."

"That a common girl from Trastevere knows anything of emperors' palaces?"

"That you would find history of interest."

She gazed up at the lacy tree branches. "When we were small, my mother used to tell my sister and me stories about the grandeur of this city. They were her version of bedtime tales. I

believe she wanted us to dream of bigger things, to believe they
were possible. So she filled our heads with tales of Nero and his
beloved Poppaea."

"Ah, such a scandal!" Raphael chuckled. "His beautiful mistress!"

"Later his wife."

"It is true," Raphael concurred.

"My mother told us of Poppaea's love of music and art. She
was as common as we are, my mother used to say, so excitedly that
her eyes danced—I can see her even now in my mind. Poppaea
taught herself the things she did not know, and managed to
become an empress. I think that is why that one was always my
favorite story." She stopped for a moment as a shadow of sadness
passed across her face, then disappeared behind a slightly embarrassed smile, which faded into one of sadness. "I miss her greatly."

"I miss my own, as well," said Raphael.

"You lost your mother?"

"As a child, sì, and my father not long afterward."

"I am sorry."

"It is a loss from which one never quite recovers, and I have
found it is best not even to try. Rather to hold the moments
inside, nurture them, and care for them fondly, but solely."

"I am told so often not to dwell on her memory, to move on in
the company of those still living," she said sadly.

"Would that it were that simple." Raphael shook his head.
"But, here or not, they are a part of us . . . and they shall be forever an element of who we become."

Margherita studied him. "Sì."

"But you have happy memories. Stories to make you smile.
Images . . . moments that are a comfort."

"It is true."

"Like the story of Nero's second wife?"

Her embarrassed smile returned, and her mood eased. "My
mother told us about *all* of the great emperors' wives, if you can
imagine—and the story of Caesar and Cleopatra. I loved every

word of them all. They were great fantasies for a little girl who—"
She stopped for a moment, then began again. "My father said she
was filling our heads with nonsense, that things like that never
happened to real people."

"And what does he say of you having met *me?*"

"Meeting you is a fairy tale for any girl, Signor Sanzio. Surely
you know that. But like all beautiful tales, there must be an end to
it. That is what he would say."

"How sad for him that he never heard the tales with happy
endings."

His eyes settled on her so earnestly then that she needed to
look away. She was quite certain that he meant to kiss her, and the
thought of that quite frightened her to death for the absolute
power behind it—and because suddenly she desired it with every
part of her body.

As if sensing her reticence, they began to walk again. And as
they did, Raphael changed the subject entirely, speaking to her
of his other new assignment, as architect for Saint Peter's—and
to that Margherita listened intently, nodding in understanding as
he spoke.

"So I see the project quite differently from Bramante before
me. He conceived the great basilica in the shape of a Greek cross,
topped by a cupola. He wished a dome more grand than the Pantheon. But I say it must be in the shape of a Latin cross. And also
Bramante's design will never hold such a massive vault as he
intended. So that will all need to be seen to and reconsidered
mathematically, as well. Rather a massive undertaking for a
simple artist as myself."

She was looking over at him. "And rather an impressive honor
for a simple boy from Urbino."

"It has been a very long time since anyone has reminded me
that there was ever anything simple about my life."

"You are, however, the product of your youth, are you not? As
you are a part of those who defined it? No matter where life has
taken you now?"

"Well, I am heartened that you find it to be so, anyway."

Again they stopped. Raphael turned to face her. Sensing his eyes upon her, Margherita turned to face him as well. The cool autumn breeze rustled the tendrils of her hair that had come loose from her cap. Neither of them could see Donato. He seemed to have disappeared.

"Why on earth should what *I* think matter to you?"

As they stood in shimmering afternoon sunlight that had begun very swiftly to descend in a brilliant gold-and-crimson ball, Raphael reached a hand to touch her cheek. It stilled there. "Can you honestly tell me, *bella* Margherita, that you know not the answer to that by now?" He spoke her name softly, gently like a prayer, as he moved a step nearer to her. Margherita's heart began to beat so swiftly that she began to feel dizzy. "Is it not obvious that I am enchanted by you?"

"And *I* am afraid of *you*,"

Instead of feeling affronted, he smiled charmingly. "*Dio*, you need not fear me!"

"Oh, I believe I must, Signor Sanzio."

They were close enough now for Margherita to feel his breath on her upturned face. She could smell the musky maleness of him as his hand stilled at the line of her jaw. Then, close as they were, Raphael very lightly moved his lips over hers in a gentle kiss.

Antonio had kissed her before. But not like this. At that moment she dared to think of Letitia and Donato, and what they did in the privacy of their bedchamber. She felt something deep and low within herself stir, something hot and very powerful. His dark eyes . . . strong corded arms . . . and such sweetly tender lips . . . The sensation became an ache. Her heart was hammering.

It was a moment before Margherita could draw herself away from the craving, but when she did it was harshly. "No!" she declared, squaring her shoulders as she stepped back from him. "You shall not have me that way!"

His response was a softly mischievous smile. "And what way is that, *signorina*?"

"In the way of all others! I will *not* be a diversion like that!"

"Is that what you believe has begun between us, a simple diversion?"

"Nothing has begun between us!"

"Then you know very little." He flipped a hand at her dismissively, and it was the first passionate gesture she had ever seen crack his smooth, and always elegant, demeanor.

"You sound like my father."

"Then your father is a wise man. You would do well to regard him."

"And *you* would do well, Signor Sanzio, not to assume that everyone in the world will be so easily seduced by your talent or your charm." Donato was upon them suddenly then, breaking the tension. Margherita turned away from Raphael. "It is late. We must go."

"*Sì,* go then," Raphael agreed, knowing he was unlikely to change her mind about anything. What his expression did not reveal was that it was also the thing about her that had bewitched him the most.

"ARE YOU ALL RIGHT, *CARA?*"

Donato broke the silence once they had returned to the Via Santa Dorotea, and sat alone in the warm, lamp-lit kitchen long after the bakery had closed, the curtains drawn protectively, cocooning them safely from the frightening new world that lay beyond. Of all the rooms in the house, Margherita liked it best here, feeling safe amid the sacks of flours, the stacks of wooden bowls, the spoons, and the reassuring aroma from the rich buttery loaves that lingered there. She held Matteo on her lap, swaying him gently to sleep with a back-and-forth movement of her knees as Donato asked the question.

"Of course. Why would I not be?" Margherita replied too quickly, and they both realized the defense in that.

"I could not help but see the way he looked at you, the way you spoke with one another in the papal gardens."

Margherita gazed out the window into the steadily darkening afternoon where a never-ending line of drying laundry flapped, and Letitia's other sons played. She could not bring herself to tell him that Raphael had kissed her, or that, the good Lord save her, it had been wildly pleasurable. Even now, at the very thought, her body ached again for his touch.

"What does it matter, Donato, hmm? Of course Signor Sanzio is handsome, powerful, sharp-tongued, and as elegant as any prince. He is the great Raffaello, after all, and I can only ever be a momentary distraction while he paints."

"How can you be so certain of that?"

Margherita clasped her hands and squeezed them tightly. "You know as well as I that I am not of his world! He could never actually care for someone so beneath his own station for more than a few trifling days, and I could never settle for a fate as a mistress! I told you all that from the first!"

"How do you know the future?"

"History is the best predictor of the future. There are mistresses, Donato, and there are wives! A man who breaks bread with dukes, kings, and the Holy Father himself does not make a wife of the woman who bakes that bread!"

"You also believed he could not intend you as a serious model for an important commission," he carefully reminded her, fingering the base of the melting candle pooling on the table between them.

"The two are very different!"

"Does not the stuff of life—of relationships between people—evolve and change?"

"Not *that* much!"

"Look to the expression in his eyes today, my dear sister. See him as I saw him today before you tell me that," Donato said more gently. "He is, I believe, entirely taken with you."

Francesco Luti and Letitia had been listening at the door. She should have known it. Margherita rolled her eyes wearily as they burst in then in a swirl of excitement. "Can it be?" her father asked, his deep voice heavy with incredulity. "That the good Lord, in his wisdom, has sought to take this unlikely moment between you and the great painter, and possibly transform it into a grand lifetime together?"

"They are fool's words you speak, *Padre mio*."

"Oh now. Could he not fall so deeply in love that he would wish to make you his wife?"

"You know well that is *not* possible, and I will thank you not to lurk around corners listening to my conversations!"

"Margherita!" her sister gasped sanctimoniously, fingers splayed across the laces at the top of her dress. "You must ask our father's forgiveness at once!"

"I owe him no such thing."

"We owe him respect!"

And Margherita believed that as well, with her whole heart. Francesco Luti had been a good and caring father all of her life. He may be a little harsh now, but he wanted only the best for his daughters.

"Forgive me, *Padre mio*. It is the events of the day that have clouded my judgment."

"Well, is it true that the great Raffaello is taken with you in some familiar way?"

"It is absolutely certain," Donato intervened with smooth assurance. "I saw it all myself. He was as taken with her as I have ever seen a man."

"This could mean a fortune for our family!" Letitia smiled dreamily.

"And the utter ruin of *me*."

"*Dio,* is that not a tired old song by now?" her sister groaned. "Your piteous droning is truly vile on the eve of something so grand! How can you see us to the very edge of so great a thing and then contemplate ignoring that it is even there?"

"We are your *famiglia*," Francesco more cautiously offered. "Do you not owe us some part of what has happened for you?"

"And what do all of you owe to *me*? Am I to be bartered like a lamb to market for a few pieces more of gold?"

"Oh truly, Margherita! It is only your body—not your soul, unless you choose to give it," Letitia countered unsympathetically. "And can you tell me bedding a great *mastro* like that could be so dreadful, especially if he chose one day to marry you? Heaven knows I would have done it myself had he glanced at me with my child that day and not you!"

"Letitia!" Francesco gasped, seeing the look of sudden shock and hurt color Donato's face.

"Oh, you know I don't mean it like that. Such an opportunity could never be mine anyway. I no longer carry that alluring look of purity so appealing to wealthy men."

Seeing that the hurt expression remained on her husband's face, Letitia whispered to Donato, put a hand over his shoulder, and they slipped silently together up the back stairs. Once Letitia and her husband were gone, Francesco sat where Donato had been and gently placed a hand over his daughter's. The soft hum of crickets, and the sounds of the boys playing in the garden beyond, filled the silence between them.

"Do you truly wish not to pursue this with the great *mastro*?"

"What I do not wish is to be made a mockery. To see my life ruined."

"It would seem to me that he is honoring you greatly, daughter."

"It would seem that way to me, as well," she conceded with a small shrug.

"Then I bid you, fear it not."

"And what would it seem if I bed him?"

"Wise women who know how to play the game become great and powerful courtesans."

"*Padre mio,* great courtesans are *not* baker's daughters from Trastevere."

"Do they not say, Margherita *mia,* that there is a first time for everything? You could become famous! You would be the first, and long remembered for it!"

"And *you* could become rich."

He pursed his lips and shrugged. "Would it be so bad? My girl, so much your mother's daughter. You are just like her, with that undefinable power to capture a man's heart and hold it forever. Signor Raphael is only a man like all the rest of us, and I believe with everything I am that he could come to love you exactly like that." He embraced her tightly, and his warm, fleshy body was a comfort. "But do not allow anyone, least of all me, to force you to do what is not in you to do."

"When I see him look at me," she said weakly, "I fear it would be easier to push back the rain."

❧ 10 ❧

ON THE FOLLOWING FRIDAY, MARGHERITA AGREED RE-luctantly to take a stroll with Antonio out toward the great green rise of Il Gianicolo, once he had finished his duties at the stables. He had said he missed her and wished to see her. Why he was calling on her in this way she did not know. He had not done so in several months. But there was to be a papal procession from the Vatican Palace to the Castel Sant'Angelo, honoring Pope Leo's guest, the German ambassador, and everyone was going out to watch the grand spectacle.

Margherita was no longer naive. She acknowledged Antonio's penchant for other women, but she did not confront him about it. Margherita also did not continue to give him hope that she loved him. She did not. Rather, she went with him because his companionship seemed a comfort to her now when everything else in her life was swiftly changing, pressing her toward Raphael. Her thoughts now, her fantasies, were all of him. Intense. Com-pelling. Magnetic. Everything about him drew her, made her think of him . . . imagine *them*.

A grown woman, she knew to what conclusion desire led. And in her private moments, her body ached for that base, sensual union with him.

Antonio Perazzi held her hand, his smile a gratified one,

believing himself firmly attached to a swiftly rising star—one who valued loyalty, thrived on naïveté, and who, conveniently, had depended upon him for years. She knew that. Understood it. Sensing it again now brought her heavily from her fantasies.

Just after they crossed the cobbled street, he paused, drew her against him, and kissed her. "This is going to be a *grand* day," he proclaimed. "I can feel it!"

"You seem awfully certain of yourself," Margherita smiled. His kiss, like the other memories of them, lingered only slightly before it faded into the moment and the bustling scene around them.

"One has to be certain to get anywhere in this life!"

When they arrived at a crowded corner of the Borgo Santo Spirito, they could hear that the lavish procession had already begun. There was the herald of trumpets, a clash of cymbals, and a heavy din of shouting and laughter from the crushing crowd of onlookers who lined the cobbled streets. Margherita shaded her eyes and saw the pope nearing in the distance, resplendent in his rich pontifical robes, seated on a great winged chair, riding high on the back of Hanno. Seated on the elephant's neck was a dark-skinned, barefoot, exotic-looking boy in a white turban and tunic, and bearing a long leather whip. Seeing the whip, Margherita's heart lurched painfully, then seemed to stop.

When the procession came more clearly into view in the shadow of the silvery sunlit afternoon, she could see that Hanno's head was down, his trunk limp as he slowly lumbered amid the ostentatious procession. There seemed so little life in the great gray animal, confined like this, such a world away from the one he had been meant to have. Margherita felt her heart lurch again at the sight.

She touched her fingers to her lips as she heard Antonio cruelly laugh. "Behold that! Is he not the most ridiculous looking beast in the world!"

"*I* think he is magnificent," she defended.

As was the custom, a great triumphal arch had been set up along the pathway. Elegantly garbed noblemen on horseback were the pope's escort. Statesmen, cardinals, and bishops followed, all in grand regalia. As the procession neared, the din and clamber of trumpeters, drummers, and pipers grew. She watched Hanno lumber on. The roar of cannon fire pierced the air with such suddenness that not only the crowd, but the elephant, was startled. He was agitated now, she could see, his trunk beginning to swing and his head jerking from side to side. Instinctively, Margherita pressed forward into the crowd nearer the street.

"*Gesù!* What are you doing!" Antonio charged, grabbing her arm in a panic, only to have her cast it off.

"He is frightened!"

"He is a dangerous beast! Take care!"

"*You* are far more dangerous to me than he shall ever be!"

Stepping toward him into the street, in the place where the turbaned boy had begun to whip Hanno to stop his thrashing, Margherita reached out a hand to his trunk. With honeyed sweetness, and tender words, she spoke desperately, but beneath her breath, the noise of the crowd around her masked her kind plea. "Poor Hanno . . . be not afraid . . . these foolish people wish only to see you . . . shhh . . . be not afraid . . ."

As Hanno lowered his head to her, the eyes of all present, both grand and common, were upon her. They stared curiously at Margherita, wondering, she could see, what power a common daughter of Trastevere possessed over so great and exotic a beast belonging to the Holy Father. Would it be like this, she wondered, feeling the weight of the city's collective gaze — the attention, the curious whispers, layered over with admiration — if she were to become a part of Raphael's life? She felt a small, odd shiver of delight. Power. A tiny spark of pride . . . *Pride.* She had known precious little of that in her life.

"Back, *signorina!* You frighten the beast!" the turbaned boy growled in a heavily accented command, glowering down at her, his dark eyes glittering with condescension as a quartet of papal guards rushed toward her.

"I was trying to calm him!"

"Arrest her!" someone shouted.

She felt the guardsmen clamp down on her upper arms in a grip like a vise and jerk her forward. "But you do not understand!"

"You will come with us!"

Another hand clamped onto her other wrist.

"Hanno was frightened! I only tried to—"

"She meant no harm! If it would please His Holiness, I shall vouch for the girl! She is Raphael's model." The voice was from a young man behind her, yet spoken with such authority of purpose that the guardsmen loosened their grip. Her expression was stricken as she turned to see the young apprentice from Raphael's workshop who had first come to the bakery on his behalf. His name, she remembered, was Giulio Romano.

Dressed elegantly now in a great embroidered jerkin, with a high ruffled collar and tilted velvet hat, which made him appear much older and more worldly than he was, and holding a large sketchpad and piece of black chalk, Giulio stood in a surprisingly authoritative posture, separating Margherita and the stone-faced guards. One of them looked up at the pope for direction, something was whispered that she could not determine, and then, in an instant, she was freed—but not before the pontiff shot her a deep and appraising look. She saw then that he had been watching the altercation all along, yet she was not at all certain by his expression, so far above her, if his reaction was a favorable one or not.

As the procession continued on, and Hanno slowly disappeared from her view, Margherita stood beside a dumbstruck Antonio as she gazed appreciatively at Raphael's assistant. "I owe you my thanks," she said breathlessly.

"You owe me nothing. The *mastro* would have wished me to intercede, and there is nothing I would not do for him."

"The sentiments of all Rome, I hear. Especially the loveliest of them," Antonio vulgarly quipped, but neither Margherita or Giulio heard him.

"I honestly meant no harm," she said, rubbing her aching wrists, still shaken by the force so suddenly brought upon her. "I felt so sorry for the animal. He looked utterly miserable reined in like that."

"I am afraid, sadly, that my sketch reflects not the proud, mighty nature, but that instead, just as you describe."

"The great Raffaello had you come out here to draw a picture of a beast?" Antonio asked with a small laugh.

"The *mastro* wishes to use an image of Hanno in a fresco he is planning of the Battle of Scipio, *signore*." Giulio narrowed his eyes on Antonio for the briefest moment. "I have drawn beggars, fools, and blind men, as well. The world, after all, is full of all sorts." Then he looked back at Margherita. "I was to make a few sketches of the elephant as he moved in procession. The animal is very dear to His Holiness and he wishes his likeness immortalized as often as possible."

"Hanno is very sweet and gentle. I wish everyone could see that," Margherita said sadly.

"I knew it!" Antonio spat. "You *have* seen that beast before!"

"Oh, do be still," Margherita snapped and extended her hand to Giulio. "No matter what you say, I truly must thank you again, Signor Romano. I am not at all certain where I would be without your intervention just now."

He nodded and then smiled. In the echo of her praise, it was the first time he had seemed even slightly boyish to her. "Perhaps one day, if the *mastro* approves, of course, you would allow me to use the *mastro*'s sketches of you for my own works. It is difficult indeed in Rome to find women who will model. Especially ones who are so extraordinarily beautiful."

Margherita smiled. No matter how it had sounded she knew what he meant. It seemed to her a high honor to be asked. "Will you be telling Signor Sanzio about this?"

"I must tell him, *signorina*, before the Holy Father's aides twist it completely in the telling."

"Word travels that fast within your sphere?"

"Signorina Luti," Giulio laughed. "You have no idea!"

As they parted, and Antonio led her away from the thinning

crowd along the Borgo Santo Spirito, she saw his suddenly mirth-less smile. "At least tell me, after that little scene, that the great and powerful Raffaello has given you some money for your trouble."

"I wouldn't tell you if he had."

"We have always been like family," he indignantly retorted, drawing up her hand between his and squeezing it so tightly that it hurt. It was the first time in her life he had ever frightened her. It was also the first time she had ever truly disliked him.

Her body went rigid as she wrenched her hand away and shot him a warning glare. "Never touch me like that again!"

"Forgive me, but it has been your custom always to tell me everything!"

"*Sì*, once it was, Antonio. But lately, much has changed—it seems for all of us." Two entirely different worlds had collided boldly for her back there on the Borgo Santo Spirito, and she had accepted, for the first time, her odd new place between them.

※ *11* ※

THE MOUNTING NUMBER OF COMMISSIONS DREW RAPHAEL'S attention in the next days. There was the work at Agostino Chigi's chapel, in Santa Maria del Popolo, and the unfinished portrait of his friend Castiglione to complete and see shipped. As well, there was the initial drawing personally requested by the pope for a for-mal portrait of his good friend Cardinal Bibbiena, and Bibbiena's bathing room was still waiting to be decorated. The papal *stanza* was finally complete after two years, but Raphael had been awarded yet another large papal commission—the pope's dining room, to ornament intricately in fresco with such grand themes as the Fire in the Borgo, the Battle of Ostia, and the Coronation of Charlemagne.

As the workshop *mastro,* he was responsible for all frescoes, paintings, and initial drawings. Raphael did dozens of quick sketches each day, and held meetings with his assistants to communicate how he wished each work positioned, down to the character placement and facial expressions. Then he handed each one over to a member of his entourage to sketch so that he might later critique it. Amid this blur of never-ending commissions and responsibility, Raphael consoled himself with the courtly idea that the genius he offered was in the inception of the idea, not in its execution. But the portrait of the Madonna for the church at San Sisto had become his obsession.

He still envisioned her standing on a pillow of clouds, feet bare, the clothing simple and elegant — the perfect combination of ethereal, exquisite and yet reality, as Margherita herself was. He wanted a human Madonna. A woman who was flesh and blood, one who could laugh and love and cry, and who would move the viewer by merely seeing her. He felt a powerfully sensual jolt surge up through him again, the one he always felt when he imagined her. His heart began to pound, and Raphael squeezed his eyes, forcing back the image.

"You called for me, *mastro?*" Giulio asked, coming into his small, private sitting room, which faced the busy Via dei Coronari.

It had been a long day of working on the large-scale drawings for the new sequence of the frescoes at Chigi's villa, and they were both weary. Sun slatted through the half-open shutters and streaked both of their faces.

"Sit with me, Giulio."

The younger artist took a small tufted footstool and drew it near to Raphael's armchair. As neither of them yet had the energy to wash, both were stained with splashes of cool pastel-colored plaster from the newly finished image of two flying angels in the first new Vatican fresco. Their hands were marked with drawing chalk from other works.

"We are very busy these days," Raphael began on a sigh.

"*Sì,* it is so," Giulio sighed too, exhausted beyond words from the strain and demands of the day.

"When you first came to my studio four years ago, you showed great promise."

"I was very young," he countered shyly. "But eager beyond measure."

"Fourteen was when I began my own apprenticeship. And in your case, the promise you showed has been fulfilled. You are now a brilliant artist in your own right."

"You have many years and experience beyond me, *mastro*."

"God delivers His great gifts in *His* time, Giulio *mio*, not ours."

"Your words are too much praise for my heart to hear. I believe I have tried very hard, and yet—"

Raphael directed his gaze straight on so Giulio would grasp the sincerity, as well as the absolute commitment there. "Yesterday, Gianfrancesco Penni thought your drawings of the women for the Borgo area of the new fresco were my own."

"It is not so!"

"Giulio, I want you to decorate and to oversee the new *stanza* on my behalf."

"For the entire room?" Giulio gulped. He leaned forward, his mouth dropping open like a hinge. For a long moment, he said nothing else. "That commission is from the Holy Father himself, for his private dining room!"

"I know well what I ask of you, Giulio, and I would not do it now if you were not ready."

"It cannot be so. Gianfrancesco and Giovanni are far more experienced than I. Should you not bestow upon one of them the honor of assisting you in this way?"

"They both have many talents, but it is your help in this I require. It is your technique alone, the delicacy of your figures, that can mirror my intent, and help me be free to move on to conceptualize our many other commissions."

"This is an incomparable opportunity for me."

"And I would not offer it to you if I did not believe you were prepared for the task."

"But how—rather, where do I begin?"

"I shall help you every step of the way. We shall meet each morning and go over concepts, other figure designs, body positioning, once we are both rested and clear-eyed, and of course I will supervise your progress all the while. He leaned forward in his stiff-backed leather chair. "You *can* do this, Giulio. I know that you can."

"Your belief in me is staggering, *mastro*."

"I only see what is already there before me." Raphael smiled kindly.

Raphael took a sip of wine and gazed out at the soothing fire, the golden flames which warmed the grand and vaulted room beyond the doorway.

"I saw your new sketches for the Madonna today," Giulio offered, cutting into the contemplative silence that had risen up between them.

Raphael continued to stare into the fire. "And how did you find them?"

"Your concept is amazingly innovative."

"And would you suppose His Holiness will be pleased?"

"At least as pleased at the model you have chosen, if not the majesty of the whole of it."

Giulio was smiling at him, seeing some of what Raphael felt, in spite of his attempt to hide it. "She *is* an extraordinary beauty. That comes through even in your rough sketches of her."

"That she is. As a model, she is beyond compare."

Giulio was still looking at him. "And as something more, *mastro?*"

Only then did Raphael turn again to meet Giulio's gaze. The boy's open worship of him created an odd place of safety for a man who needed to show caution in all that he did. "I am betrothed to the niece of one of the most powerful men in Rome. That is an honor of which I could not have dreamed as the son of an unheralded court artist in Urbino. As I was recently reminded, no mere artist has ever married so high."

"But you do not love Signorina Bibbiena."

"I do not. But I have worked very hard to achieve all that I have now. It has been my entire world."

Giulio prodded the burning wood with an iron poker so that he was no longer a nuisance by looking directly at the master, who had clearly become uncomfortable with the conversation. The flames flared. "Yet one is your work while the other is your life."

"Both have been bound up with one another for so long I am uncertain if I can see one for the other now."

"And yet you fancy the baker's daughter?"

"It is dangerous right now for me to do so in any meaningful way." Raphael lay his head back against the chair and closed his eyes. "It would only jeopardize her reputation, as well as my own standing in Rome. And there is so very much at stake for all of us just now."

"So you see her as more than a tumble or two?"

"I do not see her in that way at all, Giulio *mio*. I never have. And she would never have me that way even if I did. That is the very heart of the problem. She is unwilling, and *I* am unavailable for more." He shot to his feet, raking back his shoulder-length hair. "And it is *that* which is driving me half mad!"

❧ *12* ❧

FRANCESCO LUTI HAD GIVEN HIS DAUGHTER A GREAT deal to consider in the weeks that followed, especially since those weeks did not include another summons to Raphael's workshop. She had pushed him away, her father said. But there had been no choice. Especially when she had no idea how to battle her fear. It was a fear of what might become of her if she gave in to the power of her wildly growing and erotic feelings for him.

She thought so much of her mother in these complex days, and craved even more something she could never have again—a mother's wise and tender counsel. What would she have advised about this? she wondered. Marina Luti certainly had grand dreams for her daughters, but would this have been among them?

Might she have urged caution or encouraged her to move forward with her whole heart?

I miss you now more than ever, Madre mia . . . was the aching refrain Margherita could not chase from her mind. *What would you think? What would you have me do?*

On a cold and gray afternoon in early December, with rain clouds darkening Rome, Margherita stood beside her sister in the small, stifling kitchen of the family bakery. Her hair was pulled tightly away from her face, knotted with a limp piece of brown cloth. The body already immortalized magnificently in sketches as the Madonna was clothed now in a simple work dress of gray cotton, covered over with a white apron. As the bread oven blazed beside her, filled with new fragrant loaves of sweet bread, she and Letitia shaped more of the risen dough in two large earthen bowls for the batch to come next.

Beside them, wet with perspiration, Francesco Luti pushed the long wooden peel into the fire to retrieve the loaves that were fully baked. They were a team of quiet efficiency, each knowing their roles. But the pounding, mixing, and straining that went on daily to produce bread for this neighborhood of Rome still left them all exhausted.

Margherita leaned forward over the bowl, her face flushed with the strain and from the heat, her mind free to move around thoughts and memories of moments. She thought of Antonio, then of Raphael. There was no comparison to how she felt when she was with Raphael. The raw energy she felt when he looked at her—the *way* he looked at her, his eyes studying her with a strangely devoted intensity, and her own body reacting in the deepest places to it.

But her weakness was simply her awe of him. It must be. Raphael was not a man, not a real one whom she could ever understand. He was handsome, cultured, and intimidatingly well educated—a myth and a legend in Rome. They could never speak of the same things, never live the same sort of experiences. Still, for some reason, she had been allowed to stand in the glow of that greatness, and dare to imagine being swept away by the vitality and fire that was Raffaello.

Margherita stood straight, let out a sigh, and brushed her glistening brow with the back of her hand. Francesco shot her a glowering look of disapproval. "Attention, *cara!* Mind the dough! You know well enough what will happen to the bread if you knead it too roughly!"

"Forgive me, *Padre mio.*"

Letitia's two older boys were playing in the stairwell beyond the kitchen and the small, stifling room was shaking with the activity. Margherita thought about her existence — the certainty and predictability of it, feeling trapped by the cold, gray day beyond the thin, peeling walls. As tears welled in her eyes, she lifted her chin defiantly and forced them away. Never before had she permitted herself the sin of self-pity, and she was not about to begin today.

As she turned to fetch the dish of salt for the next batch that Letitia had begun, she saw her sister and father standing, mouths agape, at the sudden presence of an elegantly clad gentleman standing before them. He had a thick swath of silvery hair and a dignified air, and was clad in a black velvet cape and hat with a padded brim, and a heavy gold chain around his neck.

"Forgive my intrusion. I called at your door but there was no answer," he said in a richly schooled tone thick with condescension. "I am Giovanni da Udine, assistant to Raffaello, and I have come with a message for Signorina Luti."

Margherita dried her hands on a heavy towel laying beside the bowl, exchanged a glance with her sister and father, then moved forward tentatively. "I am Signorina Luti."

"*Sì,* I see that you are," he said appraisingly, clearly having seen her likeness on Raphael's worktable. He, however, was not so taken with her as Giulio Romano had been. His gaze told her that. "I have come to say that the *mastro* bids you to return with your chaperone to our studio at your earliest convenience."

"He has finished the Madonna? It has been but a fortnight."

"Alas, no, *signorina,* the work is yet incomplete. But there is enough there for the *mastro* to begin adding your skin tones."

Margherita tried very hard not to show, in the presence of this tall, self-assured artist, her pleasure at the request. While Raphael had told her he would send for her, as the days had worn on, and her life had returned to the normal, predictable pace of a Trastevere baker's daughter, she had begun to think of it all as a very fanciful dream.

"I am uncertain when that might be," she forced herself to lie. His expression was arrogant, his tone expectant. She was simply another girl, another model. "This is a very busy time for my father's bakery here, with the seasonal fruit bread now expected by our patrons." Knowing the expression she would find on his face, Margherita refused to look at her father.

"I am quite certain we could part with you for a few short hours, sister," Letitia coolly offered.

"And what of Donato?"

"My good husband told me only this morning of the stable master's pleasure at his invitation to the studio of so great an artist as Raffaello. I do believe another visit would only strengthen his standing there."

So it was decided. Margherita hesitated only a moment longer. "Will the *mastro* find Friday agreeable, perhaps in the afternoon after the last loaves of bread have been seen to?"

His nod was a courtly gesture, his costly gold chain glistening in the firelight cast from the open bread oven. "I was given leave to accept any circumstance, and occasion, you might be inclined to propose."

"Any?" She arched a brow.

"Such is the value Raffaello places upon the completion of your portrait, *signorina.*"

This man was smooth, experienced, scholarly, she thought, with his silver hair and high manner. He was certainly cautious of her—and she was wary of him as she walked him politely to the door. "I take it you are not in agreement with his opinion, Signor da Udine," she said, opening the door for him then standing beside it, with her hand on the heavy iron handle.

"It is not my place to agree or disagree with the *mastro*'s choices, Signorina Luti, only to see them to fruition in any way that I am able."

His indifference was almost palpable. "Tell him, if you please, that my escort and I shall arrive at the hour of four on the morrow, and that I understand this to be the final time he shall have need of me."

"As you wish." He nodded again. "I shall tell him exactly that," said Giovanni da Udine. And the way in which he said it made it quite clear to Margherita that he thought her a silly girl, a model of modest value, and that he cared not in the slightest whether she even returned to the workshop at all.

AS THE MOON GLOWED above the cobbled stone streets, wet with fog and rain, Raphael made a smiling and grand entrance into the crowded rooms of a thriving bordello in the Quartiere dell' Ortaccio. But even as he gave his cloak to a door guard, and stepped smilingly down the smooth stone steps his calloused drawing hand throbbed. As he and his men entered the richly appointed foyer, with its tapestry-lined walls and glittering wall braziers, his lower back ached from bending over the large sheets of paper glued together to make the cartoon. The full-scale drawing of the next sequence in the new papal room, this one for the Battle of Ostia, with its dozens of detailed figures and boats, various costumes, and the placement of the pope, had been difficult.

Before that, he had done six sheets of studies for the concept of the statuary in Chigi's chapel in Santa Maria del Popolo, and met with Gianfrancesco Penni for hours about it. He had then gone to an excavation site and met with his new advisers on the antiquities projects. Then, before returning to the workshop, he had spent the remainder of the afternoon on a scaffold in the pope's *stanza*, wetting and redoing one of the female faces in the Fire in the Borgo sequence that had not turned out precisely as he wished.

It was grueling work, he warned his staff of artists, knowing that he would not be the only one who was weary and pained. *Toil well for me and I shall reward you with all the women and drink you desire,* he had told his men. And now it was time to do just that. Rome and Florence were full of rival artisans angry at what they saw as the increasing power and influence of one man. And so, keeping a contented staff of artists became almost as important to Raphael as completing the work itself.

Earlier in the day, Giulio had a run-in with Sebastiano Luciani, whose anger was rising over the commissions he believed were owed to his own benefactor, Michelangelo Buonarroti. They were commissions Raphael's workshop had won instead. Young and still unsure, Giulio had been shaken by the confrontation, which likely accounted for the mistakes in the frescoed figure of the woman that Raphael himself had been called to correct.

But Raphael chose not to think of any of that as he sank into one of the carved chairs with tall backs that surrounded a table busy with a game of dice. Tonight he was in need of diversion. And tonight, for the first time, he had insisted that Giulio accompany him. *You can do only what you wish to do,* Raphael had assured him. *If that is but eating, drinking, watching and listening, then so be it. But to be a great artist,* he had told the boy, *you must understand all that life has to offer.* And so, out of gratitude more than interest, Giulio had reluctantly agreed to join them.

Wearing one of Raphael's costly doublets, sewn of green satin with fashionable slashed sleeves, and rust-colored hose, Giulio sank into another of the chairs at a table with da Udine and Penni, who were already sitting together, each with a woman on his lap.

"Ah, *mastro!* Play a round with us!" Giovanni urged his friend and master with a jovial wave.

"It is too early for me, *caro,* to gamble on *anything* yet."

"Have a bit of hot mulled wine," Penni called out. "And you are sure to change your mind!"

Raphael and Giulio each accepted wine in silver goblets from a servant bearing a tray full of them, just as a young girl came up beside him. She was dressed seductively in crimson fabric, with cleavage that was daringly low, and her face was painted to make her appear far older than she clearly was.

"What may I offer you, Signor Sanzio?" she asked, and the tone of the request implied more than food or drink.

Raphael regarded her closely then, an easy smile turning up the corners of his mouth. She was a surprisingly pretty girl for a place like this, with wide blue eyes, smooth skin, and full pink lips. Young, very young. She was not hardened yet by her trade, nor by the years, which made her that much more attractive to him. And, not all that long ago, it would have assured her a place upstairs with him for the rest of the evening. It would be easy enough to take her, he thought. But he had no inclination for that now, nor had he for days.

When he thought carnally of women lately—when he craved a pliant female body beneath his own now the only one he could imagine was the frustratingly aloof baker's daughter. That simple fact tortured him. It was not going to happen with Margherita. She had made that clear, in her charmingly provincial style, that she would become no man's diversion. Still, Raphael could not banish the fantasy.

"*Grazie*, but no," he said engagingly as the girl sidled up close beside him, smelling only faintly of musk and sweat. In response, Raphael took her hand and kissed the soft, warm palm sensually. "Not that I am not tempted, mind you. You are a beautiful girl."

"But there is a problem?"

He laughed in surprise. "With me? No. Nothing like that. It is rather that I am too, shall we say, distracted of late."

She sank into his lap then with a surprisingly seductive smile, and his assistants around him let out a collective bawdy peal of laughter. Raphael could feel her fingers snaking up along his thigh before he had time to stop it. "If that is all it is, Signor Raphael, I know that I can do whatever—"

Raphael pressed her hand away more forcefully. "There is a woman, you see," he whispered to her.

"We are very discreet. She need not know."

"But *I* would know. And for some ungodly reason, known not even to me at the moment, that seems to matter."

"She is a fortunate girl."

"Would that *she* realized it," he quipped with a dramatic little sigh.

"If she does not realize it, then perhaps she does not deserve you, *signore.*"

"This particular girl deserves the moon and stars," Raphael smiled, seeing Margherita's face come alive again in his mind as vividly as if he had only just left her. "But even she does not realize *that.*"

"Modesty is that attractive, is it?" she asked with a small, bitten-back smile.

"I am surprised to find it extraordinarily so," he replied, standing again to break the connection that, were he to allow it even a moment more, might well weaken his curious new resolve.

As the girl finally left him and moved back into the crowd of guests and ladies, Raphael saw the figure of a tall, slim man with intense black eyes and waves of red-gold hair emerge and approach. He had been a friend once when they worked side by side at the villa, but no longer. Sebastiano Luciani was drunk. He swayed toward Raphael from the arms of another girl who clearly recognized trouble in the impending encounter. Wisely, she turned and disappeared with the blue-eyed girl behind a heavy green velvet curtain.

"Well, if it is not the great *mastro* himself come into our humble midst!"

Raphael let a sigh at the predictably envious tone and turned to face him. "Indeed it is I, Sebastiano, and *you,* it seems, are quite drunk."

"Am I not owed a bit of revelry as reward for my work, Raffaello?" He spoke the name with disdain, the nostrils of his long nose flaring. "Or is that saved only for you who so greedily take up all of the important commissions in Rome?"

Beside Raphael, Penni laughed most raucously, glancing protectively at the other assistants. "Spoken like one whose own art is sorely lacking in design and grace!"

"I accept them because they are offered," Raphael said smoothly. "And because I can complete them. Which is not the case for all artists once offered work here in the city of the Holy Father."

"You would be well advised to watch your back, Raffaello. I am coming for you."

He arched a brow. "Are you threatening me?"

"Only your standing as the single most favored artist in Rome!"

"*Buona fortuna* to you then," said Raphael with practiced cool.

"Oh, I have more than fortune on my side. What I *have* is Michelangelo Buonarroti's friendship and support, which, very soon, shall be the death knell for you!"

So that was it. That was what Michelangelo had meant those weeks ago when they had encountered one another at the Vatican Palace. Sebastiano had never forgiven Raphael for the impression he had made on Agostino Chigi after each had done a wall panel in the banker's opulent villa. The fact that Raphael alone had been given further Chigi commissions, when Chigi had personally brought Sebastiano to Rome, was a powerful source of resentment that a fading Michelangelo intended to use to the fullest.

But tonight he was in no mood to be taunted by an envious competitor who found his courage at the bottom of a bottle. Raphael cast a last appraising glance at Sebastiano, who continued to sway before him. Seeing no impending challenge there, Raphael stood, turned, and began to stride toward the curtains behind which the two girls had gone.

But that had been a miscalculation on his part.

Not just hours, but a full day of drinking had fueled Sebastiano's rage to an incendiary pitch. Seeing Raphael turn his back to him, Sebastiano picked up a tufted footstool and swung it. The force of the blow, which hit him square across the back, sent Raphael to his knees. Before he could right himself, Sebastiano kicked him sharply in the ribs. Someone across the room screamed as Giulio, Penni, and da Udine rushed forward, diving into the fray. Seizing on the pandemonium, and the tangle of men beginning to brawl, Sebastiano lunged at him again. Raphael countered with a powerful fist. Sebastiano staggered back from the blow, surprise lighting his face amid a tangle of defensive arms and fists from Raphael's assistants.

"Stop!" Raphael called out to his men, a firm hand raised up as they prepared to pummel Sebastiano. "No good can come of this!"

"Attacking a man from behind is a great show of cowardice!" Penni boldly declared. He and a swiftly growing contingent of men were blocking Sebastiano from Raphael. "And he deserves a coward's punishment, *mastro!*"

"Ah, the great courtier, better than the rest of us!" Sebastiano jeered, breathing heavily.

"A self-perception of greatness is not a courtly attribute, Sebastiano," Giovanni da Udine countered on Raphael's behalf. "Surely Michelangelo has taught you that much, if not how to paint!"

Raphael rubbed his aching hand. His fingers had begun very swiftly to swell.

"Does the great *mastro* have an independent thought, one well could wonder," Sebastiano taunted, glancing around for a show of support in his envy.

"Looking at you, I think a great many of my own thoughts," Raphael said, masking the pain in his hand with a smoothly delivered sleight. "None of which are worth more than a moment's consideration."

"You have dishonored the greatest *mastro,* Signor Michelangelo Buonarroti, and I shall not allow it!" he called out baitingly as Raphael turned from him once again and was braced on both sides by his concerned assistants, another of whom had Sebastiano by the scruff of the neck.

"If Michelangelo is angry with me, I am certain he can fight his own battles!" Raphael called out.

"I am honored to do his bidding when he is not in Rome, Sanzio!"

"What you cannot do for yourself, you must champion in another!" Penni baited him, drunk enough and clearly itching to begin brawling again.

"Insult me at your own risk, Gianfrancesco! For I do swear, it is I who shall have the final laugh!"

"Is it Raphael's fault that your work is entirely lacking in design, color, and style?" he taunted. "A thing not even so great an artist as Michelangelo can teach you!"

"He does speak the truth!" da Udine seconded with a mischievous smile.

"Raphael is a thief!" Sebastiano pressed, an angry vein pulsing in his neck. "He openly co-opted the *mastro*'s Sistine sibyls and prophets for his own work at the Chigi chapel! I have seen it myself, seen the theft!"

"You know very well artists study one another's works," da Udine boldly defended. "Raphael has done nothing you yourself have not done!"

"Giulio, see to my horse, would you?" Raphael said as he held his throbbing wrist. "I have had enough revelry for one evening."

Outside, amid the brisk night air and daunting shadows, Raphael stood alone, wrapped in his cloak, angry that he had allowed himself to be baited—angry that of all things it was his painting hand with which he had struck. Sebastiano was more dangerous than he had considered. But now at least he had been warned. That was his thought as two men came toward him from the shadows. They were both huge men, dressed in coarse, peasant clothing the shades of textures that blended into the dull, chipped paint of the shadowy building from which they had emerged. By the dirt on their knees and hands, they were farmers, possibly workers from a vineyard.

In the light from a full moon, Raphael could see the rough features of their faces. One had pocked skin and a small mouth, his lips fat and wet. Beneath a sloping brow were deep-set eyes, red and unfocused. The whole of him was glossy with sweat in spite of the evening chill. Clearly, he was not an admirer of art. Raphael's tensed, sensing what lay ahead.

"We have no quarrel with one another," he said angrily, his injured hand throbbing. "Allow me to wait alone for my horse."

"As you might suppose, that is not going to happen," said the other man, equally repulsive in his personal filth and rotting teeth. "You have insulted Signor Luciani and, with him, the great Michelangelo Buonarroti!"

"You know nothing of art, only what an artist's money can tell you to say!"

The men glanced at one another and both laughed evilly, one drooling a stream of saliva. A sudden hand seized Raphael's collar. The blow that came after that was swift. By instinct, Raphael blocked the assault with his injured hand, his painting hand, which met an even stronger gnarled fist. Raphael felt something crack near his wrist, and the force of it brought him to his knees. A searing pain followed at the very moment the entire collection of assistants came dashing out into the night through a cone of lamplight cast from the open bordello door.

"*Mastro!* Oh, *Madre di Maria!*" Giulio called out. "They mean to kill him!" But Raphael had already faltered and collapsed onto the wet cobbled stones.

❧ 13 ❧

FEARING THE EXTENT OF HIS CONDITION, GIULIO AND the others did not take Raphael home to the Via dei Coronari, which lay farther across town. Rather, together they carried him themselves, and Giovanni led his horse, through the dark streets back to the workshop. Gently, they laid him on a pallet there, then Gianfrancesco Penni went quickly to gather a collection of models' velvet draperies and downy soft pillows used in their work to lie beneath the *mastro*'s head. Giulio brought a glass of strong wine to his lips because Raphael could not hold the cup himself, then helped him to lie back, and allowed Penni to dot his brow with a cool cloth.

Giovanni da Udine had gone to retrieve one of the papal physicians, but in the meantime they had stabilized Raphael's wounded and still swelling hand on a flat board, then bound it with cloths. They were powerless to do more. The concern in the room was a palpable thing, each artist gathered around him knowing well what was at stake in the potential damage of the *mastro*'s hand.

As Giulio sat beside him, he knew all the *mastro* would be thinking was of the hand that was so essential to his craft, and what would be at stake if there were any permanent damage to the man who meant prosperity to many more than just himself.

"Can you move your fingers?"

"*Per favore!*" he swatted at Penni, who loomed over him, his face blanched with concern. "You make too much of this!"

"But your hand, *mastro!*"

"I am well aware of what is at stake! As was Sebastiano!"

"His henchman was holding something shiny and brass-colored in his grasp. I saw it myself," Giulio said. "Try to move your fingers."

"It is painful," he revealed, grimacing even as he tried to make a fist. Raphael closed his eyes and let a heavy sigh.

"I should like to break both of his arms so that he could never paint again!"

"He is desperate, and desperation can all too easily cloud the mind of wisdom."

Giulio shook his head, still bound by his anger. "You are too good for him, *Mastro* Raffaello."

Raphael let a weak smile turn his mouth. "Not so good, *caro*. I am just a man like any other. The only difference is I have been one who has pleased two pontiffs. It is from that alone that my blessings have so generously come."

"And this envy has come from it, as well! But he shall never get to you again, by holy God! I shall kill him myself before I let that happen!" vowed Giulio Romano.

RAPHAEL WOKE from a dream-soaked sleep unaware of the time or place. It was a moment more before he moved and felt the searing pain in his hand. There was a bone broken; he could feel it. Glancing around the small workshop anteroom then, he remembered. It had been two days, but it felt as if months had passed. The papal physicians had seen him, set the hand between two of their own more precisely cut boards, then bound it with finer cloth to keep it stationary—and to keep him from painting. They had bled him, and then left a tincture to be taken upon the hour to restore his strength.

At least with his other hand, Raphael remembered, he was free to drink.

In physical pain from the beating, and mired in the heavy grip of frustration over the future of so many things—with so many depending upon him—Raphael drank great volumes of wine within the protective walls of the small room. Unwilling to return to his house, he nevertheless avoided the men who waited outside for his direction. He also avoided the papal emissaries who came to inquire every hour of his progress. Margherita and Donato were unaware of this turn of events as they came to the workshop at the prearranged time—an appointment entirely forgotten by Raphael.

The vast room was quiet, eerily so, and the door was left ajar as they came through the arched doorway. Cool, melon-pink light was streaming in across the room from the long, partially shuttered windows, and the empty studio was wreathed in shadows of the late afternoon. In the small room, beneath a window embrasure, Raphael sat contemplatively on a pallet constructed by his men, gazing out across the river and the ancient Palatine Hill beyond.

"Where is everyone?" Margherita asked tentatively, exchanging a little glance with Donato.

"I have sent them all home."

"But what of all your commissions?"

"I am not working today," he growled, not looking up at them.

"Nor yesterday or tomorrow by the look of you."

"Foolish girl!" Raphael flared. "What could you know of my life or the demands placed on it?"

"*Perdone, signore . . .*" Donato interjected in a more tentative and respectful tone. "It is the time to which we agreed. We are here for the painting— your Madonna."

And then she saw it. The splint. The bandages. "*Gesù!* You have been hurt!"

"To be precise, I am unable to paint—it is that distinction alone that matters here in Rome!"

"Surely with rest and care your hand will mend."

"And in the meantime? What will become of my commissions—*and* my men? That, of course, was precisely what Sebastiano and Michelangelo desired!"

"Would you rather we return at another time, Signor Sanzio?" Donato asked, filling the tense silence that had swiftly engulfed Raphael and Margherita.

"I believe that would be best."

The protective response had come not from the *mastro,* but from Giulio Romano, who had quietly and protectively appeared. He alone had remained to tend to Raphael's needs even after all of the other assistants had been sent home.

"Leave us, Giulio."

"But *mastro*—"

"*Per favore* go, and take Signor Perazzi with you."

Donato and Giulio glanced at one another. Giulio's face marked his concern, and yet still there was a silent understanding as they went together through the door and closed it after themselves.

"I cannot finish the work—the Madonna," Raphael finally announced in a toneless voice once he and Margherita were alone.

Still he would not look at her. He would not look at her winter dress, her mother's beautiful cinnamon-colored cloth, adorned only by a pale blue sash. He could not allow himself to see her smooth, sable-brown hair, held back by a small pale-blue kerchief that made her eyes seem all the larger and more expressive as she gazed at him, and at his heavily bandaged hand resting limply in his lap. Without thinking of propriety, or her reserve, for the first time since their meeting, Margherita went to him and knelt beside the pallet.

"I should not have raised my voice to you," he said more gently, at last turning his gaze to her, and allowing her to see his eyes, bloodshot with frustration and exhaustion. "I ask you to forgive me."

"Considering the circumstances, it is understandable."

"Do not show me your pity! I despise pity!" he raged, more to the heavens, which long had known it, than to her.

"Then what *do* you want?"

"Something other than the life I have!" He raked the hair back from his face with his good hand, and tipped his head back against the wall behind him. "A life other than the one with no family, no love, no reason even to exist, but only to paint and work to the point of exhaustion and blindness! To create only for the desire of others, on and on, day after day, then return home completely alone!"

"You cannot mean that you paint only for others! I have seen you work; it is in your blood!"

He closed his eyes for a moment, then opened them again. "Yet I work—not for my own passion now, but for theirs! The clergymen for whom I work are obsessed with finding their bit of immortality! Since they can have no acknowledged children I am there to provide them a legacy—something that will live on once they are gone! It is their absolute obsession! And all the while, I go about Rome, elegant, blithely, seeming to the world as if I have not a care in it! But as just a shell of a man whose entire life seems to have fallen apart with a small injury—as if my only value at all to anyone in this world is that!"

"Signor Sanzio, I—"

"Do you know what it is for a man to actually realize his true value?" He moved forward onto his knees, coming nearer to her, his eyes blazing with emotion. "To keep working, and working, all of the time, as if you have no life at all? The isolation that comes with this existence, the loneliness of being able to love virtually no one, because you have allowed no one to love *you*? It makes me wish to leave all of this—to go somewhere very far away . . . "

"But you cannot!" She looked stricken. "You have an enormous gift given to you by God!"

"Or was it a curse cast upon me?"

"How can you speak such self-pitying words when you are so celebrated and admired?"

"It is *Rafaello* they admire—the women, bankers, cardinals, dukes, sycophants, even the Holy Father, who have come here since I was injured, and all of them wanting to know, most of all, not how I am, but when I will paint again! Certainly they inquire, but not about Raphael—the man—the one who bleeds when he is cut, who weeps, who fears . . . and who lusts for love, as any other man!" The raw timbre of his words—and their sentiment—turned the tide of things between them then. Everything changed in that moment.

"I must go."

Margherita tried to stand. Raphael caught her wrist with his uninjured hand.

"*Per favore* . . . I bid you . . . stay."

It was then that their eyes met again fully. The last bit of daylight through the long wooden window shutters cast slatted shadows on his smooth face. His expression was dark and glittering with something she had never seen before. Vulnerability. It held her entirely captive as the sound of a sudden rain surrounded them. This was not the image or the artist before her, Margherita knew, but Raphael the man.

Her color rose beneath his ardent stare. "If it is your wish."

"Always the one in control, hmm?" he said very gently, with only a hint of mocking. "Making me think things I have never thought . . . causing me to speak words I swore I never would."

Her voice was a whisper as she dared to reach out to touch his arm. "I might have said the same of you."

Margherita's eyes moved to the door, then back to Raphael. By leaving her here alone with him, Donato was telling her that the family wished her to stay and to console the great artistic *mastro* in whatever way she chose. But it did not require their sanction. The feeling between them had changed. She saw sincerity now in a man whose mask had been stripped away. She had misjudged him. Behind the cavalier image that Raphael wanted the world to see, there was someone else entirely. He was just a man, like any other. Complex. Vulnerable. Solitary.

For a moment they gazed silently at one another. Raphael closed his arm around her, as if he were protecting her from the rest of the world—as if that were in his power to do. Then, very gently, he covered her mouth with his own. A gasp of desire rushed up from her throat as she felt his thighs against hers, his chest against her breasts. Margherita's mouth opened to his as their kiss deepened, and her body shivered with a barrage of new sensations.

When he grimaced, she saw that he had moved his hand. Gently, she drew it up to her lips and softly kissed his fingertips beyond the splint. His uninjured hand moved deftly down the length of her back, drawing her tightly to him as they kissed again.

Her heart pounded as he gently removed the kerchief from her head, her warm brown hair cascading forward around her face. Raphael took up a curl and pressed the soft, flowery scent of it, the silky smoothness, against his lightly stubbled jaw, then flinched with the strain of withheld ardor.

"It is this face that controls me! God, but you are already so much in my blood!" he murmured, finding her mouth again and drawing her to him so forcefully that she felt her chaste young body yield. "I am on fire for want of you!"

"Do you desire me only because today you feel alone in the world?"

"I desired you from the first! In that, today will be like every other, before and after! You have known that all along!"

Drawing her onto the pallet, with its array of velvet pillows, Raphael deftly slipped her dress up over her head, then the unadorned linen shift beneath. Margherita felt his own body heat as he stood next to her, and her breathing quickened. She did not resist as his own slippers, hose, and shirt came away from his taut body and fell into a pool of color onto the tiled floor, and she battled a new shiver of pleasure that pulsed through her. Her heart was racing. Her skin was hot.

"I have never loved a woman," he murmured. "Never *truly* loved a woman."

"And now?"

"Can you not see that I am entirely besotted by you? I want every part of you! And I want—*Dio*, yes desperately—I want to love you!"

She let him kiss her again, knowing what would come next, and wanting that. Wanting him as he came fully down upon her then. She felt the shock of a sudden sharp pain, but then the pain became pleasure—became exquisite. And like that, so simply, yet profoundly, she had given herself over to him, to the man behind the image. Her body, her heart, and her soul.

AFTERWARD, lifting himself onto an elbow, he searched her face, waited a beat before he kissed her again. Raphael was not certain what was happening to him. Yes, he had boldly begun this with her, but he had not been prepared for what had just happened. The way she had so tenderly stroked his face, her fingers feather-light upon his skin as he entered her. Her eyes wide and adoring upon him as he had moved inside her. Oh, the indescribable pleasure of it! She was so beautiful, so desirable . . . and he found he wanted to bring her pleasure, along with his own. To actually feel something emotionally when he took a woman was entirely foreign to him. Her gentleness and her innocence, the simple, sweet smell of her untouched flesh, had quite literally rocked him to the core.

"You are so different," he whispered, their bodies still joined—his own slick with perspiration. "So totally human . . . you are everything, and like nothing I have ever known, or touched, or craved. I want to paint you . . . to create you . . . to bed with you, over and over again! *Dio mío,* to possess your whole body and heart—yes, that most of all!"

"You speak now as if that were impossible."

He let a pained and heavy sigh. "It is complicated."

Outside, past the wall of windows, the sky, now darkened to pewter, emptied a stronger rain onto Rome as Raphael rose reluctantly and moved away from her. He could not lie with her when he told her the truth. And she deserved the truth. Only when he had dressed did he come back to her on the pallet to sit beside her, wrapped as she was in one of the model's draperies that had covered them both only moments before.

He pressed another tender kiss onto her cheek, craving the assurance of her skin beneath his lips. "You must understand, this has nothing to do with my heart. But power is everything here in Rome."

"Do you not have enough of that as most favored artist of the Holy Father?"

Raphael hedged for a moment, uncertain of how to say it to make it more palatable to hear. It had been such a long time since he had cared at all what anyone else thought or felt. Suddenly, he could not look at her. There was too much trust in her eyes. "I made a choice—a poor one, before I knew better." The breath he exhaled then was painful. He had made so many poor choices regarding women. But this had been the worst of them.

"There is a cardinal. He is the dearest friend of the pope. Cardinal Bibbiena has a niece . . . "

Margherita sat up slowly. "And so?"

"Her name is Maria." He drew in another painful breath and let it out very quickly. "We are betrothed."

Her voice was strident with the sudden shock. As the meaning slowly became clear her lower lip began to tremble. "You waited to tell me of this until I, until *after* we — "

Raphael closed his eyes, burned by the pained expression on the exquisite face that mattered to him immensely now. "I have never . . . Not with her, Margherita. It is a powerful match made by powerful men, not having anything to do with lust or love."

She cast back the heavy modeling drapery and shot to her feet, scrambling for her shift and her dress, which lay in a heap beneath the window. "Why should it when you have poor models from Trastevere for that sort of thing?"

"Before now work has ever been my only real love!" He pleaded. "The match with Maria is one I have regretted from the very first! It is a betrothal I have sought to break even before I met you! That I do swear!"

Stunned, Margherita moved toward the door, but he blocked her path. "You are well schooled and well experienced with women! Everyone in Rome knows of your reputation. I don't believe you!"

He caught her wrist and was gripping it with his good hand. "That was before I knew *you!*"

"How many have there been before me, Raphael, who heard the same protestations?"

"How many before you, I know not." He brushed the hair back from his face in frustration. "*Sì*, I told you, there have been many women. I confess I have known too many even to count! But I have never spoken of the things with another woman I have spoken of with you, nor felt what I feel with you!"

She spun away from him in the other direction, but he held her tightly. "Let me go!"

"It would be easier to cut out my very heart!"

"As you wish! You haven't a heart worth having anyway!"

"You don't mean that!"

Her face flushed scarlet with anger. "I mean it entirely!" Margherita's rich brown eyes glittered angrily at him, even as he held her tightly and very close to his own tall, ramrod-straight body.

"We sealed that together just now, you and I!"

"We rutted like animals! That was all!"

The flare of her spirit only bewitched him the more. "You are mine, as I am yours!" he murmured in a voice mixed with sincerity and sudden renewed lust. "And, by God, I'll not give you up!"

Unable to control the tears that her anger had nearly hidden, Margherita tried to twist away from him, but he only held her more powerfully, kissing the tears away, tasting them seductively with his lips and tongue. "I loathe you!" she cried in a small, choking voice as his powerful arms encircled her once again.

"I know not how or why, or what made it happen so completely, but I worship *you!*" he volleyed, pressing her back toward the window seat as the salty taste of the tears on her cheeks became urgent kisses, his mouth parting her lips, his tongue driving a rhythm into her mouth, and the overwhelming passion rising swiftly within him again.

After all the years, a lifetime, of meaningless coupling, of the terrible things he had done with nameless women in places too seamy and dark even to recall, Raphael was desperate that this woman know she was different in his life — and that he was made wholly different by her.

"Margherita . . . *pearl* . . . luminescent . . . rare." He whispered huskily the meaning of her name into her hair as he moved back with her onto the pallet, then arched over her again, trapping her beneath him. "My life begins with you, this I swear . . . I do swear it!"

As he touched her with his lips, his warm breath on her skin, he could feel her falter in her resolve against him.

"This cannot endure!" she softly cried.

"It well might."

"There is everything against it! You yourself said that work was your only true love!"

He pulled her onto her side, then slid his arm around her, moving sensually down to the small of her back, and pulling her against him, wanting her to feel how aroused by her he was already again.

"I did?" he asked, suppressing a smile.

"You did."

He tightened his hold around her and felt her suppress a little moan of pleasure. "But, alas, that was in a world before you."

"She is a cardinal's niece, your betrothed—a great prize. And I am a poor baker's daughter."

"You are a queen in my eyes. My paintbrush has not lied."

He touched the planes of her face, the tip of her nose, then kissed her again, shocked by the tenderness he felt for her, along with the driving lust.

"And what shall happen when you come upon your next Madonna?"

"You shall be the last Madonna in my paintings, *carissima*. The most remarkable, the most unique   the one the world remembers . . . and absolutely, I do swear, you shall be my only, my last love," he declared as he sheltered her once again in his powerful embrace.

LATE THAT NIGHT, in a wooden bath set in the kitchen beside the warmth of the bread ovens, in water heated over flames by Letitia, Margherita sat alone and wept silently into her hands. Her mind spun from all that had happened—how her life had been changed forever in the space of a single afternoon. And she forced herself to accept the truth. She dare not love Raphael because he belonged to Signorina Bibbiena, not to her. She could not—would not—do battle against the niece of a powerful cardinal. And when he came to his senses, when he had known enough of her, Raphael would not allow her to do it.

In the end, she had done what she had sworn not to. She had given herself to a man, and to an overpowering love that was impossible. Still, she had desired that which had happened between them, as if it had meant life itself to a simple girl whose existence had taken this sudden and dramatic turn. And even now, after she had bathed, and sat alone back in her room, in the little house with the sloping roof, and the bakery beneath, she could think of nothing so much as the touch of his hands, the weight of his body above hers, the taste of his lips, and wonder, without ceasing, when they might be together like that again.

Part Two

Overcoming me with
the light of a smile,
she said to me:
"Turn and listen,
for not only
in my eyes is
Paradise."

Dante,
La vita nuova

DECEMBER 1514

AS WINTER CAME IN ON A FREEZING WIND FROM THE north, and Rome was blanketed with a heavy winter cold, the papal court was plunged into preparations for the Christmas festivities, and in celebration of a new peace with France. Giant banners proclaimed news of a great pageant that was to be held throughout the city streets.

As soon as his hand healed sufficiently, Raphael went back to work on more of the preparation sketches, using black pencil heightened with white lead, for the pope's new *stanza*, which Giulio was overseeing on the *mastro*'s behalf. The hand that had been so injured in his fight with Sebastiano's thug healed quickly with a combination of help from the pope's physicians and an ancient remedy Margherita had made for him.

For the next three days and nights after they had first been together, Raphael never left his workshop, so pressing was the amount of work. At night, when the others had gone home, Donato brought Margherita there, returning each morning long before the other artists arrived or before she was required to help with the new loaves of bread that needed to be baked. And so the grand house with its many levels on the Via dei Coronari sat alone but for Giulio Romano, who watched over it for Raphael, and Elena, who cleaned and organized and kept order in case he should suddenly desire to return.

"May I get you anything?"

Giulio glanced up from his place in Raphael's study, wreathed in flickering gold lamplight, where he had been trying for the past quarter hour to understand one of the deeply meaningful sonnets in *La vita nuova*, by the poet Dante. He had thus far read it three times and was glad for a reason to look away from it for even a moment.

"Thank you, no," he said to Elena, who stood before him.

She moved a step nearer and he closed the book, settling its thick red leather binding on his lap. She was warmly pretty in this light, he surprised himself by thinking. Not angles and striking features, like models with whom he was familiar, but all warm curves and gentle shapes. Her eyes were big and clear and gray, with dark lashes, and she had fully defined lips, perfect for the skill of a painter's brush. The desire to sketch her face for one of the characters in the marriage of Cupid and Psyche at the Chigi Villa came unexpectedly.

"You can read Dante?" she asked, vanquishing the moment, and the notion behind it.

"Apparently not very well." He smiled. "Certainly not as well as Raffaello. You are familiar with Dante's work?"

Elena was thoughtful, then she looked away. "My life was very different before I came here," she said. "But you. Why do you try to read it? Surely you don't need it for your painting."

The open expression on her face told him that she was not being critical. Rather, she honestly wished to know. "Many of our commissions are classical or biblical themes, along with stories of love and loss, as in Dante's work. *Mastro* Raphael believes that it is not enough to re-create an emotion. An artist must know it himself, and understand it, as well if not better than the story's author does before he begins to paint."

He could see that she had never considered that, but it was also clear from her expression that he had not spoken beyond her ability to comprehend it. She moved a little nearer still, and so he politely stood, facing her. She gazed at the wall of leather-bound books behind the chair in which he had been sitting.

"Is that so for all artists?"

"No. Before I came to work for the *mastro*, I had heard it

declared by other artists that the masses would not understand it anyway."

"But Signor Raphael believes differently?"

"He has never painted for the masses nor with the notion of idealized perfection. He works toward his own desire of re-creating the thing with honesty, in order to move the viewer."

"You must be an extraordinary painter yourself for a *mastro* like Raphael to trust you as he does with these concepts."

"I would not dream of comparing myself," Giulio said honestly. "*He* is the genius. They are his ideas, his concepts, and his scrupulously detailed designs, which his assistants only see to fruition."

"But is it not you, then, by so doing, who brings them to life?"

"Perhaps, on occasion," he conceded with a small but proud smile.

"It was horrendous what happened to him. Thanks be to God that he had you to help him with all of those commissions until he had fully recovered, or no doubt everyone would be pounding at his door."

"Thank you for the compliment, but Signor Raphael has many other able assistants who have been painting far longer and more capably than I."

"Not ones he has trusted enough to invite to live beneath his roof. He told me what you did for him, staying with him by the hour at the studio those first few days, then finishing many of his sketches for him to give to the other apprentices."

Unaccustomed to adulation, Giulio awkwardly nodded to her. He had indeed done precisely that—taken the sketches to Raphael for approval, then given them to the other artists as if they were Raphael's directions—exactly in order to maintain the confident flow of the workshop.

"At a time when it is difficult for him to trust other artists," Elena went on in a voice of simple honesty. "I think he is fortunate to have you, Signor Romano. In his studio *and* here in his home as well."

As she turned to go out of Raphael's library, Giulio wanted to say that he was the fortunate one, but he realized, as her face still shone with kind admiration, that she was absolutely determined to leave him for this evening with a compliment of his own lingering between them.

POPE LEO sat regally on a canopied throne, having just dismissed the papal legate with a bored wave. Behind him stood a stone-faced page with powerfully set shoulders. The page bore the ever-present silver tray brimming with egg-washed, sugar-dusted pastries, one of which the pontiff was just then consuming with great relish. As the pope pressed the final bite between his lips, his cousin, Giulio, came through the door in a sweep of crimson, flanked by two lower-order priests, both wearing black cassocks. Cardinal Giulio de Medici stopped before his cousin, hands linked behind his back. He was younger than the pontiff, and more handsome, a fact he had worked to his advantage all of their lives. Leo's bulging eyes, with heavy gray bags beneath, and ever-expanding girth aged him well beyond his thirty-nine years.

"Ah, good cousin! Do share a sweet with us," Pope Leo said, his round cheeks bulging.

"Thank you no, Your Holiness. I have broken my fast already this morning."

Leo was surprised at that and chuckled. "So have I and yet . . . these are sweets!"

He had been this way all of his life, Giulio thought. Nothing, not even devotion or papal responsibility, compared with food. For Pope Leo, the papacy had not been earned. It was a gift for being a Medici, and the son of Lorenzo the Magnificent. He had left the play of true power to other men with more ambition than he.

"Then why have you presented yourself this day, if not to share the fruits of my good fortune?"

He dipped his head. "It is not *those* fruits of which I desire to avail myself."

The response was swift and direct. Leo wiped his mouth on a

silk cloth and cast it over his shoulder at another liveried page, as if knowing he would be there to collect it. Pope Leo envied his cousin's youth and beauty, and required his presence all the more because of it. It was rather how he felt about Raphael Sanzio, as youth and good looks were the attributes with which he himself had not been blessed. But Raphael he needed more for his incredible talent, to ornament his private world, and make his lasting mark on the Vatican Palace.

"Very well. Leave us," he sighed, brushing away the bishops and cardinals who lingered near him, as if they were bothersome insects on a warm summer day. Only the page who bore the tray of pastries knew to remain.

When the cousins were alone enough for private conversation, he said, "What is it to be this time then? Another villa? More money to impress a new mistress?"

As the pope reached up, the page bent and pressed the tray forward, a single anticipated movement, as was the plucking of a new long pastry decorated with raisins and sugared almonds, which the pontiff began to consume with relish equal to the last.

"No, no. Nothing like that." Giulio sank onto the small gold stool positioned before the pope's throne, and fastidiously straightened the length of his own rigidly starched crimson cassock. Only then did he settle his eyes directly onto his cousin's. "My own legacy is in a dire state, and I wish you to exert your powerful influence over Raphael to see that the commencement of my portrait shall be the next."

"Raphael shall not be doing any more portraits, good cousin, until he completes the next *stanza!*" he declared with an imperiousness with which he was now, after a full year on the papal throne, fully versed.

"What the devil is the problem? I know for a fact he has a staff of assistants and apprentices as long as your arm to help with the details and lesser commissions!"

The pope cupped fat fingers around his little bulb of a mouth and swallowed the last of the pastry with an audible gulp. "I am told that his attention is taken up, not so much with art, as it is with an alluring and mysterious new mistress—one who is said to be far more serious to him than any of the others. But that need not get out to Bibbiena, or the Lord God alone knows what form of delays it will create for my *stanza!*"

"You speak of the betrothal of Raphael to Bibbiena's niece?" the cardinal chuckled, sinking back and touching his own knee with a slap of incredulity. "Surely the poor foolish girl was told of Raphael's reputation with women before she agreed to the match."

"Indeed she was, and she desired him just the same."

"Be assured that he is a lusty young man who shall *always* have a mistress or two tucked away to inspire him, no matter whether *you* warn him against it or not!"

"Such things concern me not at all," the pope replied, not quite believably. "What *does* concern me is that Raphael keeps working without interruption. I have bestowed upon him enough commissions here to keep him busy for another two years at least! They are *my* legacy, the only bit of immortality I shall ever have. And my only way of blotting out the stain of my vile predecessor. And *that,* good cousin, takes precedence over all else in his life!"

"And what might Bibbiena do if he thought Raphael's eye had strayed from his sallow-faced little bird of a niece?"

"Sallow-faced or not, Bernardo is devoted to the little chit. He thinks of her as the daughter he never had. And, moreover, he believes he has bestowed a rare honor on our good Raffaello by handing that simple son of Urbino a powerful cardinal's very chaste niece on a shining silver platter. If Bernardo were to believe there was heartbreak in the offing for his little Maria, I do believe he might actually find a way to sabotage the great artist."

"Forgive me, cousin." The cardinal scratched his nose with a bejeweled finger. "But it is rather difficult to believe that a mistress, no matter how nubile and comely, could alter Raphael's ambitions of greatness, or risk the alliance he has forged with Cardinal Bibbiena. Raphael was honored by the important betrothal. I heard him tell you as much myself."

"Early on, *sì*, it was so. But that was four years ago, and for some reason an ambitious boy like Raphael has not yet seen fit to formalize that honor with a marriage. Nor does he wish to."

"Perhaps in the end he was looking for something more in a wife."

"Well, he certainly shall not find what a man such as he desires in a peasant from Trastevere."

"Trastevere! It is not so!"

"*Sì.*" The pope nodded, doubling his chin.

They cackled then, putting their heads together like two old fishwives at the mere thought of two such oddly matched lovers. "And yet my spies report that for the moment, she has entirely won him. He has her installed each evening in his studio, where they remain together until dawn."

Giulio de Medici pondered the revelation, finally relenting to take one of the remaining pastries from the quickly dwindling supply set on silver still hovering in the hands of the page behind them. He bit into it, savoring the bite. After a moment Giulio said, "Marinated anchovies are wonderful, too, but how many of *them* can you consume before the thought alone fills your throat with bile?" He pointed his finger in warning. "Mark my word and fear not, my good and holy cousin. Raphael shall tire of this one just as he has all the others."

"Apparently she is *not* like the others."

"She is a body given up to an important man's unholy desires. Why would she not become, in the end, just like all the others?"

"Because this one, good cardinal, he has painted as the Madonna!"

IN THE SHADOWS of moonlit darkness, through a small stained-glass window, and beside the pallet they had shared, Margherita watched him when he did not see her. At work again so late at night, in this utter stillness, a different aspect of Raphael had come alive before her. Now again he was obsessed, intense, and absolutely driven, but on something other than his passion for her. Sitting naked beside her, legs crossed, he was entirely focused in this silent moment on the chalk and paper he held and commanded. Raphael's stare was leveled, his body tensed, the broad shoulders hunched forward, devoted to the activity as he confronted, prodded, and caressed the paper. From it, he powerfully coaxed shapes and figures out of nothing with broad, precise sweeps of his hand.

Again, the memory of Marina Luti moved across her daughter's heart. Her mother would have liked him. And she knew now with a strange certainty that she would have approved. Raphael would have fascinated her, as he did her daughter. Knowing that gave her a warm and settled feeling of peace.

Margherita was transfixed by the energy swirling wildly around Raphael, and also at the sight of him entirely captivated. This was the private, inner dominion of an artist—the secret moment of creation, an experience as intimate and yet powerful as a sexual communion. Margherita felt herself grow warm as she watched his hand sweeping the length of the large sheet of white paper, the red chalk and his exacting strokes pulling forth the naked, recumbent figure of a woman, one arm behind her head, the other laying lazily between her legs. It was Margherita, her naked body, as she had slept beside him. She saw more fully the importance of it—what he did, how he worked, the absolute compulsion of an artist to create when the moment and the inspiration occurred. This was an understanding she knew she would remember for the rest of her life. There was power and delight in knowing that she now played a small role in that. She had never had power over anything in her life, yet suddenly it seemed she was the muse of a great and important man.

"I really must remember to fall asleep only with my clothes on," she said softly, and her mouth was curved into a slightly mischievous smile. "Soon everyone in Rome shall speak of the forbidden things we do here in this studio, and we shall become quite notorious."

Raphael glanced at her and bit back his own smile, then lay

the paper onto the floor beside his thigh. He moved onto her and kissed her lips tenderly. "You speak as if that displeases you. But the flush of your face belies something else."

"Happiness."

"Yet you are right. There is danger in this for us both. And I must protect you, *amore mio,* for as long as I am able."

"Why do I require protection?"

"Because a commodity, not only a man, has fallen in love with you—totally and entirely in love with you—and there are those in Rome with other plans for my life."

"It frightens me to death, loving you."

"Yet you do?"

"I know not why, yet I do."

Moved, he said, "Then I am the man of greatest fortune in all the world."

"You may not believe it is so when the world, and particularly your benefactor, discovers it."

"I shall never regret a single thing that is between us, Margherita *mia.* You shall never know how you have forever altered my world."

"Your world is your art."

"My world, now, is *you.*"

He kissed her deeply, sensually, then, and Margherita kissed him back with an innocent passion that still could rock him to the core. In spite of how many times, and how many ways, they had made love, or how many intimate ways he had possessed her, it surprised Raphael that unlike all other women, he had no sense of tiring of her. Nor had he built up the same walls to his heart as he always had before. Each day, she surprised and delighted him. Moreover, she still touched a part of him that was new, vulnerable, and entirely unreachable before her. Thinking of that, as his eyes roamed the length of her glorious body, Raphael felt himself flushed with desire again.

"If you ever wish to change your mind," she said with heartfelt sincerity, "I have seen what your art means to you. If it comes to that between us that you must choose, I shall promise to understand."

"It will not happen," he declared in response, with the passion of a sacred oath. He was holding her hands together between the two of them in a prayerful shape. "You have made my art come alive in a new way, do you understand that? You have given me a new motivation where I had been fading. It is said, *amore mio,* that a writer has his muse. If that is so, then I have my own artistic inspiration—and that evermore shall be you."

He left her suddenly then, driven to use the power of his passion not to have her, but to capture her like this exactly. He moved across the room to his sketchbook as she lay naked before the fire, then drew up another stub of red chalk and began to outline her body on a fresh slip of paper, as she reclined so sensually before him.

"Have you not done enough of these studies?" She smiled up at him, her body relaxed and open, her smile slim and sensual.

"Such a thing is not possible." He smiled rakishly back at her, showing her as he did how to position her arm lazily between parted legs, one knee slightly lifted, and her eyes leveled wide and unapologetically at him. "*Dio,* but that is wonderful! So erotic . . . "

"So illegal!" she softly giggled. "You cannot simply go around painting the bodies of naked women!"

"But you are not just any naked woman. You are the artist's inspiration! If I am ever asked to explain it, this is the classical representation of . . . of . . . " He paused to think of the perfect classical deity. "I know, of Diana, the goddess of love! Naked women in classical form are perfectly acceptable as artistic subject matter in Rome, you know!"

"No," she chuckled. "I knew that not."

Raphael tossed down his sheaf of paper and chalk and traveled slowly up the length of her body once again, and as he did, kissing the inside of her thighs, and the little triangle of downy hair where her legs ended. Margherita's head lolled back and her eyes closed as she gave in to the sweet sensation of his tongue on her skin.

As he tasted her, she caught a glimpse of writing scrawled beneath an earlier sketched image, sloping words at the bottom of the page. She reached for it and drew it back to them.

"What have you done to my picture?"

"I have written you a sonnet."

She was genuinely surprised. "Will you read it to me?"

"Should you not read it yourself?"

"I want to hear it from your lips as I look at the art you created above it. *Per favore,* Raphael. Read it for me."

As tentatively as a child about to recite lessons, Raphael took the sketch back and settled it on his lap. He glanced at her once more, then gazed down at the words he had written for love of her.

> *The way my heart sees you, your beauty is clear.*
> *But my very faithful paintbrush cannot compare it.*
> *My love for you weakens all else . . .*

Tears glittered in her eyes. "That is beautiful."

"It is only the first stanza. I wrote it to you when my longing for you was—unrequited."

"No one shall ever give me a greater gift."

"I certainly plan to try."

"Nothing you could ever buy for me could compare to what comes from the depth of your heart."

He had never known a woman who could say that and make him believe she meant it.

"Come home with me tonight," he said suddenly.

"To your house?"

"*Sì.* Be there with me. Talk with me, eat with me. I will read to you from the classics, to teach you. Then wake in my arms without the need to rush away before the studio opens. It is far more comfortable than here, to be sure. I have plenty of rooms for Donato there as well, and only one servant who lives with me upstairs."

"But your assistant . . . Signor Romano . . . does he not still reside with you there?"

For the moment Raphael had forgotten that, and remembering it now came with a cold jolt of other things. Another woman. In his passion to greedily possess every moment he could find with Margherita, he had forgotten Elena, and the powerful regret he bore for what had once occurred between them, there at his home.

"Perhaps you are right." He washed a hand across his face. "Giulio is as devoted a young man as you shall ever see, and his rooms are upstairs with my valet. But if it would bring you discomfort, we must think of something else so that I can see you like this every night."

Margherita rolled onto her elbows, balanced her chin on her palms, and looked with a little frown at his eyes for what felt to him like a lifetime. "This is what you wish of me every night?"

"This is what I wish for *us* for the rest of our lives."

"Without benefit of marriage?"

Raphael felt his heart squeeze. He closed his eyes and thought desperately of what to tell her—how to explain it so that she would understand. That there was still the issue of Maria and the tremendous amount of work left for Cardinal Bibbiena. Not to mention the powerful influence he could exert in ruining him—and the assistants who depended upon him if Raphael openly rejected Maria. But the overwhelming love he now felt for Margherita made all of that seem trivial even to him. That it would begin an unraveling of his commissions that could easily spiral out of control did not matter at this moment because Margherita would not understand that. He was insulting her even to try, belittling her by asking her to leave her home and come to his house every night as nothing better or more committed than a concubine.

"I *want* to marry you, Margherita."

"Marry me?"

"By my oath, I *will* make you my wife one day."

"One day."

He rolled away from her and let a heavy sigh. It was the first time in days that the euphoria of his overwhelming passion for her had been tempered in the slightest, and he felt sick to his stomach by her look of disappointment. Even closing his own eyes could not chase it away. "Tell me what I can do. I know not how to convince you—" He turned his gaze on her again as she remained there, waiting for him to explain. "I wish to end the betrothal with Maria Bibbiena, and I will. It is my vow. But there are so many artists here in my studio. Giulio, Gianfrancesco, and Giovanni are but a few who have given up their whole lives to believe in me, to follow me, to work for me . . . and if I make a stand against his niece with a cardinal as influential as Bibbiena now, when there is so much riding—"

"Your assistants—your *friends*—will all be without work. And it will be because of you."

He raked the hair back from his forehead and let a heavy sigh. "It is entirely possible for Cardinal Bibbiena to turn Chigi and the Holy Father against me as well. Michelangelo Buonarroti would be only too happy to return from Florence and take my outstanding commissions, and I will be back in Urbino searching for portraits to paint."

Margherita reached out and ran her hand across the plane of his cheek, then placed a small, gentle kiss there. "Poor Raphael. So many people wanting you for their purposes, not your own."

"I warned you that I was only a commodity to them."

"It is, as I feared, an impossible circumstance."

But it came to him then, and his eyes glistened with delight. Raphael laughed, unable to believe that he had not had the most obvious of thoughts before.

"What is it?" Margherita asked, seeing the change in his expression.

Raphael sat up and began hurriedly to dress. "I cannot tell you," he laughed happily. "Not yet. It may take some time to accomplish, but I *will* make this better!"

He helped her to dress then, and to put on her worn slippers with the little leather ties to keep them on her feet. He must attend to that as well, he thought. Her wardrobe. There were dresses, headdresses, and undergarments to be bought, and jewelry to find. Margherita Luti deserved the best that he could give her. And he wanted to give her everything.

Raphael took her chin and held it tightly between his thumb and forefinger, settling his gaze on her. "I shall send for you as soon as it is arranged. But what I have in mind may take a bit of time to organize. Can you be patient?"

She waited a moment looking at him, tipped her head, then said very softly, "You know, I find that I could actually wait forever for you."

"*Grazie a Dio,*" he murmured deeply, taking her one last time into his arms.

❧ *15* ❧

ANTONIO WAS WAITING FOR MARGHERITA WHEN SHE returned to the bakery shortly before dawn that next morning. She was stunned by his pallor and the grave expression on his unshaven face—a face that had always reflected his hauteur and self-importance. Something had actually shaken the more unshakable Perazzi brother.

Margherita drew off her cloak warily and opened the bakery door. Purposely, she had chosen not to enter the small plain door beside it, the entrance to the living quarters, so as not to draw attention to the hour of her arrival. Of course her father, Donato, and Letitia knew where she spent her nights now, but Margherita had too much pride to draw attention to that fact or to find herself in need of explanations.

It appeared that now she would be made to do so anyway.

"*Allora,* it is true! You *are* bedding with him," Antonio said flatly as he followed her into the kitchen, which was still gray in the early morning light; no loaves of bread were yet baking. She lit a single candle lamp on the table herself and took her white cloth apron from a peg beside the just lit bread oven.

"That's none of your affair," she replied, tying the apron around her waist and beginning to set out the several bowls required for mixing—trying to find something that would keep her from having to meet Antonio's judgmental gaze. "Besides, was it not you who told me to *allow* him to pursue me?"

"I thought you might lead him on for a while, get a few florins, some jewels perhaps, to help us in our start."

She stopped with a wooden spoon suspended in her hand and looked up at him, seeing the difference so clearly there between him and Raphael. "Then you did not know me very well."

"I have known you since we were children! We have always had an understanding of what we wanted in life! What would be best for our beginning!"

"You had given me the impression that we were now only to be friends."

"Oh, I say a great many things," he shrugged. "You know that."

"It was by your behavior, not your words, that circumstances changed between us." She braced herself on the table with both hands and he knew that she meant the other women. He wisely chose not to deny that. "There is not going to be a beginning for us, Antonio."

His stare became angry. "I never would have thought you would do this to me!"

"And *I* never thought you would be willing to share me for a bit of money, or seduce Chigi servant girls to advance yourself!"

"I used what we had, Margherita!" His smooth, handsome face was suddenly mottled red and twisted with anger. "And at the time, our best commodity was you. We come from the same place. We *are* the same. You cannot possibly begrudge me that!"

"Perhaps not, but neither can I respect you any longer."

"You speak of respect when you have given a total stranger your chastity, your dignity?"

"I have given him my heart along with it, Antonio."

"He will break it in two, mark my words. You were a challenge, the novelty of stout fruit bread when one has eaten too many cream-filled tarts!"

"Thank you very much for that!" she replied, sharply wounded now by his ongoing assault.

"You were always meant to be *my* wife!"

"Then you should not have pushed me toward another man!"

He slammed his fist angrily onto the table. "You owe me something for this, Margherita—at least for the shame, the jests and sneers, you have brought upon me, and which, for your lustful ways, I shall now be forced to endure with our neighbors and friends for a good many months!"

She spun around, her eyes ablaze with disbelief. "You want *money?*"

"I believe I am owed something!"

She had known Antonio all of her life, and only now did she realize fully that this man before her, so handsome and carefree, up until now the epitome of self-assurance, was a complete stranger to her.

"You are nothing like your brother."

"I have always considered that an attribute," he said nastily. "Donato allows that sister of yours to drag him around by the nose, and he is not the better for it. He shall never do more than muck out stables the rest of his life!"

"Get out, Antonio!"

The brittle, angry tenor came from Donato. He stood at the bottom of the staircase with Francesco and Letitia, all dressed to begin the day's batches of bread. All three of them had heard the cruel exchange.

"Not until I get what I came for!"

"The only thing you shall receive here is a thrashing!" Donato promised as he charged at his younger brother, taking him up by the collar.

"I agonized for a long time whether I was doing the right

thing," Margherita said. "I am glad you came here today, Antonio."

"You shall not get away with shaming me, Margherita Luti!" he warned as Donato thrust him toward the door. "That, I promise all of you!"

THAT EVENING, Cardinal Bibbiena stood before his niece and rolled his eyes, impatiently watching her weep into her bony hands. Tender feelings were largely foreign to him, yet he felt them for her. Maria had been with him here in Rome since the age of nine. His brother and sister-in-law, who remained at the family seat, the grand Palazzo Dovizi, in Bibbiena, believed a better match could be made for their homely daughter nearer to the base of power.

At first, a ward had been a family obligation Bernardo had taken on grudgingly. But somewhere along the way, although now he remembered not where, Maria had become like a daughter to him. The child of his heart. The one he would never have.

To her, he became the caring guide she could not find in her own father.

Through the years, Maria rarely saw her parents. She depended upon her uncle for all things. Within his tender feelings was a wild need to protect her, along with his own strong desire for her success. Initially, he had wanted the marriage with Raphael for the prestige it would bring him. But Maria's infatuation with Raphael had made a love match into a fatherly desire.

Its unraveling now pricked him because it wounded her.

As she wept before him, he glanced up at the painting, *Saint Jerome in Meditation,* that he had given to her for her suite of rooms at his villa on the elegant Via dei Leutari. He folded his arms across his chest.

"If you are quite finished, *cara,* you must dry your eyes and decide what we are to do about all of it."

The cardinal had left the Vatican and, accompanied by papal guards, rode his own great chestnut stallion, with the ecclesiastical blanket beneath his jeweled saddle. A biting winter wind cut through his cape and cassock as he crossed the Tiber to the family villa where Maria lived in appropriate splendor.

He had found her in this grand room, dotted with niches full of priceless urns, the walls ornamented with religious paintings. It was the anteroom to her bedchamber. Maria sat on a hassock, covered in midnight-blue silk, before a raging fire in the grand stone hearth. She was as limp as an abandoned rag doll, and he was losing patience. Her woebegone sobbing, at this point, was grating on his nerves. Even worse, it was tugging at his heart.

"What is there to do but concede?"

"Concede?" he bellowed, his reedy voice echoing through the cavernous room. "To a baker's daughter? *Dio mio,* child! Those are not the words of a Bibbiena! Can you not for a moment reflect upon *that?*"

"How can I do anything *but* reflect? Reflect on my future— the one without Raphael in it!"

He knelt before her, clamped his hands on her shuddering upper arms, and gently shook her in the shadows cast from the fire. He hated loving her this much, and the weakened state to which it brought him. He did not wish to be vulnerable to anyone.

Consciously, he worked to control the volume of his voice, and the anger it bore. "You *must* save this betrothal, Maria. Your reputation is at stake. The family name is at stake. Your honor will be lost if someone so well known as Raphael withdraws his petition, and then it would be virtually impossible to find you another important match!"

Helpless tears cascaded down her colorless cheeks. "Can you not go to the Holy Father? Plead my case before him?"

"Even the Holy Father cannot make a man wish to marry you if he does not, Maria. Besides, they had words about you last autumn, and His Holiness noted great resistance from Raphael on the subject of moving forward with the marriage."

"Then I am lost!" She began openly to sob again, a shallow, mouselike squeaking. "And I do so love him!"

"That, my girl, is your first mistake," the cardinal coldly declared, standing fully, once again, over her. "Marriages for our kind have nothing to do with love. If you manage to change his mind by outlasting this newest infatuation of his, you would do well to learn that Raphael has an artist's temperament. He is wildly driven, incredibly self-absorbed, and absolutely bound by virtually insatiable carnal passions."

"Uncle!" Maria gasped, fingers splayed across her mouth, and tears running over her bony knuckles.

"It is time you grew up, *cara mía*. While it is those qualities that create some of the world's most incredible art, it is those same qualities that shall require a wife to tolerate and understand many things."

"Such as mistresses."

"Many of them, in all likelihood."

Her owlish, tear-filled eyes widened. "Do you believe he will never find me comely enough to love? That I can never be enough for him, even once we are wed?"

In a fit of frustration, he pummeled the leather-covered arm of the chair beside her hassock with his bound fist. "Maria, wake up, I bid you! He may well yet, by some intervening miracle, marry you! If we are patient, careful, and very wise he may even, if the Lord smiles upon your union, get you with a child! But Raphael Sanzio will never be faithful to you! He is simply not capable of that sort of devotion to anyone's desires but his own! If you go along much further with the childish notion that things can be any different than that, you will, I believe, chase him as far from you as he can get, and swiftly!"

He paced the room for a moment, his words resonating between them. "So, it is for you to decide. Is it the naive storybook version of a husband you desire, or is it Rome's greatest prize, the lauded artist—the *mastro*—upon whom you shall keep your sights absolutely set upon winning?"

She wiped her nose on a lace-edged handkerchief, then blew into it until her nose was red. "I still wish him as my husband, Uncle."

"Even as he is."

"*Sì*. Even as he is."

"Very well. Then let us do as it requires. *All* that it may require, shall we?" he calmly declared.

THEY WALKED together unnoticed through the narrow, busy streets of Trastevere, Raphael's olive-green velvet hat tipped down over his brow, and his head kept low as they arrived at the little cobblestone piazza and the small parish church of Santa Dorotea.

"Come," Margherita smiled, motioning him inside.

"The two of us in a church?" he chuckled. "After what we have only this morning done with one another?"

"I would like you to meet someone," she said as they climbed the wide stone steps to the carved and weathered doors with large brass handles.

Entering the sanctuary was soothing to Margherita. This warm, candlelit cocoon of silence and peace was where she had worshipped, confessed, and paid homage to her dead mother for the final time. It was reassuring to be back here, even for a few moments, when so much about her life now was changing.

Margherita moved down the center of the church toward the nave, between two banks of old wooden chairs. She walked toward a heavily jowled man, a priest, in a long black cassock, who was removing the melted candles and puddles of hardened wax from brass holders beside the altar. He never changed, Margherita thought. Padre Giacomo was the picture of calm kindness, with his compact body, balding head, and heavy gray temples above the dominant jowls. She felt her own smile broaden as she neared him, and as he looked up with soft, silvery blue eyes, recognizing her.

"*Santissima Maria,* it is good to see you, child," he said as they embraced, and then he held her out at arm's length as a proud uncle might do, assessing the changes in her these past months that she had not come to the neighborhood sanctuary. The glowing smile on her face spoke volumes.

"I have missed hearing Mass with you," Margherita said. "And I have missed your wise counsel, *padre.*"

"It would seem you have done admirably without it," he said, smiling over at the renowned artist garbed extravagantly in the exquisitely rich olive-green hat and a cloak with fur collar and cuffs, his hands, cleaned of paint, now dotted with rings. The priest was clearly anticipating a proper introduction.

Raphael was surveying a large unadorned niche beside the altar. He turned abruptly, his expression wide and piqued with interest. "A panel of the Assumption would look marvelous here," he said, pointing to the space. "And perhaps a small, gold-framed Madonna over there."

"Would that this parish could afford such masterful adornments, Signor Raphael."

His lips stretched into a smile. "You know who I am then?"

"Does not all of Rome know the great *mastro?* I am Padre Giacomo," he said, smiling affably.

"Margherita has told me much of your kindness to her after the death of her mother, *padre.* I feel as if I know you already."

"I am honored to be thought of thusly." He lowered his eyes deferentially for a moment then looked up again, his smile broadened. "And so to what do I owe the pleasure of this memorable visit?"

"I needed to be back here," Margherita confessed. "I wished Signor Sanzio to be here in this place, to see and feel that which is special to me in my neighborhood."

"Then I am honored by the presence of both of you." He put the dried candle wax into the burlap bag he held, then said, "I have little to give, but I would be honored to share a humble cup of wine and a bit of Luti bread in my private rooms with the great *mastro* and the woman who has brought him into our simple little church."

Raphael smiled. "The fare you offer would be most welcome indeed, Padre Giacomo," he replied elegantly.

They sat together in the small, curtained-off room behind the chapel, with its unadorned whitewashed walls and a small leaded-glass window with iron handle, speaking of art, the church, and Margherita's perfectly exquisite simplicity as a Madonna. "I remember her as a little girl. It feels like only moments ago," he said proudly.

"I wish I had known her then," Raphael responded with a smile. "What was she like?"

"Oh, charming indeed! Always that, with those great round eyes of hers, and her husky little laugh. Yet with her unmistakable spark of fire from the very first. There was a time when she was a very little girl that she hid behind my altar table at Mass, simply because she wished to be sure to hear me properly, so devout was she as a child. Margherita, do you recall that?"

"Of course," she giggled. "My father scolded me soundly for it!"

"And now she is a beautiful woman, grown and self-assured, with a fascinating new life before her. And I can only imagine the magnificence of our Margherita here as she has been painted by so great an artist."

"Then you shall come to my workshop to see it for yourself."

"Such a thing would not be possible!"

Raphael tipped his head. "You do not wish it then?"

"Rather, I cannot fathom it. I am a poor cleric, *signore,* unsuited for leaving the predictability of this little square where I am known and tolerated, I am afraid."

Raphael bit back a kind little smile, placing a finger over his lips for a moment, a large gold ring glittering there. "Then how will you ever approve the altarpiece of the Assumption that my assistants and I are going to paint for your altar niche?"

"But why would you do such a thing?" The cleric's stubby fingers splayed out across his mouth. "Surely you have other more pressing commissions from patrons who can pay you what your talent is worth!"

"Because Signorina Luti values this place, and you, *padre*. It gives me the greatest pleasure to make her happy. And your other little niche over there cries out from above for a small Madonna. I find I am drawn to paint that for you myself."

"Neither I nor this little parish church will ever forget this, Signor Sanzio. If you ever have need of anything, either of you," he declared with the greatest sincerity, "know that you have but to ask."

SIX WEEKS LATER, after the coming of the new year, a package was delivered to the church of Santa Dorotea in Trastevere by a well-dressed young courier who had come from the workshop of *Mastro* Raffaello. Inside the package, Padre Giacomo found a small, circular, painstakingly detailed Madonna. Garbed extravagantly in blue silk with a turban and a rich green silk shawl, she had been painted looking directly at the viewer, her eyes full of confident, serene love for the playful child she held. The model for the Christ child, Padre Giacomo knew instantly, had been Letitia Perazzi's littlest son, Matteo, and in the background, her next youngest, Aldo, had been painted as a young Saint John. The Madonna was unmistakable . . . beautiful and timeless.

The face of the Madonna belonged to a simple peasant whose family sold bread. It was Margherita Luti.

※ *16* ※

IN THE BLAZE OF A CRIMSON SETTING SUN, ON A CRISPLY cold afternoon, Raphael stood at the corner of the excavation site at the Domus Aurea, once the property of the infamous Roman emperor Nero, now nothing but rubble and ruin. Dozens of workers in loose-fitting muslin shirts belted with leather, buff-colored hose, dusty shoes, and soiled caps filed in and out before him, like a busy parade of ants. They were coming and going with baskets and barrels full of soil, stone, and loose artifacts painstakingly retrieved at what had been called the Golden House.

The once-breathtaking marvel had taken up vital city space and so, tragically, had been filled with tons of dirt by a subsequent emperor, Trajan, to make way for his own great vision, and what was to become the massive and splendid Colosseum. The only way into the cavernous remains now was to be lowered in a basket, eased down by heavy ropes.

Overseeing this excavation, and several other ancient preservation sites around the city, was part of Raphael's duty as commissary of antiquities. *As if I needed yet another honor,* he thought to himself, weary from the hours last night that he had passed at the Vatican Palace, laying out the next sequences in the fresco series in the pope's *stanza.* There were the hours after that which he and Giulio had spent in consultation about other figures and their placement. He had not seen Margherita, or even his own bed at the Via dei Coronari, for two nights. He was weary to the bone, yet his day was far from over.

At this very moment, Giulio and Gianfrancesco Penni were at work on the *stanza,* and Giovanni da Udine and a staff of assistants were several corridors away beginning the animal and fruit decorations of Bibbiena's long-awaited bath, called a *stufetta.* In style, it was to be a companion to the corridor Raphael had already completed for the powerful cardinal in the ancient theme from the Domus Aurea, which Bibbiena loved. So broad had Raphael's reputation become that there was a stack of unopened letters from kings, dukes, and princes around the world, pleading with him to paint their official portraits, and more work in Rome every day. And all the while, Michelangelo was in Florence, still scheming for a way to usurp Raphael's dominance, through his ambitious student, Sebastiano Luciani.

"Are you ready then, *signore?*"

The voice of the beefy-faced, dust-covered workman beside Raphael brought him from his thoughts. "Ready as I ever am to do *this,*" he replied of the claustrophobic, swaying ride, plunging him into the dark and musty mélange of throat-clotting rubble, sand, and dust. It was down to glimpses of a magnificence long ago destroyed and entombed.

Raphael clung to the sides as the basket was slowly lowered by four hard-armed, sweaty-faced workmen into a small circular opening into the ground, a single lamp held for light.

He was fascinated by what treasures and mysteries these depths still held from a long-ago age, but getting there always unnerved Raphael. The close darkness, the dank odor, and the pervasive lack of fresh air made him think too much of a coffin, of death itself, and what it would be like to be entombed. It was this place that reminded him too much of his fear that like his mother and father, he might die young, leaving things in his life unfinished. It had been a frequent fear until he met Margherita, who had revived him in so many ways. Raphael shivered and braced the basket more tightly, feeling the sudden drop in temperature of the Domus Aurea, like the catacombs . . . like a funeral chamber.

The basket swayed and jerked as it dropped him very slowly into the vast primary space, aptly called the Octagonal Room. Other baskets full of dirt and rocks had been lifted daily from this vaulted expanse for over two years, and yet the true floor still remained buried beneath several more feet, a time capsule of remaining art and artifacts—things not considered important enough to have been pilfered by Trajan's men.

He would give Margherita a palace one day, like this had been. He was driven to honor her, and to remind her at every turn, with the most wonderful symbols he could find, her absolute necessity in his life.

The most costly, the most beautiful—and the most rare.

Because that was what she was for him.

As Raphael stepped from the large basket, workmen in their soiled and sweat-stained shirts moved busily around him, their arms loaded with baskets of earth. Another tried to hold open a set of plans on large sheets of parchment for the excavation as Raphael stood in what was once the magnificent center room.

The roof had once been a great dome, with a huge oculus to let in light. This had been the very place, it was said, where the infamous emperor spent his last days before committing suicide.

Advisers had detailed for Raphael the great palace the Domus Aurea once had been. Built by Nero after the great Roman fire, it had been ornamented to bursting with paintings, frescoes, fountains, and elaborate furnishings. Even now, here and in the adjoining rooms newly unearthed, there was evidence of the once-opulent interior. Decorations were of gold leaf, marble, and gems; some ceilings of fretted ivory. The small remembrance of that faraway time, the breathtaking yet heavily damaged ceiling frescoes, were only now being restored under his careful direction. It was those frescoes, in particular, that had inspired the previous pope, Julius II, to begin the work, sending artists down to copy the ancient style, which they then reproduced in places in the Vatican. Raphael had done that for Bibbiena's corridor, a tribute to the cardinal's interest in this place and its hidden treasures.

Raphael stood now, amid flaming torchlight, glancing up at the men on scaffolding who, at his direction, worked to save the delicate artistry. Floating above him were images of Ulysses offering a cup of wine to Polyphemus and, at the center, Achilles at Sciro before the Trojan War.

In the stone wall of the Octagonal Room, as in the room beyond, there was a hole three feet around through which one needed to crawl to access the other rooms. The entire Domus Aurea was a labyrinth of darkness, dirt, and dank odors, all of it accessible only to those willing to move through the pitch-black maze. That was the worst, Raphael thought. Stiflingly close, frightening in its ability to make one feel entombed. He crawled quickly on his hands and knees, balancing a single small brass lamp that swung the small gold shaft of light as he inched forward toward the next room.

Dropping into this second room, he saw another large group of men, these working by flickering gold lamplight at restoring the plaster in a critical corner of the foundation where it was crumbling. This had been the Nymphaeum. It was an impressive room even in its state of destruction, with a coved roof, barrel vaults, niches for statuary, and the remnants of a large water feature designed to replicate a waterfall, where ladies of ancient Rome might sit and reflect. As Raphael stood brushing the thick layer of dust from his own hose, an unshaven man with tousled black hair, thick dark eyebrows, and a mud-covered shirt approached with a welcoming smile.

"How goes the work, Nicolò?" Raphael asked the supervisor.

"Very well indeed today, *signore*," he replied, pointing to the delicate yellow fresco.

It must have been, Raphael thought, glancing around, a magnificent room in its day, with walls covered in large sheets of polished marble, all long since removed. But the ceiling frescoes that had survived here as well, albeit in a poor state, were the real value to Pope Leo and Pope Julius before him. The pontiff wished to see the design, called "grotesqueries," duplicated in his Vatican corridor, which was why he had continued to finance this tedious and massive unearthing of Nero's buried palace.

"And strangely enough today, after all of our work, and your direction," said the man called Nicolò, offering forth an article held delicately between his meaty thumb and forefinger, "we found this."

Raphael narrowed his eyes and held up his small oil lamp, focusing on a delicate gold ring, set with a perfectly square, bright-red ruby.

"It was discovered here?" he asked incredulously, looking at the rubble, the dust and the shadowy darkness. *The room of Poppaea and Nero* . . .

"Indeed, *signore,* it was. Inside what was once a small pool."

"After Nero, Trajan had these rooms stripped of everything valuable he could find."

The supervisor's smile was wide, his front teeth stained dark beneath a heavily veined bulbous nose and those overpowering eyebrows. "Apparently he did not find *this!* Nunzio, working over there, found it at the bottom of those baths early this morning. This Nymphaeum was, after all, a place for elegant Roman women to sit and reflect upon their great beauty, was it not?"

Raphael began to smile incredulously, rolling the small perfect ring around in the palm of his hand, watching it glitter and catch the lamplight. Could there be a greater coincidence, a thing more symbolic in its rightness?

"It was," he agreed, a little breathless at the exquisite gem.

"I suspect Trajan and his men were so worried about all the larger articles that they never thought to sift through the layer of dirt covering the women's pool."

My mother used to read to us about the emperor's wives . . . particularly Poppaea, wife of Nero . . .

Raphael felt as excited as a child about this ring, and his thought, most powerfully, all at once, that Margherita would adore it. It would be the most perfect, unexpected gift. Here in this place where he saw eerily, and often felt, his own death, came to him instead a symbol, a sign of the life he was meant to live now—a symbol that had come from the toil of his other world. Was there really any greater sign than this?

This ring, from this place particularly, was meant for Margherita's finger. She was the symbol of his new, fuller life, and this ring, from here, was the proof of that. His fear and apprehension of this place gave way to something pure and uplifting, symbolized in a single ring, ironically from the very reign of which they once had spoken.

"Perhaps it belonged to Nero's wife," the man speculated, seeing Raphael still examining the exquisitely delicate ruby ring. "That would be something, would it not? A piece of Rome's history tucked away here, forgotten for the grander things that were sought by greedy men. Thus, perhaps the fates intend it for another very special hand."

"Perhaps they do," Raphael agreed, unable to take his eyes from the ring.

"The connection to Emperor Nero is certainly possible, but

likely only through his conniving mistress, Poppaea, with whom he built this place."

The cool, calculated voice behind them filled the air, and at once the room felt chilly and tense. Raphael and the others turned to find Cardinal Bibbiena standing behind them, hands steepled piously, as if in prayer, his lips turned up into the slightest hint of a calculated smile. Raphael had been so taken up by the ring that he had heard nothing, and had not seen him approach. Bibbiena had clearly been down here first.

"She *was* later made Nero's wife," Raphael reminded him.

"Indeed, after he had broken the heart of his *true* wife," Bibbiena continued in the patient tone of one speaking with young children. "In his chronicles of the infamous emperor, Suetonius writes of a ring given by Nero to Poppaea, the scheming harlot who stole the emperor from his good and loyal mate, Octavia. That would make the ring nothing more than a pagan bauble."

"Perhaps the emperor was not well matched with his first wife, Your Grace. And perhaps Poppaea was his true love—which would instead make the ring a symbol of great importance."

"Yet a man who does not honor his commitments is no man of any real honor." Still smiling shrewdly, his owlish eyes glittering in the bright torchlight, he glanced up at Raphael's shocked expression. "As Poppaea favored power, not the riches and perfection that drove her husband, the ring was said to be a single ruby set in a simple band of solid gold. Perhaps it was tossed into the Nymphaeum pool by a servant loyal to poor Octavia, where she believed it would never be found."

"Your Grace spins an impressively creative tale," dared Raphael.

"Yet a plausible one, nonetheless." He held out his own heavily jeweled hand. "May I?"

With a furtive glance toward Raphael for approval, the stout workman surrendered the ring to the cardinal. Bibbiena's thin-lipped smile broadened as he took it into the palm of his hand, turning it over until it caught the lamplight.

"Exquisite. This would be quite a valuable little relic," he murmured, forgetting his reserve.

Raphael felt his chest tighten, and an odd sense of dread begin to seize him. What could a man like Bibbiena want with yet another piece of jewelry?

"The Nero connection seems highly unlikely after all of this time," Raphael said with a feigned indifference that he fought to maintain, knowing instinctively how fate had led him to the ring, intending it for Margherita's hand. "So many other emperors here since then, so many other years."

"It was well buried, *signore,* perfectly preserved by pure chance," Nicolò reminded, unaware of the growing hostility between the two men.

The cardinal lifted a single eyebrow. "And stranger things have happened."

"Perhaps. But, in either case, the Holy Father should be allowed to determine its authenticity and value for himself." Raphael now held out his hand.

"I shall see it to the Holy Father, Raphael, when I dine privately with him this evening."

"Your Grace's offer is a gracious one, but *I* am the Holy Father's commissary of antiquities. It is my responsibility to supervise its transport."

Bibbiena lowered his eyes, setting his gaze on Raphael. "Do you not trust me, Raphael?"

"It is not a matter of trust, Your Grace, rather one of responsibility."

"An odd stand to take, considering your stand on your *other* responsibilities."

Raphael gritted his teeth. Bibbiena had meant his relationship with Maria, and the disquieting silence between them was charged heavily with animosity. "Still, Your Grace, I really must insist." He held out his hand, his eyes leveled on the gaunt, harsh face, so like Maria's.

There was a hint of malice in Bibbiena's eyes that grew to

something very strong. "Tell me, *Raffaello*, were it yours to give, would this be something you would intend for my niece? She is, after all, still your officially betrothed."

"I intend nothing other than seeing it to the care of the Holy Father, to be dealt with at his pleasure, Your Grace," Raphael said, his eyes narrowed.

"You have no idea of the value of something like this! You could not possibly!"

Raphael studied the cardinal for a moment, straining to remain calm. "But this is not about the ring—is it, Your Grace?"

"Precious things deserve to be in the care of those who understand their value."

"Like your niece?"

A little gasp sounded, but Raphael did not know from where it had come.

"Very well," Bibbiena conceded. A tense moment later, he surrendered the ring, then turned away in a whirl of crimson. "It shall find its rightful hand soon enough, pray God," he declared with a slim, sardonic grin Raphael could not see, but one he certainly felt.

Raphael glanced back down at the ring, already warm and reassuring in his own hand. "*Sì*, pray God," he repeated as the cardinal and his assistants turned and headed for the circular hole in the side wall, the only way to escape the dank, rubble-filled room. But it was clear as he went that the two men had very different intentions in mind regarding the future of this newly discovered gem.

❊ *17* ❊

RAPHAEL SAT WAITING FOR ELENA IN HIS OWN GRAND kitchen on the Via dei Coronari until she finally appeared, her arms laden with food to prepare for the evening meal. The market had been hot and crowded, and now she was late, and weary.

Elena wore a white linen cap, a white collar, and an apron over her gray wool underdress. There was a leather belt and pouch at her waist in which she kept the market money. But no jewelry adorned her hands now. That had long ago been sold to see to her family's survival. Hanging over her arm, once draped by rich damask, were a bag of potatoes and a large silvery fish. She looked up and saw Raphael settled into a wooden chair beside the newly lit kitchen fire with a goblet of wine in his hand.

It was clear to her, by his troubled expression, he was waiting for her. Only once had Elena seen the *mastro* here in this vast room, cluttered with stained copper pots hanging from a heavy, open-beamed ceiling, bowls, plates, and kettles. She was un-nerved by his presence now. It had been many months since they had been alone together. And that one time had changed her life forever.

"It is not your custom to return home so early, *signore*," she nodded and quickly turned away, busying herself with laying out the onions, fish, and cheese she had just bought. "Forgive me, but your supper is going to be a bit late this evening."

"That doesn't matter," he said, his smooth voice changed by a slight tremor.

She was relieved he was not angry with her, but she feared what his being here again could mean. "Then have you come to request something special for your meal?" she asked thinly, pray-ing silently that her hunch was wrong. "The market was particu-larly busy today, but there was some lovely—"

"It is nothing to do with food," Raphael replied, interrupting her as he shifted uncomfortably on the stool.

Her heart began to race, and she felt ill. The kitchen suddenly became hot and close—this place held a memory she did not wish to revive. Elena felt her face flush. How could she tell the *mastro* that what had occurred only once—that foolish evening after her youngest sister had died so suddenly—had been the worst mis-take of her life? Tell him that and she was certain to lose the employment that entirely sustained the rest of her family. Yet here he was in her kitchen, wanting things to be as they were, drinking his wine in great gulps . . . waiting for her.

Elena's face must have been positively etched with panic because the moment she turned toward him, Raphael shot to his feet, the silver wine goblet tumbling from his hand and clattering onto the worn stone floor.

"*No!* Oh, no! I've not come about—" he declared loudly at first, then stopping himself in midsentence so that he would not need to speak the words. She saw his face pale, and an awkward moment of silence fell heavily between them.

"Pray, may we speak frankly?" he bid her in a lower, more strained tone. He moved a step nearer, across the chasm of the room, as well as through the awkward breach the past had created.

The throbbing beat of her heart still had not slowed, nor had her fear of what would come next. Wiping her hands on a kitchen cloth, she sank against the long wooden table topped with mixing bowls and a collection of wooden spoons.

"If you wish it, *signore.*"

Elena tried to look at him, at his self-assured stance, the breathtaking elegance of his clothes, which, every day, set him far above her life now. Yet she simply could not see anything but the rush of images. The two of them here in this kitchen, atop the long trestle table, entwined, where the bundles of onion and package of cheese now lay in a hurried heap.

Raphael ran a hand behind his neck and glanced around the vast kitchen that saw little use most days. "The fact of the matter is that there is a woman."

Another? she longed to ask him. But she wisely avoided saying that.

"I had heard it said," she replied instead.

Elena carefully watched the instant expression of self-defense change his face. "Where do they speak of such things that you might hear? At the fish market beneath the Portico of Octavia? Or the vegetable stalls of the public market at the Piazza dell'Aracoeli?"

He was quickly defensive, bordering on the very edge of anger. "They speak in many places of the girl who has won your heart. There is great interest in it, *signore*. And you are, after all, a most important man in the city."

"So they repeatedly remind me."

And then very suddenly she began to understand. Her heart beat very swiftly. She could not afford to lose this position. "I am no threat to her, of course."

"The point is that Margherita is different. Special to me and—" Raphael stopped himself in midsentence, and she could see suddenly that he believed he had offended her. "Not that you are not special. You have kept a good house for me these past two years. It is just different with her."

She understood, and within that lay her worst fear. "You do not wish her to know of all the other women? Of the diversity and number of us, perhaps?" she asked with a hint of resentment bleeding through her calm tone.

"It is one thing, Elena, to know of them, and she does. But it would be quite another for her to have to see one of them on a daily basis, once she enters more fully into my life."

Elena grew very cold, as if an unexpected draft had swept through the room. He meant to relieve her of her employment here. She felt the burden of foolish naïveté weigh profoundly on her. Still there was the responsibility of her mother, her siblings, her duty, and in that she could allow herself no pride.

"Signor Sanzio, *per favore*," she bid him, her mouth having gone absolutely dry with the panic. "You must know I would never speak a word of that. I do swear it. It is not a circumstance of which I am proud even to recall for myself, much less to speak of to others!"

When he looked away from her, she went on, feeling the words tumble out over her desperation, her hands extended before her in a pleading gesture. "I shall never be wanted as a wife now to any honorable man in Rome! There is nothing left for me! *Per favore, signore!* At heart, you are a good and decent man! I implore you not to take away the one means I have of feeding my family!"

She saw how struck he was by that. The small pained expression, the way his eyes narrowed, as if he had never fully considered the effect of his actions on any of the women he had bedded, until this moment.

"Forgive me," he said in a deep tone, and she knew that he meant it as he ran his hand once again behind his neck in a nervous gesture. "There have been many things in my life I have not considered for how taken up I have been with finding success. I used you in a moment of my own weakness, which is an appalling excuse, I know, and yet, for it, I am still truly and completely sorry."

She wanted to say that the weakness had been hers as well, that had shock and pain not clouded her judgment she would never have given him something so precious to her as her virtue. Especially not in the desperate, unthinking way that she had. But he loved another now, and the past could not matter to him. Being rid of the reminder seemed his greatest concern.

In the silence that had fallen once again between them, Raphael drew out a small wooden chest with leather straps and a silver clasp, which he then handed to her. "This should contain enough to help you and your family for a good while, at least until you can find another suitable circumstance. I really do wish you to have it."

She felt the bile rise up into her throat with such force that she nearly vomited. Surprising even herself, Elena burst into tears. They flooded her gray eyes, clouding her vision as they rained down her round, pink cheeks.

"I am no whore to be paid off!" she managed to sputter, feeling her knees begin to buckle beneath the weight of so stinging an insult.

"I did not mean it like that!"

"If you had not taken me here in this very room, would you be offering me money?"

"I am *trying* to make amends, and perhaps not doing the best job of it, but you have entirely twisted my intent!"

"And *you* have misjudged my character!"

He gripped his forehead in frustration and wheeled around. "You have *no* idea how I regret what happened! What a dreadful mistake it was! But what can I give you? What will you take as restitution? You have but to name it!"

"I wish only what you have already agreed to with Cardinal Bibbiena! My position in this house, and my ability to care for my family!"

"Anything but that!"

"Then you do not regret it enough! I may now live in the poorest quarter of Rome, but I am not a whore, Signor Raphael, to be paid off for the regrettable use of my body! I am Elena di Francesco Guazzi, daughter of a once-great man!"

She used every ounce of courage she could call up, determined not to look away from him. "I have kept your house, lit your fires, bought your costly wine, and changed your linen after more nights of debauchery with women than I care to recall! I have only ever desired to make an honest living, and one day, by God's grace, to marry a modest and *forgiving* man! But by one incident of my own foolish and sinful lack of judgment," she cried, squaring her shoulders at him, "it appears I am meant to lose the opportunity for both!"

Elena did not give him time to speak another word. She had said, she knew, quite enough for one night. With the hem of her plain skirt swirling at her ankles, she turned and went out of the kitchen. She slammed the heavy door behind herself with a great punctuating thud.

GIULIO ROMANO sank against the wall of the corridor outside the kitchen, feeling as if he had just been hit suddenly in the solar plexus. He had suspected there might once have been something between Elena and the *mastro,* but he had not expected to learn the lurid details of it like this. He closed his eyes, trying to blot out the image of the pretty girl who shyly made his favorite broad beans and bacon, then insisted on leaving the room as he ate it. He had believed her shyness was because of him. Now all he could think was of her lying back on that wide, scarred kitchen worktable, over which he had spoken to her many times, her body surrendering to a man who had cared nothing for her.

Giulio had always loved Raphael, and more than that, he had respected him greatly, but now he felt the overpowering urge to do more damage to him than Luciani's henchman had.

And yet what he had heard brought understanding. Now it all made sense. Why she refused to sit and speak with him for more than a moment here and there. He balled his hands into tight fists. He knew, of course, about lust and overpowering physical desire, because he had always so strongly denied himself, no matter how many temptations Raphael had set before him. He had never wanted the cheap whores of the Quartiere dell' Ortaccio, but a real love to one day sate his passion. And for that, Giulio had always told himself, he could wait, no matter how much the *mastro* had said the opposite would improve the passion in his art.

Giulio had never loved anyone enough to be certain of precisely in what direction his true heart lay. What he felt now for Elena was not a matter of the heart, surely, but rather a strong urge to see her protected. That urge was rooted not in passion, but in compassion, he told himself. And yet it was enough to entirely occupy his mind at that moment. As he walked silently away from the kitchen, Giulio Romano felt compelled to do something about what he had heard beyond the door. The only question was what.

❈ 18 ❈

IT SNOWED ON SUNDAY, AND ALL OF ROME CAME OUT TO see the dusting, like powdered sugar, that melted the instant it hit the ground. But the cheering effect on the citizens was still the same. It was something magical. Something that could take most of them, even for a moment, from the drudgery of their daily lives.

Exhausted, Raphael rode his grand horse toward the workshop from the Vatican Palace, the hour being much later than he had hoped. There had been trouble in the fresco with the likeness of Agostino as Cupid. Raphael simply had not been able to break away from it. One of the layers of plaster had not been properly mixed by an apprentice and so they had needed to dash to remove it, then repaint the section before it was allowed to dry. But that had not been his day's final appointment.

Raphael had finally been given a private audience with the Holy Father this evening, hopefully to secure the Domus Aurea ring. The pope had been preoccupied of late with the issue of his alliances with Spain and France, and this had been Raphael's first chance in weeks, since first seeing the rare gem, to speak about it. Once he was received by the pontiff, however, Cardinal Bibbiena emerged from a small side room, his hands piously steepled, and proceeded to entirely commandeer the meeting. Questions were asked in rapid succession about his progress on so many commissions that Pope Leo tired completely before Raphael could ever speak a word about the ring.

He had no idea whether Bibbiena intended the ring for himself, or why, but Raphael left the Vatican Palace that evening knowing absolutely, by the cold, unforgiving expression on his face, and his piercing stare, that Maria's uncle meant to stop him from having it. He also came away with the distinct impression that he may well have crossed the wrong cardinal.

THE ASSISTANTS all fell silent as Margherita entered the workshop. It was early evening when the wind whipped through the narrow, tangled alleyways of Rome, and felt like sword blades beneath the heavy blue cloak she wore. In an instant, all eyes among Raphael's great team of artists were turned away from her, as if she were not even there. Smug indifference chilled her to the bone in a way the wind had not. To them, clearly, she was just another conquest of the great *mastro*.

"He is not here," one of them gruffly called out to her, turning back to his panel. It was the silver-haired da Udine, his voice echoing across the vaulted chasm. Da Udine had made it clear he did not like her. And he apparently liked her *here* even less.

"When is he expected?" she forced herself pleasantly to inquire as he continued to paint, his back still to her.

"The *mastro* is a powerful man who does as he pleases, *signorina*. One is wise to expect little of him in that regard, since his mood can change as swiftly as the weather once something suits him no longer."

Or someone was what he had meant. But a pointed inference, she had begun to learn, was more powerful than a direct hit.

She took a step forward, forcing herself not to shrink from his challenge. The effort was so great that she felt herself begin to tremble. "I shall wait."

"As you wish," said da Udine coldly, still refusing to regard her.

"It *is* as I wish, Signor da Udine."

Wish it, sì, she thought when no one spoke further, and she sank onto a little wooden bench beside the door. *Yet all of this, and everything else, is far beyond anything I might ever have bargained for.*

MARGHERITA was waiting for him as they had planned, in the little private room in the workshop where there was now the pallet, blankets, and a spray of fringed velvet pillows. But he could tell by the expression on her face, the moment he came in, that she had grown weary of the evening routine that had become Raphael's salvation from the work. It had also become his one powerful obsession.

"Forgive me, *amore mio,* but the delay could not be helped," he said with a sigh as he held her shoulders and gently kissed her cheek. Her skin was cold to the touch and her expression was strangely distant. She was tense when he took her into his arms.

"It would be easier to bear, waiting for you, if I were not greeted each evening by the indifferent stares of your many assistants and models."

She had chosen the word *indifferent,* but what she had meant was *contemptous,* particularly the glance of Giovanni da Udine, the oldest and most intimidating of the group. Every time she came through the heavy workshop door, he made it apparent, with his rolled eyes and half smirk, that she was merely another trifling girl there for the *mastro*'s pleasure. Nothing more.

"I know how difficult it is for you to come here," he said patiently as he kissed the soft place beneath her earlobe.

Inwardly, Raphael cringed at the mention of it. Elena had not yet left the house on the Via dei Coronari, in spite of the tense and silent three days it had been since their conversation. It was difficult, she said, to find other employment in Rome, along with accommodations like those she had found with Raphael. When she would not take his money, he did not have the heart to put her out onto the street.

"Cardinal Bibbiena guaranteed this employment with you to my mother," she told him stubbornly just this morning. "And, as I have done everything here that he told me I would be required to do, I see no reason to leave hastily."

"But I must be free to entertain who I like in my home!" he had barked in frustration.

"I do nothing to threaten that."

"Your mere presence here threatens that!"

"Perhaps you should have considered the consequences before you chose to take my virtue."

"May the Lord help me, I assumed you were not so virtuous, as you did nothing to stop that regrettable event!"

"You are Raffaello! Does not every woman do as you bid them?"

"No, Elena. Not every woman."

Raphael shivered, pressing away the memory of their angry exchange, kissed Margherita's forehead, and pulled her close to his chest. He was gratified to have her near again, fed by her calm presence, and the needed energy he gleaned from that alone.

They kissed deeply before he said, "Come. I want to show you something."

Raphael took her hand and led her out into the studio, which was empty now of the artists and models who so unnerved her. Here, in the flaming salmon-pink light of early evening that glittered through the open shutters, she saw it. On an easel beside his own worktable in the main workshop was the completed Madonna at last. Margherita gasped, seeing herself as the Virgin Mary standing barefoot on a celestial bed of clouds with two figures kneeling in adoration around her. On one side, the image of Saint Barbara, and on the other, Pope Sixtus II. She had never seen anything even close to this, nor, she knew, had anyone else. She was stunned.

"It is . . . exquisite."

"You find it so?"

She looked at him and saw plainly his need for her approval in this. "Truly I do."

"You trusted me and I did not wish to disappoint you. I wished it to be entirely unique. As you are."

"You have done that, Raphael, and so much more. I don't know what to say."

"The expression in your eyes is better than any words."

As they stood before the easel, Raphael's hand on her shoulder, the door was held open by one of two velvet-clad servants, allowing entry for the elderly man with flowing snowy hair and beard whom they were attending. Turning to see who was approaching, Raphael's face lit with a sudden beaming smile.

"Ah, *bene!* My dear friend, at last you have arrived!" he said, embracing the elderly man, then he turned back to Margherita. "I wish for you to meet a very dear friend."

The sage old man with a hooked, veined nose and bright blue eyes smiled kindly down at her. "Signor da Vinci, may I present Signorina Luti."

Wearing a knee-length coat and tunic of green-and-gold brocade, gold hose, and a gold embroidered hat with a wide, upturned brim, he stood elegantly before them, his face a network of fine wrinkles. But he regarded her just as Raphael had at the first, with that same critical artist's eye. Of course, like the rest of Rome, she knew the name Leonardo da Vinci. He was a revered master who had created beautiful works, including *Adoration of the Magi,* a fresco of the Last Supper, and a portrait of a mysterious woman people called La Giaconda.

"It is a great pleasure to be met with such beauty on a cold March afternoon," he said in an aging, slightly rusty voice, yet one still full of grace and charm. "But a true friend of Raphael's must call me Leonardo."

"I would be honored to do so."

"With me, you must only be yourself." He smiled at her with courtly aplomb.

"If you can judge a man by his friends," Margherita said smoothly, feeling herself begin to smile, "then Signor Raphael is a fortunate man indeed."

"I see the level of company you keep has improved here in Rome, along with your talent, *caro amico,*" he said to Raphael with a growing smile. "Most impressive indeed."

It was the first time anyone had placed value upon her besides Raphael, and did not look askance at her presence in his life. Margherita found it a pleasurable sensation, and she found da Vinci a charming man. "Leonardo has come to see the completed Madonna, as we spoke of it many times while it was being painted. It is so much the better to have the model here, as well."

The old master stroked his chin as his gaze fell upon the Madonna painting, still smelling of linseed oil and wood fiber. "Brilliant, *caro.* Original . . . evocative . . . truly a stunning work."

"There is no higher praise than that which comes from you," said Raphael. "With Bramante dead now, and Michelangelo against me, your approval means more to me than it ever has."

"I can see that the girl has inspired you."

"More than that, she has forever changed me, Leonardo."

Da Vinci smiled at them sagely, understanding now. "Ah. You are in love with one another!"

"Forevermore."

Leonardo looked more closely at Margherita then. His eyes were tired with years, yet still they were filled with a long life's wisdom. "Then I bid you tread softly upon his heart, child, for Raphael may have convinced the world of how cavalier he is, yet he is an innocent to the cost of a broken heart. And I would not expect the Holy Father to look kindly upon one who impedes the work of one he considers his personal artisan."

He smiled as he spoke the words, but there was, nonetheless, a warning in them.

"They have nothing to fear from me, Signor da Vinci," she softly responded as she turned to gaze up adoringly at Raphael.

"I painted a woman myself once . . . long ago . . . Like you, it was her eyes that captured me most, and that which I hope I offered to the world."

"I remember her," Raphael nodded, smiling. "And I have studied often the sketches you allowed me to make from her—her figure placement, the turn of her head . . . the eyes, and her curious smile. Your work shall always be an inspiration to me."

"Sì, that is the one, my Mona Lisa. She became a representation of many things, a challenge to me. But, your *signorina* here, she is from your heart. You will do many great works of her."

"It is my passion now."

Margherita bit back an embarrassed smile. Raphael looked at her turned-up lips and thought, suddenly, how erotic it felt to kiss them. To taste her tongue in his mouth, and to feel the innocent passion that so freely came to him when they made love. She had brought him back to life in so many ways. At times, she made him feel like an innocent himself when they were alone.

"Take great care then that your sincerest wish is not at odds with the desire of the Holy Father, and those around him," da Vinci warned with a rheumy cough. "For you know there is great

power in that Vatican Palace. And I fear the tide of your good
fortune could turn quickly if it is suspected that you were no
longer entirely committed to their desires, first and foremost."

Raphael had taken her hand and was rubbing his thumb
against her palm. He could feel her shiver as he said, "Many
thanks, old friend. I shall consider myself warned."

AFTER LEONARDO had departed into the grainy gray Roman
dusk, Raphael and Margherita were alone again. Seizing the privacy, Raphael pushed back the artist's drapery lying on their pallet,
and pressed her into the folds of cool linen beneath, in the private
little sanctuary off the main workshop. Without words, Margherita
fell willingly beneath his smooth, tender hands and reveled as he
touched the soft skin of her neck with gentle fingertips. As Raphael
began passionately to kiss her, their bodies bound by one another,
both in the state of half undress, the sound of a door swinging back
on its hinges out in the main workshop brought a sudden and
frightening stop to the moment. Margherita's eyes widened at the
sound of rustling skirts, and Raphael turned toward the second
door to see who was so unexpectedly there . . .

❦ 19 ❦

IT WAS THE FIRST TIME MARIA BIBBIENA HAD BEEN TO
the workshop in months. Raphael did not invite her here, nor did
he seem to appreciate her presence when she did, on occasion,
visit, bringing him a basket of warm bread, figs, a chunk of thick
yellow cheese, and wine for his dinner. But as there was little
other excuse to see him, he being so entirely taken up these days
with all of the feverish activity in his life, it was the only excuse
left to her. She would come here with an offering basket of his
favorite things and hope that even if he was not appreciative, at
least he might be hungry.

The two women attendants who accompanied Maria, richly

attired in their own quilted and jeweled winter gowns, which matched her black velvet with long fur collar and cuffs, were dutifully silent. The expressions on their smooth, pretty faces were passive as they followed her. Maria knew that they, too, had heard the gossip about her betrothed and his new common model.

Maria squared her painfully thin shoulders, which, like her telltale bony collarbone, were masked by layers of rich black velvet and a wide band of fur. She did her best to hold her head high, but her nose was running again and she felt weakened by the daunting performance that lay before her.

She had suffered many illnesses in her twenty years, and a general sense of ill health pervaded her world. There were daily tinctures, ointments, powders, and plasters, and endless consultations with new physicians, herbs, and special food. Her thin, ash-blond hair and pale-lipped smile could only hide so much. Still, the dignity of the house of Bibbiena thrust her forward, a proud, slippered step at a time, followed by her entourage, onto aged stairs that gave a small creak with each footfall.

It was quiet when they entered through the main workshop door. She saw that everyone had gone home for the day. Even the young apprentice who usually remained to clean paintbrushes in pails of water across the vast, easel ornamented room was nowhere to be seen. Yet Maria knew Raphael would still be here. It was not so late for him, with so many commissions to balance. *Long after everyone is asleep,* he once had told her, *here I remain. It is, after all, my name and my reputation that suffers if I cannot find a way to satisfy them all.*

Maria ventured forth toward his small, private room. She had found him there once before late like this, pouring over account books. Maria knocked once; then, when no response came, she turned the iron handle of the little room and pushed open the door.

There before her was Raphael and a woman, with hair like sable-colored satin, long and graceful, curved over her bare shoulders. Both of them were naked, yet covered by the same amber artist's drapery, and lounging sensually on a pallet on the floor. But what shocked her the most was the expression on his face. It was one of complete exultant desire for the woman whose bare leg was twined with his own. To her credit, Maria thought, disdainfully, the peasant girl, once seen, had the manners to cover herself.

She must have gasped before her fingers moved up and splayed across her mouth because Raphael shot her a stunned glare.

"Dio mio!" he cried out, bolting upright. "What the devil are you doing here?"

"Clearly, I should not have come," Maria managed to respond, fingers still splayed across her lips, as her eyes settled on this newest rival—the common girl from Trastevere whom he preferred as the model for his Madonna.

Maria spun on her heel, the hem of her gown swirling out behind her. The only sound was a rustle of skirts. To his credit, Raphael rose, called out her name in a tone of concern, then tried to go after her. But Maria's male attendant and guard, a solidly built Tuscan with a square face and a flat nose, blocked the door to the room as soon as Maria had gone out of it.

"Allow her to go with her dignity, *signore,*" he said with surprising command. "Follow her, if you will, but only once you have your clothes on."

Despite their wild trembling, Maria ran as fast as her legs could carry her, her eyes clouded with tears.

"What a fool I am!" she sobbed against the butter-yellow stone facade of the building once she was out on the street. An icy winter breeze buffeted her.

"If he wants you he will come after you, *signorina,*" the groom said kindly. "And if he does not—"

"If he does not, it is the end of my life!"

"You must not speak such words!"

"What other can come from me?"

"Those saying that you shall rise above this, and above him, and you shall go on, if he desires you not!"

Maria turned her head and looked at the guardsman through

tear-clouded eyes. She had never, until this moment, truly regarded him. He had worked for her family for many years and she did not even know his name. When she looked into his soulful green eyes now she saw that they were full of kindness and a remarkable concern.

"What do *you* know of such things?" she sniffled.

"I know what I see, *signorina*. A lovely girl who deserves better than to chase rainbows."

"You believe Raffaello to be a rainbow, do you, *signor guardia?*"

"He may well be one for *you.*"

"I find you impertinent with me and I know not even your name."

"I am Alessandro, Signorina Bibbiena."

"From what family?"

"Agnolo, of Montalcino, *signorina*," he nodded, hands stiffly at his sides. "Am I less impertinent to you now?"

She tried not to smile, but it was useless. He proffered a handkerchief, which she accepted as her two ladies emerged and gathered on the street behind her. The meaning of his family name was *gentle as a lamb*, and for all of his strength as a guard she could see that in him.

"Only mildly impertinent now."

"Improvement is a worthy thing." He bit back a smile.

"So it is, Signor Guardia Alessandro Agnolo. Now, if you please, see me home. I find I am feeling very tired."

❧ 20 ❧

MARCH 1515

DONATO TOOK HER GLOVED HAND IN HIS OWN AS THEY stepped along in the chilled March air, and through the crowded streets of Trastevere. His smile was a strange one, Margherita saw. They walked silently, arm in arm, passing a large bronze equestrian statue in the center of a small piazza. A flock of pigeons flapped their wings, some of them abandoning the statue as Margherita and Donato passed.

"Where are we going?"

"You must learn to like surprises if you are to remain a part of a great man's life!"

"Where we are going is to be a *surprise* for me?"

"A rather grand one, I should imagine."

They next passed through an arcade and into a narrow street still full of medieval houses, each with Gothic windows and broad balconies. They passed a little church with a fine rose glass window glittering like a jewel in a single burst of afternoon sun through a gray sky. Around them, old women in heavy cloaks filtered out past the carved doors into the street. Donato's eyes twinkled with the merriment of a summer's day in spite of the wintry air.

"*You* know what it is?" she asked, putting a hand on his arm, as they walked through a carved archway between two buildings and out onto the grand Via Alessandrina. They passed two brown-clad monks, their lowered heads covered in wide straw hats, and a collection of musical instrument workshops before they came finally to the portion of the street housing stately villas. Situated on the corner was a particularly imposing four-story house of terra-cotta and stone.

Suddenly, Donato stopped, kissed her cheek with brotherly affection, then slowly pulled open one of the huge and heavy front doors, which had a coat of arms carved above them. With a long, low creaking sound, the doors revealed a grand vestibule with a soaring ceiling, Doric columns, marble floors, and sweeping staircase that lay beyond. The rich aroma of leather and old books spilled out onto the street around them as Margherita gasped.

"What are you doing?"

But before he could respond, Raphael came toward her across the marble floor of the imposing foyer, his shoe heels tapping and his smile wide. Extending his arms, he enveloped Margherita, kissed her, then drew her into the warmth of the house.

"Well? Does it please you?" he asked with the happy expectation of a child. "If you are not pleased, then, of course, I will sell it immediately." Before she could answer, he led her into a large room dotted with art to the left of the foyer. Its vaulted ceiling and broad, painted beams made her gasp.

"I do not understand," she told him as she looked back from a room appointed with more luxury and grandeur than her mind could conjure.

"It is for you. It is your new home. *If* it pleases you, naturally."

She frowned slightly, trying to digest all that he was saying, and all that it implied. "As your mistress?"

"As yourself, Margherita. Only ever as yourself. To give you the privacy you deserve, from my assistants, or anyone else. To accept or decline whatever visitor you wish. Including me."

"You?" she smiled in disbelief. "You, who would be responsible for it in the first place?"

He was smiling back at her with delight in his weary eyes. "I love you, Margherita. I do not wish to keep you like a prize, or like a servant. I wish most of all to marry you, and I have meant this house as a show of that declaration."

"Signorina Bibbiena will never give you up."

He wanted to say that he had asked Maria yet again to terminate the betrothal, but betraying Margherita with a lie would be to sully something pure and special.

"I have not seen her since she came to the studio and found us," he answered truthfully.

"Is it her cardinal uncle you fear?"

Raphael let a sigh and drew her down onto a divan with carved wooden legs and covered in French tapestry. "I care not for myself if he is angered by the truth. I can always find work painting portraits."

"But your men, good men like Giulio." She saw the concern in his eyes. "Spare me not, Raphael. Truth matters to me as loyalty does to you." She waited a moment. "Do you truly see a time when you shall be free of her? I have no wish to dream for something that can never be."

He pulled her close and kissed her deeply. "I know not when or how, but before the day I draw my final breath, you alone shall be called wife to Raphael of Urbino."

JOINED BY Padre Giacomo and Margherita's family, Margherita and Raphael celebrated her first night in the new house on the Via Alessandrina, which was home, as well, to the Spanish ambassador. The house had been a palace, a city dwelling for the powerful and influential Caprini family a decade earlier. Margherita had told Raphael in the hours after it began to sink in how happy this would have made her mother. For so simple a woman to see dreams become reality for her daughter would have meant the world to her.

"Oh, how I wish she could have been here with me to see this," Margherita whispered, with tears in her eyes.

Raphael smiled kindly and glanced at the ceiling. "I believe she *is* here, *cara*. I've always felt my own father around me at times like this."

Margherita smiled through her tears. "It makes me happy to imagine it could actually be so."

In the grand house, Letitia went from room to room touching furniture and picking up costly candlesticks to see if she might, from their weight alone, determine their cost. As she did, Francesco Luti sat proudly in costly garments that did not suit him, but pleased him, and sank more deeply into a studded velvet chair of hunter green, allowing himself to be catered to by Margherita's new servants, who had come with the price of the house.

A stone-faced man, with a beaklike nose, leaned over the patriarch with a silver platter laden with rich slivers of almond frittata, marzipan, and, beside it, delectable sugared fruit. Donato stood silently near the fire drinking costly wine, shaking his head in disbelief, and trying his best to keep the feet of his four sons off the costly furnishings.

As he watched Margherita's family basking in their sudden, newfound fortune, Raphael's mind wandered from the joy of see-

ing Margherita's open shock and delight to darker thoughts of
Maria. It was her expression, when she had seen them together in
the studio. He had no wish to hurt her, and yet he had seen by her
face that he had done just that. His instinct had been to go to her
directly afterward. But after the plea from her guardsman, he
thought better of it. He had always believed Maria deserved better than the political marriage her uncle was foisting on her.

Raphael sank back into the deep, tapestry-covered chair,
crossed one leg over the other, and continued watching Margherita
and her family. He studied their easy way with one another—the
rhythms of people with a rich, shared history. He was mesmerized
by it, and a deep sense of longing for his own family began to fill
him. It had been so many years since he had shared in a family
meal, boisterous, loving arguments, the laughter of children, or
expressions, ages old, that made him feel twined with others in the
deep fabric of experiences.

Drawing to him his small leather folio, which held several long
sheets of paper and a piece of blue chalk, that he always carried,
Raphael began to sketch fragments of the scene before him:
Donato's torso twisting around in response when Letitia called to
him from across the room . . . Jacopo, the oldest child, his face
hinting at manhood, yet still bearing traces of the soft roundness
of youth . . . and portly Francesco, the patriarch, his full lips
twisted up in a wine-induced chuckle, his eyes dancing mirthfully.
His face was still unmistakably defined by years of work, sacrifice,
hardship, and loss. It was only as Raphael formed the precise
shape of Margherita's smile, with rapid exacting movements, that
the images began to melt and he could no longer see. Glancing up
again at Margherita, laughing joyously at something precocious
Matteo had just done, Raphael realized that it was not fatigue but
tears that were clouding his eyes.

WHEN THEY had all drunk too much wine to be sent home, the
servants saw Margherita's family to the several guest chambers on
the second floor while Raphael led Margherita to the third-floor

suite that would now be theirs. While they dined downstairs, Raphael had seen that the chamber was filled with flowers—white winter roses framed with fragrant rosemary. Margherita gasped when she saw them and sank back against the closed door.

"It is for you. All of it, for you," he murmured, unwinding her hair from the neatly tied knot at the back, then lifting a handful of the shiny waves and kissing the spot of her neck just below her ear. "I am going to paint another Madonna of you."

Margherita smiled. "I thought we agreed to only one."

"We also agreed to end *this* after the first time!"

He kissed her hungrily then, pressing her back against the closed door, his hands playing over the length of her body.

"What sort of Madonna did you have in mind?"

"From the sketch I did tonight as you held little Matteo. Your eyes, your face . . . it was perfect. And something else," he confessed, his breath coming now on a ragged whisper. "There is another gift I have in mind for you one day soon."

"You have already given me far more than I could ever deserve."

Raphael ran his hands down the length of her body, feeling the curves beneath the layers of fine silk that she now wore, uninterested in waiting to have her on the grand canopied bed across the room. "That is simply not possible. And this particular gift . . . is as fated as we are. I knew it the moment I saw it."

"As you knew with you and I?" she whispered then, betraying a little laugh as a guilty child would.

"Exactly as. Until we are able to marry, I mean to shower you every day of your life with the evidence that you are everything to me. I want this gift for the absolute rightness of it. When I am able to obtain it for you—and, mark me, I one day will—it will symbolize our formal betrothal."

It felt powerful and forbidden this way—wildly exciting—to take her against the door as he might with one of the whores in the bordello. But this time they would do it while speaking of Madonnas, and love, in the shadow of the magnificent painted Virgin that had at first brought them together. Propped on an easel beside their bed for one day more before it would be shipped to San Sisto, tonight it would remind them most pointedly of his gift and her beauty.

"In the meantime," he murmured into her hair as he cast off his hose and lifted her gown, "I will show you what to do with me. I will show you everything to pleasure us both, *mio grand amore.*"

❧ 21 ❧

AT FIRST SHE DECLINED TO RECEIVE HIM. SIGNORINA Bibbiena was resting, Raphael was told by the square-jawed groom in a blue velvet tunic and gray shirt and hose, who opened the heavily carved doors to the cardinal's villa on the Via dei Leutari on the chilled March morning. But Raphael would not be dismissed. He did not love her, but neither did he wish to dishonor her further so publicly by allowing her to believe they were still betrothed when he was now living openly with another woman. Whatever the repercussions, he at least owed Maria the truth. In this, Margherita made him wish to behave honorably — even if he could not honor his commitment.

"I must see her."

"She is not receiving guests," the guard repeated, his stony expression never changing. He was the same guard who had stopped Raphael outside of his workshop when Maria had left crying that dreadfully dark day.

"I am not a guest. I am Raffaello."

"I know who you are, *signore.* Lately, there is not a person in this house allowed to forget it."

Raphael glanced behind himself at the entourage of artists from his workshop, and a few noblemen, all in their velvet capes, hose and slippers, who did their best to follow him about Rome, from Chigi's villa to the Vatican Palace, hoping to bask in the glow that seemed always to surround him. The remark they had overheard had not been intended as flattery.

"Either you see me to Signorina Bibbiena, or doubt not that I shall find my own way," Raphael warned. "Do you wish to make a scene? The cardinal will soon hear about it if you do."

Like a hidden key to a lock, the ploy worked. The servant turned and stiffly proceeded up the torch-lit flight of stone stairs.

Maria was in her bed when Raphael entered her richly wood-paneled chamber. Along with a retinue of young ladies, she was listening to a performance on the lute played by a young man in a parti-color costume, half gold, half green. Propped up by a collection of gold and blue velvet pillows, he could see that her nearly skeletal frame was covered by thick layers of concealing fur. Her face was masked with powder, the color of roses, to hide the gray pallor of her skin. It was clear in this drafty room so close to the river that there was no bloom of good health around her, and that the people were more a comfort than frivolous entertainment.

Seeing Raphael at her door, Maria only nodded, but the lute player instantly ceased his playing, and all eyes were then turned critically upon him. "I seek a private word with you," said Raphael.

"I seek not the same with you," she replied coldly as he approached the foot of her bed where two small spaniel dogs lay curled warmly at her feet.

"Shall we discuss the matter of our betrothal before these others then?" he stubbornly pressed her, knowing instinctively he would win with her, as he always did. It was a circumstance he never thought much about, or cared about, before now, when she looked so weak and ill, so vulnerable. Still, this must be done. Reluctantly, Maria nodded again and the others withdrew—all but the commanding guard, who seemed to have a suspiciously inappropriate expression of concern etched into the straight angles of his face.

"It is time for us to speak of that day," he said once they were alone and he had moved to her bedside.

Maria coughed into her hand. It was a moment before she responded. "It is one thing for me to learn to quietly tolerate your infidelities," she said achingly. "It will be quite another to speak of them with you."

"It cannot be an infidelity, Maria, if you and I are not wed."

"We are formally betrothed," she volleyed weakly, "which you well know is as good as married. I have waited for you such a long time, Raphael, and betrayal, no matter the law, wounds the same."

"Forgive me for hurting you."

"I cannot. It was a vision that will be with me forever, you there wantonly with that girl, heaped together, bare and tangled, like rutting dogs!"

"She is not just a girl, Maria. I am in love with her."

Pressing her face into her hands, Maria began to weep. It was at that moment, and for the first time in his life, Raphael thought what that emotion would feel like—the cold absolute of betrayal. He heard her words echo back at him as if they were his own. How might he feel, the question came to him, if it were Margherita before him, the same declaration on her lips as were now on his?

"I have treated you poorly these past years," he said very tenderly. "I hate that I have never once considered your feelings, and now that I have, there seems to be nothing I can do about it."

He rubbed a hand behind his neck awkwardly when she made no reply. Now that he had opened the wound it would be better for her to hear all of it. Steadying himself, Raphael glanced around the elegant room, with its fringed carpets, painted beams, ornate inlaid chest, and grand carved bed. On the bedside table were combs of ivory next to a collection of foul-smelling, silver-lidded jars.

"I intend to marry her, Maria."

When she looked up, her tearstained face was set. "You will marry me. It was agreed to by our families, and both of us."

"No," he said very gently. "I will only ever belong to her."

"You have belonged to me for four years!"

"Not truly. Not my heart. She is the only one who has ever possessed that."

They were quiet with one another then. Awkward strangers. "I am asking you for my freedom," he finally said.

"My uncle would never agree, even if I did," she warned in a wounded voice that came just above a whisper, and Raphael knew that she was probably right.

"Can you not reason with him?"

"Not about that. It is not that he finds you so pleasing as a husband for me, as that he despises the notion of losing."

"He is right to see me for what I am, for your sake," he said, then tenderly kissed the top of her head. "I swear to you, I wish you only happiness, Maria."

"I could have had that with you."

"I would have broken your heart. You deserve better than that."

He turned to go, and as he did she called out to him. "Watch your baker's girl very carefully, Raphael, for she will not be safe once my uncle hears news of this."

"I shall consider myself warned," he replied, trying very hard to conjure his old, very cavalier smile as he considered the harsh change in Cardinal Bibbiena. The expression of pure hate in those eyes was symbolized now, it seemed, in a small, hotly contested ruby ring.

THEY WERE working on the Battle of Ostia sequence in the pope's new room. The water-based pigments they were spreading onto the freshly spread moist lime plaster were changing colors in a way Raphael did not like, but Giulio had taken charge, ordering some of the apprentices to remix a batch of new shades while others began to layer over the work with new plaster to begin the area again.

"I heard what you did for Signorina Luti. The new house," Giulio cautiously began as Raphael stood behind him, hands on his hips, amid the collection of water-filled buckets, paint pots, and brushes. "What a splendid gift."

"If I could give her the world, Giulio, I surely would."

"So she will no longer need to come to the studio to meet with you."

"No."

"Or ever then to the house on the Via dei Coronari?"

Raphael turned to look more closely at the artist he considered his heir apparent, studying him for nuances as he would a model. "You are inferring something are you, *caro?*"

Giulio picked up a moist cloth and wiped his hands. "It concerns Elena, *mastro.*"

Raphael's face changed swiftly, brightening as the question crossed his lips. "Has she found another circumstance at last?"

"I ask you as a personal favor to allow her to remain with you."

Raphael looked away from the scaffolding and the work going on above them. He turned his attention to Giulio then, trying to study the intent behind the request. After a moment, Raphael led him out into the corridor with a firm hand. When they were alone, Raphael breathed deeply and leaned against a wall beside a large window barred outside by an iron grille. He looked reflectively out at the ordered courtyard with its fountain, sculptures, and ornamental hedges.

"Forgive me, *caro,* but I cannot permit that," he replied in a low voice, fearing the spies who were frequently around. "I can have nothing that might endanger things with Signorina Luti until we are married."

"But you said yourself you have been truthful with her about your past with women."

"As I told Elena herself when we spoke of this, it would be quite another thing for the woman of my heart to be faced with the evidence of so great an indiscretion right in my household. The truth, Giulio, is that I despise myself for what I did to the girl. I have tried every way I can think to make amends but she has refused me, and so now I would prefer to think it never happened."

"Elena will not speak of it. She told you so herself!"

Raphael turned his gaze upon Giulio, his eyes widening in surprise. "You were listening?"

"Not intentionally, no. But the result is the same. I regret that I did, but I heard your exchange myself and I know that Elena wishes greatly to remain in service to you. And work for her is essential."

Raphael had begun to pace across the polished parquet flooring. *"Per l'amor di Dio,* Giulio! I cannot help that! I offered her money but she refused me! What more than that can I do?"

"Allow her to keep what she needs as payment for what you took from her!" Giulio leaned forward, his body tight. "I am asking as a personal favor, *mastro.* Allow her to keep her dignity by believing the words both of you spoke, that it was a mistake, that it is finished between you and in the past."

"And if Margherita were to discover it, and discover that I maintain the girl still?"

"The only three who know of it have a vested interest in keeping it concealed."

"You, Giulio *mio?* What is your interest?"

For the first time his confidence faded just slightly as Raphael looked at him in open surprise.

"She comes from a good family and she does not deserve what will happen to her if you do not change your mind!"

He lifted a brow. "You have not answered my question. Have you come to care for the girl?"

"Not in the way you mean, *mastro!* I have little time for a life of my own. What I have is dedicated to our work, of course."

Raphael stroked his chin, considering that. All of these weeks Giulio had lived with him so that he might not only separate him from his father, but introduce the naive boy to all of a man's pleasures, which he had been avoiding. Now Giulio appeared to have done it on his own.

"When the heart is involved, things can change."

"I have some small concern for her, that is all."

"Forgive me, *caro.*" His hand fell away from his chin. "But I have too much to lose if I change my mind."

Giulio had never confronted Raphael. He had never confronted anyone. But something had changed. Whatever it was, it had been sudden within him, oddly profound, and it involved Elena di Francesco Guazzi.

"Then *I* cannot remain as your assistant."

"Surely you do not mean that. We have so much work before us. Work I could not fathom completing without you."

"Then respectfully, *mastro,* change your mind in this."

"This is a new life for me, Giulio. Signorina Luti has given me that life, shown me a heart I never knew I had, hope, love . . . She is everything to me. You ask too much."

"I have heard it said that *everything* comes with a price," Giulio dared to say.

"If you were anyone else, Giulio, *anyone,* I would not even entertain such a threat! I need not answer for my choices to anyone. Do you understand that?"

"I have lived in your shadow long enough to know it well."

Raphael looked at him incredulously. "Can it be that two souls so alike as we must part over this?"

"I could not remain with you knowing she had gone, and why."

"And I would lose my own life rather than risk losing Margherita! She would despise me if she knew how base and self ish I had been with that vulnerable young girl for my own pleasure! *Dío,* I despise myself!"

A moment passed. Raphael cleared his throat, glanced around, then settled his sight on a pillar through the window and across the courtyard, in order to steady himself from a blow he had not seen coming. He could not look at his assistant. Giulio was so like him, and so quickly had become a part of the demanding and tumultuous process that was Raphael's life. Giulio Romano had entered the complex and demanding works in progress, yet found the pace—and quickly made himself indispensable. He was the best, his brightest star. Raphael could not imagine any loss in the world, save Margherita, that would be more heart-wrenching than losing Giulio Romano.

"There will be a handsome severance to tide you over until you find a new studio, which of course you quickly shall," he offered, his breath painful in his chest, knowing well that Sebastiano would snap Giulio up in a heartbeat.

"That will be much appreciated, *mastro.*"

Neither man moved. Raphael, still focused on the pillar, then rubbed his hands together, but he would say nothing more, in spite of how he ached to do so. Everything was over suddenly for the sake of a servant girl with whom he had once made a drastic mistake. A mistake that had just cost him dearly.

GIULIO WAS gathering up the few belongings he had at the house on the Via dei Coronari and preparing to take them downstairs when Elena appeared at his door. They were alone in the house now.

"You are leaving?" Elena asked. She stood in the doorway dressed in an elegantly simple costume of pale-green. Her hair was tucked beneath a matching cap, and her head was tipped against the doorjamb.

"*Sì.*"

"You have found another circumstance then?"

"Not yet. But I will."

"Then why not wait until you have?"

He stopped and turned to her. He was still disappointed, and it showed in his pure, youthful features. "It is complicated, Elena."

It was the first time he had spoken her name aloud, and in a familiar way. The sound of it resonated, stopping them both. "I must leave here, that is all," he added, knowing he could not possibly tell her the truth.

Giulio ran a hand behind his neck as she studied his expression, her light-gray eyes cautious and discerning.

"I have become rather accustomed to having you here," she said in an amazingly frank and open tone that stunned him. "You have kept me good company in the early evenings before I return home."

He turned to her. They were separated by an inlaid chest at the foot of his bed. "You always seemed rather uncomfortable by my nearness," he told her truthfully, feeling an odd sensation that it truly mattered what she said next. As he waited, watching her, Giulio felt the hair prick at the back of his neck, realizing that Elena was the first girl he had ever been anywhere alone with in his life. He knew now how much he desired that.

"Although I was unaccustomed to it, it became necessary for me to work. Cardinal Bibbiena was my mother's childhood friend. She was able to call in one last favor with him, which is the only reason I was given a circumstance with Signor Raphael. My discomfort has been less with you than with reconciling myself to that fate."

He was, for a moment, moved to apologize for being forward enough that she was reminded of her family's social and financial decline. But when he tried to speak them aloud, the words would not come. Confusion, and the barrier of his own long-held control, stopped him. The charged silence then became something awkward, full of things aching to be said. But neither had the power to say them.

"I wish you well then," Elena said thinly.

"I fear he shall be rather alone without either of us. We were, both of us, his true friends," Giulio said, yet knowing that Raphael would be too taken up with his new inamorata to notice it, or to miss the presence of either one of them, for the moment at least.

✢ 22 ✣

SILVERY LATE-AFTERNOON SUNLIGHT SLANTED IN THROUGH the high arched windows of the vastly impressive stables as Antonio swept straw into a pile for Signor Chigi's best English bay. As he did, a group of men in close conversation came through the stable doors and moved steadily nearer to him. All of them were grandly dressed in knee-length capes of velvet and brocade, and wearing small hats trimmed with feathers and jewels. And he could see, at last, that the man in the center was Agostino Chigi himself. Antonio had seen the banker at a distance one other time, but he had never had occasion to be this close. He felt himself go suddenly cold and his skin turn to gooseflesh at his nearness to such power and influence.

He could hear them speaking of the pope's hunting party, the opulence of it, where great, brightly colored tents were erected and then filled with tables, chairs, food, wine, and musicians to entertain his guests. Imagine a life, he thought, leaning on his shovel, where one had the luxury of time and education to recall such banalities in a walk through the stables. As one of the horses whinnied, he knew this was his chance, a pivotal moment for a simple stableman who craved better, and strongly believed that he deserved it.

Antonio moved forward on firm legs that nonetheless began to buckle with anticipation as they neared him in their fine cloaks, braided with silver thread and jewel-spotted fingers. Antonio nodded deeply, hoping his reverence would sugarcoat the warning he intended to deliver.

"My great pardon, *signore.*" He felt the words pass across his lips, yet the sensation of them like this, spoken with such deference, was foreign. It was not his custom to openly defer to anyone. He held his breath and waited for one of them to react. They did not.

"Signor Chigi, *per favore,*" he called out to them again, summoning what he could from his own shallow well of bravery.

To his relief this time, as he had no other strategy, they stopped directly before him. In an instant, their collective, critical gaze was upon him. Antonio felt his heart race wildly, but he forced himself to stay absolutely calm, divining that they would respect the appearance of outward dignity in another man.

"What is it, boy?" asked one of them, a portly, silver-haired man with pockmarked skin and a bulbous nose.

"I desire a private word with Signor Chigi," he said as boldly as if he had a right to ask for such a thing. There was a moment of silence and then the men—five of them, including Chigi—began to laugh at the absurdity of the request.

"Go back to the dung you were mucking out, boy!"

"Now, now, Frederico, that was unnecessarily harsh," Chigi chuckled beneath his breath as he lay a long finger upon his dark beard.

"Surely one must know his place here," the bald man argued.

"It is a private matter concerning Signor Raffaello," Antonio interrupted, unwilling to lose this single opportunity.

Chigi arched a thick black brow. "It seems to me his bold spirit has earned him a moment of elevation from that place," he decreed with boastful magnanimity.

"As you wish." The bald man shook his head disdainfully. "But we dare not be late to meet with the Holy Father because of this."

"I will give him but a moment to state his business." Chigi took a few steps away from his companions and Antonio followed. They were facing a wall of horse stalls, each with carved and grandly painted doors, housing some of the most shining, expensive animals in Rome.

"I warn you, boy, before you speak a word more, I will not look favorably upon idle gossip," Chigi warned.

"I come not with gossip of the artist but firsthand knowledge, Signor Chigi."

"You must understand, boy, how unlikely that would seem."

This was it. He would have no other opportunity. Antonio felt his lungs constrict. "He is bedding my betrothed, and he claims now actually to *love* her."

Chigi barked out a sudden harsh sound, throwing his head back in ribald laughter until tears came to his eyes. "Would that I had one of his paintings for every time I heard *that* of the *mastro!*" He shook his head. "Forgive me, boy—"

"The name is Perazzi, *signore. Antonio* Perazzi," he said, feeling his own sense of indignation rise up no matter how he tried to suppress it.

"Well, in any case, you would do well to understand that to be the oldest tune played in Rome, Antonio. I am sorry for you if you have been hurt by the loss of a girl, but, mark my words, she

will return to you, for there will be no other option once he has
tired of her. She will return less of an innocent certainly, yet far
more capable of keeping you happy beneath your bedcovers!"

Chigi was still laughing as he turned to walk away, shaking his
head amid small bursts of laughter from himself and the others.

"He has bought her a house on the Via Alessandrina," Antonio flatly announced, now loudly enough for all of them to hear.
"Her father tells me she keeps him from his work night and day,
and that he rarely returns now to his studio."

It was that last revelation that stopped the great banker, who
realized that he had seen only Raphael's assistants working on the
pope's new frescoes for many days, and that Raphael was still only
in the beginning stage on the new fresco at his villa. For the rest
of it, all Chigi had seen so far were various sketches and drawings.
As his own wedding to his mistress drew ever nearer, Chigi
intended the frescoed Marriage of Cupid and Psyche not only as a
representation of the event, and a gift for his bride, but to adorn
the wall for their magnificent wedding banquet.

The thought that Raphael might be too distracted to complete it angered him greatly.

"What is in this for you?"

"The return of my woman, *signore*. Only that."

"As I said, she *will* be back when she begins to bore him."

"Sooner will be better than later. And humbled to me for this
humiliation will be better still."

"You are a bright man, Antonio Perazzi," Chigi smiled thinly,
scratching his beard, "and not a little brave to confront me with
this, as you have. They are assets I value."

Antonio nodded respectfully. "Many thanks, *signore*."

Chigi moved near to him again, put an arm around his shoulder as an old friend might, then said in a very low voice, "Can I
trust you to be my ears and eyes in this matter until it is resolved?
Bring me more evidence of this if it continues on?"

He wanted to say that he would indeed—for a price. But
Antonio thought better of being mercenary with the second most

powerful man in Rome. If he were patient, there would be a handsome reward when the time was right.

❧ 23 ❧

MAY 1515

SPRING WAS WELCOME TO ALL BUT THE HOLY FATHER, who was taken up with his dangerously mounting financial debt. The pope was made particularly angry by his advisers' inability to solve the continuing crisis. In light of his fiscal complications, and his excessive spending, the need for the sale of indulgences had created greater complications than he had expected. The growing voices of dissent had begun to alarm the usually jovial pontiff and make him susceptible to great bouts of temper.

Those who knew him well walked a fine line. They could try to obtain an audience with him early enough in the morning to find him well rested, or late enough in the afternoon to see that he had consumed enough food to mollify him. So it was when Raphael came to the pontiff's private audience chamber, along with two of his assistants, who bore for their master the newly finished draped image of Margherita Luti as the Madonna.

As Giovanni da Udine set it on an easel, then peeled back the black velvet covering, the image unfolded before them all. Light hitting darkness. Supple shapes. Softened angles. Muted, innovative color. And at the center—the face. Soft, luminescent. And the eyes, so penetrating, were inescapable to the viewer.

From his velvet-covered papal throne, Pope Leo glanced at Cardinal de' Medici, who sat in a chair of embossed leather with gold studs placed against a tapestry-covered wall. Then he turned his critical gaze upon Raphael. There was a heavy and awkward silence in the private rooms of the pontiff, with its heavy wooden desk, prie-dieu, and creaking wood-plank floors.

"Does the finished product please Your Holiness then, or do

you, perhaps, desire alterations?" Raphael finally asked, breaking a dangerously long silence as the pope and his cousin studied the painting.

Pope Leo glanced at his cousin, then looked up at Raphael. "It is a masterpiece, my son. A true, breathtaking masterpiece. Look at how the Madonna hovers above the clouds there," he pointed. "Celestial, and yet she is everywoman. A woman, a Madonna, who is real in her beauty and emotion. She . . . her face . . . " He bent his head. "For some reason she makes me want to weep."

"I am honored that Your Holiness is pleased." Raphael bowed reverently.

"Rather, it is that I am—enchanted." The pope turned back, settling his bulging-eyed gaze on Raphael, who stood, hands clasped behind his back, in grass-green summer satin. "So this is the model of whom you spoke?"

"It is."

"I should have known to trust your instinct in this, Raffaello *mio*. Her face will bring great solace and peace to the worshippers at the church of San Sisto."

And he, not his predecessor, would be credited for delivering it to them. It would become yet another symbol of this pope's legacy. "I pray Your Holiness is correct."

"I am a wise man, Raphael, named pontiff by the intervention of God Himself, and so I am never wrong, as my words come through me directly from Him. And you would do well to heed them."

"Your words of wisdom are gold to me, Your Holiness," Raphael wisely replied, with just the proper tone of schooled humility to flatter a vain man.

"A pleasing thing to hear." Pope Leo smiled in response. "Then, let me say that it has come to my attention, my son, that, of late, in spite of my rather stern warning, you have become distracted from your work for us here, and elsewhere."

Raphael studied the face of the pontiff. He had not expected this. He was set off balance by it, which he knew was the purpose.

Raphael searched his mind for the diplomatic response. He had seen the pope's increasing edginess of late, and on occasion been the victim of it.

"Is Your Holiness displeased with some of my other work?"

"Not yet," the pontiff replied, reaching up for the ever-present tray of pastries. After a moment, his fat hand hovering, he chose one, stuffed a portion of it between his lips, and slowly chewed. Then he spoke again. "But we are concerned for your ability to fully concentrate on that to which you have previously committed."

Raphael looked at the cardinal, then back at the pope. "May I ask from what foundation Your Holiness's concerns arise?"

Cardinal de' Medici whispered into the pontiff's ear, then turned his gaze to the window. "You are behind schedule on Signor Chigi's wedding fresco, are you not, my son?"

"A few weeks, perhaps, but I did not promise its completion for yet another—"

De' Medici leaned over and whispered to the pope again, never looking directly at Raphael. "And the decorated *stuffeta*, when was that due for Cardinal Bibbiena?"

"It is a challenging time, Your Holiness," he truthfully admitted. "My position as commissary of antiquities, which of course is a great honor, takes a large portion of my time, as do my drawings and the architectural planning for the new Saint Peter's."

The pope's bulging eyes twinkled. "As does a new woman!"

"I shall not allow anything to interfere with my work for *you*. Your Holiness has my word upon it," he said, not wanting to become engaged in a new debate over Margherita. "Your next *stanza* will be completed by month's end."

"A man of honor must never promise what cannot be delivered."

"Your Holiness speaks wise words as always, but it shall be done."

"It is a blessing then, I should imagine, that you have the able hand of Signor Romano to oversee this, and assist you in all else.

We have seen much of his work here, and it is obvious to all who have why he holds so high a place in your studio. Delegating competently, we too know well, is as important as creating."

Warily looking for some sort of trap set cleverly here between the two men, Raphael glanced at the face of Cardinal de' Medici. Was it known, he wondered, the estrangement of the artist and his talented young student, Giulio Romano? Since coming to Rome, he had never taken time for himself. Now that he was trying to balance work with a small glimmer of a personal life, the town was in an uproar.

The pope's inferences could not have been more clear, and Raphael felt the weight of expectation and consequence pressing down upon him: his allegiance to the pontiff versus his love for Margherita.

But how could he reconcile them and not endanger one for the other?

"We have heard it said that there is a new woman in your life. Did we not long ago speak of that in the most serious terms, you and I?"

Raphael felt himself tense, yet he struggled to keep his composure. "I believe we spoke of my former penchant for loose women, Your Holiness, and your wish for me that I repent from knowing them. And I have done that in favor of love."

"*Love,* is it? Can the powerful want of fleshly delights not urge the logic of the mind to believe almost anything?" he patiently asked.

"Respectfully, this concerns my heart, Your Holiness—more than anything."

The pontiff finished munching a round, sugar-covered pastry and absently brushed away the crumbs that had pooled in his ample lap. "And what of the cardinal's niece, the girl to whom you are formally betrothed?"

"I can no longer stay true to that pledge, and I have told her so."

"And what? Do you intend to *marry* this . . . this girl who models for you when she is not baking bread in Trastevere?"

"You know of Signorina Luti?"

"Does not all of Rome, my son? I am told it has become quite the scandal."

Raphael conceded that with a nod. "My greatest desire is to marry her, Your Holiness, and vanquish any scandal."

Deep in thought, Pope Leo rubbed his fleshy chin between his thumb and forefinger as the room fell silent. "Entirely out of the question," he finally decreed. "That will not be possible."

"May I ask why?"

"The reasons are many. First, we have not known of another important *mastro* such as yourself who has ever entertained thoughts of more than the involvement of a casual mistress in his life. Not Michelangelo Buonarroti, nor Leonardo da Vinci, certainly. Work can be the only true passion for men like you in order to remain successful. That is the first important reason."

Raphael longed to point out that both men had long been known as partaking of the same private pleasures as Il Sodoma, and that, therefore, marriage had not tempted them. A wealth of young and handsome boys roamed the halls and chambers of the Vatican complex in the presence of this powerful cardinal or that, but he dare not speak it.

"And the other reason?"

"The other is Cardinal Bibbiena. He will not allow you to shame his niece and dishonor his family in that way when you have been her betrothed for several years already. The cardinal is furious enough with you that there is such public talk of another woman, and one of such scandalously low birth, in your life."

"There will be less talk if I am allowed to marry her."

"Out of the question! No. Now that is the end of it. We shall entertain talk of it no more!"

Raphael could see the pope was becoming angry. The red of his face had deepened to a passionate crimson. But he would not—could not—let this issue die. He had never in his life wanted to marry anyone, or even to be with anyone forever, until he met Margherita. He would rather go against the great powers in Rome—Agostino Chigi, Cardinal Bibbiena, and the Holy Father himself—than lose the love of his life.

"SO WILL YOU AWARD him the contract for yet another *stanza?*" Giuliano de' Medici asked his brother once Raphael had been dismissed. "Or will you toss a bone at last to poor Michelangelo?"

The pontiff drew yet another pastry from the tray, an oblong, sugared thing, dotted with almond slivers, and chewed slowly before he replied.

"Alas, I have growing concerns over Raphael, brother. The once quiet gossip about this woman has grown swiftly to a roar here in Rome."

"Talk of it *is* everywhere," Giuliano de' Medici confirmed. "Agostino came to me last night with the same complaint. Raphael's immortal soul is surely in jeopardy."

"It is not his soul but rather my legacy that concerns me! He must keep working!"

"Chigi had been told by a source that the woman, this baker's daughter, of all things, has seduced Raphael to such an extent that he is rarely even at his studio. Not so long ago, he practically lived there!"

Pope Leo gazed back at the painted Madonna. "Perfect as a model or not, it appears this comely *peasant* has, at the very least, altered our Raphael's good judgment, putting the completion of our most important commissions at risk, and endangering his standing with Cardinal Bibbiena."

"That niece of Bernardo's does mean the world to him. The only time I have ever seen anything close to a human side of him is when it concerns Maria. I cannot think that he will let this go if Raphael means to carry on with his strumpet much longer."

"But what can we do? Lust is a very powerful emotion—or so I am told," the pope observed.

"As to Michelangelo and Raphael, it has long been a personal contest between the two. Buonarroti certainly has been fanning the flames of gossip, even from the distance of Florence."

"Ah, *sì*," the pope nodded, doubling his chin. "Did it not become so while Buonarroti was working on the Sistine Chapel and Raphael was just down the hall doing our Stanza della Segnatura?"

"Indeed it seems to have begun there, each of them spying on the other's work and comparing it to his own. Now it has become a further contest with Michelangelo's second, Sebastiano," admitted the pope's brother. "Perhaps we shall gain more from a distracted Raphael if he feels the pressure of competition."

"Threaten him? As if he is no longer the only fair-haired boy in the eyes of his Holy Father?"

"Precisely."

The pope began to smile. "There is something Raphael wants . . . something he has asked me for. A ruby ring that was uncovered at the Domus Aurea. I suspect it is for that girl. I have always given him his every desire in the past. But what if— "

"Thought out like a true Medici!" Giuliano coldly laughed. "Before we take a more drastic course of action, why not do as you suggest. Put him in his place a bit, with the notion that disappointment can actually befall him like everyone else. Then let us sit back for just a bit longer, and see what Raphael will do."

MARGHERITA was sitting alone in the library, with its soaring bookcases and heavily musty smell of time and old leather. She was trying to read a copy of Ovid's writings on love when Raphael found her. He stood for a moment watching her finger moving slowly over the words, her head bent in concentration. He was filled with a new wave of love for her, seeing the furrowing of her brow into an absolute frown of determination.

"I wonder if Nero's Poppaea had this much difficulty!" she chuckled, glancing up and seeing him.

Raphael knelt and took up both of her hands, not responding to her query. "We must speak of a serious matter."

"You are troubled?"

"Only by the nature of the confession now before me."

"You feel you have made an error about this house?"

"Never that!" he smiled grimly, pressing her hands together and bringing them to his lips. "You are where you absolutely must be. No, this concerns a time before we met. A different girl. She kept my house for me on the Via dei Coronari."

Margherita studied the expression on his face before she said, "And this girl who kept your house held some portion of your heart, as well?"

"Elena never possessed my heart. It was only an indiscretion by a lonely, overworked artist, with more lust than judgment, an act that was regretted by both of us soon afterward. So regretted and feared, in fact, that I asked her to seek employment elsewhere after I met you so that you might not discover it."

She sank back, her lips gently parting as she closed the book and settled it onto her lap. "I see."

"In it, I was so unspeakably selfish, Margherita. I hate even to say it for the truth there, but I fully see now that I sacrificed a young woman's livelihood, and her virtue, so that I would not risk your ever meeting her," he confessed, feeling like a boy suddenly in his desire for forgiveness and understanding. "And I lost Giulio over it as well."

"Your assistant is gone from the studio when you are drowning in work? But why did you not tell me that?"

He thought for a moment. When he spoke at last, he looked at her squarely. "I was ashamed, Margherita. Giulio had befriended Elena while he was staying with me. In addition to being a brilliant artist, he is a sensitive soul, and he could not bear to see me make an honest young woman suffer like that because of my own sense of shame and regret. He said that if I insisted on turning her out, he, too, would be forced to look elsewhere for employment."

Margherita was struck. She had known only a little of Giulio Romano, but she had seen how essential the young man was to the *mastro*'s success. "Did you truly believe I would not understand?"

"I know not what I believed." He washed a hand heavily over

his face. "Only that it has been many years since I have felt any deep emotion at all toward anyone. I was greedy with it, Margherita, like a man who has gone too long without water and then suddenly finds a fresh cool stream." He drew in a breath. "I was so wrong. I know that now."

"Then you must do what you can to change it."

She spoke so simply and full of conviction that he felt cleansed by it. She was right, of course. "And the girl, Elena, you will not blame her or be disturbed by her presence?"

She reached out to caress his face. Her own expression was full of kind understanding. "Poor Raphael, caught between so many things, and so many people. Elena was someone from your past. A moment. I hope to be a lifetime, *amore mio*," she said tenderly. "She need have no fear of me—*if* she will take *you* back, that is."

Raphael pulled her forward and kissed her deeply. "You always make me want to be a better man." He smiled when they parted. "I will try to find her at once, and I will do my best to apologize, whatever her response."

"Whatever her response, it is the right thing to do."

He smiled as he shook his head. "For a man who once believed it was the rest of the world that needed what *I* had to offer them, I am finding that I was actually in need as well. I certainly do need both of them in my life," he confessed, kissing her again. "But my need above all others has very swiftly become *you*."

24

ELENA WAS SHOWN INTO THE LARGE LIBRARY ON THE VIA Alessandrina, with its ancient books and windows of colored leaded glass—blue, red, and green—in geometric designs. A candle chandelier hung from its center. The space was enormous, giving the impression of great power. Its large and heavy carved doors were closed behind her with a sharp and fateful click, leaving her in the shadows and sunlight that filtered through the glass. She stiffened, and forced herself to prepare for what would come next. Then she saw that it was Margherita, not Raphael, sitting before her beside the fire, in a tall chair of embossed leather with silver studs. She had faced other disappointments. Surely she could face this.

Elena was not alone in her trepidation. Everyone in the house had wondered why Margherita had insisted on speaking privately with the former house girl. Particularly Raphael, who, along with the others, was not admitted to the library when Elena arrived. After a moment, Margherita lay her book onto a small side table, stood, and advanced toward Elena, who had begun, quite noticeably, to tremble.

"You asked to see me, Signora Luti," said Elena in a tone that came just barely above a whisper. She had wisely chosen the title for a married woman, rather than that of a young girl, out of respect.

"I did." Margherita steepled her hands, once covered in baker's flour, now ornamented with gold. "So then." She exhaled, and waited for a moment. "You are Elena."

"I am, *signora.*"

The two women faced one another directly as Magherita walked slowly into the colored light cast from the windows, the odd turn of fate obvious to both of them now. Elena born to privilege, reduced in circumstance by fate. And Margherita born into poverty, elevated now by an unlikely love.

"What is it you would want with me, may I ask, Signora Luti?" Elena haltingly asked, as frightened by the question itself as the response.

One heartbeat, then two. The small fire in the hearth crackled, then flared in the silence as each gazed upon the face of the other. "I shall be blunt. It is my wish that you accept a position as my personal attendant and companion."

A hand splayed across Elena's mouth, and she blurted out before she could think, "I could not!"

"Your assets are wasted in domestic chores, here or anywhere else," Margherita calmly said, beginning to deliver the small speech she had been practicing all morning. "I know of your family and your background, Elena. But much about all of our lives has changed these past months." She straightened the folds of her skirts and continued. "There are few I can trust in this new life. Among those few I count Giulio as a kind and honorable soul. He believed in you enough to leave Raphael over your dismissal, which is certainly a good enough indication of your character."

"Forgive me, *signora,* but to serve *you* of all people!"

"I wish you not to serve me, Elena. Rather, I believe I would benefit from the companionship of a steady ally to help me navigate this frightening and complex world in which I find myself and which, most days, frightens me quite to death. And someone to teach me to seem like a lady when I am presented to Signor Sanzio's friends. A circumstance I have thus far avoided, but which I must face, sooner or later."

"But you are a lady, Signora Luti. The finest!"

"Not one like you, taught from birth."

"It is difficult to believe that you would do this for *me,* take this chance, considering all things."

"It is no more difficult to believe than that you would help me learn what I need to know." Margherita smiled tentatively then. Her dark eyes were full of sincerity. "I need someone I can trust, Elena. The fact that Giulio trusts you is enough. You would begin as my lady's maid and companion. The rest beyond that is ours to make between us for ourselves."

"But what happened between—"

"Let us speak not of such things that cannot be changed, and which have no bearing on tomorrow. As a foolish young girl, not so very long ago, I believed it was unseemly for a woman to earn money to help her family. Knowing of you, of your determination, your spirit, and your pride, I am ashamed of that view, Elena. Ashamed when, looking at you, I see how noble a thing it can be. So rather than look to either of our pasts, let us begin a new history—if you are willing."

Margherita then indicated a chair beside her in which she

wished Elena to sit. After a moment's hesitation, Elena sank onto the edge of the tapestry-covered chair, with its finely carved arms and legs. "So tell me then. You truly grew to womanhood in this sort of luxury?" Margherita asked her, glancing around her own magnificent library, still in awe of it.

"Indeed, it was so. And yet I have learned through my own transformation that it can all vanish as quickly as it comes. No lady must ever forget that, no matter how secure she believes herself to be."

"I see that we have more in common than anyone else might believe." There was another moment of silence, this one fueled by contemplation.

"Will you agree then?" Margherita finally asked, watching her.

"If you are absolutely certain it is what you wish."

"I could not be more certain."

Elena nodded deeply, deferring to a girl who once might well have deferred to *her*. "Then it would be my honor to serve you, *signora*."

"It is my better hope that we shall not be mistress and servant, but rather one day that we shall become friends," Margherita said, her words full of sincerity. "It seems I need a *true* friend above all other things if I am ever to move forward, as Signor Raphael wishes me to do."

"HOW CAN YOUR HEART be so good?" Raphael asked her later. They lay together in the grand tapestry-draped poster bed, listening to a soft summer rain beyond the shuttered windows of the dark-wood bedchamber they shared.

"It is not a question of that."

He turned onto his side, propping himself up on an elbow and looking at her amid the candle glow that flickered and danced around them. "It is to me. I am the painter, yet it is you who see clear through to *my* soul."

She ran a hand along his jaw. "Elena is a kind and gentle girl. I did nothing you would not have done for love of me."

"You do things every day for me, Margherita, that my mind could never have conjured."

"Flattering words that seem most unlikely."

"Very likely, alas," he disagreed. "And true. Before there was you, I lived nearly every day of my life enjoying what the world, and the people in it, could do for me. Appalling as it is to admit, I came to feel entitled to that at every turn . . . and I got it nearly everywhere I looked."

"Until a baker's daughter on Il Gianicolo turned away from you."

"Until that day." He smiled. Then his face went suddenly serious. "And because of it, I wish to give you something extraordinary."

"Speak not of that again. You have already given me the world. What more could I desire than what I have this very moment?"

"I told you that I wanted you to have something," Raphael insisted. "The meaning of which you shall understand the moment you behold it. A thing," he mused, "as rare and irreplaceable as you are."

"I see you have something particular in mind," she remarked with a little half smile.

"Oh, indeed I do," said Raphael, never having forgotten the exquisite ruby ring, and his many cautious inquiries to Pope Leo on its behalf. Now that the pontiff was so pleased with his new Madonna, it seemed unlikely that anything—or anyone—would prevent him from possessing the ruby ring that was meant absolutely for Margherita's hand. Not even a vindictive man like Cardinal Bibbiena.

❧ *25* ❧

SEPTEMBER 1515

AS SUMMER TURNED TO FALL, AND ELENA DI FRANCESCO Guazzi became Margherita's companion, Giulio Romano and Raphael were reconciled. There was too much at stake, with all of the outstanding commissions, for them to stand on past angers. Giulio returned to the studio by day to work on the elaborate frescoes in the pope's private dining room, and at night he returned to his suite of rooms upstairs at the house on the Via dei Coronari. While he spent most of his time with Margherita at her new house, Raphael maintained his former address out of respect for the woman he still was not free to marry.

His personal conflicts now resolved, Raphael forced himself back into a rigorous routine of work, trying to appease the various factions who had come to question his dedication. Giulio had heard a rumor that was swiftly spreading, that the pope was entertaining the idea of awarding a new and important commission to Michelangelo Buonarroti.

Not only that, but Agostino Chigi was said to want Sebastiano Luciani, of all artists, involved in ornamenting the room where the Marriage of Cupid and Psyche was nearing completion. This, after Chigi had refused him work, in favor of Raphael, for several years. The potential danger in that could not be overlooked.

A softly growing whisper of a downfall was in the air, but Raphael alone could not stop or confront it. The whispers of it were as forceful as the wind, and as impossible to contain. But in spite of the danger there, Raphael would not give up the love of his life.

Trying to stem the potentially dangerous tide, Raphael worked like a demon late into every night. Only then, his vision blurred and his painting hand aching, would he go, exhausted, hungry, and ravenous with desire, to spend a few passionate hours with Margherita. He would rise then in the early morning darkness once again to tackle, full force, the great volumes of work that awaited him.

In the months that followed Giulio Romano's return to his life, Raphael's production of masterpieces once again peaked, particularly in his use of Margherita as model. He sketched her first in red chalk, then painted her several times more as his

Madonna. Particularly, he became intent on turning the sketch he had made that first night in her new house into a finished, richly painted Madonna. He envisioned her seated in a chair, holding Matteo Perazzi, looking directly at the beholder, as any other dedicated mother might do, in clothing that bespoke a common life, not divinity.

The portrait, done in a tondo format, painted within a circle, felt magical the moment it began to burst forth from his paintbrush. It was swiftly praised by those fortunate enough to view it. But, amid all of the Vatican work, the Chigi fresco he was straining to complete, and the intricate and laborious designs of Saint Peter's, the project that still obsessed him through the next autumn was to paint Margherita. This time, however, she would not be the Madonna; rather, he wished to paint her as herself, in portraiture, as he had done for Maddalena Doni. As the elegant, noble woman of calmness, dignity, and grace that she had become.

"I cannot possibly wear *that!*" she laughed incredulously, seeing the opulent gown laid out on her bed on a warm Sunday in September. With the sun through the long, half-shuttered windows, it lay there like spun gold and jewels, the sleeves thick layers of billowing snow white silk and intricate gold thread.

"But of course you can!" Raphael smiled devotedly at her. "You must. I absolutely mean to paint you in it!"

"The world would laugh at a peasant girl dressed up as so grand a lady!"

He took her chin in his hand and leveled his eyes on her with absolute adoration. "You are a grand lady, *amore mio*. The fine lady of Raphael di Urbino."

"Ah, the things you can almost make me believe," she wistfully sighed.

"Believe them only because they are true—for to you, I would not speak otherwise."

There was an easel set up in an alcove of their large bedchamber, in which he maintained a carved Venetian desk topped with art supplies, pots full of paintbrushes, ink, pens, and boxes of different colored chalk, and white lead for highlighting, so that he might sketch or paint at any hour or moment he wished. In spite of it officially being Margherita's house, Raphael's presence was everywhere in it. Many of his finest clothes were in her dressing chamber and his favorite wine now filled her cellar. Quick chalk sketches and various studies of Margherita, Donato, and the children lay scattered in almost every room as sources for possible future subjects.

"Signorina di Francesco Guazzi!" he called out to Elena, who seemed properly to always be lingering nearby in case she was required. She came forward from the small dressing room beside the bedchamber, now dressed much better by Margherita in a billowing gown of azure silk with fashionable sleeves slashed with gold and an azure velvet cap.

"See Signora Luti into this new gown at once, *per favore.*"

He gasped when he beheld her a few minutes later walking slowly toward him. In the last of the afternoon sunlight through the tall windows it would not have been possible to do otherwise but feel astonished. How was it, he wondered, that she always made him breathless? She always made him want—no, ache—to ravish her, and that sensation was only heightened with the days. Looking at her now, that desire was mixed with a need to paint her, to create on canvas what he saw, felt—what he ached to possess forever. Her face in that light was luminescent, her head held so high and gracefully that she looked, he thought, like one who had actually been nobly born.

With a soft grunt of intention, Raphael strode across the room, drew up a straight-backed chair, and set it near enough to the window to catch the afternoon light. First must come the sketch, the way he intended to position her, but this crystal, honeyed illumination, like liquid jewels, had already inspired him.

Raphael sat her down, moving her body, her limbs and neck, looking at each part of her with a critical painter's eye: the tilt of her head, the placement of her arms, the exact cast of her gaze. Still, he could not take all of her in, could not process the loveli-

ness of her for the voluminous richness of the fabric that had
enveloped her. The play of light over the skin of her exposed neck
and face was opalescent, shimmering.

He sank before her onto his knees, heels beneath him, a
sketchpad in his hands, and a stub of blue chalk staining his fingertips in the other. Once he began, his hand moved wildly over
the blank pages as his eyes went back and forth from the paper to
her. In an instant, his expression grew wild, his own color heightened, and he could feel his heart hammering the rhythm of
excitement against his rib cage.

Sketching a subject had never seemed erotic to him, not even
the women of the bordello who had allowed themselves to be
used as models for a few extra scudi. He had never had the same
wild sexual urge build within him as he gripped the chalk more
tightly, pressed it against the paper, moved it in a rhythm that in
and of itself was arousing, as he looked at her, studied her. Re-
creating her. Arousing him.

"There, *sì*, like that . . . look at me now . . . *sì, bene*. Your eyes
must be directly upon me!"

Raphael bolted to his feet and took the light Spanish lace
shawl from the back of a chair and put it over her head like a veil.
She was not the Madonna to him now but secular and courtly.
Serene and elegant. Sensual in the reserve that was implied. Just
the thought of her warm, sweet skin beneath those layers was
powerfully erotic to him now, to a point that he could not think
or work but only feel the desire. He was hard, his face was flushed,
the blood having rushed swiftly to every extremity he could feel.
His hand felt on fire as he gripped the chalk so tightly between his
fingers that it snapped in two.

He tossed the pieces onto the floor, along with the sketch, and
came back up onto his knees, clutching her waist and bringing her
forward. His lips moved across her skin, giving in to the warm
swell of her breasts where they met the silk, the beads, and the
lace at the bodice. Elena, who had come into the room behind
them, saw them as they were, and silently withdrew.

Driven, Raphael pressed Margherita back onto the heavy velvet bedcovers. He did not remove the dress or the veil, but only lifted them and the chemise beneath. Then he drew down the delicate lace drawers, tossing them onto the Turkish carpet as he looked to see the beautiful triangle of downy hair, and the private place it hid, waiting there for him alone. Falling to his knees, her hips firmly in his hands, he ran his tongue slowly up her inner thigh until she gasped with guilty pleasure. As his fingers traced the path that his tongue had found, he saw the line of blue chalk from his fingers branding her bare skin in a fresh, erotic way. Even the scent of her flesh, freshly washed, sweetly musky, was a new and powerful element of this addiction.

A single drop of perspiration fell onto the chalk, then dripped in a wet blue line to the place near her navel, mingling, pooling there. Margherita glanced down, seeing it too, her lips parting at the sight. The effect of that on what remained of his reserve was lethal.

Afterward, gently stripped of the costly gown, which now lay neatly at the foot of the bed, they lay naked and drenched in their shared perspiration on the rich, smooth damask bedcover, and Margherita began very softly to laugh.

"Can this be the surprise you had in mind for that gown?"

"This was spontaneous, and a surprise even to me, I assure you."

"It is a pity you got a streak of blue chalk on the skirts, as I fear it will be impossible now to clean."

"Ah, but every time you wear it, I shall feel ardor rise for the memory of how it got there!"

Margherita blushed. "I cannot wear it again."

"Wear it now," he bid her. "Come to dinner with me."

"And where would we dine?"

She saw the moment's hesitation, a flash of uncertainty before he smiled at her. "I dine with Signor Chigi each Saturday, and often the Holy Father attends. From now on, I wish you to accompany me when I do."

The expression that changed her face just then belied, she knew, only a small portion of the terror she felt. Seeing it, Raphael took her powerfully into his arms. "You need not fear any place where I am with you."

"Even the great Raffaello cannot stop their cruel whispers and their raised eyebrows when they see your companion is a baker's daughter."

"Can we not stop them, the force of us, together?"

"I bid you humbly, *amore mio.*" She glanced around at the absolute splendor in which she now lived, the elegantly appointed cocoon that insulated her from the hardships of life. "Do not force me when I have faced so many new changes in my world already."

"I ask, I shall never insist. Nothing gained from you that way would ever please me."

"Then the answer is no. I want not fame, nor notoriety, from what we have together."

"And what are we to do with this most opulent new gown?"

"May I not wear it only for you?"

"Tomorrow you must pose for me and, *sì,* I bid you, wear it again."

"And will it end between us as it has today?"

"Only if I am very fortunate indeed!" Raphael smiled.

MARGHERITA came unexpectedly into the bedchamber, where Elena was laying out the gown and headdress her mistress was to wear first thing tomorrow to visit Padre Giacomo, and to offer what help she could to the poor of his parish. Elena jumped, and the beaded headdress clattered to the floor. But the moment she saw Margherita standing before her, her face blanched, ringing her hands, Elena's fear dissolved. Margherita was ghostly pale, her body rigid with concern.

"You must teach me to dance!"

To Elena's complete surprise, Margherita reached out her hand and clasped Elena's in her own. "*Per favore,*" she said in a tone of gentle pleading that shocked Elena almost as much as it moved her. "I have avoided it for as long as I was able, but I must know enough not to make an entire fool of myself when we are guests at Signor Chigi's coming wedding."

Elena was genuinely surprised. It was spoken of throughout Rome as the event of the year. "You will attend?"

"I would do anything to get out of it. But I cannot. It is the *mastro*'s wish that I accompany him."

"Of course we will all see that you look lovely."

"But eventually I will have to speak! If I cannot dance like the others, I will not succeed, and if I do not do that, Raphael will *know* I can never sustain my place in his life!"

Their relationship, in these first weeks, had been full of such twists and turns, Elena thought, neither of them ever fully in command. And she respected Margherita immensely—for respecting her. "I can teach you what you wish to know."

"*Grazie a Dio!*" Margherita groaned. Unexpectedly, she pulled Elena to her in a sudden, very fond embrace, and began to laugh. "What would I do without you?" Margherita asked, her countenance changed entirely by what Elena imagined was relief.

"Respectfully, *signora,* I am beginning to ask the very same thing about *you.*"

RAPHAEL and Leonardo da Vinci rode out of Rome together, Raphael on horseback, his aged companion in an elegant curtained litter, pulled by horses and a formally clad horseman. The wind was heavy against them as they neared Monteflavio, where Leonardo intended to look at a large farm that was for sale. In it, he required, he said, the advice of a trusted friend. That was the expressed reason for the journey. But the elder artist also wished to seek advice from the younger on an entirely different matter. Although Raphael had once been an apprentice, and now had eclipsed him in promise and importance, still the friendship, the connection, unlike that with Michelangelo, had never wavered.

At the end of a long dirt trail that melted into a vast open hayfield, they stopped, dismounted, and left the horses to graze for a moment beneath the warm country sun. They stood beneath the shade cast from the last fragments of an ancient chestnut forest. Beyond were jagged purple hills dotted with old stone convents and ruined castles in their craggy niched terraces.

"The truth is that I have had an offer," Leonardo revealed as they walked across a rock-strewn path leading to the remains of a small Roman bridge. Beside it lay the dignified ruins of a once-proud chimneypiece, along with a stone staircase leading to some rich Roman villa, long ago destroyed.

"A generous one, I hope."

The cool autumn breeze tossed back the edges of both their riding capes and tousled their hair, one man's snow white, the other still bearing the rich umber hue of his youth. "The offer is from the new king, François I. His Majesty has invited me to come and live in France as artist in residence, accorded all honors and privileges thereto."

"A very generous offer indeed," Raphael observed as he leaned casually against the trunk of a tree. "And will you go?"

"I am considering it."

"You would be greatly missed here."

"By you, perhaps. But it is the sunset of my artistic years in Florence and Rome, Raphael, and you bask in the full summer sunlight of those days. Little but shadow remains for everyone else."

"Very poetic, but vastly untrue," Raphael tried to joke. "There will always be room for the man who taught me technique and portraiture. I still use many of your sketches of posture and attitude when I begin a new portrait of my own."

"It was the musings of an old man and yet, alas, the sad truth."

"Then why buy a farm all the way out here if you wish to go to France?"

"An investment for the future if the king should tire of me there."

"You have, it seems, thought of everything."

"Age brings with it perspective, if nothing else, Raphael."

They walked back through the grass a few paces. "So it goes well with your *signorina?*" Leonardo asked, changing the subject as they prepared to continue the journey.

"Better than I have ever had a right to hope."

"You certainly seem content. But perhaps a bit distracted, might I say, from all of your work."

"For the first time in my life, my personal happiness exceeds my drive to paint. If only—"

"If only?"

"She is not—" Raphael stopped again, unsure of an expression that would not lessen her dignity. "Margherita is not comfortable in many of the circumstances in which I find myself in need of engaging," he carefully confessed, not wanting either to belittle her to this man he so respected, or even in his own thoughts.

"She has lived a very different life than you."

"But that was in the past. We are equal now. She has a fine new home, clothes, and all of the respectability—"

"That you can buy for her?"

"She is my partner in all things."

Leonardo looked over at him. "In your mind perhaps," the elder artist sagely observed, his eyes heavily lidded by experience and years. "But you must be patient, for changing the costume changes not the person beneath."

Raphael thought of the rich white gown that to him had transformed her—its elegance and cost a mask of beauty for the baker's daughter beneath. "I am invited to attend Agostino Chigi's wedding in just over a month's time, but I have put off responding because—"

"Because you must take her with you."

"She has always declined to accompany me anywhere publicly. It is the gossip that she says she fears."

"Insist the first time. If you mean to have a life with her, do what you can to press her to reconsider. Perhaps something less daunting at first. Gossip shall never cease if those with wagging tongues have mystery upon which to build their talk. Take her there proudly," Leonardo advised. "And in time the tale of the artist and his love shall be an old and familiar one. Only then are they bound to move on to someone new."

"Wise words, but the reality of that is a difficult thing to wait for."

"Nothing shall be so difficult for either of you as that first time. They shall grow accustomed to the notion of your mistress as your wife, just as they did with Agostino Chigi's less-than-noble inamorata."

"But Agostino is a patron with power over the pope. I am only an artisan indebted to him and his minions."

"Then you shall need to be twice as clever, and thrice as insistent."

A quarter of an hour later, they rode together down a long causeway surrounded by olive groves and rows of sentinel junipers, then passed through a vine shaded archway. The property, on a hillside with a sweeping view over the fields and wooded forest beyond, was flanked by richly sculpted marble pillars and two great marble lions.

Raphael chuckled, glancing around. "A *farm,* is it?"

"A rather grand farm," da Vinci admitted with an endearing little shrug.

Raphael held the reins of his elegant Spanish jennet as it pawed the dirt, then helped da Vinci from his litter once again. The two men stood facing one another in an open courtyard in the shade of vine leaves, the wind shaking them like hundreds of small emerald flags in the afternoon light.

"If the offer to go to France pleases you," Raphael said sadly, "I hope it is what you wish it to be. But be assured, your presence in Rome shall be sorely missed." He fondly embraced the old man. "By Raphael Sanzio most especially."

Weeks later, in the late autumn of 1515, Leonardo da Vinci left Rome for France, to live there as an honored guest of the French king, François I. Leonardo was installed at Blois, on the property of the king's magnificent château, in his own grand manor. Raphael received several letters back over the next years detailing life at the French court, full of gossip and intrigue. Leonardo was old but well cared for and respected. His opinion, he wrote, was sought on many matters. Raphael read those first letters with a bittersweet smile. It was, he believed, a fitting finale for a true artistic *mastro*.

❧ 26 ❧

NOVEMBER 1515

"I THANK YOU FOR THIS, *CARISSIMA*. AND YOU LOOK magnificent," Raphael declared, gazing in admiration at Margherita. She had come into the music room of their house at last, seeming to float toward him, dressed exquisitely in a new white damask gown—strikingly similar to the one in which he had painted her, smiling her serene Madonna smile.

"Your friend Leonardo told me, before he left for France, that I should try at least to be a part of your world. And so tonight I shall."

"You have worked greatly for this."

She wanted to say that he could not begin to imagine how hard she had worked for this first public event—the dancing instruction, the etiquette lessons, and the exhausting drills in polite conversation—nor how nervous she was to attempt to use them all in one night. But that would have ruined this moment for him. Raphael touched her cheek with the whisper of a kiss.

"They must all know, sooner or later, that you are meant to remain in my life."

"I do not suppose it shall be easy."

"What in life worth having ever is?" he asked her, and she knew it was true.

"My mother would have been very fond of you."

"I wish very much that I had known her."

Margherita pressed a hand to her heart. "She is with me here, every day of my life. And I know she believes I have done the right thing in loving you."

He extended his arm gallantly to her. "Well, then? Shall we go and set all the tongues of Rome to wagging by our presence together?"

"I suspect you could do little else, appearing anywhere with a Trastevere baker's daughter!"

"That is certainly not how I see you, *amore mio.* Nor shall it be what the rest of the world thinks." He led her toward the foyer where a velvet-clad servant held open the front door for them. The cool night air soothed them both as they walked out amid a canopy of stars.

"At the moment," said Margherita. "I would settle for amusing even one of your very important friends."

"YET AGAIN, *more* delays?" Agostino Chigi bellowed, his deep voice echoing through the cavernous stone rooms of the Castel Sant'Angelo. "Impossible! It cannot be! This is entirely out of the question!"

Cardinal Bibbiena stood with the imposing, black-bearded banker, who was dressed in finery of olive-green velvet edged in silver. They were the first guests to arrive for Chigi's weekly mid-day dinner, this one given across from the Vatican Palace at the ancient papal fortress. They stood together, draped in white silk, in the library hall, with its soaring ceiling, massive windows, and large banquet table, while the pope's favorite buffoon, Niccolò, entertained in the corner.

Bibbiena's hands were clasped piously, and the expression on his face was one of rigid contradiction. He was biting back a victorious smile. "Alas, it is so, I fear," he said patiently. "That is the news I was given, and I come to you with it only in friendly warning. Signor Sanzio has told His Holiness that he needs more time with everything. He says it is due to the slow progress on the architectural drawings for Saint Peter's, and his work with the antiquities, about which I do not mind confessing to you, *caro,* I believe him to be far in over his head. And yet it is also my belief that the excuse is merely a tactic to mask . . . *other* things."

"But my wedding is in four days' time, and you tell me that the fresco in the very room where we will banquet shall not be complete, when Raphael himself assured me that it would be?"

"I fear it may well be so."

So mired in angry disbelief was Chigi that he saw no ulterior motive in Bibbiena's patient explanation. "This cannot stand! I am a man of great power, and this fresco is my legacy, my story! He will have his assistant—that Romano fellow, someone—see it to completion or there will be hell to pay!"

"Perhaps you shall effectuate that. And yet does it not mask a greater problem?"

Chigi looked imperiously at him. "That girl!"

"*Sì.* Still that girl. For a common tart with no family of note, she has managed for some time to entirely disrupt his life, his work, *and* his reputation. What, one might be given to ponder, will that do to the value of his work?" He sighed for effect, paused, then said, "Would that my poor niece had managed to marry him before that girl came along. But alas—"

"This is an abomination, that a Trastevere peasant could supersede someone so important as myself!" blustered Chigi. "And I had an agreement about his work for me long before he discovered *her!*"

"Sentiments I assure you that I share with you, Agostino *mio.* You could certainly take this up with him at dinner today," Bibbiena offered.

"The great Raphael is going to grace us, at last, with his presence when he has been so taken up with his whore?" Chigi asked sarcastically, still fuming with indignation.

Then, unexpectedly, Margherita herself entered the room on Raphael's arm.

Everything fell to a sudden, bitter hush. Bibbiena saw Margherita go very pale as all eyes in the grand villa were, at once, turned upon her. Then low murmuring voices began to fill the marked silence. Soft snickering behind raised palms followed, chins lifted loftily in judgment. Bibbiena thought for a moment she meant to turn and run. Or perhaps that was merely wishful thinking. Alas, she was still moving forward on Raphael's arm, looking nothing at all like his niece. She was undeniably exquisite in a rich white damask gown, ornamented in beadwork and gold thread, and her face . . . breathtaking.

Puttana!

"Apparently he means to bring the objectionable girl along as an accent to one of these dinners of revelry and comedic entertainment!" the cardinal cautiously replied behind a raised hand.

He quirked a smile. If his informants were correct, there was a presentation about to be made at this gathering, and the cardinal decided now, with that in mind, that the Luti girl's introduction into their world could not be more well timed.

As the hour wore on, he watched them seated together, amid the first trays piled with almonds, figs, and chunks of rich yellow cheese. He was sickened by the current that pulsed between them, the low whispers and the smiles they exchanged, as they repeatedly glanced at one another and then giggled like children.

Bibbiena was still tormented by the fact that Raphael had not paid a price for breaking his niece's heart. Yet anything he did — any public reprisal he might set in motion — would come back too boldly on him, and reflect poorly on his own eventual papal bid. No, his actions would need to be surreptitious. Careful. As in everything he did — as it was with the favors he had called in with Cardinal de' Rossi, encouraging him to speak glowingly to Pope Leo of Bibbiena's work so that he might stand out just now from the other cardinals.

It was Maria's place beside Raphael. His niece should be here. Not this girl. The pope's buffoon, dressed in a brightly colored costume, with hair dyed the color of fresh carrots, entertained them near the fireplace hearth, but Bibbiena could enjoy none of it.

Before the meal, as most of the guests sat staring at Raphael's mistress among them for the first time, the pope raised a hand to speak. By the gesture, his guests were immediately silenced. The buffoon bowed and left the room. The music and the clink of glasses faded softly away.

"Bernardo," Pope Leo intoned in his high, thin voice. "We are told many good things, of late, about your work. Finding the tone of our official position in the letter to Emperor Maximilian is extremely important, yet you keep such successes so nobly to yourself. Your selflessness is pleasing."

Pure brilliance! He would owe Cardinal de' Rossi for this. Bibbiena made a mental note of it as he smiled politely. "My thanks for the high compliment from Your Holiness. But the work is its own reward," he smoothly replied.

"And yet it is still my wish for you to have something, Bernardo. A token of my gratitude and pleasure with you and your exceedingly important work."

He lay a meaty jeweled finger to the side of his chin, enjoying his magnanimity. "You know I am much interested in the excavation at the Domus Aurea, the endless examples of ancient art left there, in spite of the cruel destruction."

"I have seen the exquisite frescoes there myself," Bibbiena concurred, a sweetly toned dig forming on his lips. "As you know, those ancient works have driven my desire for similar decorations by our own, very busy, Raffaello."

"Occasionally there have been gifts smaller than frescoes that history has offered up to us—other glimpses back to the exquisite grandeur and beauty of ancient Rome left for us to behold." As he made the slow pronouncement, Pope Leo withdrew from the small, plump finger of his own left hand a delicate, square-cut ruby set in a band gold. "This was found at the Domus Aurea of Nero in excavations which our good Raffaello has ably overseen for us. Spoken of in the writings of Suetonius, as the favored piece of jewelry for Nero's wife, if it is *that* ruby ring, it would be, as you might imagine, priceless." He leveled his protruding, bloodshot eyes on Bibbiena. "As *you* have made yourself to this papal court."

Smiling, Bibbiena took the ring as the pope extended it to him, and held it up to the light. Not exquisite, but lovely enough. Nevertheless, by the look on Raphael's face just now, it was priceless and would suit his purposes well indeed.

In a social strata where everything was said and done for the effect of gain, Bibbiena was pleased that this presentation of something from the pontiff's own person had been made in the very presence of the scoundrel and his peasant mistress themselves. He felt a spark of victory in that, and more than a hint of pleasure.

Bibbiena bowed deeply, causing more guests at the table to turn from their private conversations, as he held the ring up to the light in a dramatic gesture.

"It is exquisite. And so difficult to believe that down there, amid all of that rubble, so delicate and beautiful a thing—" He broke off with appropriate awe. "And yet I cannot help but think Your Holiness is the only one who should wear such a fine and rare jewel."

"Perhaps it is so," Pope Leo conceded, his fleshy cheeks swiftly bulging as his expression became merry. "Were it not for my great affection toward you, and a strong desire to reward your loyalty."

"With benevolence and grace, Your Holiness leads us in all things," said Bibbiena as he slipped the ring onto his own finger and then lifted his goblet of wine with the same hand so that the gem might glitter a little more brightly in the candlelight.

RAPHAEL SAT SILENTLY on the other side of the pope, watching the scene play out, his anger and shock breeding in him a curious detachment from the scene. It was the ring meant for Margherita's hand, the one he had tried for weeks to obtain. He had personally petitioned the pope—a thing to which His Holiness had, at first, easily agreed, simply because his favorite artist desired it. A bold statement indeed that this—the only thing he had ever asked of a pontiff who asked much of him—should be so publicly presented to someone else. In particular, to the uncle of a woman he had spurned.

Raphael touched his chin where a small, neat brown beard now grew beneath a trimmed mustache. He studied the pontiff, seated across from him. Something very odd, an undercurrent of danger, was beginning to swirl around this particular collection of people. Instinct told him to be cautious until he was absolutely certain who he should fear, as he saw Bibbiena lean across to speak with Margherita.

As great silver serving dishes of sugar biscuits, marzipan, pine nuts, quail, and sweetmeats were laid across the surface of the vast, linen-draped table, they saw bread that had been gilded set beside shining silver saltcellars and vases of fresh flowers. There was a velvet-clad boy playing something melodic on a lute across the room near the fire. Raphael reached beneath the damask table cover and found Margherita's small hand, which he squeezed reassuringly. Both of them saw the cardinal prop the palms of his hands conspicuously on the surface of the table so that his rings, especially the ruby ring, would glitter in the candlelight.

"The ring is exquisite, Your Grace," he heard Margherita very softly remark, knowing nothing of its value to Raphael. They were the first words she had spoken to anyone but Raphael all evening.

She was straining, Raphael knew, to adopt the appropriately modulated tone to be used with so important and intimidating a cleric as the one who sat stiffly only two guests away from her. His heart squeezed with pride, and he willed himself not to intercede. This must become a successful evening for her—never mind the ring—and she must do it on her own.

"And it seems I have your Raphael to thank for it, *signora*," Cardinal Bibbiena replied with an imperious gleam.

Raphael set down his goblet of wine and listened more carefully, the hair on the back of his neck suddenly prickling in warning.

"After all," Bibbiena continued, stabbing a piece of white fish with his gleaming silver fork, then settling his gaze very directly on Raphael, "was it not you who brought it up yourself from the ruins of Nero's house?"

Where do you mean to go with this? He felt the caution surge up inside him. "It is so," he carefully replied.

"Well, there you see? The credit for my gift then is exclusively yours."

"I am glad the ring pleases Your Grace."

"And so at least one Bibbiena is victorious against a Sanzio in something."

He had been played like that lute, Raphael realized. The cardinal knew he had valued that ring, and now he sat there beside him, so smugly pious, twirling it around on his own cold, reedy finger. Raphael had long been wary of the cardinal's power. His wariness had increased once he had sought to leave Maria. But he had not truly feared him until now—now that there was Margherita, vulnerable and unaware, between them.

MARGHERITA glanced at Raphael across the room half an hour later as he stood, arms crossed over his chest below a bronze medallion he wore on a heavy chain. He was deeply engaged in conversation with another cardinal. This one, called Inghirami, was a short, stout man, nearly bald, yet with the shadow of a beard on his double chin, and one unfocused eye. She allowed herself the slightest self-satisfied smile then, and drew in the first full breath she had taken since the dinner began. *Madre Maria!* She was actually surviving this! She had not spilled any wine or spoken too quickly, nor even said the wrong thing.

She watched Raphael and the cardinal speak intensely of the great architectural debate concerning the mammoth size of the planned basilica for Saint Peter's, and whether or not, once complete, it could actually stand. The artist and the cleric spoke intensely and quietly, standing there holding their jewel-encrusted goblets, only a few feet from the Holy Father seated in his silk-covered dining chair. Raphael was wrapped in an elegant doublet of aubergine and gold thread, his toque tilted in the stylish French manner. She was dressed like a princess.

This was her world now, she thought, as unbelievable as that still seemed.

That world had shifted entirely from one of baking endless loaves of bread in a stifling kitchen, and wondering daily if they had earned enough money to feed them all, to an existence of deciding upon shoes with pearls or beads, attending to the needs of various servants, reading books, engaging in fascinating discussions, and making choices on more new gowns than she could count. She had fine jewelry and two very fashionable French headdresses. These trappings, and Elena's patient lessons, had recast the uncertain peasant girl from Trastevere like a layer of blue wash on one of Raphael's paintings. By his devotion, she had been transformed, and she almost dared to believe that she was actually on the pathway to becoming someone appropriate for him. For example, the handsome young painter Sebastiano Luciani, with his sharply assessing black eyes, had dined near her and treated her with the greatest respect. He inquired as to her opinion of the Castel Sant'Angelo, and her new very elegant home, as if they were the most natural of subjects.

She found very quickly that it was difficult not to like Sebastiano, his sense of humor, and the way in which he so quickly put her at ease. Once Raphael, on her other side, was taken up in conversation elsewhere, Margherita was grateful to have had Sebastiano ask a cardinal if they might trade places.

Margherita had no idea what had made Raphael so tense after the presentation to Cardinal Bibbiena, but she was beginning to understand the sometimes volatile and always changing temperament of an artist. And because of the kind attentions of the dining partner on the other side of her, she had been given no opportunity to ask him.

A slim hand on her shoulder brought her back to the moment.

Margherita turned around to see a lovely woman with shining honey-colored hair and a kind smile standing beside her. She wore a dress of rich, dove-gray silk, and her hair was braided with tiny sapphires.

"Ours are complicated men who have dared to love beneath expectation," she said sweetly. "Our ranks, as those who love them in return, are few."

When Margherita looked puzzled, she added with an easy smile, "I am Francesca Andreozza, betrothed of Signor Chigi."

Margherita had heard about her from Raphael, as well as about Chigi's other mistress, Imperia, who had battled valiantly for the title of Signora Chigi. Francesca, like herself, was common. And in the beginning she had been treated to the very same social rebuff.

"I am Margherita Luti."

"Of course. All of Rome knows who you are. But only *I* understand what it is like to *be* in your shoes."

"Perhaps you have a point." Margherita found herself smiling. "I would be most fond of a sound ally."

Trust was a difficult thing for Margherita to risk in a world so new to her, and thus so fraught with danger. But she, too, could benefit from an ally. And Raphael would be proud of her, she determined, having found one in his own patron's fiancée.

"I would like that."

Francesca clasped her hands. "Splendid! Then tell me you will come to supper with me next week. We will have a more private opportunity to speak of things then."

"It would be a pleasure."

Francesca smiled. "And it has been one for me this evening— meeting you."

The entertainment began. The pope's buffoon was making everyone laugh with his antics set to music played on a lute and a flute set up near the fireplace hearth. Francesca was distracted then by another guest. Alone now, Margherita felt brave enough to seek a breath of fresh air. This really had been the most extraordinary event.

The stone wall around the castle had large open bays, each with a more magnificent view of the city than the last. There were small stone benches beneath each one, upon which to consider the grandeur. As she walked past these little niches in the stone, amid the cool afternoon air, Margherita still could not believe that she was actually a guest in a place like this—that she had not embarrassed herself or Raphael, and that a part of her now was actually enjoying the experience. She kept walking, the fragrance of the air reviving her, steadying her after the fright and anticipation that she had carried with her to the vaunted Castel Sant'Angelo a mere two hours earlier. Perhaps one day they could learn to accept her, after all, as Signor Chigi's mistress now was accepted. Stranger things, she knew, had happened in the long history of Rome.

Margherita descended a small flight of stone steps entering a charming little enclosed inner courtyard peppered with fat, gray pigeons. It was decorated with fountains and stone pots spilling over with geraniums. She sat on a stone bench supported by two carved lion's heads and, for the first time today, felt herself fully exhale. A pleased little smile followed.

"Hoping to escape, Signora Luti?"

Margherita turned with a start toward the voice that came at her from the shadows. It was her dinner partner, Sebastiano Luciani. He was smiling casually as he leaned against a stone pillar, arms crossed nonchalantly over his chest. She realized, with a little jolt of her heart, that she had not heard him behind her.

A moment later, he moved toward her and sank onto the same small bench. "Because, if you are, I will warn you that you would find it a frustrating and unsuccessful endeavor. These walls around us are fortified to keep us in, as well as to keep the common world out."

"I needed a breath of air."

"I should not wonder! They can be a daunting lot, all of those starched robes and crucifixes." Margherita smiled at that, but she was uncertain how further to respond. "Of course, as you can see, I wear no ecclesiastical garb, so you are free to be as open with me as you like."

How did he know what she felt? In spite of all her lessons, was she still that transparent? She knew Raphael did not like him, but she did not understand why. He certainly was the most approachable of all the guests, and a fellow artist, beside whom Raphael once had worked. Raphael must be wrong about him. Raphael had spoken of his temper, driven by their competition. They had quarreled, Raphael had told her. But Sebastiano simply could not be guilty of those other awful things. And Raphael had always admitted he had no absolute proof that Sebastiano was behind the plot to injure his hand.

"If it is any consolation," he continued, gazing up at the broad, cloudless sky above them, "you do look far more at ease than I would guess you feel in a place like this. I did not sleep for two days the first time I was in the presence of the Holy Father."

"I suspect we will share *that* fate," Margherita smiled.

"To share any fate at all with you, *signora*, I should consider myself a fortunate man indeed."

Margherita was unsure if the comment had been flattery, or if something more had been implied. He was certainly more worldly than she. At the very moment her mind filled with the question of what the comment had meant, and how to respond as other women might, a voice cut into the awkward silence.

"What are you doing with *him?*"

The tone of voice was cold, the stare icier still. Raphael stood before them now, his body a ramrod of pure anger. Margherita reacted to it defensively, having tried all evening to make the right choices, say the right things. In that moment, she felt foolish and slightly afraid.

"It was nothing! Sebastiano found me wandering and he was simply being polite."

Raphael arched a suspicious brow. "Sebastiano, is it?"

"Forgive me, *amore mio,* but is that not how *you* refer to him?"

"*I* am not an unmarried woman!"

"Were it in my power, I would not be so, either!" She had spoken too quickly, and she regretted it the moment she saw his expression change. She knew he was doing everything in his power to receive the Holy Father's approval in the matter. "Raphael, *per favore,* it was harmless. He truly was only trying to be polite."

"Odd, when it has been a very long time since he has been anything near polite to *me!*"

"You make too much of a small thing."

He took her arm above the elbow, gripping it, neither of them noticing Sebastiano's slim, satisfied smile.

"Come," Raphael commanded. "We are leaving."

"But—"

Raphael turned back suddenly, his face changed in a way she had never seen before. The stare he gave his rival was darkly menacing. "Leave her alone, Sebastiano! This is only between the two of us!"

Still smiling, Sebastiano shrugged. "Perhaps not."

"Touch her, and I swear by all that is holy, I will see you dead! And, unlike you, *I* will need no henchmen to do the job for me!"

"Threats so lack creativity, Raphael," his rival yawned, his lips lifting into an unattractive sneer.

"It was not a threat! You may consider it an absolute certainty!"

RAPHAEL did not speak to Margherita again until they were home, alone in her bedchamber with its massive bed and soaring beamed ceilings. A fire blazed and crackled in the hearth, lighting and warming everything in the room, especially the tense expressions on both of their faces.

"What was *really* wrong with you today?" Margherita asked, an arm placed gently at the small of his back. She had taken off her shoes and jewelry, but she had no wish to call Elena to undress her until she and Raphael had discussed this. It felt like a great and sudden barrier between them.

He raked back his hair and stared into the fire as she sat down on the needlepoint hearthside bench beside him. "I petitioned the pope once again to allow us to marry," he confessed.

The fire cracked and flared. "He is still against it, even though Signorina Bibbiena acknowledges the end of your betrothal?"

Raphael nodded somberly, unable and unwilling to tell her the full truth. He could not tell her that Pope Leo had angrily decreed a peasant girl to be too far beneath him for anything but a passing dalliance. His request alone, said the pope, was a grand insult to Cardinal Bibbiena and his much-loved niece. The pope had hotly declared that a marriage between them could never be ordained by God. That he must concentrate on the work . . . *always the work* . . . and forget her.

"It doesn't matter," Margherita soothingly told him, with a hand across his shoulder, their faces made golden by the flames.

"But it *does* matter! Without our marriage, none of them will *ever*—"

She knew what he meant to say. The thing that would not leave his lips for love of her   that the patrician class of Rome, the nobles and the powerful clergy, would never accept her, no matter for how many breathtaking Madonnas she posed, or how she enriched his life. She would forever be a peasant who had dared to ensnare a man far above her station by the power of seduction.

Raphael sagged against the hearth, then hung his head. "I *will* marry you, by God in his heaven!"

"I know you will."

He turned to her then, his face alive and burning with his frustration. "We will go to Urbino! There we can be wed with no protest from anyone!"

"And when you return here to the city, then what? Will you not have jeopardized all of your important commissions?"

"I care not a whit about any of them if it means they come before you!"

"The lives of your assistants then?"

"What of *our* lives, Margherita? What of us?"

"But you have me already." She smiled comfortingly in the glow of the fire beside them. "And it shall be so, until you wish me in your life no longer."

Her reassurance was not the balm she hoped. His expression still bore the torment of the uncertain and dangerous future he saw before them if they remained unmarried.

"That is not the point. What I wish is to honor you by our formal union."

"I know. And I will wait for as long as it takes," she said soothingly, running a finger along his cheek. "Perhaps the next pope—"

"His Holiness is only gluttonous, not old! There is no hope for us in that! And in the meantime, with all of the men of Rome, like Sebastiano Luciani, who see you as fair game—"

She tipped her head. "As if I have no control in that matter at all?"

"But they are men who know well how to manipulate!"

"And I am not wise enough to defend myself?"

"You could not begin to defend yourself against the clever words or intent of one of them!"

She stood then, stiff with indignation. "A victim, am I? A mere possession, allowing myself to be taken? If you believe that, Raphael, then you do not know me at all!"

He reached out for her hand but she jerked it away. His eyes were a color she had never seen, and frightening. "Sebastiano challenges me in all things! Many here in Rome do! I must remain vigilant to the daily threat, and I must protect you!"

Margherita's face went ashen, something deep changing within her as she moved across the bedchamber, twisted the iron door handle, and drew back the door. "You brought me into this competitive world of yours! You entreated me to become a part of it, to learn it, and compete in it using my *own* skills, even knowing what determination that would take!" When she looked at him, her eyes were deep with sincerity. "Raphael, I love you with all of my heart, but you must learn to believe in me, and to trust me!"

He stood slowly, gazing at her with the distance of the room, and the weight of misunderstanding, between them. "You are putting me out?"

"It would be best if you returned for tonight to the Via dei Coronari, or to your studio, giving us both some time for . . . reflection."

He went to her, arms extended. "Margherita. Do not do this—"

Her hand went up in defense. Tonight, she had walked among cardinals and bishops, and sat in the presence of the Holy Father himself, as one who was actually entitled to do so. It had taken her a personal strength she had never even known she possessed, and now she was entirely spent.

"Have we not both said enough for one evening?"

As they looked at one another in the silence of her question, Margherita saw the torment of a complicated man, besieged by people who only wanted to take from him. Even so, he had chosen to trust her, and to love her. She was, he said, his only bit of family now. But in their time together, she had also come to know the tumult of creativity and self-doubt that defined his world, and she could not allow herself to be caught up in that dangerous current. Her duty, she believed, was to be the light, the beacon, and the bit of reason he needed to keep him from his own dark demons.

"As you wish." He nodded soberly, coming to stand before her at the open door. The lamplight from the corridor beyond, for that moment, bathed them both in a single cone of shimmering gold. Very lightly, Raphael pressed a kiss onto her cheek. "I shall speak no more now. But I do bid you, consider well what I have said, and do not trust those who have not *earned* your trust. I did not easily learn that myself here in Rome, but eventually I did learn it well."

"This night, *amore mio,* I will be unable to think of anything else."

❧ 27 ❧

EACH WEEK WHEN SHE RETURNED TO THE BAKERY AND the little house in Trastevere to visit her father, Margherita came with baskets of gifts. There were always gold florins for each of them to spend as they chose, and sweets for her young nephews—especially little Matteo upon whom she doted. Fine new dresses were sent for Letitia, and new, well-made shoes for her father, along with a comfortable new bed brought in from Venice. Raphael's personal gift to the family had been two young, able-bodied men he hired to help in the family bakery so that the burden might be lifted from Francesco.

While Margherita had offered her sister a position managing the new house, Letitia preferred being a big fish in her little pond in Trastevere, where she could boast about the family's newfound fortunes. In addition, Raphael had offered to take Donato from the Chigi stables and give him the position of attendant and personal guard to Margherita for the long hours when he could not be with her himself. It was a position Donato gratefully and swiftly accepted.

In spite of the envy on her sister's face, and her father's growing avarice, Margherita felt honor bound to share her good fortune, not only with her family, but with Padre Giacomo and the little parish church that not so long ago had been the center of her world. As the months passed, the visits to Trastevere became shorter—yet their requests greater. And the time they all wished to spend on the Via Alessandrina was increasing as well. There was always much to discuss. Letitia petitioned for two new beds for her growing elder sons. And Donato could not possibly make do with only the two new doublets designed by Raphael's own tailor—not now, when he was known to have an affiliation with the famous artist, Letitia insisted. And if Letitia was going to be expected to spend time socially in her sister's company, the dresses she wore, like Margherita's, would need to reflect her changing status. When she left the bakery, or they left her home, her head full of new requests, Margherita felt not regret or sadness, but only relief to be away from them.

Her world had changed, and now so had she.

As Raphael had warned her, there were actually very few whom she could trust, and, in spite of Letitia's grating behavior, she was grateful to have Donato there as support as she tried to navigate in this new and far more complicated world.

After a visit with Hanno in the Vatican gardens, Margherita walked along the muddy cobbled street with her new companions, Donato and Elena. Margherita felt the safety in numbers and did not travel through the city without the constant companionship of them both. And she preferred walking, rather than riding the lovely horses Raphael offered. It was easier to maintain her dwindling anonymity by being among the people on the streets.

It was a pleasant day for so late in November, and a blaze of gold sunlight shimmered down on the cobbled stone piazza through which they passed on their way back home. Today had brought a more difficult visit to the bakery than usual, and thus her time with sweet-tempered Hanno, who still sank to his knees for her, and wrapped his trunk around her arm, had been welcome.

With so many things pressing on her mind she did not see the collection of finely gowned patrician ladies coming toward her. Nor did she, at first, hear their low, cruel whispers breaking the silence on the quiet square.

"By my troth, it *is* her!"

"No!"

"I would know that trollop anywhere!"

"Tart!" they tittered. "And out like this, as proud as you please!"

"They say Signor Raphael has bought her a fine house, and he spends more time there with her than at his work for the Holy Father!"

"I have heard it said that she has the impudence to continue posing as the great Virgin Mother while there is nothing left of the virgin about *her!* She is even called *signora* now!"

They cackled like hens, not looking directly at her, but speaking loudly enough to be certain she could hear them. Donato slowed his pace when a dirty-faced boy crossed their path, hand out, hoping for a coin from the finely dressed man. Margherita only wanted to be away from this place and from these women, knowing that they meant her nothing but harm. As the two factions drew ever nearer, and Donato was distracted searching for the coins, she felt her body tense.

When Donato kindly patted the boy on top of his head, handing him what coins he had with him, the ring of four women, all in their sweeping velvet finery, stopped, as if having cornered prey. It was a great irony, Margherita thought, that they had all just emerged from a little stone church at the opposite end of the square.

"She is not as comely as I would have thought," said one of them, a stout, silver-haired woman with a long hooked nose and faintly pockmarked skin. "But she does have those eyes everyone speaks about."

"Eyes or not, I would know Raphael's harlot anywhere!"

Realizing at last the danger, Donato faced them head-on, tall and confrontational. "Is there a problem?" he asked in a deep, commanding voice that shook even Margherita with its implied threat. Surprisingly, once again, they laughed.

"Not for us. But then we are not making a sow's ear into a silk purse!"

Again there was a chorus of cruel tittering that filled the peaceful square. Donato put a protective arm around Margherita's shoulder, and Elena followed them as he steered her away.

"Flee if you will!" another called out in an acid taunt that echoed through the little piazza. "But you cannot outrun the gossip that has filled this town!"

SHE WEPT until there were no more tears. Then she vomited a vile mix of despair and frustration that came up through the depths of her innocent belief that love could solve all things, heal all things. Yet it was not Raphael who smoothed the hair away from her face and stroked her arm until the trembling ceased — it was Donato. Brother. Friend. Now confidant.

"I am a laughingstock in Rome!"

"They are old, bitter women. You must not take them as anything more."

"It is all coming undone, Donato! There will be no marriage, no honor . . . no resolution to this! I should never have allowed myself to love him for what, in the end, it shall do to us both!"

Donato turned her away from the corner of the building and held her arms squarely as Elena waited silently beside him, her own expression grave with the shock of what had just occurred.

"Don't speak that way! Raphael adores you, and you *do* love him!"

"The forces against us are great! I was a fool to believe anyone besides Raphael could ever accept me as I am! And where is the future in it for the two of us, Donato, if they cannot?"

"WELL, THEN? Will it be completed in time?" Cardinal Bibbiena pointedly asked, gazing up at the mammoth fresco in the great hall of Chigi's villa. Scaffolding was everywhere, with paint pots and draperies littering the elegant inlaid marble floor. A collection of apprentices were beginning to prepare the pigments with the wedding but a day away.

"It is still my hope," Agostino uncomfortably replied.

"Where is Raphael now? Half the morning is gone already!"

"I was told by one of them over there that he is taken up this morning at the Domus Aurea, but that he will be here."

"Something simply must be done about this disturbing new

trend," the cardinal said in a carefully modulated tone. "I don't like it at all."

"He certainly is not the artist he was, not so long ago," Chigi concurred with a tilt of his head. "It seems that Raphael's dedication is at issue, if not his skill. Although the outcome of the fresco, even in this state, you must admit, *is* brilliant."

"Yet one must ask, is there nothing that can be done to set him back on the proper path for us? The unfinished works are mounting. He has yet to complete the *stuffeta* promised to me long ago, or to begin my portrait—never mind the things he has not attended to for the Holy Father."

Chigi stroked his black bearded chin as they stopped beneath a second arch and gazed out at the gardens. It was clear he had not seen it as the same mammoth artistic crisis Bibbiena had—until now. "I suppose it is the fault of that peasant girl he is rutting with, hmm?" said the cardinal.

"Who else? She has changed much in his world—and by extension, in ours."

"Raphael seems to care about nothing so much these days as painting Madonnas."

"Rather a vulgar sort of irony, would you not agree?" quipped Chigi.

"The Holy Father has told him more than once he may not marry her, yet it does not seem to have dampened his ardor."

"Perhaps that ardor shall lead to a bad end, which, given the scope of his enormous talent, would be a tragedy for all of us indeed."

"Something well worth stopping—*if* there were only a viable way."

"*Sì.* Would that he had never found the baker's daughter for his model in the first place!"

"Or," said the cardinal, "that she had been possessed of the good sense to know that he was well out of her league."

They strode together back across the room, the cardinal's arms linked behind his back, the still incomplete fresco like a punctuation mark above them. Bibbiena was immensely pleased with himself. He had played the part of a sage friend quite to the hilt, then planted the seed that sooner or later, God willing, would bring him, and his poor Maria, a bit of compensation. The timing was not important, so long as it happened.

❧ 28 ❧

RAPHAEL KNELT ALONE ON THE SOARING SCAFFOLDING in the grand loggia of the Chigi villa. Around him were dozens of lamps and flickering candles to illuminate the wall enough so that he might continue working through the night. Still, the lateness of the hour already had altered the way he saw the shades of color on the fresco. It was the *Wedding of Cupid and Psyche,* and the many faces of those attending the wedding party were painted lolling at the grand banquet table in their classical costumes.

Giulio had done the outlines, the shapes of the figures, and their faces, and Gianfrancesco Penni had fashioned the lovely flowers and garlands as ornamentation. Now, this day before Chigi's wedding, the work was still incomplete. The irony of Chigi's marrying his mistress—happily sanctioned by Pope Leo, and officiated by Cardinal Bibbiena—was a bitter pill to Raphael as he worked.

With only three weary assistants to aid him in this candlelit darkness, Raphael pushed back his anger and fought against the rapidly drying plaster. Dried streaks of color covered him up to his elbows and splattered onto his face and neck. Raphael worked with quiet intensity while a young apprentice knelt beside him to hand him pigments, water, and different brushes, and another waited below to quickly mix whatever he would require.

Raphael knew that Agostino was less than pleased with his progress. As friendly as the banker seemed, Raphael was to Agostino Chigi as he was to Cardinal Bibbiena, to the pope, and to Cardinal de' Medici: a creator of great works that would further their status and earn them immortality. They may pay him exorbitant rates, and tout him as a great artistic master, but, at the end of the day, Raphael was their servant.

That cold truth made him think again of Margherita and long for her as he pressed daubs of pale pink into the slim cheeks of the frescoed mythic bridegroom. Since Margherita had come into his life, Raphael had seen a coarsening in those who had hired him, particularly Agostino, and a resistance from all of them to any sort of delay, no matter how explainable. To their minds, it was not an overabundance of work, but an overindulgence of lust for a girl that caused it. The peasant girl, they called her. The baker's daughter. *La fornarina.*

THE HUNT had been long, cold, and very taxing, and Pope Leo was hungry—a state that always put him out of sorts. Yet Agostino knew, as the pontiff pushed the first silver fork full of freshly cooked trout and almonds between his rosebud lips, it was the perfect time to launch the plan.

"Ah, my son." Pope Leo smiled as he chewed. "Tell me. Have you confessed and prayed, in preparation for your wedding tomorrow?"

"I only hope my house is nearly as ready as I am, since there shall be so many there to behold it if it is not."

The pope looked at him, his blue eyes bulging, and now ate a pastry in two large, cheek-swelling bites. "There is a problem with your grand and lovely house?"

"The fresco of Cupid and Psyche, to ornament the wall for the wedding party, perhaps will not be so grand. I do not mind telling Your Holiness that I left my Francesca in something of a state this morning, seeing that it was not yet complete."

"Not yet complete?" Pope Leo gulped. "Is it not being painted by Raphael's team?"

"It is . . . even as we speak."

"And still it is unfinished?"

"The apprentices did what they could, but the *mastro* wished to complete the faces himself. It is my only hope now that it be at least dry by the time it is unveiled, so as not to embarrass my bride."

"This is a scandal, and not at all worthy of a *mastro* like our great Raffaello!"

"Yet a *mastro*, I am afraid, increasingly taken up"—he grimaced as if the thought alone had physically struck him—"by his mistress. A woman so common she could never understand the rigors of a schedule like his."

"That baker's daughter *still*?"

"They say it is so, Your Holiness. He seems not to be able to work at all with her so present in his life, distracting and disrupting everything."

"He certainly has found many reasons these past months to miss your little dinners."

Chigi leaned toward the pontiff, who was brushing crumbs from his white brocade cassock. "I am loath to say it, Your Holiness, but Cardinal Bibbiena tells me that his commissions, too, have been stalled, and I have heard you say yourself that you are frustrated over the delays in the work at Saint Peter's. It seems we *all* share in Raphael's unsettled new life."

Pope Leo jerked forward, then sprang onto his feet in such an uncommonly energetic burst that it caused the tray of pastries, held above his shoulder, to fly up, then come clattering back down, crashing onto the tile floor. "This cannot continue! We have much work for him that he *must* complete!" He blustered, his heavy neck rattling beneath his red little hairless nob of a chin.

"Perhaps if they were allowed to marry, she would become less . . . alluring. The bloom, as it were, being well off the rose."

"Out of the question! Absolutely not! I shall never permit it! If this is Raphael's way of maneuvering me into a change of mind—by not working, as a means to threaten me—he shall see he is sorely misguided!" As the pontiff bellowed, bits of pastry flew forth onto his stiff cassock and across the room.

"Such a girl is not suitable, nor will she ever be, no matter how he dresses her up, or in what manner he paints her!" He was angry now, blustering, a vein in his forehead pulsing as he raged. "More than that, allowing such a thing would be a great insult to poor grieving Bernardo. The cardinal's niece, God save her innocent soul, is heartbroken because of Raphael's appalling preoccupation with a peasant! Och! I had hopes that this would play itself out, but this really is an abomination! It would be far better for him if she were gone from his life entirely!"

Chigi lifted a finger to his neatly bearded chin, as though something had only just then occurred to him. "There *is* one way to be done with this entire business, *and* have our Raphael returned entirely to us, Your Holiness. Although it is arguably a way perhaps not altogether pleasing in the sight of God."

Pope Leo slumped back into his chair, his corpulent body spent by his sudden outburst. "Perhaps you should allow *me* to be the judge of what Almighty God might find objectionable."

Chigi nodded with a respectful smile. "It is as Your Holiness wishes."

IT WAS the end of autumn, late November, and the trees bristled with the sound of the wind through the last crisp, dead leaves. Shades of gold, red, and rich umber accented the rural areas of Rome as scattered patches of dandelions died away, their stalks bowing with the weight of the dead blossoms above them, yet still swaying them in a rhythm with the cool breeze. Clouds moved overhead like pillows across a richly azure sky as Giulio and Elena walked together away from the raucous clamor of the busy market at the Piazza Navona. Here they were far from the prying eyes of anyone who would know or care that Raphael's chief assistant and his mistress's companion were alone together on a Sunday.

"You are happy with Signora Luti?" he casually asked her.

"She is not as I expected," Elena replied.

"You mean that she is common?"

"No, I had already heard that." They stopped beneath an ancient stone archway where they were protected from the full force of the wind. "There is actually something quite *uncommon* about her."

"In that, you are not so very different from her."

Elena turned away from the sudden flattery, but he brought her face back with a gentle finger beneath her chin. It was the most bold move he had ever made toward a woman, and he felt his own uncertainty redoubled as he did.

"You must not speak of such things," Elena murmured.

"But you are not married, nor do you belong to another."

She turned away again. "And yet I did, unalterably."

"You speak of Raphael."

"Who it was does not matter. What's important is how unsuitable that foolish moment made me for the future." She turned back around then to face him, her expression hauntingly sad. "You are a good man, Giulio, with many challenges of your own to face. I would not want to become a complication for you."

He took her hands as the buttery yellow sunlight, mixed with vibrant orange, played across their shimmering faces. "Elena, you are the first person to make it all seem perfectly simple. What I want in my life." He felt himself exhale very hard after the words left his lips, realizing then that he had forgotten to breathe. "I have come to care deeply for you."

"This can lead to nothing honorable for you because of my past," she warned. "And because we serve the same *mastro*."

"I bid you, let it lead only where it will."

"We are impossible. As impossible, some would say, as Raphael and his Margherita."

"I shall never believe that." He moved to press a gentle kiss onto her lips. He had never kissed a girl before, and her mouth beneath his brought a surprisingly powerful sensation. As he pulled away, afraid of it, he was prepared to tell her that he was in love with her. But something else stopped his confession. From the corner of his eye, Giulio Romano saw, across the bridge, a figure and a face he knew. It was Margherita. She was on horseback, riding behind a man.

"Not Sebastiano!" Giulio groaned, the expression on his face one of horrified shock. "And Signora Luti on his very horse! I recognize the cloak and hood! The *mastro* would kill him with his bare hands if he saw them together!"

"You do not think that the *signora* and Sebastiano are—"

"I know that she and the *mastro* had quarreled a few days ago, and that she sent him away. Beyond that, I know not what to think!"

❧ 29 ❧

RAPHAEL WAS TO BE A GUEST AT THE MARRIAGE OF Agostino Chigi to Francesca Andreozza, and he meant for Margherita to accompany him. Francesca and Margherita had become sudden friends, and so her presence would be accepted. But more than that, Raphael wished to prove to the world that his relationship with a common woman was no less worthy of papal sanction than Chigi's. The ceremony would commence in the late afternoon, when the setting sun was pink and rich and at its loveliest, glittering upon the Tiber.

He stood while being dressed by his valet in a rich doublet of wine-colored brocade with a jeweled chain at his waist. His dark hair and neat beard were tamed with fragrant Turkish oil. Raphael heard Margherita's angry words again. They echoed through his mind . . . *You do not know me at all!*

He could not vanquish the thought of her warning: *I will not join you in your fear of everything and everyone who exists beyond the walls of this house* . . . Still, he was giving her the time she wished, and the incident would soon be forgotten. He was certain of it. Raphael knew he had been foolish to express his fears about Sebastiano without her knowing the root of it. The artistic rivalry in Rome between himself, Sebastiano, and Michelangelo was a deeply complex thing to understand if one were not an artist. He knew that Sebastiano would like nothing better than to steal Margherita away. Her naive kindness would make her a splendid pawn in this vicious game.

The motivation was evil, and the bitter battle had long since gotten out of hand.

But she would not allow that, he reassured himself. Never. Not Margherita.

Once dressed, Raphael reached for a small chest on a carved table beneath the window, and opened it. The curved lid, with leather straps and brass studs, squealed on its hinges. A pearl necklace glimmered on a bed of crimson velvet. It was not the ruby ring he was determined to give her, but until he could, the pearls would look splendid against her smooth, fair skin. The rope of pearls, with a diamond clasp, had cost a small fortune, but until they were free to marry, Raphael needed to keep reminding her exactly what she had come to mean to his life.

When Giulio came in, Raphael turned and flashed a smile, feeling happy and in command, wearing his new, costly Florentine doublet with the fashionable silver braid. He looked, he knew, every bit the cavalier, the refined Raphael Sanzio whom the world believed him to be. But as Giulio neared, Raphael saw a flicker of something out of place on the smooth, handsome face of his trusted assistant. Something was wrong.

Raphael closed the jewelry chest and set it back on top of his bed. The smile faded. "What is it, *caro?*"

Giulio stepped back, his eyes narrowed. He seemed to want to say something. He began, there was a hesitation, then he said, "A long day only, *mastro*. I oversaw the finishing touches at the Chigi villa but an hour ago."

Raphael was not immediately convinced. "Is there something with your father again?"

"I have not seen my father for many days, nor do I wish to."

Raphael studied his young friend for a moment, more anxious suddenly than before to leave for the Via Alessandrina to be with Margherita, to be reassured again that the words she had spoken had meant little. And yet he had known Giulio long enough to understand that there was something more to his mood than simply a difficult day of work. Raphael felt a cold rush of fear.

"Very well then," he stubbornly said, determined not to dwell on it. "If you have something to tell me, I trust you shall."

"It shall always be so, *mastro.*"

"Then let us be off to fetch Signora Luti, and attend Signor Chigi's wedding!"

"HAS THE MATTER been seen to then?"

Cardinal Bibbiena stood behind Agostino, who was admiring his own wedding ensemble before a long mirror framed in gold. Chigi glanced at Bibbiena's reflection first, then turned to face him directly. They were in a large dressing room on the second floor of his villa. A cool wind blew in through a bank of open windows. Beyond the heavy rounded oak door was the commotion of servants, clergy, family, and guests, all preparing for the ceremony that was to take place in less than an hour.

"*Sì,*" he replied. But a hesitation filtered in through his reedy tenor. "It is only that . . . After all, Bernardo, Raphael does seem to love the girl."

My niece loved him, and knows great heartbreak because of it, Bibbiena thought, feeling that undesirable wrenching in his gut. But he chose not to say that.

"Remember, Bernardo, I, too, fell in love with a woman of low birth. Certainly the woman I will marry today was not immediately seen as a suitable bride for one of your circle."

"You know well, Agostino *mio,* that this is very different. Raphael serves the Holy Father, who craves more than anything a legacy, and a bit of immortality only Raphael can give him. In that, you possess a freedom he does not. So it had to be this way," Bibbiena reassured him as he clamped his cold, bony fingers on Chigi's broad, silk-draped shoulder.

"And if our plan is uncovered?"

"The Holy Father believes the plan to be of his own design. That is best to protect both of us, having the pontiff involved so deeply as he now is."

"And I suppose it shall have been worth it, what we have

done"—he shrugged, his tone full of reticence—"*if* we can have Raphael return to creating the volume of work we have all come to expect."

"I bid you not to look at things in so gloomy a fashion, Agostino." The cardinal smiled his thin-lipped, menacing smile. "You know our Raffaello. Now that the deed is done, how long do you truly believe it shall be before he sees the baker's daughter as but a pleasant little memory?"

RAPHAEL was late to Chigi's wedding. He had already missed the ceremony, having gone too late with Giulio to Trastevere to collect Margherita, and whisper to her words of contrition. He had wanted to go himself rather than to send for her after their angry exchange. But when he and Giulio arrived, she was nowhere to be found. Francesco Luti had not seen her, he said, surprised by the painter's sudden presence there. Nor had Letitia.

"I assumed she was with you by now," said Donato cautiously. "That painter, Sebastiano, took her home for me, as she was not feeling well, and he luckily came upon us as we were leaving the Vatican gardens. She had wanted to visit that elephant again."

"What happened? Was she taken ill?"

"She was only weary, and distracted, *signore*. Not ill." Donato chose not to reveal that the cruel women on the piazza had been Margherita's undoing.

"But why the devil did you let Sebastiano Luciani, of all men, escort her?"

Donato tipped his head, waited a beat. "Because, *signore,* he had a swift horse. We were on foot, and I knew not how to deny the offer from a grand man without appearing rude."

Raphael's eyes had filled with a growing panic, glancing back and forth at each of them, as Giulio stood behind him in the doorway. He had pushed his concern away before hearing that. But there could be no doubt that something had gone very wrong.

Now Raphael burst into Chigi's palazzo, past the stone-faced guards at the gate, and took the wide marble steps up from the courtyard two at a time, his wine-colored cape flaring out behind him. Giulio was running, out of breath, close at his heels. Raphael's heart throbbed with dread, unaware of anything or anyone but finding Margherita. Someone here must have seen her or Sebastiano. There had to be an explanation. How did Sebastiano, of all people, come upon Margherita—his love—at just that precise moment?

The guests were already assembled at the banquet table beneath the newly finished fresco he had designed. The table was piled high with gleaming silver dishes laden with mounds of food and great crystal decanters of wine. He realized only then that he had missed the actual wedding, which would do nothing to ingratiate him to the already irritated Chigi.

But he could not think of that. Not now. In a wild-eyed panic, Raphael scanned the crowd for the presence of his rival. If Sebastiano was the last to have seen her, then Raphael would force him to reveal where she had gone. This bitter feud had gotten dangerously out of hand.

As he scanned the faces of wedding guest after guest, amid a crescendo of laughter and happy conversation, none of them yet realized he was even there. Nor did they notice him as he moved around the servants bearing an elegant orgy of food on gleaming silver trays. There were grand dishes piled with steaming lampreys baked in pie, pomegranates, dressed anchovies, fresh green almonds split and served on vine leaves, candied fruit and marzipan, but all of it was a blur. His face as he searched was stricken, his mind darting back to their quarrel four days ago.

Had there been anything at all in her words, or their inference, he asked himself frantically now, to foreshadow something serious? Had she been more than a little angry with him? He had seen too little of her since to answer the question with certainty.

"Ah, well!" said Agostino grandly, a golden goblet held in midair at the moment of seeing Raphael standing near the wide doorway arch. "As they say, Raffaello *mio*, better late than never! Oh, but do sit down, and tell us what brilliant piece of work has kept you from us, as the meal has already begun!"

"You must tell me, have you seen Sebastiano?" he asked, the words leaping from his mouth like sticky fruit, the panic in them obvious, and his face gone pale with fear.

"Well, no. Now that it is mentioned, it seems yet another of our great artisans has not had the grace to be prompt to my wedding celebration." He set the goblet down and kissed his new wife's cheek. "A bridegroom who was not so deliriously happy as I *could* take offense at that, you know."

Once again, Raphael scanned the faces of the wealthy and powerful guests assembled before him, all of them seeing his panic and reacting with whispers and lifted eyebrows, even as they chewed and drank and laughed.

"What is it?" Cardinal Bibbiena asked, glancing up from an intense conversation across the table with Cardinal de' Medici. His elbow propped up the hand from which the brilliant ruby ring glittered. "Has something happened?"

He tried desperately to keep his tone modulated, but the words left his lips in a staccato tenor. "I cannot find Signora Luti!"

The whispers rose to a sedate crescendo as the pope stood, with the aide of his two ever-present secretaries, one on each side of him. Raphael could not breathe for the spasm of fear that shot through his lungs, then raced back up toward his heart. She would not do this . . . she would not simply disappear . . .

If you believe that, Raphael, then you do not know me at all . . .

The pope's expression was grave. "Come, my son." It was not a request, but a command. "And Agostino as well. Be good enough to join us."

GIULIO ROMANO paced the corridor outside the loggia where the banquet was going on. Tiny beads of sweat formed on his brow and he wiped them away with the back of his hand. Laughter and the clink of silver and glasses spilled out from the loggia before him, but Giulio did not feel like revelry. He had withheld what he had seen from the *mastro,* and so he had betrayed him, the man who had given him everything.

All afternoon Giulio had silently prayed that there had been some mistake. That when they arrived in Trastevere, Signora Luti would be there, but not with Sebastiano, and all between the two of them would be forgiven. He had wanted to tell Raphael when they heard that she had not returned home or to the bakery. He *knew* he should have told him, but what could he possibly say? Could he be the one to tell the *mastro* that the love of his life had gone off with his greatest rival?

It was a revelation Giulio simply did not feel his heart was strong enough to make.

Instead, he told Signor Chigi. The great banker, and Raphael's close friend, surely would know better than he what to say. And so Raphael had gone outside with a dour-faced pope and Signor Chigi to hear what would likely be his undoing. *Forgive me,* mastro, Giulio was thinking as he paced. *You mean the world to me. You are everything. Too much for me to be the one to break your heart.*

THE THREE WALKED somberly outside onto the ornate balcony, with its carved stone balustrade and small, ordered gardens beyond. A light breeze blew the briny scent of water, and the odor of fish in the stagnant Tiber, up at them. As they stood facing the twisting dark water below, Pope Leo reached out and placed his hand on Raphael's shoulder. His touch was firm.

"It will be easier on you if I am direct, my son. The girl is gone."

The effect was immediate, and lethal. Like bile rushing into his mouth, Raphael tasted betrayal on a rancid swell of bitterness — something, he thought strangely then, of what Maria must have felt. And then what followed . . .

It cannot be . . . I must not . . . There is a mistake!

"Gone?" The word came out in a short bark of disbelief. "What do *you* know of it? Gone where? Why?"

"It plagues the heart, my son, to be the one to tell you this, but I have had my staff following your *signora* for several days now. I was advised to expect something like this. And, alas, their warning appears to have been an accurate one."

The words seemed distorted, unbelievable. As if it were a part of a very poor joke.

"To be blunt, my son, as a clean wound heals most swiftly, I shall tell you that as she left Rome, she was seen on horseback in the company of a man."

Raphael searched his fear-plagued mind, thoughts and memories racing through it. She was his love. It had been a small disagreement, nothing more. Yet that same betrayal hardened now in his throat, refusing to be ignored. Hot, corrosive. Betrayal he tried powerfully to refuse.

"It is a lie!" His eyes were wide with panic. "Have you checked Hanno's enclosure? She often goes there when—"

"Raffaello *mio*," Pope Leo soothed. "*Per favore,* she is not with the beast. Do not make this more difficult upon yourself. She was never worthy of this kind of pain."

He sank against a carved stone pilaster, his knees buckling beneath him, still unable to breathe. He touched the cold stone very lightly. *Dio . . . Dio!* "She was worth everything to me," he mouthed very softly in an aching tone.

"You would not be the first to have misjudged a woman's value, Raphael," Agostino Chigi carefully interjected. "You are a wealthy man now. Women of her class could be motivated to appear exceedingly accommodating, until they had received a sufficient amount of . . . compensation."

He still could not breathe. His lungs were still constricting with a hot, heavy force. "She never asked for anything, and she allowed me to give her very little."

"Yet she was, for a time, companion to the great Raffaello, and perhaps that was enough."

Raphael looked at Pope Leo through glazed eyes. "Was the man Sebastiano?"

"I'm afraid we do not know the man's identity for certain, my son. But it is odd that Signor Luciani is not here now when he, too, had accepted an invitation."

Raphael raked both hands through his loose, long hair and

exhaled a first deep, painful breath—one that seemed to scorch his lungs. "Who told you of this?"

Chigi and Pope Leo exchanged a glance. "It was your assistant," Chigi revealed. "Giulio Romano came to us not long ago, concerned about how you were to be told."

The wound deepened, tore at his soul. *Not Giulio, as well?*

"Was he absolutely certain it was Margherita?"

Murmuring a Latin prayer and raising his fat, ring-dotted hand beneficently toward Raphael, the pope somberly said, "My son. There is no doubt at all about the girl. He says he knows her face well. Let us now pray for your soul, and for deliverance back to the ways of the Lord for the poor misguided girl, wherever she now may be."

Part Three

Thus does my infinite
passion for her torment me.
Her beauty is blinding
in its splendor.
Unfriendly has become
my hand,
and now I am unable
even to work . . .

From a sonnet
by Raphael Sanzio

✤ *30* ✤

WERE THEY DAYS, OR HOURS?

Time was like colors in a fresco, running together. Time had drifted by without marking itself for Raphael. Or perhaps it was he who did not wish to know how long she had been gone.

He had not slept nor even drunk the wine Elena and Giulio continually left out for him, a palliative that might have cauterized this open wound upon his heart. He could not stay at the house on the Via Alessandrina, or even at the one on the Via dei Coronari. There were too many sketches and Madonnas of her at them both.

Piercing shards of memory, jagged as glass, tore at him as he moved through the city, head down, wearing a wide brim hat, not seeing people, or the tall shadow-making buildings on the endless tangle of city streets in which he wanted to lose himself. He needed to be far away from all of the things that might remind him of her. A new rush of anguish shook him. The thoughts crept into his mind, day and night. Relentlessly. Excruciatingly. It was, all of it, wrong. This could not be, his heart repeated over and over in a heavy, painful drumbeat. Yet still, catlike, the thoughts crept in. Had she truly been so restless for marriage, and he too hopeful for "some day" to have seen her displeasure? Had someone else offered more, or offered it more swiftly? Where was Sebastiano? It had been days since anyone in Rome had seen him. Could she really have been blind to his motives? The imaginings behind Raphael's eyes, when he could not push them away, showed him fearsome things. Disappointment in her gentle expression when

she last gazed at him. Hurt in her tone at the papal pronouncement about her.

At the end of yet another street, he turned and went up a set
of wide stone steps, passing a stout street vendor in shabby
clothes hawking ripe lemons with a loud, pagan call. A few steps
on, a dirty-faced, shoeless boy stood with his eyes wide and his
hand out. Walking along a Roman road of stone blocks laid by
Julius Caesar's men, Raphael pushed away the tormenting
thoughts of regret. Yet even as he did, they always returned,
redoubled in force. *I should not have listened to the doubts she raised. I
should have taken her to Urbino and married her there. I should never have given
her a chance to question us!* That drumbeat stayed in his mind, until he
could not think, eat, sleep, or paint. He felt now like the beggars
crowding the filthy, shadow-darkened Borgo near the papal
palace through which he roamed. Shiftless, purposeless. Empty.

He was not certain how he had gotten there or why, but many
days, Raphael found himself inside the Vatican gardens, standing
outside the large enclosure that housed Hanno, the pope's great
exotic beast. His mind wound back to the times Margherita had
insisted they visit the creature. He remembered her gentleness
with him, and the animal's response, the way he pressed his trunk
against her shoulder in a show of affection. She had been gentle
with him. She had shown him respect, as she did with everyone
she met.

"Do you miss her, too, I wonder?" he quietly asked. "We're not
all that different, you and I. Possessions of the Holy Father. Here
at his will, brought to do his bidding . . . caged, controlled.
Trapped. She saw that in you. Where they saw your novelty, she
saw your sadness."

Swathed in heavy fur against the early winter chill, a woman
approached him then, moving quietly along the path. He had not
heard her until she was very near, which caused him to turn with
a start. It was Maria Bibbiena, gowned in blue velvet with wide
fur cuffs and a matching patterned velvet cloak. Her hair was
dressed in a fine gold net. A ring of servants stood nearby; one of

them, a tall, commanding guard Raphael remembered, held the reins of her horse.

"Have you followed me?" he growled, gazing at her through red-veined eyes.

"Forgive me, but I felt I must speak with you," she said, her pale mouth trembling at the sight of him. "I wanted to tell you how truly sorry I am. Sorry I mean, about the baker's daughter abandoning you."

"She has not abandoned me!" he barked, his body going rigid in defense as the cold winter wind whispered through them both.

"Then where is she?"

"I don't know! But I will *never* believe—" He stopped himself, knowing it could not be right to reveal any part of his heartbreak to her.

"*Per favore,*" she bid him in a thin voice. "Come home with me, Raffaello *mio*. I will see you warmed by a cup of spiced wine and we shall sit beside the fire and talk, as we once did. All will be forgiven. Our betrothal revived."

"Nothing can ever be between us as it once was, Maria!"

"You sound so certain of that."

"I am."

"But she has gone!"

"Not from my heart," he said achingly. "No matter what has happened to her, she will never be gone from my heart!"

He saw that her gaunt cheeks were red and chapped and that she was shivering. Raphael felt a deep pang of regret looking at her like this. Regret that he had hurt her. Regret that he had been so foolish long ago and toyed with her heart—a heart he had broken without meaning to. In the end, she had been betrayed, as he now was.

"I thank you for your concern," he said somberly, taking up her gloved hands between the two of them, and squeezing them with a memory of the small affection he once had felt for her. "But I must be alone now, I bid you. Leave me to my sorrow. Find another life for yourself."

"My life is with you. *I* was your betrothed, Raphael. Not her."

"Set me free, Maria," he urged her achingly. "I beg you, set me free of your heart! It is the only thing I have ever asked of you!"

"And the only thing I cannot give."

"*Per favore* . . . do not make me hurt you anymore!"

She reached up to touch his cheek. There were tears in her pale blue-gray eyes. "It would not be possible, Raffaello *mio,* for you to hurt me more."

MORE DAYS . . . more hours . . . Walking . . . searching . . . No rest. No work. No answers. Only memories and questions to his companions, of what had driven her away. The wind gusted and the rain surged through his clothes, pelting his face, wetting his eyes so that he could not tell the rain from his tears.

Day after endless day, he walked aimlessly through Rome, up Il Gianicolo, hoping to see her there, where they had met. But she was never there, nor were the answers to why she had gone, or where. On a day like all of the others, one that felt like decades, Raphael stood alone at the top of the hill, wind whipping through his cape and doublet, shaking his fists at the God above him who had allowed this to happen.

"Have I not done all that you have asked of me, *dio mio?* Have I not served You . . . Honored You . . . painted You!" He wailed aloud like a man gone mad. "If you have had enough of me this is surely a sign! My art . . . my painting . . . All of it is gone with her!"

Strollers came upon him and were staring, but he could change nothing—feel nothing, but the desolation. From how great a height had he fallen. Now there was nothing left of his work, his life, his heart, but fragments, like pieces of shattered glass. It was finished, all of it. And so was he.

AN ODD SILENCE that had descended across the vast workshop. The assistants and apprentices still showed up for work every morning, yet after a few days, their direction lost, they simply collected, gossiped, cleaned brushes, murmured their regret, and waited for news, as if the fate of Margherita Luti, a woman they had disregarded, somehow mattered to them after all.

Everyone knew what had happened, yet no one dared to speak of it, for how they had all looked askance at her. The baker's daughter was just another of the *mastro*'s trifles, they all had believed, and they had behaved accordingly. Particularly the disdainful Giovanni da Udine, who had placed bets on the tables in the bordello as to how long she would last in Raphael's life. Beautiful, mindless, inconsequential, he had said—and he could not have been more wrong.

As the days wore on with no answer to the mystery, the consequences of Margherita's disappearance affected not only Raphael, but the entire group of artists. He was not there to lead them, to teach them—or to bring them work. Without the *mastro*, there was nothing for them. Over a bottle of wine, they collected, shiftless and uncertain, sitting together on stools, chairs, and painting props, their cups half drained, their hope of a happy ending to all of this dwindling by the day.

"I suppose some of us misjudged her," da Udine grumbled awkwardly, breaking the tense silence of another uncertain afternoon.

Only Penni glanced up from his cup. "We could have been nicer to her when she was here. I, for one, never even tried to speak to her or give her a smile."

"It is clear now she was good for the *mastro*," one of the young apprentices dared to say, and several of the assistants nodded silently in agreement.

For the first time, Giulio came across the room to sit among them, since he was as lost as they all were. "She deserved better than she got from the lot of us," he said, shaking his head.

Da Udine shot him a defensive glare, and, for a moment, there was another tense silence. "You are not saying, I hope, that you believe it was our fault that she went away!"

"I am saying it well could be, Giovanni. And if she ever returns to him, I believe we must tell her that."

"I am not one to admit such things." Da Udine shrugged grudgingly. "But perhaps it is so."

"Do you suppose she will ever return to him?" Penni asked Giulio, who they all knew to be the closest to Raphael. "Looking back, they really did seem happy."

"I suppose that depends on where she has gone—and why. And, for the moment, only the Good Lord knows the answer to that. For the *mastro*'s sake, I hope he finds out the truth before the mystery of it destroys him, and all the rest of us along with him."

"WHAT DO YOU MEAN, things are not improved?"

Cardinal Bibbiena bellowed the question with uncharacteristic ferocity, having lost all decorum. He stood at the back of the cold and soaring basilica of Santa Maria Maggiore beside Agostino Chigi as the wave of parishoners filed out past him after Mass.

"Sadly, it is true. And, for that matter," Agostino confessed with an impotent shrug, "I would say that things are actually much worse! In truth, Raphael barely works at all. His assistant, Giulio Romano, admitted to me that *mastro* Raffaello wanders the streets aimlessly, as if searching for her, and rarely sets foot in the studio at all these days. The Holy Father's *stanza* and the antiquities projects go unattended. The assistants, Romano, Penni, and da Udine, have tried their best to cover for him, to work around his prolonged absence, but before long it will be an impossible thing to hide. I tell you, Your Grace, it is as if the very spark has gone out of the man."

"Over the loss of that *peasant girl? Impossible!*" he hissed.

It was not supposed to be this way. This was entirely wrong. All of it. His plan had been so well thought out. So completely flawless. As everything was about his life. He had been a cardinal for many years, and he had grown accustomed to the glory, the wealth, and, in particular, the power. Power to control people and things as he saw fit. And he most certainly did not like feeling stripped of any of that, as he did now.

"Have you spoken with him? Reasoned with him about his duty to Rome? To the Holy Father?"

"Regrettably, Your Grace, there is no reasoning with a broken heart."

"Foolish words!" he snarled. "Where is his pride? He is Raffaello!"

"He is first a man who was in love with a woman. One now gone from his life."

Bibbiena wrinkled his long face as if smelling something foul, then he shook his head distastefully. "So what do you propose we do now, Agostino?"

"I fear there is only one thing that *can* be done, Your Grace."

They were looking directly at one another. "You cannot mean—"

"I mean it entirely."

"That is not possible."

"Then, in all likelihood, neither is the completion of our projects."

"This has been a disaster." Bibbiena turned away, nervously twisting the ruby ring. "I will not indite myself in this mess, nor shall you."

"Then how?"

He pivoted, his eyes glittering hatefully. "I should imagine you shall have to convince the Holy Father that the two of you need to confess to Raphael what was done—and why."

Chigi laughed bitterly. "And then hope with both of our hearts that Raphael chooses to forgive us?"

"I do not suppose he shall do much of that, in this case." Bibbiena leveled his eyes and clasped his hands. He nodded to the nameless worshippers filing past him as he spoke beneath his breath. "Rather, if there is hope of salvaging the work, I think, we had all better begin very intensely to pray for forgiveness from the Almighty—and particularly, from Raphael."

ELENA AND GIULIO waited late into the night at the house on the Via dei Coronari for Raphael to return. The veal and onions she had cooked for him had gone cold, and the grand house was a silent tomb, crackling with anticipation. In nearly twenty days, there had been not a single word at all from Margherita Luti. When they glanced at one another now, Elena looked quickly away. There was still something between them. They both felt that. Adversity had only intensified it. But there was danger in it for Elena. He was another artist. Another potential mistake. She had risked her family's welfare once that way. She would not do so again.

As they sat alone with only the occasional comment and the sound of the crackling fire between them, a forceful knock sounded at the door. Giovanni da Udine stood in the gold lamplight cast before the door, his ruddy face showing that there was news.

"Enter!" Giulio hurriedly bid him, pulling him inside. "What is it? What has happened?"

"It is not Sebastiano who has gone away with her! At least he is not with her now!"

"How do you know that?"

"Gianfrancesco saw him with his own eyes just now down on the Piazza Navona. And he was very much alone."

Giulio washed a hand across his face, then looked over at Elena, who stood back near the shadowy stairwell. The thought came to them both at the same time, but it was Giulio who spoke the words.

"Then, if Sebastiano is not with her, what has become of poor Margherita?"

❧ 31 ❧

JANUARY 1516

"OH, BERNARDO, THIS IS TOO MUCH! NOW IF WE ARE TO confess involvement, you and I, Raphael will surely be more unwilling to work than before!" wailed the rotund pontiff. "It is his art that was making me immortal! His hand alone that was meant to give me a legacy! I *must* have my legacy!"

His plump face was covered in a sheen of perspiration, and his small lips were pursed in frustration. As he sat on his crimson-draped papal throne in the bedchamber at the Castel Sant'-Angelo, a sandy morning light filtered in through the single oval window behind Bibbiena.

Cardinal Bibbiena had been blunt about the plan's swift unraveling. Bluntness lessened the blame, he long ago had discovered, and for Bernardo Dovizi da Bibbiena, self-protection had always been one of his primary goals. Self-advancement was the other. Without them, he was simply another of the ambitious cardinals who vied for scraps of attention from an often distracted pontiff.

"It is certainly a tragedy, Your Holiness," he said with the greatest caution.

"We have made an error in it! I was too taken up with everything else to have seen it, and now of course I must apologize, and appear contrite, when I care nothing for his common little tart! Or else he may never paint for any of us again!"

The once jovial pope had been weakened by the problems that had engulfed his papacy of late. On one hand, a new and ambitious young king was on the French throne, and thus Milan was threatened with war. King François I promised to take the city, so now Pope Leo needed to strengthen his alliances with King Ferdinand of Spain and Emperor Maximilian. On the other hand, the pope had reluctantly made an Englishman, Thomas Wolsey, a cardinal, hoping to persuade Henry VIII to join an alliance against ambitious France. But the worst blow to the pope was not a political one. Suddenly, he had lost his beloved brother, Giuliano, Duke of Nemours, to fever—one of the people upon whom he had greatly depended for advice and support. That had weakened the pontiff emotionally in a way that nothing else could.

"We must tell Raphael the truth, mustn't we?"

Bibbiena struggled to find his own tone of contrition with the pope when what he still desired greatly was to gloat. Now, finally, Raphael was as miserable as he had made Maria, and he wished that to continue for as long as possible. But, as always, there was his self-advancement to consider, and that must come first.

"I fear you are correct. He must be told, Your Holiness."

"Then we must pray to God Almighty for a sincere appearance when we do, or he may never create anything for any of us ever again!"

THE MOMENT came later that same afternoon.

In the soaring frescoed *stanza,* Pope Leo hoped to remind Raphael what was at stake. Several of his cardinals pleaded with him to let them take the fall by manipulating the truth. The Holy Father was, after all, to be protected at all cost. There was much debate about the point, but at last Pope Leo convinced them to accept his own scheme. Coming directly from him, with a calculated, albeit feigned, show of remorse, it might just soften the heavy blow. And the less damaged Raphael was by the wound, the more likely he was, in time, to forgive.

Maintaining their creative workhorse was really all that mattered, and Pope Leo would do anything—say anything—to achieve that.

Raphael's face was ghostly pale, his expression grave, and his eyes bloodshot from lack of sleep as he was shown into the papal audience chamber. He had not changed his clothes for several days, and the rich burgundian fabric hung on him now, rumpled and soiled. His usually neat chestnut-colored hair was tousled and uncombed, his beard ragged.

When the pope motioned to him, he sank onto the edge of a golden chair fringed in crimson velvet tassels that had been brought before the throne. "It concerns Signora Luti, my son. Her whereabouts, and why she has gone."

A sudden spasm of pain crossed Raphael's face. *Dio mio . . . Let it not be . . .* He shot to his feet, his body a ramrod of tension. He glanced over to Agostino Chigi, then to Cardinal de' Medici, the pope's cousin, both of whom bore the gravest expressions. These men he had known and trusted—they were involved?

"What do *you* know of it?"

Pope Leo flinched then shifted uncomfortably. As it was unseasonably warm, the hair at the nape of his neck was wet with perspiration, as was the small dent beneath his nose. "We—I wished you to work, you see, and you were not working. Not enough, and—"

"Per l'amor di Dio! No!" His heart was slamming against his ribs. "I am a man, Your Holiness! Not just a servant to answer to your pleasure!"

"The decision was unwise with regard to you."

Raphael felt himself begin to unravel as he stood in stunned disbelief. These men for whom he had toiled and sacrificed, men he had respected and admired. Raphael's tone when he spoke again was flat and very cold. "Where is she?"

"But will you understand what we have done, Raphael *mio?* First, tell me, if she is returned to you with our most sincere apologies, might we go on as if it were but an error in judgment?"

"Tell me where she is, by God Almighty, or I—!" he shouted fiercely, forgetting everything. This man before him he saw not as the Holy Father. This place, the Vatican, was not sacred, but a prison of lies and deceit that had trapped him and horribly punished his beloved.

"First, you must know that she has been well cared for!"

"She has been your *prisoner!*"

"We did it for your own good, Raphael. We only meant to keep her until this obsession of yours had passed and then, of course—"

"I bid you, Raphael, do not let your anger keep you from hearing what the Holy Father has to say!" Chigi tried to intercede on the pope's behalf, his hands held out in a pleading gesture.

"Speak no more! I shall listen to none of your lies! I was a fool for both of you! My heart, my soul, went into my creations for you here, and yet you sought to pluck out that very soul that painted for you, worked for you! Believed in you!"

"Raphael!" Chigi gasped at his impropriety before the Holy Father.

"Where is she, damn you?" he demanded again furiously. "Say only that and not a word more! The confession of the details is too vile for even our good Lord above us to hear! Tell me, by God, or you shall never see me or any of my work again!"

"She is held at La Magliana."

Raphael staggered back. "Your hunting lodge?"

"She has not been harmed!" the pope himself repeated. "You will find her well there, I promise you!"

With a final angry stare of sheer disbelief, Raphael turned away from them and went out the door, his cape flying as he neglected the deferential bow to the Holy Father.

❧ *32* ❧

SHE HAD NOT LEFT HIM. THERE WAS NO OTHER MAN. This was a most foul dream. A nightmare. Impossible to comprehend. Looking into the face of a friend, he saw now an enemy, and the betrayal from so unlikely a source was like poison in his veins.

"I shall ride with you!" Giulio called as they stood outside the Vatican Gates, where two grooms held Raphael's saddled horse. The winter wind tossed their hair and the edges of the cloaks they wore. "I bid you, *mastro.* I must make amends to you—*and* to Signora Luti for not revealing sooner what I knew."

"Allow me to go as well. I owe her my life for the chance she has given to mine," Elena said. She seemed to have come out of nowhere but she must have been with Giulio, he realized. Raphael shot her a surprised glance, and was prepared to deny her when she added, "If she has been injured or violated in any way, *signore,* anything of a"—she struggled with a phrase that would not upset

Raphael more—"of a womanly nature, she may feel more comfortable if—"

"But you have no horse!"

"Elena can ride with me," Giulio declared. "My horse is tied to
the ring just over there."

"But of course," Raphael amended, grateful for her caring.
"Thank you, both."

As a show of solidarity and support, the other artists joined
them then, and they rode with fearsome speed. The cold wind
lashed at their faces and tossed their hair, but Raphael felt none
of it. His breaths were shallow, and even that scorched his lungs.
She was alive, praise God Almighty in His heaven! And she had
not left him!

Raphael's heart crashed over and over against his ribs, beating
a rhythm of fury, relief, and anticipation of what he would find at
La Magliana. His only hope now was that she had not been
harmed and that she would not blame him for what she had
endured because of his connections, rivalries, and commitments
to powerful men.

La Magliana was an estate on the edge of a vast wooded hillock
outside of Rome. The broad expanse of sky above was heavily gray,
threatening an ominous winter rain. Raphael brought his horse to a
hard gallop, churning the dirt and dust into a great cloud down the
long causeway behind him. They knew him here. They had hosted
him as the pope's guest many times. That the friars here, those
pious men of God, had knowingly kept a woman—*his* woman,
against her will, tormenting him, likely frightening her, and nearly
destroying his soul. All of this ran through his mind as he leaped
from his mount and stormed through the gates of the grand stucco-
covered facade of La Magliana.

THE ROOMS accorded her were not entirely objectionable.
There was a large canopy bed covered in tapestry fabric, a warming fireplace inscribed with the name of Pope Innocent VIII, a

game table for solitaire, and a sweeping, desolate view over the woodlands. And yet this place still was her prison. Margherita sat on the window embrasure, clutching her rosary, arms around her knees, as she had for hours, days, now weeks, trying to find anything in that flat, unending vista before her that might tell her where she had been taken. But, as always, it was fruitless.

She remembered little about her actual abduction beyond the sack placed over her head, and the strong, acrid smell of old wool. There was the draft of damp air, and the chill held in by the heavy building stones, a building she longed to escape, but she was reminded daily that she could not.

Everything from that point on was a gray sort of nightmare. And all of it had happened so fast. So disjointedly. A shadowy barrage of images and sounds came at her now when she tried to make sense of it. She remembered Sebastiano offering her a ride on the back of his horse. Then the brief struggle later, the heart-thumping fear of the unknown, and then total darkness. When she woke, it was with a piercing headache, nausea, and vision that did not entirely clear for several days. She had been drugged somehow, and the only possible way involved either Donato or Sebastiano, the two men who had been her companions that day. Knowing in her heart that Donato could have had nothing to do with this, only one unthinkable choice remained.

"... And in the meantime, with all of the men of Rome, like Sebastiano Luciani, who sees you as fair game ..."

She squeezed her eyes, trying to push back the always looming sense of stupidity that pelted her cruelly about it. Why had she not believed Raphael? Trusted his opinion of his rival, at least? There was still so much about his world that she did not understand. She had been a fool to push him—and his fear—away.

Margherita moved from the window and began to pace across the wide wood-plank floor that echoed her every step. Most days, most long hours, it was the only sound she heard. Food came to her twice a day, brought by a plump-faced friar, his head and face cleanly shaven and his stout body garbed in drab brown robes, with a heavy crucifix suspended to the middle of his belly. His thin lips always moved in silent prayer as he set down her tray, steepled his hands, and left the room.

As the unending days wore on, she longed to ask the monk to play a game of cards with her, even to speak to her of the day, the hour—or when she might be freed. Yet always it was the same reaction. A polite, stone-faced nod and withdrawal from the room. The click of the latch and turn of the heavy iron key had become sounds both fearsome and depressing. Depressing because they meant that someone had wanted her out of Raphael's life badly enough to have had her abducted.

What had he been told? She had wondered that most of all. Did he believe her dead? And was she meant to be? If he did not believe it, would he ever find her here, well hidden, far from any city or town? It was too vast here, too isolated. But they had not harmed her. Only held her, with no end of any of it anywhere in sight. Tears of futility pooled in her eyes, and she brushed them away with the back of her hand. She would not cry again. She could not give into the panic. She was a prisoner, and she would be a prisoner, for as long as her captors desired.

As she paced now nearer the door, Margherita heard footsteps in the corridor beyond. They were heavy, masculine steps belonging to more than one man. Her heart quickened. It was a sound she had not heard here before. Only the gentle pacing of the soft-sandaled friars ever broke the monotony of silence. Suddenly her eyes were wide, expectant. Her first thought, the one that followed the sound, was one of fear that danger was near. She thought to hide, but in this single vast room that was impossible. Her hands flew to her mouth to stifle a cry as she heard the familiar sound of the lock, the turn of the handle, and then the impossible. It was no dangerous stranger but Raphael, with Giulio Romano and three other men, who thrust back the door powerfully and burst into the room toward her, all of their shining swords drawn. At last, she thought. At last he has come . . .

MARGHERITA SOBBED IN relief against his chest, and Raphael wept silently into the softness of her unbound hair. The fragrance of it, of her skin, the assurance there, was like honeyed wine to a man who had begun to believe that he might never know his love again. At first, he held her at arm's length, tears clouding their eyes. He was tender with her, as if she might break. He held her face in his trembling hands.

"Are you . . . well?" he managed to murmur on a tone of such painful relief that his voice quivered, falling into a whisper.

"I am," she said in reply. "Now."

As he pulled her tightly to his chest, more tightly than he had ever held her before, Margherita saw Elena standing beside Giulio Romano and the other men. "Are you in need of anything of a private nature, Signora Luti?" Elena shyly asked, her eyes wide with concern and care. None of them knew what had been done to her here, or by whom.

Margherita could only shake her head for the barrage of emotion that pelted her and the tears that filled her eyes. Raphael still clutched her tightly to him, both of their bodies trembling with emotion. "Leave us, all of you. Just for a moment. And ready the horses as soon as they have had a drink and a bit of a rest. I want us not to remain here a moment longer than necessary!"

A stolen glance passed between Giulio and Elena before she looked away. Wordlessly then, Raphael and Margherita wound their arms around one another, then anticipated a freedom she had not known, for the cruelty and ambition of men, for over a month's time.

❧ 33 ❧

AS RAPHAEL STOLE QUICKLY AWAY FROM THE HOUSE, heading alone toward the stables, someone suddenly jerked him back. Giulio held fast to both of Raphael's shoulders. A short, pearl-handled rapier glinted from Raphael's hand in the last of the afternoon sunlight.

"Leave me, Giulio! This does not concern you!"

"If you go, it would be a fool's journey that would only lead to your ruin, *mastro!*"

Raphael's face blazed with murderous intent as he threw off the firm hands of his assistant. "That does not matter as long as Sebastiano is ruined along with me!"

"You cannot harm him!"

"Harm? I mean to *kill him!*"

"You cannot!"

"Stand aside!"

But Giulio only clamped his hands more tightly. "I will save you as you have saved me!"

"I thank you for your fidelity," Raphael said, his chest heaving, and his face gone red with anger and exertion, "but these are two very different things! I will do this to avenge Margherita!"

"You will be doing it *to* yourself!"

"Let me go, Giulio!" Raphael growled, still struggling.

"I cannot, *mastro.* Do not ask that of me!" They struggled for a moment more, there on the street, but Giulio would not relent. "Go back inside, *mastro.* Signora Luti needs you now far more than you need to do this!"

"Giulio, step aside!"

"*Per l'amor di Dio,* think of Signora Luti!"

"I shall ever think only of her!"

"Then do not leave her alone! What sort of existence would she have without you to protect her?" When he did not respond, Giulio leveled his gaze upon Raphael with great seriousness. In that moment, things had turned and the student had become the master. "Be with her, *mastro*. Go upstairs and be with her. Signora Luti needs that now—she needs *you* far more than she needs revenge!"

THE PUNCH came out of nowhere. Antonio Perazzi was catapulted up and backward through the air, then landed sprawling in a pile of straw in the Chigi stables. One of the huge horses whinnied in response and pawed the ground, and the bag of oats Antonio had been feeding them sprayed the ground. It took a moment for his vision to clear and another to realize that the blow had been delivered by his own brother, Donato.

"What the devil was *that* for?"

"For Margherita, you lout! I would kill you myself to avenge her if the damage were not already done!"

"I don't know what you're talking about, brother," he lied, rubbing his jaw and struggling for the breath that had just soundly been knocked out of him.

"Spare me the lies, *brother!* The fishmonger's daughter boasted of it all herself. She was so proud to have her former rival put in her place!"

"Anna would never—"

"Never what? Betray you? Hell hath no fury like a woman scorned, they say—or for that matter, a woman preceded by another in the heart of the man she loves!"

Antonio struggled to stand but stumbled back onto his knees. "This is preposterous."

"Is it? I would have said it was preposterous that my own brother would actually betray his childhood friend—and mine— for the sake of revenge! That is what *I* would have thought preposterous!"

"It was not for revenge, it was—"

"It was what, Antonio? Why would you do this?"

"Because I wanted her to know suffering as I did!" Antonio spat, unapologetic. "Are you pleased now?"

Donato shook his head, lowered it, and stepped back. "That is pure evil."

"How can you side with *her*? I believed we would be married! That *I* would share her fortunes *and* her life! She always loved me! Always obeyed me, only to torment me in the end!"

"You are wretched, brother! Any woman was always fair game to you! It was that way since we were boys! If you wanted it, you took it! It mattered not a whit who you hurt or how! You were the papal spy all along!"

"And I would have succeeded as well, if not for the great Raffaello!"

"If he had just *used* Margherita, you mean, and not fallen in love with her?"

"*Sì,* as he did with countless other women before her!" Antonio declared, his hands extended in a pleading gesture. "I had it all planned out!"

Again, Donato shook his head. "I see that you did. But plans change."

Antonio's expression suddenly went cold. "Better to escape with some pride, than to consign myself to sniffing after her and doing her bidding for the rest of my life!"

"As I do, you mean?"

"Strike me again, if you will, but *sì,* brother, precisely as you do!"

"I might have hit you again for Margherita's honor." Donato paused a moment as if contemplating his next move. His face compressed into a frown of open disgust. Then, instead, he simply turned and walked away. As he moved to leave the stables, pushing through the crowd of men who had gathered, Donato made one final volley.

"But I find now that you are not worth the effort. You deserve what you get!"

❧ 34 ❧

MARGHERITA WATCHED RAPHAEL PACE THE LONG ROOM like a caged animal, still violently angry. The rage at their betrayal—men for whom he had toiled and sweat, men with whom he had broken bread, laughed—prayed, brought forth in him a kind of dark rage she had never seen before.

"Talk to me, *mio dolce amato*," she softly bid him from the bed to which he had carried her himself and lovingly lay her. He had removed her gown, and covered her over with rich bedding. He came now and sat beside her, but the tension did not leave his face even as he took her hands in his own.

"We must leave Rome. I must be away from this place. There is no other answer!"

"*Amore*," she soothed.

Giving in to her touch for only a moment, he then pulled away. "You shall not pacify me in this. I will never forgive what they have done!"

"Raphael, your talent is too great. Do not allow this incident to be the focus of your life."

"*You* are the focus of my life!" He thumped a fist onto the table beside their bed. "And they knew it!"

"They wanted you to themselves. Their wish is the magnificent art they know you will create. They lost sight of their good sense in the face of that."

Again he began to pace, his body still taut with anger. "They made their choice, Margherita. They chose art over honor, and I choose *you* over all else!"

"And yet you cannot leave here. You are needed to glorify this city, to leave your mark on history as it is meant to be."

"If I ever do feel like painting again, I can do that anywhere. Florence was very good to me before I came here. Perhaps I will return and help to beautify Florence instead of Rome."

"Is Michelangelo not there?"

"As we have seen, I have rivals everywhere. But I shall not be a fool with your safety now. *Dio mio,* if anything else were to happen to you, I —"

"They would not dare to visit any more harm upon me! Surely I am safe now that this has occurred."

He shook his head. "But I feel such hate! I know that if I remain, my work for all of them would be as dark and ominous as my heart!"

"Unless they could repay you. Some sacrifice on their part like the ones you have made for them . . . " She paused as the thought went on forming in her mind.

"Nothing could ever fully do *that.*"

"Nothing at all?" She glanced up at the open-beam ceiling and paused, willing herself not to mention a marriage between them, even though she wanted it desperately. When that day came, it must be his doing entirely. "Consider it at least, *amore mio.* You are meant to be here in Rome, to work, to paint as you have. There is a sense of rightness with you and this place, with your assistants, and all that you have accomplished. I feel that in my heart as strongly as the love I bear for you. Do not let me be the reason for that to come to an end."

Raphael went to her then, took her in his arms, and held her. She kissed his cheek tenderly, then moved her lips onto his, their mouths brushing tentatively. Yet swiftly, the tender kiss between them changed. The desire powerfully intensified. A moment later he stopped, pulling forcefully away.

"It is too soon for you." he declared, standing to back away a step from the bed. "You must rest."

"I feel quite well. Honestly, I do." She smiled sweetly, holding out her hand to him, feeling him shudder. "I want us to be as we were. *Just* as we were."

"I could not bear to . . . What I mean, is that I am afraid to hurt you in some way . . . "

"That would not be possible. I adore you, *mio dolce amato.*"

Again he sat beside her and ran a hand along her cheek, then down the length of her arm. Breathing heavily, he searched her upturned face with his eyes, his heart thudding. "Are you certain?"

"Entirely."

A moment later, consumed completely with her assurance, his mouth bore down on hers, as though something wild within him had been unleashed. Aching for the familiar ecstasy of her warm, silken flesh joined with his, a low, agonized groan tore from his throat and he cast the heavy brocade coverlet away from her, then pressed her back into the spray of downy pillows.

Raphael slid his hands along her hips to draw up the muslin nightdress she wore. His restraint abandoned now with her loving approval, Raphael's mouth traveled hungrily down the column of her neck to the swell of her bare breasts, the small, tawny nipples. As he tasted her skin with his tongue, he strained to stave off the intense release that was taunting him at the very moment he entered her. Yet the flood of familiar and reassuring sensations was his undoing, and he was powerless against the overwhelming rush. Her scent, her touch, the feel of her heart beating wildly beneath his was emotional ambrosia.

"No one shall *ever* hurt you again, I pledge you that! Not ever!" he heard himself declare on a deep and ragged breath at the very moment she wrapped her legs over his thighs, and he lost the very last shred of his own fragile control.

Afterward, as they lay quietly together, Raphael felt reborn. There was only the sensation now of complete and total peace. The excruciating uncertainty, and the pain of the past weeks, were behind them both. They spoke softly, kissed, and held one another into the early hours of the morning, then made love again, neither of them wanting to be a part just yet of the outside world that had tried to separate them.

Finally, as dawn drew near and the room was flooded with shades of fuchsia, pink, and gold from the sunrise, Margherita turned and, with the tips of her fingers, tenderly touched his face where the small, neat beard now grew fuller. "Did you truly ever believe that I had left you for someone else?" she gently asked him.

"It was not unbelievable to me that another man should want to steal you away."

"But my heart is here, Raphael." She touched his bare chest, and her lips gave a tender smile. "For better or worse, my life will be forever bound with yours."

"For better or worse?"

"Which of us knows the future, *amore mio?*" Margherita said. "But no matter what lies ahead for us, I wish only to be always by your side."

"SHE WAS RETURNED to him?" Maria Bibbiena gasped at the news. "Traitorous fools! My uncle promised me he would never forsake our cause!"

"I am sorry, *signorina,*" declared Alessandro, the Tuscan guard who now accompanied her everywhere. "Yet it is so."

"I allowed myself to believe—for the briefest of moments— that with her gone, Raphael might actually come to . . . " She did not speak the words that she had allowed herself to hope for his love. She sat alone in the gardens of Cardinal Bibbiena's garden on the Via dei Leutari, surrounded by bare trees, prepared for winter.

"He will start those wild ravings about marrying his baker's daughter again. My uncle will be exceedingly angry!"

"Perhaps it is time you see the future for what it is . . . and what it is not?"

"Who are *you* to advise me?" she cried angrily. "You are a servant in this house!"

"I am indeed, *signorina.*" He nodded gallantly. "I have forgotten my place."

Maria immediately regretted her tone. She was weary and frustrated, and she had lost that valued thing for which she had fought for many years. "No. Forgive *me,* Alessandro," she bid him sincerely. "It is *I* who have managed not to see the future right before my eyes, for how I have allowed the past to blind me."

"It is the letting go that is the most difficult." His eyes glittered at her. "Unless you are letting go of one thing in order to cleave to another."

Their eyes met. His gaze held her powerfully. There was so much calm control about him, she realized fully only then. His dominance over her had been gradual, subtle—and complete.

"Do you mean something in particular, Alessandro?" she dared finally to ask.

"Of course, it would not be proper for a guardsman to advise a lady."

"But for just a man to tell *just* a woman?"

"Would that those were our circumstances—Signorina Bibbiena."

He touched the back of her hand as it rested on the arms of the black iron garden chair. He had never actually touched her before.

"And if they were, *caro* Alessandro? What might you say to me then?"

He waited for a moment, considering well his reply. "If the circumstances were different, I might say that giving your full heart to someone who does not desire it is closing it off to someone else who might."

AS THE SUN SET on the city and its ancient ruins, a cold winter rain brought a new pressing chill to the air. Elena lay another log on the dwindling fire in the massive hearth that dominated the *mastro*'s bedchamber. He and Margherita were downstairs at dinner. The flames flared as Giulio Romano closed the door behind himself and sank onto a rush-seat stool beside her, his face bathed in the umber light of the fire glow.

"That was most kind of you to want to accompany Signor Raphael and me yesterday as you did," Giulio said in a voice rich with admiration.

His eyes sought hers with the greatest tenderness as Elena prepared Signora Luti's sleeping garments.

A gentle smile played at the corners of her lips when she saw how he looked at her. "Signora Luti has always said there are few in her new life whom she can trust. She trusted me, so I could not forsake her."

"You were meant in this world to concern yourself with dancing and parties, and making a good match. Not with making up beds and arranging nightclothes."

"I have told you before, those are fanciful dreams from the past, Giulio. Believe me, I am grateful for what I have here." She tipped her head to the side as she looked at him. "And I never thanked you properly for what you did for me with the *mastro*. You should never have risked your own place with him because of me."

"There is nothing in the world I would not do for you."

"Or for Raphael?"

He stood and took a step toward her, closing the modest gap between them. He placed a hand over hers on the bed, atop Margherita's silk-and-lace nightdress. She did not turn her head, did not acknowledge the powerful connection she felt between them. "Do you ever think about him that way now?" Giulio asked her with a blistering openness that surprised her.

"Never. Nor, I imagine, does he."

"Then do you yet think of me?"

Only then did Elena turn her lovely plump face, with her expressive gray eyes, to his. Through them, she saw an open admiration that both startled and frightened her. Yet he was still beyond her reach. The most trusted assistant to the famed Raffaello. A brilliant artist himself. She must not allow herself to believe that there could be the same sort of magical ending for her that there had been for Signora Luti.

"Do not," she murmured softly, as he took her hand very tightly in his own and tried again to kiss her. "You deserve better than me."

He lifted a hand to touch her hair, then fixed her with a pure and honest gaze. "We, all of us, are scarred in some way by this life, Elena. Different wounds perhaps, but the same effect on the soul."

It was painful to look at him. "I have told you, no good man should want me now."

"*I* want you, Elena. I want you very dearly—as my wife." Leaning forward, Giulio brushed his lips against her soft face. The tenderness she felt from him just then nearly broke her heart. "But I am content to wait until it is what you desire as much as I do."

❊ 35 ❊

RAPHAEL WAS RELIEVED NOT TO BE PRESSED ANY FURTHER concerning a reconciliation with Pope Leo. Politics and tenuous alliances, which had distracted him through the autumn and then winter, were made worse by what the Holy Father's aides referred to as "the unfortunate event with Raffaello." But whatever the cost of what had happened, for Raphael it was higher.

Quite simply, he could no longer paint.

Even as the commissions piled up, and the existing works went unfinished, Raphael spent all of his time with Margherita. No matter who bid him, Raphael would not return to the work-shop, nor visit the Vatican Palace. Even Giulio was denied a pri-vate visit with the *mastro* during those dark first days, if he meant to discuss painting.

Months later, in the spring of 1516, Giulio came to the house again to speak about a problem he had found with the frescoed image of King Charlemagne in the pope's new room. But once again, Raphael insisted he leave if the subject matter did not change. Having announced Giulio to Raphael and Margherita, Elena inclined her head with the greatest respect. Then she withdrew, and closed the large carved doors, leaving them alone again.

"You must return to work sometime, *amore mio,*" Margherita observed, poking the long thin needle through the needlepoint hoop on her lap.

Raphael closed his book with a small snap. "I have sufficient money, and thus I am bound by no such command."

"Yet you are."

"I have told you, I am finished with painting!"

She set down her work and came to sit at his feet, her hands on his knees. Gazing up into his troubled face, she gently declared, "I will not allow you to quit."

Raphael raked the hair back from his face. "I have lost my passion for it, Margherita! I do not feel it any longer—not down in my bones! It is not there—that urge—the absolute drive that once absolutely moved me to create!"

"It shall return. It is too much a part of you for it not to."

He shook his head and looked away. "You have too much faith in me."

"It is what God has put me here to do."

It was a weak smile that broke the tension between them then. "Once I could not convince you that I was even trustworthy."

"That was a lifetime ago."

Then, in a seductive move that surprised them both, Margherita very slowly began to unlace and remove the top of her dress. In their time together, with his guidance, she had learned well the sensual arts, and this now was a slow, seductive dance meant to entice him. She watched his eyes widen and his lips part slightly, but he said nothing as the silken fabric fell away from her breasts, pooling at her waist.

"Paint me," she bid him. "Like this . . . paint *all* of me."

He turned away. "I tell you, I cannot."

Margherita took his hand and placed it on her bare breast. He looked at her again, and she softly smiled. "You can!"

From a ceramic cup that held a collection of brushes on the worktable beside them, she drew one out and held it out to him. "You can," she said again. "I want you to paint me precisely this way . . . the way you have made me feel with you . . . the way you have changed me . . . made me able to be wanton and free."

"*Amore mio,* I—"

"Allow me to see this part of myself through your eyes—your hand—now. Not a Madonna this time, nor a lady . . . but as your partner, your lover—the woman of your heart."

"But I do not *want* to begin again!" he said with a catch in his voice. "I want to punish them all!"

"Yet in that, do you not punish yourself most of all? It is who you are! What you are!" She drew up his hand and ran it down the line between her breasts, across her navel, and up her skirts to feel the place where her legs came together. For a moment, she let her head tip back, luxuriating in his touch, her unbound hair falling across her shoulders. He took in the soft scent of roses that clung to her always. Then she looked up at him, open-eyed and committed. "Tell me you cannot see me painted in this way. Sensual . . . free . . . Tell me you cannot paint the woman *you* created!"

"The woman I only helped you become," he corrected her in a rasp that marked his mounting desire.

She held the brush out to him again, undeterred. "Paint me this way for *us,* Raphael. Show me myself as you see me—as you experience me."

He drew her to himself powerfully then and kissed her, hard and hungrily, pressing himself fully against her bare breasts. "Margherita Luti, you are an extraordinary woman!"

"A woman in love."

He kissed her again, with a rough urgency. "In love with a man who worships you!"

His hands encircled her then, sensually, as he ran them over the curves and planes of her body, her arms and thighs, as a blind man might, but she pulled away even as a surge of desire coursed through her. "Sketch me first. Begin it!"

Reaching over onto his table, she drew up a sheet of paper fastened to a hard sketching board and handed it to him. "Do it for *us!*" she coaxed seductively.

"I cannot think for want of you!"

"Use that desire! Channel it into that urge you once knew to create! Seduce the paper!" She ran a finger along his neck. "Caress the chalk between your fingers as though it were a part of my flesh . . ."

He rolled his eyes to a close and took the chalk, groaning with impatience, knowing that for all of his life, he would never have enough of her. "You are a cruel vixen!"

"Draw me . . ." She kissed his earlobe, taking it gently between her teeth. "Then, afterward . . ."

THE FEVER WAS SUDDEN.

Maria had suffered this malady in the stifling months the summer before, and this summer, only months away, apparently was to be no exception. As mosquitoes up from the stagnant Tiber swirled around the cardinal's villa on the Via dei Leutari, Signorina Bibbiena's ladies collected around her wide black oak bed with its twisted posts and canopy. Three papal physicians and Cardinal Bibbiena himself gathered across the room to discuss the seriousness of the matter. Candle lamps flickered and smoked in the grand, drapery-darkened room, casting shadows on the heavy furniture.

"I don't understand! She was well two days ago when I left her! What have you to say?" the cardinal barked out at Costanza Giacolo, his niece's senior most lady.

"Perhaps it is still her heart, Your Grace. She was never entirely well. Not really since her meeting with Signor Raphael in the Vatican gardens last winter," the distinguished woman calmly offered. "We tried to discourage her from going there, as we all knew she would see him at the elephant's enclosure, but it was when his mistress had gone missing and—"

"You *tried?*" he bellowed. "Why did you not succeed?"

"Signorina Bibbiena said she must see Signor Sanzio to remain hopeful about things, that her future depended upon it. I did not think, Your Grace, to argue that, as she has tried for so long to revive her betrothal."

"Raphael Sanzio! Och, how I rue the moment I first heard that name!"

He shook his head and turned from her, despising excuses almost as much as he despised weakness. Maria watched him passively from her bed, feeling his displeasure with her, at her failing. Yet she saw how he meant to make this, if he could, Raphael's fault. She had sought to do that herself the day she had come back, wounded and rejected, from the studio. Certainly her battered heart had opened the door. But her own physical weakness, this yearly susceptibility to illness, was only the fault of her own body. She could blame no one else for that.

But would he?

Maria looked at her uncle, his ambition a brittle mantle upon his bony shoulders. He had been driven for so long to succeed that to the world, he had become a sharp-eyed, vastly unkind man. To her, however, he was simply Uncle Bernardo, the man who had cared for her, who played games with her as a child, who calmed her fears, and the one person who cradled her when she cried. No one but Maria had ever seen that tender side of him—the side he fought against. The side that frightened him because it threatened his heart—nor would they, now.

Maria had seen his wrath meted out upon others before when his goals were not achieved. Someone would pay the price for this new illness she now endured. Either poor Costanza or Raphael—or both of them. Maria regretted that. But then, there really was no way to stop Uncle Bernardo when he directed his mind to something. Dedicated absolutely to his love of her, he would nevertheless be an angry bull charging an enemy.

She watched him leave the room without returning to her bedside. She was ashamed that the next sensation she felt was one of relief. She no longer despised Raphael. That all seemed long ago, and somehow insignificant now, compared to the need to confront her own mortality.

As she watched the cardinal go Maria noticed Alessandro

standing just outside the door, her strong and quiet guard. His presence there made her smile, and she whispered to Costanza to have him brought forward to her bedside.

It was odd how handsome Maria now thought him. He had been in her household for so long, and she had rarely taken the time to notice his many kindnesses. "Come and sit with me," she weakly bid him as he neared.

"Oh, *signorina*, it would be unseemly."

"To the devil with what *seems* to be proper! *Per favore*, Alessandro. Sit with me."

Glancing at her waiting women, he sank reluctantly into the hard chair, fashioned with nail studs around leather, that had been placed beside her bed. "*Allora*. Speak to me of things as you did today, honestly. I find it most pleasing amid all of this boredom."

"But Signorina Bibbiena, you are ill."

"Oh, Alessandro, I have been ill for half of my life, and for most of that time people have been afraid to speak truths to me. Perhaps that is why I was, for a time, allowed to believe I could make a man like Raphael Sanzio love me."

"Surely you know how an artist like that is. That is not your fault."

"*Sì*, I know it. And, sadly, I know now that he truly loves her, and that no one shall separate them."

"Forgive me, *signorina*, but His Grace, your uncle, does not seem to know it at all."

"The cardinal sees what he wishes, Alessandro. I believe he has suffered from knowing only ambition from the time he was very young. It has led him to see nothing else."

"He has become a very rich and powerful cleric."

"But what of the man? Is there not a life of pleasure and happiness one must try to find as well?"

"Apparently power is a comely enough bedtime companion."

Maria laughed softly, then the laughter faded as she settled her eyes upon him. "I find it would have been pleasing to have known you earlier in my life, Alessandro," she said. "I only wish I had opened my eyes to really see you there all of these months. In that, I believe, I am not so much better than my uncle."

"Speak no more of these thoughts," he bid her, knowing how many waiting women might hear their words.

"Perhaps I should not say such things, but my illness gives me a certain confidence that nothing I speak now shall have the power to come back to haunt me."

"That is a thought I cannot bear."

Maria reached out to put her slim, veined hand over his as it rested on his own knee. "We are worlds apart, you and I."

"I serve you, *signorina*. Our worlds could only ever be joined by my devoted service to you."

"I should have liked to know what it might have been to serve *you*, as a man desires. I find now, looking at you, that I regret I never came to know that particular earthly pleasure."

He glanced across the room at the curious ladies who stood close enough to have heard the words they spoke. *"Signorina,"* he said, urging caution in his tone.

"I have had much time to reflect these past days. And I see now that I did not experience that same curiosity, alas, regarding Signor Sanzio—in spite of believing absolutely that I loved him."

He leaned very close to her. "These are dangerous words, Signorina Bibbiena, for a servant to hear from so noble a lady."

"And in that, perhaps, I know a little of how Signor Sanzio feels about *his* love, after all." Maria smiled up at his strong, kind face, etched with concern for her in a way she had never seen on any other. It seemed incomprehensible that this man, this guard, for whom she was unreachable, still could actually somehow have come to care for her, or she for him.

"I am weary now, Alessandro, and in need of rest," she said, unable to spend another moment on so peculiar and unexpected an emotion. "But would you stay with me, here, like this, and speak softly to me until I fall asleep?"

"If it is your wish."

"It is one of them at least, my good friend," Maria said.

TWO DAYS LATER, Maria Bibbiena, the cardinal's niece, and the woman once officially betrothed to the eminent papal artist Raphael Sanzio, was dead. Her premature death was a blow to her family, but most especially to her uncle. Cardinal Bibbiena blamed only one man, and thus sought to bar Raphael from the dignified and stately funeral he had arranged.

Raphael attended in spite of the directive against him.

Once the intimate Vatican chapel was packed to capacity, before an elegantly carved coffin, high on a velvet-draped bier, Raphael slipped inside through a carved side door and up into the balcony. Alone and attired in black, he had considered it his duty to be here amid the cold stone, the echoed whispers from the mourners, and the dark elegy sung from the choir stalls beside him.

He had not loved Maria, but he had always respected her. She deserved that respect now. Standing silent and still as the Holy Father began the funeral Mass, Raphael looked down, searching the faces in the front of the chapel. Shaken and pale, Cardinal Bibbiena stood beside Cardinal de' Medici, cousin of the pope. Twice Bibbiena seemed to falter, and de' Medici had reached out to steady him. The powerful cardinal had never seemed quite capable of tender emotion, Raphael had always thought. Looking at him now, with a tug from his own feelings, he knew that he had been wrong.

Maria had been loved deeply by someone after all.

After the funeral Mass, a throng of Roman nobility walked in solemn procession from the chapel to the shaded and lovely burial site within the highly private Vatican grounds. Amid them, a tall and dignified servant, unknown and unregarded by most of the mourners, stood well behind them. But Raphael recognized him immediately, for they had met at his studio once, when Maria had run off weeping. The man's head was lowered, and his hands were clasped so that no one of importance would see the tears for Maria shining in his eyes. But Raphael saw them, and understood. Watching him now, it seemed to Raphael that in the end, Maria Bibbiena had actually come to know the great love of not one, but two devoted men.

❧ 36 ❧

APRIL 1516

RAPHAEL WAS WORKING EXCLUSIVELY ON THE NUDE POR-trait of Margherita when he was summoned by guards to the Vatican Palace, to a meeting with the pope's cousin, Cardinal de' Medici. It had not been an invitation this time, but a command.

The cardinal's spacious Vatican apartments were grand, vaulted rooms, scented with incense. The walls, decorated with religious portraits, were hung in heavy gold frames. Raphael made a necessarily deep yet perfunctory bow to the cardinal. Seated in a tall, leather-covered chair, studded in silver, the Medici response was direct and without flourish.

"It is the Holy Father, Raffaello."

"This is not another plea for a reconciliation between us, I hope."

"That is not why I have summoned you here."

"When he stops his excuse making and agrees to a date to per-form my marriage to Signora Luti, then I shall begin to entertain the *concept* at least of a reconciliation. But before that—"

"Raphael . . . "

"His Holiness is not ill, I trust?" Raphael asked indifferently. Even though it had been several months since Margherita's kidnapping, he simply could not find it in his heart to reconcile with his former patron.

"It is his heart. Some say it is beyond repair over all that has happened, primarily with you. Following your estrangement, things began to go very badly for the Holy Father. There was the sudden passing of his brother and then the loss of his key alliance with Spain—and the threat which now poses following the death of King Ferdinand. He feels he is meant to lose everything dear to him as payment for what occurred. Now even his favorite Hanno has suddenly become ill."

That alone surprised Raphael, and altered his tone. "The elephant is unwell?"

"His Holiness has come to favor dearly that gentle beast, almost as if he were a lapdog or pet marmoset. Since he was brought to Rome, the Holy Father has visited Hanno each and every day. The visits seemed to bring him a sense of peace through all of the turmoil and talk of war that has plagued him. Now that one last bit of joy is about to be taken from him as well."

"Is there nothing that can be done for the creature?"

"The doctors have tried everything. He has been bled and given every purgative possible, but to no avail. The jungle beast, we are told, shall not survive this. Death is imminent."

Raphael thought not of the pope but of Margherita's affinity for the animal, and how she would feel knowing he would die. "I am sorry for the Holy Father," he forced himself to say. "But there is certainly nothing I can do about his circumstances."

"Pardon me, Raphael, but you *could* go to the pontiff. Visit with him as the friends you once were. You would help a great deal with the Holy Father's outlook on all the more important matters. You could use the animal's unfortunate circumstance as a beginning between you."

"I cannot."

"That simple?"

"He tried to take from me the thing most dear in my life!" Raphael said contemptuously, wholly unable to stifle the furious words pressing forth from his heart. "And still he refuses to allow us to marry for no other reason than his own dislike of the woman I have chosen!"

The cardinal shrugged. He drew in a measured breath. There

was a moment of consideration before he replied in a voice full of piety. "His Holiness is not a well man, Raphael. The thing he craves most in the world now, at this difficult juncture in his life, is your forgiveness. He is not beyond paying you any price if it will return you to your former state with each other."

"*That* state can never be. Not exactly as it was."

Cardinal de' Medici arched a brow, and drew a finger to his chin. "But some approximation, perhaps?"

Raphael wheeled around, hands on his hips, his voice full of contemptuous challenge. "Get me the ruby ring, which His Holiness knew well I desired, yet gave to Cardinal Bibbiena, *and* guarantee not only Signora Luti's absolute safety, but her invitation to all events to which I am invited. Tell him that he must sanction our marriage as he sanctioned Agostino Chigi's. If he will consent to do all of that, I will visit him."

Cardinal de' Medici nodded calmly. "I shall present your terms at once. I shall return to you with a reply by nightfall."

"You do that," Raphael replied, knowing what the response must be. Too much power, greed, and ambition swirled around the pontiff. His Holiness would never take away the ruby ring from one of his dearest friends.

THE RESPONSE came long before evening fell. Two hours after Raphael left the Vatican Palace, a small leather box was presented to him, carried personally by a somber-faced Swiss guard in his brightly colored uniform and plumed steel helmet. Beside him stood Cardinal de' Medici. The exquisite ruby ring from the house of Nero glittered up at him from a small bed of blue velvet. Raphael heard himself gasp.

"His Holiness wishes greatly for there to be an end to the animosity between the two of you," de' Medici announced. "He has sent me to say that if this act shall achieve that, he is exceedingly content at the prospect. And, after an appropriate time of mourning for Signorina Bibbiena, so as not to insult His Holiness's dear friend, Cardinal Bibbiena, he will approve of, and sanction, your marriage to Signora Luti."

Raphael took the small ring from the swatch of velvet and held it up. It glittered in the light with the same brilliant intensity it had the first time he had seen it. It truly was breathtaking, perfectly suited for Margherita's slender finger, with the same rightness about it there had always been. He felt his rage begin to subside. The ring had been meant for her always, and it would be hers at last.

"I shall consider the matter," he replied with a caution that he still could not vanquish. He must remain in control of all this until the day he took Margherita as his bride. It was not only for her protection . . . but his own.

"Excellent." Cardinal de' Medici nodded piously. "In addition, the Holy Father would have you consider the question of when you might be willing to return to work on the Stanza dell'Incendio."

"I bid Your Grace not to press me. I shall inform the Holy Father when I will return to work."

Raphael knew he was certainly pushing his luck, but he also knew he was the one who held all of the cards. The great and powerful Pope Leo, and all of his cardinals and henchmen, he had decided, should know it as well before he gave them what they wished.

NOW THAT Margherita was finally alone, with Raphael having gone to the Vatican, the entire group of them went to the Via Alessandrina and stood together on her doorstep, an unlikely lot. Potbellied Gianfrancesco Penni, with his unruly mass of red-gold curls and ruddy face, stood beside Giovanni da Udine, who appeared tall and awkward here, his silver hair smoothed away from his face. He especially was chafing. Behind them were all of the other artists and apprentices from Raphael's workshop.

"While it is long overdue, we mean to apologize for our treatment of her. But will she see us?" Penni asked Elena, who held the front doorjamb and gazed in surprise at the great collection of men in their painter's loose white shirts, hose, leather belts, and boots. "Knowing that the *mastro* has gone to the Vatican, hopefully to reconcile with the Holy Father, we saw an opportunity at last. We are here to plead for a fresh start with Signora Luti."

"I would blame her not at all if she declined," Elena replied. Giulio had told her how coolly they had all treated Margherita in the early days of her courtship with Raphael. "It has been months you have waited for this! And some debts as they mount are simply too high to be paid!"

"And some are better off simply forgiven." The words had come from Margherita herself, stepping off her staircase, the hem of her dress clinging to the last stone stair. Elena turned to look at her, just as the men did. "Show them in, Elena," she calmly directed, elegance defining her now, richly gowned as she was in amethyst-and-ivory brocade. "And see them to the library, *per favore.*"

The men, largely out of work since the kidnapping plot was revealed, shuffled across the glossy marble floor and the richly woven Turkish carpet. They stood bunched up beside the fireplace hearth, above which hung one of the small tondo paintings of Margherita as the Madonna. It was a silent reminder of her power, not only over Raphael, but over all of them.

"We would have come before now, and we should have. But we thought an apology for our behavior toward you would be precious little and far too late, especially after what happened," said Penni, the designated spokesman. "But now, with things changing all over, and perhaps a new era beginning for us all, we *needed* to try," he added as he stood a step forward, away from the others. "You deserved better than how we treated you, *signora.*"

In spite of the surprise, Margherita felt a smile tug at her lips. He was using the designation *signora* now, not in ridicule but rather in deference to her. Margherita took it as a show of respect.

"We will all simply go on from here."

"*Grazie, signora,*" da Udine nodded, surprising Margherita—and himself.

"Raphael has good men who care for his welfare. I did not fault any of you for that."

"We should have shown courtesy to the lady whom the *mastro* loved." Penni pressed the apology. "He certainly has been selfless enough with all of us to have expected that from us in return."

"Well." Margherita clasped her hands and searched each of their faces with a smile of her own. "We have all of the time in the world to change our course with one another now, do we not?" she asked, a gentle smile lighting her eyes.

Each of them nodded their agreement, and reached out in turn to take her hand.

MARGHERITA was sitting at her dressing table when he came into her bedchamber very late that night. He saw her face reflected in the lamplight. It was freshly scrubbed, her hair parted in the center hanging long and soft around her face and across her shoulders. Raphael drew near and rested a hand upon her shoulder.

Seeing his reflection behind her, Margherita reached up to her shoulder and took his hand.

"Did it go well today?"

"Better than I expected. There is something we must speak of. But first, I must tell you of Hanno." Raphael despised having to tell her the truth of this.

Seeing his expression, she dropped her gaze. Silence passed between them for a moment. "He has died."

"*Sì, amore mio.* It is so."

"*Grazie a Dio.*"

He watched her exhale deeply, as if a great burden had been released from her heart. "At last his spirit is free."

"I believe that as well. I am relieved you are not upset."

"Hanno has been imprisoned too long for that." She shook her head and waited for a moment. "And the Holy Father, how is he about it?"

Raphael shrugged. "He is distraught, of course. I believe Hanno's death, on the heels of his brother's untimely passing, has softened him greatly. At least it appears so."

"And how is that?" she asked him as he sank onto the bench beside her. Gently, he touched a long tendril of her hair and brushed it behind her shoulder, then he kissed the bare skin that had been covered beneath it.

"Cardinal de' Medici came to see me today."

"The pope's cousin?"

"Through his visit, I believe I have at last found a way to forgive them."

"If it is *your* desire finally," she softly smiled, "then I am well glad of it."

"There will be changes, however," Raphael said, reaching into a pocket of his doublet, his lips curving into a slow smile. "And he shall agree to them."

"Such as?"

"Perhaps I shall have the Holy Father agree to bury me in the Pantheon one day, with you resting beside me, so that no one shall ever forget. Unlikely or not, we two are, forever, lovers," he said wistfully.

Smiling, Margherita shook her head. "You speak too much of death for one so young."

"Perhaps I shall die prematurely. I have always felt that I would. Even when I was a boy, I believed it."

"I will not hear that!"

"My father used to tell me the same thing, yet he died young as well. Death is the natural order of things. To live, and to die . . . We cannot avoid it, you know."

"Well, they would certainly never bury *me* in the Pantheon, no matter what the Holy Father might assure you."

"They would not *dare* to do otherwise. Remember, *amore mío, I* am Raffaello!"

The suggestion of a smile lifted the corners of her mouth. "And *I* am the woman whose daily task is to try to remind you of your responsibility in that. Not an easy task, reining in a creative soul, I assure you!"

"True enough," he conceded with a smile. "So the more immediate changes from the Holy Father and the others will be in how they deal with me—and how they treat *you*. In the interim, I believe I have found, at last, that certain something that our private painting of you has been missing." At last, he held up the ruby ring to her, glittering brilliantly in the candle glow. "The single article that will transform it into a *wedding* portrait."

Margherita gazed down at the ring shimmering there, but did not move. A moment later, she looked up into Raphael's eyes and saw the devotion redoubled now after what they had together endured.

"Will you do me the great honor, at last, Signora Luti, of becoming my wife?"

Her expression changed. Her lips parted just slightly, and her eyes began to fill with tears. "But the Holy Father—"

He pressed a single finger, with great tenderness, against her lips. "When you are my wife, nothing shall threaten you ever again."

Tears glittered in her eyes like the precious jewel he still held up in offer to her. "Are you certain?"

"Before I met you," he gently corrected her, the love open and telling in his voice, "I had no life. By Maria's unfortunate death, I am free now from the shame of having broken my betrothal, which tainted the future for us. So there at last is nothing in our way."

Raphael held her and raked his fingers from the crown of her hair down through the length of it, settling his hand at the small of her back and whispered against her cheek. "I have never wanted anything so much as I want this with you. Margherita, you are my lover, my friend, my muse—and now soon my wife."

When Margherita turned fully toward him on the bench, Raphael took her hand and slipped the ruby ring—the jewel from another age—onto her slim finger. "This ring I give to you is something extraordinary. From the uncovered palace created by Nero."

"The one given by the Holy Father to Cardinal Bibbiena."

"But never meant for his hand. It well could have been worn by Poppaea herself. Its worth is priceless, its connection to your heart symbolic—which is the only sort of ring good enough to be a token of the love I bear for you."

He kissed her then, more deeply, drawing the thin cotton shift down over the smooth curves of her shoulders and breasts, pooling it at her hips.

"I want to enhance the sketch we began," he said adoringly, "make it a true portrait."

"A portrait of me naked?" she gasped, a soft chuckle of disbelief following.

"*Sì*," he replied. Her beautiful breasts were bare and inviting, only for him. "We began it as a sensual game between ourselves, to help me begin to work again. But along the way, it has become something greater." His voice quickened. "I intend this painting of you to be my masterpiece!"

"But it would be indecent to anyone who saw it!"

"That is just the point. Come, I will show you," he directed, holding a flickering candle lamp as he led her into the small room he kept there.

Inside, set up just beside their bedchamber, he led her onto a divan covered over in red velvet, a silvery shaft of moonlight coming in through the stained-glass windowpanes behind it. Margherita gazed up curiously at him as he lit several more lamps, then began to mix paints.

He looked up at her as he worked, his eyes wide, the passion to create entirely returned. "When we began our life together, I could see you only as the Madonna. Pure. Sacred. One-dimensional."

She bit back a smile. "I was *never* perfect."

"My artist's eye found you so."

Raphael then busied himself with finding props that would define the composition he sought. The same turban to cover her hair as in the sketch, the same slip of gauzy fabric over her navel, and an artistic device he had already included in his design for the painting—an armband, that would later be painted as though etched with gold, words declaring undeniably that this work, and this woman, were forever the possessions of Raphael Urbinas.

"You meant it as a means to get me working again, and I thank you with my life for that. But in these months since, it has come to symbolize so much more than that." He touched her cheek tenderly. "I mean this to be a wedding portrait, only for the two of us. A gift to you, to be hung in our bedchamber—an image of how my heart sees you, since I speak better with my paintbrush. But down through the ages, once both of us have gone, I wish people to see it and know how desperately a simple painter was changed by love."

She was still smiling as he fixed the turban over her hair, fastening it with a costly pearl brooch, then slid a silver band edged in blue thread up over her wrist, onto her bare upper arm. Unable to resist then, he sank to his knees before her, kissed her neck, his mouth trailing down to her bare breasts.

"And so for this *wedding portrait,* how is it you see me exactly?"

"I see you as a seductress—the only one I *can* see, or will ever see. A womanly vision. The queen of my heart, a whore, a temptress . . . everything. All the elements of you that are precious and private between us. *Dio mio,* what would have become of me—of Raphael the man, if I had never known you?"

"Well." She softly chuckled. "Put that way, how could I deny you such a portrait?"

"The style, the tone, the colors must be entirely new," he declared, kissing her again. "Yet I know, even before it is complete, that this is the work I will always hold most dear to my heart, because it was the first and only one I painted entirely for *you.*"

❧ 37 ❧

MAY 1517

A YEAR PASSED, AND AS THE SPRING CAME ONCE AGAIN,
Pope Leo was too sequestered and too consumed with his own
tribulations to commit to a date upon which he would sanction
and perform the marriage between Raphael and Margherita, even
though he had already agreed to it. In the short term of his
papacy, Pope Leo's excessive spending on revelry and costly artistic projects had bled the papal coffers dry. The manner in which
he sought to replenish the funds had only increased the scandal,
and with it, his problems.

Following the revelation of a conspiracy against the pontiff's
very life, perpetrated by a number of his own cardinals, Pope Leo
had unwisely chosen to punish them by demanding excessively
large sums of money from each of them—money he desperately
needed, not only for the building of Saint Peter's, but for the
intricately frescoed rooms at the Vatican Palace. He had also continued the controversial practice of selling indulgences, which
raised to a fever pitch the anger throughout Rome and the other
dissatisfied Italian city-states. The pope could attend to no other
duties, Raphael was continually told by the papal secretaries, until
this serious matter was under control. When that might be, he
was informed, was anyone's guess.

In spite of Margherita's assurance that she would be content
to have any priest marry them, Raphael was insistent that it be
the Holy Father. Not only had the pope performed Chigi's marriage to a commoner, thus setting a precedent in Raphael's mind,
but after the kidnapping, it was symbolic. To fully heal old
wounds, it must be Pope Leo.

Still, as they waited, with Margherita's love and constant
encouragement, Raphael had gotten back to work, full force, and
he was too excessively committed to press the situation when the

Holy Father pleaded for his patience. As spring turned to summer, and summer cooled to autumn, Raphael, as always, worked
on several commissions at one time.

Two days before Christmas of that year 1517, as a gesture of
friendship, trust, and reconciliation, Raphael accepted from Cardinal de' Medici, the pope's cousin, his most important commission thus far, marking his full return to work. He was to paint the
Transfiguration on a large panel as an altarpiece that would hang
in the cathedral of Saint-Juste, in Narbonne, France, part of the
cardinal's archepiscopal see. It would be, Cardinal de' Medici told
him, the crowning glory of not only his art, but of Pope Leo's papacy.
What he did not tell Raphael, at first, was that the Holy Father
had agreed to see a second highly prized commission for a companion piece, The Raising of Lazarus, given to Sebastiano Luciani.

When he discovered that, Raphael bounded up the grand
stairway of the house on the Via Alessandrina, his face white with
rage. With a knotted fist, he rapped at the door of the little art
studio beside the bedchamber, where Margherita generally took
her afternoon *reposo* with her father and Letitia, for the view of
the piazza and the reasonably fresh breeze it offered. This time,
however, she was alone. The door crashed against the wall, shaking the house.

"You will not believe what he has done this time!"

Margherita came to her feet, her rich blue silk skirts unfolding
around her legs, the hem sweeping the tile floor like gentle waves.
"What has upset you, *amore mio?*"

"His Holiness is trying once again to control me! Of all the
artists in Rome, his cousin has given a commission for a companion piece to *my* Transfiguration to that bastard Sebastiano!"

"Perhaps he feels it is time to end the grudge between the two
of you. After all, it has been such a long time, and are we not
stronger together even than before?"

"Yet, from Florence, Michelangelo still stirs the pot between
us daily! Bitter old fool! I still cannot trust his lackey, Sebastiano,

and I will *not* risk your safety by trusting in the very men who sought to destroy us!"

It was only then that he became aware of something. As he had come into the room, Margherita was standing beside the finished painting of herself, yet unframed, still on his easel, her eyes shining with tears. He had been so angry entering the room that he had forgotten he had left it here, and it was clear she had just seen it, now that it was complete.

In the wedding portrait, he had painted Margherita as voluptuously as anything she had ever seen: a beautiful smile highlighting her face, a turban on her head, her breasts bare. But it was the newly added details that moved her. On the finger believed to lead to her heart, he had painted the exquisite ruby ring. The band painted so seductively onto her arm now bore words: *Raphael Urbinas,* the brand of the great master—his signature, his sign of possession to all the world.

"You've *signed* it?" she asked through her tears, unable to break her gaze from the signature band he had painted onto her arm in such shades of bright blue and gold that it could not be missed by the viewer.

"One of the few I ever have. It rarely felt right to do so until now. It was never something with which I wished to ornament my work as other artists do. But as you can see," he smiled, and his face was full of adoration, "in style, tone, and subject matter, this is like nothing I have ever painted before." He kissed her deeply. "You have inspired that change, Margherita *mia*—you!"

"No one who sees it shall ever believe it is a true Raphael painting, you know. In it, you have broken all of your own artistic rules."

"Just as I have broken all of the other rules, it seems, by falling so desperately in love with you. This is meant to be our symbol of that fact." He took her in his arms. "This painting is a proclamation that I adore you more than life itself." He shook his head, then looked back at her, his eyes bright with devotion. "*Dio,* the things I have done for love of you—things I never believed I could. I have reached new heights of daring in my work—your

Madonnas . . . the concept for the Transfiguration . . . all of it, I owe to your encouragement."

Margherita wrapped her hands around his neck, and he encircled her waist. For a moment, her expression grew serious, as Raphael whispered, "By God's grace, and your patience, I am yours now completely."

They shared a kiss, and in it she felt the full promise of the future they would have together at last. Even so, Margherita had learned enough of this complex world of Raphael's to know that anything could happen between now and the day they married. She must be wary of that. In the meantime, another token of reconciliation was presented to Raphael the very next day by Margherita herself, along with her dear friend Francesca Chigi.

"WHAT IS *he* doing here?" Raphael's face swiftly grew red and his expression angry.

When he returned from the workshop that evening, there were guests in his drawing room, and they were the last two people in the world he expected to be there. Agostino and Francesca Chigi sat together in tapestry-draped chairs set at an angle near the fire. Seeing them, Raphael paused in the doorway as Margherita moved near, her expression one of openness and love.

"Will you not hear him out, at least? He is, after all, one of your dearest friends in Rome."

"He is nothing but a traitor to me!" Raphael raged, pivoting back toward the staircase before Margherita stopped him with a gentle hand.

"There will be no end to it, *amore mio,* until *you* say it is so. You have the power now."

"They took that power away from me when they imprisoned *you!*"

"It is in the past, Raphael! Francesca is my friend, and I am hers. It is a torment to us both that we cannot say the same of the men we love."

Raphael was still white with rage, his body coiled in anger. "He has yet to show a single bit of remorse for what he did!"

"Forgive me—I bid you. I was horribly wrong."

The voice belonged to Agostino Chigi. When Raphael turned back slowly, he saw the elegant banker standing, hands extended in pleading, his expression one of sincere regret. Raphael had not expected that.

"Was the kidnapping a plan of your design?"

"I am as guilty, surely, as if it were, since I chose not to object to it." Agostino moved a step nearer, then stopped, seeming to think better of pushing too hard and too swiftly. "I cannot change that I agreed to the action, Raphael. But I was just as wrong for not speaking out against the plan, and for that I can only plead guilty."

"Bibbiena planned it, did he not?"

"*Per favore,* it is not for me to indict others, Raphael. Only to make amends for my own actions. I do despise myself for what I did. Truly!"

"If you are wanting full forgiveness right now, this moment, I warn you I cannot give it."

"I would settle for an open door between us, and the time to see where it may lead."

Francesca and Margherita exchanged a glance in the uncertain silence. The fire cracked and popped. Shadows danced on the high painted walls.

"Signora Luti has forgiven you?" Raphael cautiously asked.

"She says that she has."

"You all misjudged her greatly."

"We did indeed."

"If Signora Luti wishes to spend time with your wife, then I shall not object."

"And perhaps one day you will begin to accompany her again to my home?"

"We shall see, Agostino. I will not close the door, but the most I can say for the two of us is that we shall see."

Part Four

To lose time

is the most

displeasing

to he who

knows most.

Dante

❧ 38 ❧

BY THE SUMMER OF 1519, MORE THAN THREE YEARS AFTER Margherita's kidnapping, the massive scale and intricacy of the Transfiguration had become Raphael's new obsession. Knowing that he was now openly competing with Sebastiano, whose work on the companion, the Raising of Lazarus, was progressing more quickly, he began to consider ways to stall the unveiling of his competitor's painting before his own. It was a move Margherita wholly opposed. Desperation, she said, was beneath him. He was, after all, she reminded him, the great Raffaello, and Michelangelo Buonarroti was still out of favor and living in Florence.

Hoping to bring him a more full sense of peace to balance his ambition, Margherita reminded him daily of the richness of his life. He was now an integral part of a new family, and there was healing in that. Not only did Francesco Luti and Donato pose often for male studies at the workshop, but they all dined together regularly as a family at Margherita's house. Crowded around her table, they broke bread, drank wine, argued, and laughed like any family for hours on end. Raphael particularly reveled in spoiling Matteo Perazzi, knowing he was still Margherita's favorite nephew.

In addition to family life, the broken bond of friendship with Raphael and Agostino had begun to mend. At the instigation of Chigi's wife, Francesca, Margherita was made a frequent guest at the villa, and spent many happy hours in the company of Francesca's three children, who considered her an aunt. But something always weighed on her—the fact that in all of the passion and all of the years, Margherita had never been able to give Raphael his own child.

"Are you sorry we have not been blessed in the way Francesca and Agostino have?" she finally asked one night as they lay together in her bed, gazing past the open shutters and up at the full moon in a black night sky.

Raphael smiled at her. "We still might be one day."

"My courses were never regular, even when I was younger. And then, all of this time with you and I . . . I have just never believed I was meant to bear a child of my own."

Raphael was silent for a moment. "You would make a splendid mother. I've seen you with Matteo enough to know that absolutely."

"Letitia was so taken up in those early days with the other three boys, I suppose I always thought of him as my own."

"It showed." He smiled. "And he does adore you."

"As I adore him."

"Will he be enough for you, do you think?"

Margherita touched his cheek and then smiled. "You are all I have ever truly needed, or ever will," she devotedly said.

But by spring of the following year, the pope's counselors had once again informed Raphael that the Holy Father would need to delay the performing of Raphael's wedding. The postponement was due now, they said, to the pope's all-consuming political maneuvering to secure an essential treaty between himself and King François I against the powerful and dangerous Emperor Charles V. After the battle for Milan, Pope Leo understood the power of the French king, and felt he could take no chances. Politics and scandal had worn down the beleaguered pontiff, who had spent the past two years struggling to expand the states of the Church, and Raphael was strongly advised not to press personal matters.

As he worked at an intensely frenetic pace in the busy workshop that had sprung back wildly to life, Raphael saw nothing, felt nothing, breathed nothing but the powerful images of the risen

Christ and the compassionate apostles around a boy possessed for the Transfiguration. He ignored the strange chill that he could not shake, along with strange alternating bouts of sweating and fatigue.

There was no time for illness, he told himself.

Not now when everything had finally fallen into place.

Giulio Romano filled in the details unfolding on his huge panel. The concepts, however, were from the mind of Raphael. He had used Donato Perazzi as the model for the figure of Christ himself; his tall commanding body and the gentle lines of his face were just right for the feel of the piece he wished to achieve. Francesco Luti was forever immortalized now as the balding and tired-faced Saint Andrew. And beneath the Christ figure, amid the apostles and the chaos of the healing of the demonic boy, a strong female figure was painted from behind.

Early on, in preparation sketch after preparation sketch, Margherita herself had posed for this character. When the actual panel was begun, Raphael painted her first, like the axis of the piece, so that artistically everything else would flow from her. Of this great altar panel, like his life, she was the center force.

On a day late in March 1520, now that the work was nearly complete, Raphael stood, his arms crossed over his chest, studying the work. He was feeling oddly dizzy, and not a little disoriented. He had forgotten to eat today, that must surely be it, he was thinking, as the shapes before his eyes began to change, to darken, to cloud over.

Raphael! Come and help me lift this panel! And the brushes! I want only boar brushes, you know that!

He turned with a start, feeling his skin go very cold. It was the voice of his father. *His father!* Raphael saw a figure behind him but the image, the face, was distorted, as if through rain-washed glass. He blinked hard, feeling as cold, suddenly, as ice. Still, the sensation was strong and unmistakable. In his mind, he was a boy of twelve again, with his father in the studio at the ducal court of Urbino, where his own artistic life had begun. The ache for a figure

long gone from his life was powerful, overwhelming. And everything grew darker still. The cold sensation was taking him over,
yet he could see now it was not his father, and not Urbino, but it
was Giulio Romano behind him.

"Are you all right, *mastro?*"

Raphael lost his balance and sank for a moment onto his
knees, breathing heavily. "Fine, Giulio, I am fine. A bit tired, perhaps."

But he was flushed and his eyes were bloodshot, the pupils
mere pinpricks. His father's image and the memories around it
dissolved like rain.

"Allow me to see you home. *Signora* will have my head if I do
not!"

"Where is she?" He could not seem to remember that, either.

"On her way to the Chigi villa for the afternoon, at Signora
Chigi's invitation. You are to join her there."

"Perhaps you should have her sent for, Giulio," Raphael grimaced. "I find I am feeling a bit worse than at first I thought."

ANTONIO had changed. It was the first thought Margherita had
sitting astride her horse, looking down at him standing in the
gravel courtyard of the Chigi Villa. She took the hand he extended
to her, then descended elegantly from her saddle.

He stood before her in his stableman's livery, a little paunch
now straining over the leather belt, and his eyes less steely blue.
Her second thought, seeing him again now for the first time in
over a year, was that the ambition had gone from those wild eyes.
It must be the result of his yearlong marriage to the daughter of
the fishmonger from the Portico Octavia—one of the many girls
with whom he had betrayed Margherita.

Now it was Antonio, of all the Chigi servants in the world,
who took the reins of her sleek bay horse, caparisoned in a blanket of azure velvet, and topped with a fine Portuguese leather
saddle studded in silver. Elena and Donato, Margherita's constant
companions, had already dismounted. They stood waiting, watch-

ing the rare exchange between two strangers who once, long ago, had been the closest of friends.

Margherita lingered a moment in the sun, wearing a gown of rich topaz satin with gold embroidery. Her shining hair was held back by a matching cap, and her hands were ornamented with jewels. Looking at Antonio now, she felt none of the fondness she once had. Nor did she feel any longer like the naive girl from Trastevere who he had so avariciously pushed toward this new life. This brief encounter was a heady moment of triumph for all that their inequality implied.

"*Signora,*" he said, at last releasing her finely gloved hand from his own. He was forced, by protocol, to defer to her with a formal bow. Her horse stamped at the graveled ground.

"Signor Perazzi." She nodded coolly in return, betraying nothing.

Though they did not speak beyond the greeting, her eyes, in that single instant of connection, said to him, *You did not think I would succeed. You wanted me to fail because you have failed. But I have survived, with Raphael's love and guidance to protect me* . . .

Margherita felt a sudden chill course very powerfully down her spine then. *But have you truly?* a small, strange voice inside her asked. *Are you yet his wife? Will you ever be? Are you truly safe until the day that you are? Take great care with how you hold your memories,* the small voice taunted. *They may well deceive you as much as your enemies ever would.*

Margherita looked up keenly at Antonio as Elena took her silk shawl and then properly straightened the skirts of her dress. Antonio had been so handsome once, and had seemed to her so full of promise. Now he was a stranger—one she could add to the very long list of those in Rome she did not, and could not, trust.

Margherita moved away swiftly then, away from a life that had abandoned her long before she had left it. Without looking back, she walked through a shaft of sunlight, across the courtyard, toward the front doors of the magnificent stone villa—an entrance through which Antonio would never be allowed to pass.

She would think no more of Antonio, she decided as she walked. All she would consider now was joining her love, and the other noble guests, for Francesca Chigi's afternoon concert—a world away from the little bakery that lay just a few steps, through the Porta Settimiana, in humble Trastevere.

STANDING in front of Raphael's enormous and impressive *Galatea,* Francesca Chigi warmly greeted Margherita with a genuine embrace. The two women had become close friends these past years since her marriage to Agostino. Francesca understood Margherita in a way no other could—the challenges she had faced, the ridicule and the determination it took to hold her head up in society, had bonded them. Her husband's involvement in Margherita's kidnapping was only ever referred to as "that former unpleasantness between our men."

It was the way both friends wished it.

Francesca Chigi was a beautiful woman—tall, very slender, with thick wheat-colored hair, which she wore braided and clipped above wide-set, cornflower-blue eyes. Agostino had met her in Venice, and their scandalous affair, before they married, had produced three children. In spite of her humble origins, she was, he declared, the love of his life. Not only had he built this villa for love of her, but he had fought to marry her, the same way Raphael now fought with the greatest determination for Margherita.

"I am so pleased you could be here," Francesca smiled as minstrels dressed in elegant costumes played airy music on a raised dais behind them. "And do let me have a look once again at that ring about which all of Rome is buzzing! It is truly all the talk, you know, after what Raphael has dared to do!"

Margherita felt her stomach seize up. All eyes in the room seemed suddenly upon her.

"What do you mean?" she hedged, her body on guard, even with a friend. Such had become her life among the powerful of Rome.

"Oh, come now. We have all heard that Raffaello has painted you wearing it—and, for that matter, precious little else! A bold move indeed to think of the emperor's ring on a finger like yours or mine for all eternity!"

How did she know such a thing? Raphael would never have revealed it, and he had painted the wedding portrait in his private studio at home . . .

The hair on her neck stood on end at the prospect. Margherita's mind wound over thoughts and connections, ways this might have happened, as she stood reluctantly holding out her hand and doing her best to appear casual. The ancient gem glittered before all of them.

It came to her then with a cruelly hard blow. *Antonio!*

The man she had left behind. The one who had never quite forgiven her. He was the single link, through the family connection of Donato, between the privacy of her home and the Chigi Villa. Antonio had discovered the portrait's theme through her meddlesome sister. Of course, that was it! Letitia never had learned to hold her tongue when there was something interesting to speak about, and she was certain Antonio had been only too willing to listen to her.

The sense of anger rushed at her then, mixing with private memories, vulnerabilities, and the sweeter times of their youth. Her face flushed, she steadied herself, and drew back her hand.

"It really is a small thing," she said, struggling to keep her voice steady. "An ornament to the greater work only."

"But what a remarkable ornament is your betrothal ring! From Emperor Nero?"

Francesca took her shoulders and leaned forward with a clever smile.

Margherita forced herself to laugh blithely so that everyone might hear. She had learned enough of this world to do at least that. "And in uncovering much of my body in order to be painted, I hope it is *that* state which the viewer remarks upon, rather than the ring, or the chill I took posing for it shall have been for naught!"

As laughter erupted between them, the tension of the moment dissolved. This was not the first time she had charmed them. Francesca had won her place among them with her wit; now, too, had Margherita.

"You know," Francesca softly warned, pulling her away from the others, "Cardinal Bibbiena is still wildly bitter over losing the ring to you. A brilliant move, I say, for someone to get the better of *him!*" They walked a few steps more, Francesca still tightly gripping her shoulder.

"I am sorry to hear that. I would have hoped by now the bitterness of the past would be behind all of us. Considering events, there was much to be forgiven on *all* sides."

"How quick you have become, *cara.* You have delighted everyone." Francesca smiled. "But still you dream a fool's dream. There are those, to this day, who still do not accept me as Agostino's wife, and from whose anger I shall never consider myself entirely protected. I fear it may well be the same for you once Raphael marries you."

"I have grown accustomed to the ridicule. His love and important place here in Rome protect me from more than that." As she spoke, Margherita casually hid her hand at her side within the voluminous folds of her elegant topaz gown. "In that, I am kept safe."

Walking together, they arrived at the collection of chairs facing the garden and the river beyond. Margherita glanced around, anxious to see Raphael. As bold as she tried to be, Margherita was not at all certain she was capable of convincing everyone of her self-confidence.

"Sadly," Francesca murmured fervently, "women such as we are never completely safe." She leveled her wide blue eyes on Margherita's with such gravity that Margherita felt her blood run absolutely cold as the two women linked hands. "Never completely let down your guard to any of us."

"Even you?"

"Even me."

"I thought . . . ," she hedged. "I believed that we had a deep—"

"Friendship? Make no mistake. I, too, am at the mercy of the man of my heart. His alliances, his life, determine all for me."

There was no point in not asking. "Did you know about my abduction before it happened?"

"No. But I cannot honestly say that if I had, I could have, or would have, done anything to stop it."

"That seems such a bleak picture you paint."

"Yet it is the truth, and the fate for women like us. Follow the will of our men and we survive. Go against them and all shall be forever lost."

Margherita shook her head and looked away at the line of elegantly clad guests still filing in from the entrance hall. "Raphael trusts my opinion," she tried to disagree as they sat down together in rich tapestried chairs positioned to hear the musicians. They had only just begun to play a new tune for the guests already seated in rows of chairs behind them. "He would never forsake me in that way."

"Everything changes, Margherita," Francesca warned. "And *never* is a very long time."

The musicians had played two of their lighter tunes when Margherita felt a firm tap on the top of her shoulder. A strange premonition rushed at her, bleeding through the serene facade she had worked so hard to project, even before she turned around. Giulio Romano was behind her, his face gray and his expression very grave. She knew instantly, even before he spoke, that something was very wrong. He bent low to whisper to her.

"You must come at once, Signora! *Dio mio,* it is Signor Raphael!"

❧ *39* ❧

APRIL 1520

AT FIRST, THE PHYSICIANS AND A COLLECTION OF PAPAL guards barred her entry into her own bedchamber. By the time Margherita found Giulio, and they were able to push their way past the barrier of men, it had been well over an hour's time since she had first been summoned home.

Passing the three somber papal physicians, who shook their heads in regret, she felt herself tremble with an ominous fear. Once past them, Margherita crept softly toward the bed, up on its platform, enclosed by heavy tapestry curtains, where he lay. The bed they had shared. The room was dark in spite of the early hour. Candles were lit. The table beside him was littered with all manner of medicines and potions in glass bottles and jars the physicians had already brought. It had not been long, but they had still gotten to him first, she thought in horror. The physicians had made choices for him before she even knew what the sickness was. She was firmly made inconsequential, and so quickly, she realized with great foreboding as she moved nearer the bed.

AS IF SENSING HER APPROACH—knowing it from all others— Raphael suddenly opened his eyes. He reached out to her and she sank beside him onto the bed. He was so horribly feverish, she thought, in shock, as his fingers laced with hers.

"I left you only a little weary this morning. What wicked thing have you done since we parted to bring on such heat?" she asked, feigning indignation to make him smile. Yet only a flicker of one crossed his face before she saw him grimace in pain replacing it.

"It was more than that," he confessed. "I have not felt well for over a fortnight."

"And you did not tell me?" she asked with an uncertain, half smile.

"And now I fear I am not going to be able to keep my vow to you," he said, struggling for breath. His voice came as a low, croaking sound she did not recognize. Tears leapt to her eyes at the mere suggestion, for she remembered well the vow. "This is not going to end well, *amore mio*."

Margherita put up a hand and backed away. "Do not say it, for I will not hear you!"

Raphael took her hand and with great difficulty held it tightly. "Margherita *mia* . . . my own precious gem, *per favore* . . . you must listen." He drew in another difficult breath, and there was a small pause before he could continue. For a moment his eyes rolled to a close. When he opened them again, he quietly said, "There are plans to be made . . . for your safety . . . We must speak of them."

"I will not!"

"*Cara,* why will you not hear me?"

She shook her head and wrapped her arms tightly around her waist. "If we speak not of it . . . if there are no plans . . . " Tears rained in ribbons down her cheeks. "Then you cannot leave me!"

"Margherita," he crooned to her, and brought her near to him once again with all of the strength he had in his hand. "I *am* going to die. I have seen this sickness, the fever, a dozen times myself in this city from the great cross section of people who have posed for me! Pretending otherwise cannot change what is!"

"This is fool's talk! You will *not* die! You are young and strong, and there is so much yet for you to do!" She chattered with nervous resolve through her tears, as the papal physicians sent from the Vatican Palace waited across the room. They rung their hands in frustration and murmured in low, derisive tones about her even as she held Raphael's hand. "Saint Peter's is nowhere near complete! There is the portrait of the Holy Father and his cousin and nephew . . . and your Transfiguration—"

He drew in another difficult breath, then released it. "I finished the work two days past," he revealed. "And when I cough . . . there is blood."

"No!" she cried out bitterly. "You see death, but I see only an illness! A small setback! I shall take care of you, stay with you every moment, and in time—"

"See it for what it is, I beg you! For your own safety, let me plan for you! Knowing that you are safe is the only thing that shall bring me peace!" he murmured, then began to cough. "I am not afraid to die, *amore mio*. I will welcome the new life I will have with—"

"Your life is with me!"

"*Sì* . . . and it has been the *best* life . . . the very best . . . "

As Margherita leaned over to embrace him, she could feel how weakened he had swiftly become. He was limp in her arms, as if already he was slowly beginning the process of leaving her. She wiped another flood of tears from her cheeks with the back of her hand, and glanced at the physicians who stood cruelly in judgment of her, refusing to come forward or to counsel with her on his condition. "We must be married! Then they will listen to me, and I will know how to help you!"

His eyes were heavy and he needed to sleep. She knew that he must sleep a great deal if he was to conquer this fever and whatever else was trying to conquer him. "Believe forever that was my dearest wish . . . " he said faintly, as his eyes fluttered to a close. "To make you my wife."

"I do believe it," she whispered back, close enough at that moment, to feel his labored breath on her face. *His breath . . . life . . . as long as there is that, there is hope . . .*

She bid Elena, who lingered with Donato in the shadows nearby, to come forward. In a low tone, Margherita said, "I must leave for just a little while. Will you stay with him while I am gone?"

"Of course, *signora,*" she answered with her own tear-filled eyes.

"Do not leave him alone with those vultures over there for even a moment, no matter what they tell you."

"No, Signora Luti. I shall stay with him until you return."

She looked next to Donato. "Go with me to Trastevere?"

"I would go anywhere you wished, you know that."

Once she saw that Raphael had fallen into another sleep, Margherita quietly left his bedside and moved across the vast bedchamber to the place near the door where Pope Leo's best personal physicians were still gathered, discussing the gravity of the artist's condition in their hushed tones.

"Per favore," she pleaded. "I know what you think of me, but can you not at least tell me there is something that might be done for him!"

There was a moment of silence before one of them, a stout, elderly man with a puffed chest, turned to glower at her. "We shall tell *you* nothing, *signora*. And you would be well advised, at this stage, to do what you can for yourself, for he shall not survive this."

Not so long ago, everyone who entered this house would have rushed to obey her, masking their disdain of the way Raphael lived his life so blatantly with her in order to ingratiate themselves to the *mastro*. But no longer. Their bold response was painfully ominous. "Care not for me," she cried through her indignation. "I accept that! But, I bid you, help *him!*"

"Would that we could. But it has gone too far. The fever will not abate."

"No!" Her face blanched as another physician dryly spoke.

"We speak the truth. Raffaello is greatly favored by His Holiness. If any of us could save him, for that reason alone, we surely would."

Her hands were covering her mouth. "There *must* be something! *Dio,* anything!"

"Signora Luti, you are not family. As he said, you are nothing in this discussion," proclaimed another of the physicians, a grizzled man with a noticeable paunch. "Now kindly remove yourself from our midst."

"You are wrong! I am going to find a cleric to marry us, and then I will be family, and *you* will regret your treatment of me!"

"Pitiful woman." The first physician shook his head. "Do you not know there is not a single cleric, much less a respectable citizen in all of Rome, who supports what you have done to the great *mastro?* You, a lowly girl, with your wanton ways, have corrupted his entire being—and now brought about his death, as surely as if you had plunged a knife into his heart!"

She shuddered in the echo of his words, as if those venomous murmurings alone held the power to destroy her, and had begun to do just that. Cupping her hands tightly over her ears, Margherita pivoted away from their accusing expressions and harsh stares.

"*Signora,* see the truth for what it is!" he cruelly called out as she dashed from the room. "Raphael's life is nearly over now. Do what you can to save yourself."

"DO YOU not understand, I must marry her!" Raphael declared with a quavering voice as Giulio leaned over his bed after Margherita had gone. "She has waited for so long in good faith. I *must* make her my wife in case something should happen! If this illness is—"

"You cannot possibly take that risk, *mastro mio!* Think of it! Cardinal Bibbiena is still full of rage over his niece—over the ring—and he is the senior-most cleric in Rome while the pope is away in Florence!" Giulio quietly urged, huddled close to Raphael at his bedside. "If you were not to survive this, and leave Margherita with the one honor his niece never had, you will not be able to protect her. He will make the rest of her life a misery! I have heard it whispered so myself!"

He grimaced, fighting for strength. "But she is *meant* to be my wife!"

"Is she not that already in your heart?"

"It is not the same thing for her! Without a true marriage, she will be forever thought of as a whore! My mistress! Margherita deserves better than that!"

"Let not your heart cloud your judgment, I bid you, *mastro.* The cardinal is an old and vindictive man who loved no one in this life so much as he did his niece! He will not be kind to Signora Luti if she is the widowed Signora Sanzio!"

"Then find me someone, Giulio, I bid *you*—as my most trusted assistant, and my friend! Find anyone who will marry us in secret before it is too late! She must know I did not let go of this earth without keeping my promise to her! It is the last request I will ever make of you!"

As he closed his eyes, falling into a short, fitful sleep, Giulio left his side and went to stand in the *mastro*'s private work area beside the bed chamber. Beyond the heavy velvet drapery, he could hear the team of Pope Leo's physicians struggling to save the artist's young, important life with a wild, mysterious collection of potions, purgatives, and bloodletting. Through tear-misted eyes, and the sound of their low, concerned conversation, Giulio faced the final painted image of Margherita—what he knew to be her wedding portrait.

There had been such joy, such hope brushed into that image. A new painting style marking a new chapter of their lives. Each brushstroke of the master reflected that. As an artist himself, Giulio understood the passion. He knew what this painting, and this woman, meant to Raphael, for it was precisely how Giulio would wish to immortalize Elena.

Giulio brushed the tears away with the back of his hand as he looked at the serene smile. There was the sensually scant costume, the ruby ring painted onto the finger that symbolized the route directly to the heart, and he felt as if he were intruding on something very private even by looking at it.

He turned then to a large black leather folio of sketches and studies. They were more priceless than even Raphael's paintings because, while the paintings were so often a collaborative effort within the workshop, these images were always fashioned solely from the hand of Raffaello himself. In their revelation to the world, there was yet more danger to Margherita; and as his final homage to the one who had never forsaken him, Giulio

Romano would do for her what Raphael could not. He would protect her.

"God save you, what are you doing with those?" Elena gasped.

He did not look up at her, but kept on. "I thought you were not to leave the *mastro*'s side."

"I have come away only for a moment, hearing movement in here. And still you have not answered me."

"I am destroying the last of what might harm Margherita."

"But his works . . . they are irreplaceable!"

"They are private sketches of her, and the *mastro* would want her safe at any cost—even this."

Elena went to him and drew his gaze. Only then did he sigh, and for a moment they held one another. Adversity brought them closer to each other than they had ever been, but neither felt comforted or passionate. They felt only the unspeakable sorrow of something tragic and impending.

"Is there no hope for him?"

He drew in a painful breath, unable to look at her any longer. "None at all. The doctors say it is only a matter of days."

"*Gesù, Madre Maria!*" she cried. "What shall become of us all once he is gone?"

❧ 40 ❧

"MY SON, RENOUNCE HER, I BID YOU," BIBBIENA MUR-mured gravely. His deeply cultured voice, like an incantation, came on the wings of a dream, and Raphael struggled to open his eyes. But it was no dream. "Renounce what you have done, lo these many years, dearest boy, so that I may at the least offer you absolution."

Elena stood back from the bed as the cardinal had ordered her to do, but with Margherita and Donato still gone, she would not leave the room. Like a jackal waiting to attack, Cardinal Bibbiena had arrived at the precise moment when Raphael would be alone, and thus at his weakest.

Raphael's eyes opened slowly onto the gaunt face of a man whose own cold and piercing eyes were wide with expectation. The cleric had actually dared come here into this place, where all of Rome had said sins were so openly committed.

"Never!" he rasped. "I would rather burn forever in the fires of hell than do that to her . . . "

"And so you shall, if you do not listen to reason!"

Bibbiena sank onto the edge of the bed where Margherita had been only hours before. He waited a moment, collected himself, then began again. "I have loved you, Raphael, as a son. And, indeed, there was a time when you nearly were that, until—" He paused again, glancing heavenward, seemingly to mutter a prayer. "That is, of course, in the past now. Shall you not, Raphael, my dear son, clear your soul now with me?"

"I would not do it . . . ," Raphael breathed with great difficulty, his gray pallor gaining a slight hint of color from his conviction, "if you were the last priest on this earth!"

"And indeed I may well be!" Bibbiena growled, then glanced at the door through which every cleric in Rome but himself had refused to pass for the sin that had taken place in this room.

Maria Bibbiena's rival was notorious and despised all over the city, and in that there was some cold comfort to the cardinal, who had done all that he could to see them parted. The only thing he had not considered until now was their parting by death.

"Can you not see that no respectable man of God will enter here? And with the Holy Father delayed in Florence, he will not be able to marry you. He will *never* marry the two of you!"

"It was his promise."

Bibbiena's eyes were cold. "Well, he did not mean it. As you did not mean your promise to Maria."

Raphael reached out suddenly to grip Bibbiena's arm. His hand was surprisingly strong. "Then *you* marry us, Your Grace! If you care a whit for my immortal soul, as a good and pious cardinal, declare us and our love respectable as a favor for our past affection. Do this for me!"

Bibbiena arched a sharp gray brow of surprise. "I understood no one but the Holy Father was acceptable for that task."

"We both know I will not live to see his return from Florence. *Per favore,* let me die in peace, having made her my wife . . . knowing, thus, that she will be safe, protected by your power and grace."

"I am afraid I cannot do that," Bibbiena calmly replied. "You are not well enough with that fever to consider properly such an auspicious step. Once you recover from this, if you—"

"I am not going to recover!" Raphael weakly groaned. "You know that, as do I!"

"I shall certainly pray for that nonetheless, as well as for the future of your immortal soul, my boy."

"I am sorry I did not love your niece the way you had hoped, Bernardo," Raphael admitted with the familiarity he and the cardinal once, long ago, had enjoyed. But it was too late for many things, and nostalgia was among them.

"*Allora,* we all make costly choices in this world," said the cardinal. "And indeed, you certainly seem to have made yours. One that shall live with you through all eternity now."

MARGHERITA covered her head as she and Donato entered the cool, shadowy sanctuary and absolute stillness of the small parish church of Santa Dorotea, into which she had not passed in over a year. Warm and gentle memories of another lifetime came at her swiftly amid the heavy fragrance of incense and candle wax, enveloping her like a familiar, warming shawl. It quickly gave her a sense of safety, peace, and protection she had not felt for a long time. Both of them made the sign of the cross before they advanced to the altar where the kind old cleric, Padre Giacomo, stood lighting long white candles.

She was embraced tenderly by the old man, who had always refused to remind her of how notorious she had become. "Is it true what they are saying, child, that the great man is very near his end?" he asked.

Margherita stiffened. Even the suggestion of it was intolerable. "He is ill, it is true, but he will recover, *padre*. I must believe that."

"Then why have you come here if not for prayer and solace?"

"To recall the favor you promised years ago. I implore you now, I *beg* you, to come to the Via Alessandrina and secretly marry the two of us!"

Now it was he who looked stricken. He touched the tarnished silver crucifix hanging at his chest and shook his head. "Impossible, my child."

"But why? I have known you all of my life, Padre Giacomo! You have dined in my home, celebrated together with me! You shared my grief as we buried my mother, and my good fortune at Raphael's love!" She pressed him with the greatest determination, for her life seemed to depend upon it.

"And there is no one else in all of Rome who will do it?"

She lowered her eyes for a moment, then she looked up again and touched his arm. "No. And so I beg you. We wish to marry quietly, we *must* marry, in order for me to have any voice at all in his treatment! The papal physicians can find no other option to fight this fever, and thus insist on bleeding him repeatedly, which is only stealing the last of his strength! He needs another course of treatment, I can feel it, and yet the physicians will not even speak with me! And now that they believe the end is near, none of the other clerics will consider marrying us so that I can help him, for the risk to their reputation!"

"Do you value *my* reputation less than theirs?"

She struggled for a moment with the notion that she had insulted him. "I had hoped our family connection might be worth the risk to you! And you promised Raphael himself!"

"It was a courtesy offered at a very different time, Margherita."

"Then I will pay you whatever you ask!"

"Margherita." His voice was controlled. He spoke as if she were a small child requiring his utmost patience. "Cardinal Bibbiena is my superior. He controls all. I would be ruined, or worse yet, sent abroad for defying him. Surely you understand that neither your money, nor Raphael's, would be of help to me then."

"But before the cardinal, are you not first a disciple of God—one who must answer to what is right and good in His eyes?"

The old parish cleric put an arm across her shoulder and began to lead her back toward the door with Donato. His head was somberly lowered as he silently followed behind them, the crucifix on his chest swaying with each step. "A disciple of God, *sì*. It is that for which I strive each day of my life. But I remain only a weak man."

"You truly are our last hope."

"Forgive me, Margherita, but I am not strong enough to battle all of them, and give you your desire. Yet there is one thing it is within my power to offer you. A refuge . . . a place to go if you should find yourself in need. The convent of Sant'Apollonia. They have been known to take in young women who, in a troubled time—"

She knew it well. It was the convent across the street from Raphael's own workshop. The bitter irony of that was too much just now. "Speak no more of that! I will not run away from this!"

"But what will you do then?"

"He will *not* die!" she declared. It felt entirely disloyal to her to think otherwise.

Padre Giacomo tried to take her hand. "But what if he does, child? Must you not make some provision for that? Think at least of the convent of Sant'Apollonia as a refuge if you find no other. I bid you, keep that option close to your heart."

She drew away in anger. "I have no future without Raphael, so it would not matter what would become of me if he were gone!" Those words were spoken to him but resonated within her. Her life truly was over if Raphael died. That would be the end of her. She simply could not go on without him.

The old cleric must have seen that in her eyes, because he reached out again and clamped a hand firmly onto her shoulder. His words came as gently and full of meaning as a caress. "Consider that you *are* married to one another, *cara mia*. Such is the great depth of your love for one another. Consider that God sees you as the bride of Raphael already, and only men have kept you from a legal union which He has already sanctioned."

"Oh, will you not consider marrying us?" she pleaded, tears of desperation spilling onto her cheeks. "For all of the years and friendship between us!"

"I wish I could make that matter more than my own fears, *cara*. I truly do. In that, I am sorry I am not a better man, and a better priest."

He did not wish to hurt her, she knew, and yet his refusal had been as deep and cutting as any knife wound. Everyone had turned their backs on her. She had flouted convention, and now she would be made to pay for it. But none of that mattered at all, because there was no higher price to pay than losing Raphael to death.

MARGHERITA came soundlessly into the small studio beside her bedchamber. Her heart ached with a wrenching pain, knowing that she could do nothing to help him. As she moved beyond the door, she saw Giulio and Elena. They were standing together in a deep embrace.

"What are we to do?" Elena was asking in a low tone.

He murmured something in reply that she did not hear, and then they were silent.

What Giulio and Elena felt for one another was not a surprise, nor did it upset her. But it was the sight of so many torn drawings and sketches being tossed into a roaring fire that drove her forward, her hands gnarled into fists.

"Cease this!" Margherita cried out. "I forbid you to speak of *Mastro* Sanzio as if all hope were lost! Giulio, you are his dearest friend! He will recover from this, and when he does, he will need all of our love and support! How can you—"

"Forgive me, *signora*." He bowed reverently to her. "But because he is so dear to me, I must honor him now. I *must* protect him, and all that he values, when he cannot do so for himself."

"Destroying his work is protecting him?"

"It is protecting *you*." He touched her shoulder in a supportive gesture that was very like the one that had come from Padre Giacomo. "Many of them are private sketches of you, *signora*—the woman Rome sees as having brought this illness about. They will not be so tolerant of you once he is gone."

She covered her face with her hands. The pain was so great that she almost could not bear it. "I love him more than my own life, Giulio," she said softly, achingly. "Do they not know that *he* loves *me*?"

"They care not who or what he loves. Raphael always knew that. They care only for his creations . . . his great talent. To them he is not a man but an artist."

"May the Good Lord forgive them, for I never will!"

"I bid you on his behalf, *signora*—go to your family. Speak with them. Protect yourself," Elena pleaded. "If the *mastro* does survive this, there will have been no harm done, and you will return to him."

Margherita hung her head, her lungs so constricted with grief so that she could not breathe. "I cannot go back, Elena. None of us can *ever* go back." They did not want her back now. They had made that clear. Margherita glanced up at the two of them before her, their faces mirroring the sorrow she felt, her sister's declaration from years ago creeping now back into her mind. It was the moment she had realized she could never go home to the bakery or the life she once had lived there.

"*Sì*, they respect you now, but mark me, sister: If anything should ever happen to your beloved artist, you will be a pariah in Rome! Ridiculed, laughed at!" Letitia had cruelly blustered then, seeing Margherita just after her return from abduction. "Neither Father, nor Donato and I, can allow ourselves to be caught up in *that*! The bakery would not survive—nor would we!"

Margherita shivered now, remembering her sister's words. After all she had done for them these past years, none of it mattered in the end.

Like everything else in her world, that was over as well.

She turned then and walked very slowly toward the door, remembering little Matteo's face, and feeling her heart squeeze as she did. Such innocent sweetness still about him. Like the son she would never have with Raphael. *Dio,* how she missed that boy. He had wept the last time she had seen him. Had he known somehow that they would never see one another again?

Over her shoulder, Margherita said, "Make certain you burn all of them, Giulio." Then she pulled the heavy door to the small studio closed behind herself for the last time, and for a moment everything was silent.

❧ *41* ❧

GOOD FRIDAY, APRIL 6, 1520

ANOTHER FOUR DAYS PASSED SLOWLY AS RAPHAEL LAY IN a continuously fevered state, waking briefly, only to fall sleep again without moving for hours at a time. Margherita sat beside him, holding his hand and mopping his brow with a series of cool cloths from a basin. She refused to leave even as one sour-faced papal physician after another consulted on his condition and spoke coldly of his imminent demise, as if she were not there.

Every hour the pope had an aide sent to the house and then ride swiftly to Florence so that he might be constantly apprised of Raphael's condition. She could hear the physicians, in their low tones, speaking with the aides, as they stood near the door, knowing full well she could hear their every word. Repeatedly, they whispered that it was hopeless. It was overindulgence of physical pleasures, declared one. He had seen all of these signs before. The unrelenting fever was killing him, another was convinced. Certainly the severity and duration was sufficient to make it fatal.

But none of the physicians could be absolutely certain what it was that pulled Raphael steadily toward death.

They also spoke about the clerics who would not set foot in this room to give the pope's favored artisan the last rites, unless he were to renounce his unholy alliance with a whore. If that woman were to leave him, it would be considered, they said. But if she remained, no cleric would go against the dictates of God. Not even for a pope's favored artist.

The cutting words wounded her, but not half so much as the reality of seeing Raphael motionless in the bed beside her. He was not improving. As the days wore on, he had fewer moments of lucid consciousness, fewer moments of recognizing anyone. Much of the time, he called out to his father and spoke of Urbino, and works which he had assisted with as a boy. The Lord had relieved him of his pain by bringing back his youth, and for that she was grateful, but the part of him she had lost was the greatest part of her own heart.

As an ever-changing collection of Raphael's assistants and apprentices, papal guardsmen, and Agostino Chigi himself held vigil at his bedside, his condition went unchanged. In desperation, and knowing no other effective treatment, the physicians continued to bleed him, hoping at least to release the poisonous ailment that was swiftly killing a young and vigorous man. Margherita had seen from the first that the treatments only weakened him the more. She held no power to stop them, but as long as he called out for her, they could not force her to leave his side.

Finally, on the sixth of April, Margherita was worn to sheer exhaustion. Giulio convinced her to take a few hours of rest in a quiet room next door. Unable any longer to function, she hesitantly complied and lay now, just before dawn, in a deep, unmoving sleep. As he had promised her he would, Giulio took her place and sat silently beside Raphael's bed, watching the sun slowly begin to rise through the window shutters.

"What day is it, Giulio?"

Hearing the voice he had not heard for several days, at first Giulio believed himself to be dreaming. But it was Raphael, gazing over at him. "Good Friday, *mastro*."

A weak smile edged up the corners of his mouth just slightly. "How ironic and fitting that I should die on the very day of my birth. I was actually born on Good Friday as well."

"You will not die today," Giulio trembled, reaching for Raphael's now cold hand as tears pressed forward from the back of his eyes. "But you will go to live in the house of the Lord . . ."

"*Sì,*" he sighed, then closed his eyes for so long that Giulio believed for a moment that he had perished.

He looked so old and so weary. His youthful face had been ravaged already by this mysterious illness for which he had been repeatedly bled in a last desperate attempt to save his life. Yet in his weakened condition, the loss of blood had only hastened the outcome, which all now knew was imminent. He lay very still now, a full, dark mustache and beard disguising his once-handsome features, and his eyes sinking ever more deeply into their sockets.

"See her cared for, *caro amico*. I bid you with a heart that aches. Make certain she is safe," Raphael pleaded hoarsely. "You are the only one I can ask . . . the only one I can trust."

Giulio leaned more closely, fighting off a new wave of sorrow. "You must rest, *mastro*."

He gripped Giulio's hand with surprising force — the last he possessed. "She will not be safe if you do not find a way to protect her!" Raphael strained to say.

"Worry not. On my honor, I shall protect your Margherita with my own life."

"Swear it, by your oath!"

"I do swear it."

"I shall still worry . . . Peace cannot be mine until I know what will become of her . . . " He drew in a crackling breath. "Her useless family will never have her back once I am gone, and she has nothing more but trouble and ridicule to bring them."

"Another liaison perhaps. Someone to protect her?"

"You know well that no one with any authority would have her just now," Raphael strained to say, and in his tone there was heartbreak. If he could not have her, he wanted someone else at least to protect her.

"There is another choice. For a time anyway. A choice that will surely make her safe, though not an easy one."

"Then tell me, Giulio," Raphael faintly bid him. "Before it is too late . . . I must know of it . . . "

RAPHAEL LAY perfectly still, his eyes closed, dreaming, sleeping, and feeling his body go slowly very cold as he was bound by thoughts he knew soon would be his last. *So much left to do . . .* So many moments to share . . . children. . . . paintings . . . Like any other dying man, he wished he had done things differently. Perhaps if he had lived a different way, this . . . Ah, but then this was exactly the end he was meant to have.

Pushing away the regret, he saw her face in his mind, sweet, soft, so exquisitely lovely, and he wondered what would become of her, where life would lead her. But he wished more than any other thing that he could go with her, that there could be a place for them, somewhere between this strange mortal world and heaven. Yet Raphael knew even in this hour that his life would live on in her . . . in the paintings they had made together . . . the images she alone had inspired. Margherita Luti was his slip of eternity.

MARGHERITA had only slept a little more than an hour. But seeing Giulio's stricken expression and Elena's eyes flooded with tears when she woke, she knew that her decision to leave Raphael's side was one that would haunt her for the rest of her life.

Dashing back into the bedchamber, she saw that the candles had only just been extinguished, their small trails of acrid smoke filling the silent air as the pale first morning light came softly in through the now half-open window shutters. Horrifying to her was the sight of Raphael's empty bed.

As Margherita glanced sharply around the room, at the faces, the vacant bed, the smoking candles, everything began to move in slow motion. *If no one says it,* she thought desperately, *then it cannot be true.* Yet she knew by the way Giulio held Elena so tightly to him that the unimaginable had actually occurred. She was numb, yet her mind ran in circles. He could not be gone . . . He was meant to recover—they were meant to survive this as they had everything else that life had cast cruelly at them.

As Giulio moved back from the bed, Margherita went to him. "*Signora,* I must—" Giulio tried to say, his voice breaking.

"Say nothing! I am not ready for condolences! Nor shall I ever be, because for me he shall never be gone!" Margherita felt them back away from the bed. She saw Elena's tears, but she could not comfort her. She had nothing left to give to anyone.

When she heard the door click open, and saw Cardinal Bibbiena come into the room, her own blood went deathly cold. Of all the people in the world—all the clerics—he had the fewest reasons to be here. When she looked to Giulio for an explanation, she saw, to her horror, that his face had changed.

"Forgive me, Signora Luti," Giulio began loudly enough to be overheard. "But I was not extending a condolence. Rather, it was an explanation as to where Signor Sanzio was taken while you slept." She watched him draw in a deep breath, then exhale it. His voice was brittle, changed. This was not the man, the artist, or the friend she knew and trusted. "At the end, the *mastro* saw things more clearly. He renounced you in those last moments of his life and therefore was removed from this room in order to receive absolution."

"No . . ."

"He became convinced in his final moments that the fate of his immortal soul rested on that fact, and he did renounce you to me."

"He would not have done that! Not ever!"

"How each of us sees things as we go to meet our Heavenly Father, alas, is known only to us," Cardinal Bibbiena said quietly from across the room. "Surely you can see that it is better for his immortal soul, and your future, that Raphael disavowed this unholy alliance of yours. Surely you are not still so selfish, *signora,* that you cannot admit that."

Giulio's words were an echo in her mind. *It is protecting you . . .*

Looking at the bitter cardinal, in his starched crimson robes, his face tight with hatred, then glancing over at Giulio, she understood why he had changed. Raphael's dear friend was protecting her from Cardinal Bibbiena now that Raphael could no longer do it himself.

42

MARGHERITA WALKED ALONE TOWARD THE GIANT PANtheon on the wide, cobblestone piazza where it had sat majestically since the first century. With its massive white stone columns and arches, this great architectural marvel of another age still stood, the echo of emperors emanating from its very bricks and mortar. A light rain misted her face and hair as well as the dark cloak and hood that shrouded her in anonymity. She would allow no one to accompany her. She had forced even Donato to remain behind, relegated to the task of supervising the packing of her belongings for charity.

She had told them in a weakened voice, breaking with anguish, that she must see him one final time, in spite of the risk the crowds would bring. She had not been there with him to hold his hand or comfort him as he slipped quietly into death. For that, she would never forgive herself. Now, by order of the pope, Raphael lay in state in the very center of one of the most grand buildings in Rome. As she approached, his words of long ago were bittersweet in her mind.

Perhaps I shall have the Holy Father agree to bury me in the Pantheon one day, with you resting beside me, so that no one shall ever forget, unlikely or not, we two are forever lovers."

She had smiled when he said it, thinking then that he must surely live forever. His work, after all, was timeless, and therefore he would be as well. The great Raffaello created magic and spun dreams. With him, her own had come true. For a time. Now, like the dust of angels, he was gone forever, and so were her dreams . . .

She pulled the dark cloak closer around her face and stepped into the crowd. They were waiting to move forward up the wide steps so that they might pay their last respects to a great artist most of them had never seen in life. She mingled among them— the devout, the curious, Rome's poor and its elite—their grief a balm on her raw anguish. As one of them, she was a nameless, faceless woman hoping to pay homage. Yet she did so to the man rather than the artist.

Finally she was close enough to see beyond the doors. Upon a bier, draped in black silk, a body lay—her own beloved. *So he truly is gone,* she thought, seeing a finality in it now she had not allowed herself before. At his head, like a magnificent headstone, was the epic final work, sweepingly painted. It was the *Transfiguration,* with herself as a model in the foreground. Margherita felt her knees weaken so that she nearly collapsed beneath the weight of what never should have been. The culmination of his artistic life, he had called this work. And something more. The work was his last. Her heart squeezed so painfully that she felt she would faint.

As Margherita was pushed on a wave of anguished faces and outstretched arms, ever nearer the large carved doors, she caught sight of one she recognized. A face that caused the halting of the very breath in her throat. Anna Perazzi was looking directly at her, and beside her was her husband, Antonio.

"What is *she* doing here?" the woman called out in a rough tenor more befitting a man than any sort of comely woman, and loudly enough for others to hear. Instinctively, Margherita lowered her head, but it was too late. She had barely glimpsed Raphael's body upon its bier, certainly gotten nowhere near enough to ease her broken heart, to gain one last sight of his beautiful peaceful face, to bid him a restful sleep.

"It is a horrible sin, her being here!" Antonio's wife cruelly declared.

Rather than quieting her, Antonio merely looked away from Margherita, as if they had never known one another at all. The crowd turned angry, charging at her. "*Puttana!*" they called. "You did this to him! *You!*" They swept her up into their spiteful midst, as if the power of a wave had taken her over, swallowed her, and now cast her very forcefully down the steps and away from the Pantheon.

Cast onto the cobbled courtyard like a beggar, she collapsed into a heap on the paving stones. Someone kicked her as they passed, though she did not see who. Then she was spat upon from the same direction. Another blow, and another. But the pain in her heart was beyond anything they could do to her.

Just as suddenly, Margherita felt sturdy hands draw her up from behind and begin to tug her from the midst of the angry, swelling crowd. It was only when they were out of the piazza and onto the quiet and narrow Via Madalena that she turned and saw Donato.

"I knew I should have come with you," he murmured as she sank limply against the protective depth of his broad shoulder. Trembling and weeping, she stood with him in a narrow shadowy street that smelled of urine and despair, so close to the place where Raphael lay in state with as much solemn dignity as any king. Raphael had been loved by Pope Leo. She had not.

Margherita Luti had come from nothing, and now she was nothing again.

In the end, as she had declared she would, even Francesca Chigi had abandoned her. She could not risk her standing, she said, or her husband's. Although she had expected it, the loss of that friendship, to Margherita, was devastating.

Donato held fast to her as they slowly made their way along the Via Madalena back toward the house on the Via Alessandrina for what she knew would be the final time. She could not remain there. The place held too much of Raphael for her not to have seen his face, heard his voice, around every corner.

"Take me to Giulio," she said flatly. "I am ready to go wherever he has arranged."

Donato's voice was reed thin, his expression grave. "You have Raphael's riches, do you not, to buy yourself a new home? Begin a new life, without doing something so drastic?"

Margherita lowered her eyes, shook her head, and wrapped her arms tightly around herself, pain, loss, and despair moving through her, seizing her so forcefully that she almost could not breathe. "I took nothing like that from him."

"You are not serious."

She did not tell them that Raphael had drawn up a new will several months ago, leaving everything to her. Nor did she tell them that she had destroyed it, returning the original will, with Giulio Romano as principal beneficiary, to its rightful place among his papers. She would have no use for his money where fate was taking her, anyway.

"His final will was made before our meeting," she lied. "When he fell ill, for their hatred of me, no one would amend it for him. So it is true. I have only the clothes on my back, my wedding portrait—grand irony there to torment me—and this ring."

Margherita glanced down at the ruby ring glittering on her finger, a painful reminder of a time that was now as buried from the light as the ring itself so long had been. "I want to die with him," she achingly whispered.

"You do not mean that." He tightened the arm around her shoulder. "We shall work something out."

"It does not matter now. The part of me that was worth anything Raphael created. That person is dead along with him. It is the end, and I wish it to be so. Simply that, nothing more."

EPILOGUE

THERE WAS NO RECOURSE. IT WAS OVER.

Giulio had told Margherita that he would take her wedding portrait for safekeeping until she chose to leave the convent. But she would never leave this place. She knew that, as he did. They had spoken in tender, hopeful terms as he bid her a farewell at the imposing convent gates, and both of them, for an instant, had tried to smile. Yet neither of them had managed to fool the other. They had each loved Raphael too much.

And she understood fully why, in the end, he had helped Raphael forsake her. Although he asked for her forgiveness, Margherita assured him there was nothing to forgive. Giulio had done it to protect her from those powerful forces who would want to blame her for the past, and now for the *mastro's* death. Chigi. The Pope. Cardinal Bibbiena. Danger could come from many directions. She would be safer as the vanquished, not the victor. Both of them knew that.

The warmth of Giulio's embrace lingered on her shoulders even now that he was gone, back into the tangle of streets, back to his own art, to his own life—hopefully to a future with Elena. They were meant to be together. That much was as clear as it had been for her and Raphael.

The sound of his name on her heart, in her memory, as he first had spoken it to her, brought a fresh stab of pain. *I will always treasure you . . . always love you . . . Wait for me . . . I will come to you soon . . . soon . . .*

She walked alone then back across the ancient stone floor of the convent of Sant'Appolonia and into the abbess's chamber.

The old nun sat at her desk, unmoving. Unable to look at the ring a final time, Margherita slipped it from her finger, feeling its cool, reassuring band move across her knuckles and then, one last time, touch her fingertip. It had not been off her hand since Raphael had put it there. Now the ring would be gone from her life forever, as he was. Fitting, she decided then, for this ring could only ever remind her of what she had lost.

Margherita reached across the desk and lay the ring before the stone-faced abbess. Her face betrayed none of the anguish, none of the loss, only resignation. It had been like a sweet, beautiful dream. Now it was over.

The abbess folded the ring into a dry, bloodless hand, and Margherita heard it land with a small clink in the bottom of a drawer, now a meaningless ruby and chunk of gold. A moment later, the old woman, her face dry and pale as straw, stood and held out her hand. Glittering there in the pale afternoon sunlight was an unadorned gold band, the ring that would mark her new life and make her now, like all of the others here, a bride of Christ.

Margherita hesitated for a moment, glancing at the band, seeing the stark reality of its meaning before her.

"It is our custom for there to be a ceremony," the old woman announced matter-of-factly. "But the others here do not know you yet, and, because of your notoriety, we may well keep it so. Under the circumstances, your time here may be made easier by that. We shall simply say you have come to us a postulant from another convent."

Margherita did not respond, but her answer lay in her own outstretched hand as she reached up to take the other ring she now would wear. *I want you to be my wife, Margherita Luti. I want that more than anything in this world.* She squeezed her eyes, determined to force away the sound of his voice, determined not to think anymore of the past, or of what might have been. *Wait for me . . . Per favore, amore,* she thought instead as she slowly slipped the gold ring onto the same finger where the ruby ring had been, pushing it down with the same determination with which she once had vowed to love Raphael Sanzio forever.

Eternity with him . . . it really was not all that very far away.

FOR THE LONGEST WHILE, Giulio stood frozen, the wedding portrait before him, still on its easel, as if the *mastro* might at any moment return to add a finishing touch to the beautiful innovative image of Margherita. The style was so new and daring, so full of Raphael's sense of creativity. Giulio felt his eyes well with tears as he thought of the life in this portrait—life Raphael no longer possessed. Suddenly, he slammed his fist very hard onto the *mastro*'s worktable, sending several paintbrushes skittering to the floor.

It was not supposed to end this way, the *mastro* so in his prime, with so much yet for them to do. No one had ever been better to Giulio, nor believed in him, more than Raphael Sanzio. He owed his very life to the man who saw talent in him before he saw it in himself.

Giulio shook his head. No one understood the complexity of an artist's life—the brotherhood Raphael had created within his studio, the safety to paint, to create . . . to realize a bit of immortality at the end of a paintbrush.

He glanced up at the painting again just as the afternoon sunlight filtered warm and golden across the vaulted studio and, like tender fingers, moved across the painting itself. A caress from heaven, thought Giulio with an infinite sadness. One last goodbye to his beloved . . . a final message delivered to Giulio as the sun on the painting moved down like a pointing finger, casting a shimmering highlight upon the painted image of the small, perfect ruby ring. And in seeing it, he knew what he must do. For Raphael—for the woman Raphael had loved. To protect her now that Raphael no longer could.

Drawing in one deep breath and then another to give himself courage, Giulio looked with steady determination for the right shade of paints among the *mastro*'s colors to begin mixing a flesh tone. *Her* flesh tone . . . *I will do this for you,* mastro . . . *I promised you I would protect her, and I shall* . . .   Pushing himself to do something that felt, on the surface, like an invasion, a corruption, Giulio then took a slim, boar-bristle brush from Raphael's worktable and dipped it carefully into a cup of freshly mixed paint. The silence was deafening in the old house where the echo of Margherita's rich, warm laughter still clung to the walls, and had so recently warmed the place.

How cruel a thing was fate, he thought, pressing small neat daubs of flesh-colored paint onto the canvas with precision and care. Onto the image of her finger. Her ring. As he gently daubed and worked the brush, it began to disappear as if moving back into the canvas just as quickly as Raphael had left this earth. As though it never had been. As though his fervent commitment to her had never been, either.

Now the serene, smiling face began to change in his mind. By his actions, it was no longer a wedding portrait. Now she was only a girl, scantily clothed, sensually posed. A model. An ideal. The ring was gone. This painting could not harm her any longer. The same could not be said for the other factions in Rome who still wished to do her harm. He had been right to propose to the *mastro* what he had. It had brought Raphael peace in those final moments. The convent of Sant'Apollonia was the only way left to protect her.

And to tell the world publicly that, in the end, he had disavowed her.

When Giulio had told her the truth, that Raphael, with his final breath, had approved an order to protect her, she simply gazed blankly out the window that faced onto yet another cobbled piazza with its splashing stone fountain. Then she walked alone down the stairs, prepared to find her fate in a convent she had never seen, with women who would never really know her. There was no voice left in her to change that. There was nothing left for her to say.

AS A HEAVIER RAIN FELL now across Rome, Cardinal Bibbiena watched with quiet satisfaction the exhumation of his niece's coffin from the little cemetery inside the Vatican walls. The hem of his cassock rippled like crimson waves and yet he stood stone still—eyes fixed on the goal. What a stroke of good fortune it had been that Raphael's strumpet had found the good sense to lock herself away in a convent. Clearly, it was where the girl belonged, her comely face hidden from the rest of the world. It truly was the first decent thing she had ever done.

"Where will we be taking the body, Your Grace?" asked the grimy, gray-bearded man, leaning on the handle of his rusty shovel, and mopping a sheen of perspiration from his brow.

"To the Pantheon, of course," he declared with a pious smile. "My niece will rest beside her beloved, the magnificent Raffaello. They shall be together now for all eternity. At last things are as they should be. In time, my ring shall be returned to me, and the world shall forget there ever was a baker's daughter. It shall be as if *La Fornarina* never existed at all."

Author's Note

🕸

LIKE THE CLOSING OF A BOOK, THE DEATHS OF SEVERAL important figures in Raphael's world came swiftly after his own. Agostino Chigi died suddenly four days after Raphael. Francesco Luti was dead by June. Pope Leo X perished the following year, and Cardinal Bibbiena died a mysterious death twenty days after the pontiff, thus taking many of the true keys to this moment in history with them.

In 1529, Elena di Francesco Guazzi at last became the wife of Giulio Romano. Romano went on to have a distinguished career of his own following Raphael's death, until his own demise in 1546. Of the many artists who trained in Raphael's workshop, Romano is considered by scholars the most noteworthy, his style and brilliance so like the master's that many of their works are still disputed to this day as being by the hand of the other. His own works—including the portrait of Joan of Aragon—hang in the Louvre in Paris, the J. Paul Getty Museum, the Metropolitan Museum of Art, and other major museums. Sebastiano Luciani, Michelangelo's student and Raphael's great rival, is better known historically as Sebastiano del Piombo, the title he received in 1531 after he was appointed to the office of *piombo,* or keeper of the papal seals, by Pope Clement VII—formerly Cardinal Giulio de' Medici, cousin to Pope Leo X.

The purported bakery of the Luti family on 21 Santa Dorotea in Rome remains standing and is, today, a restaurant. The only potential confirmation of the fate of Margherita herself was uncovered in 1897, when historian Antonio Valeri described a sheet he viewed, torn from a ledger and later destroyed, containing the name of postulants at the convent of Sant'Apollonia, now gone, with the entry, "Today, August 18, 1520, Margherita, daughter of the late Francesco Luti, a widow, was received into our institution." After that entry, Margherita Luti disappeared forever from the annals of history. And Maria Bibbiena, not Margherita Luti, lies buried in the Pantheon in Rome beside Raphael Sanzio.

About the Author

DIANE HAEGER is the author of five previous historical novels, including *My Dearest Cecelia* and *The Secret Wife of King George IV.*

A Readers' Guide

THE YEAR IS 1514. RAPHAEL SANZIO, THE DARLING OF THE Italian art world, has grown accustomed to having Pope Leo X wrapped around his talented little finger. Raphael's innovative portraits, altarpieces, and frescoes have so enthralled Rome's elite art collectors, in fact, that his archrival, Michelangelo Buonarroti, has stormed off to Florence to lick his wounds. Yet trouble is brewing for the *mastro*. With dozens of commissions from imperious, impatient clients piling up in his bustling studio, Raphael's energy is flagging. Exhausted and bitter from churning out one masterpiece after another on demand, he yearns for the inspiration and creative freedom he enjoyed before fame wreaked its havoc on him.

Meanwhile, Margherita Luti, a baker's daughter, dreams of a gilded life outside the stifling confines of her family's humble reality. When a walk along the Tiber River brings her face-to-face with the legendary master artist Raphael Sanzio, her predictable life lifts off its axis and is recast inalterably. For four years, the *mastro* has scoured Rome in search of the perfect model to sit for a painting of the Madonna to grace the new Sistine Chapel. In Margherita, Raphael finds at last the timeless beauty he craves. So begins a fraught courtship that will blossom and consume them both—sending shock waves through the upper echelons of Rome's clergy. For Raphael is ensnared in a politically charged betrothal to a senior cardinal's niece, and his attempts to end the engagement not only enrage the pope and his powerful cronies, but place his beloved muse, Margherita, in mortal danger.

The following questions are designed to direct your group's discussion of this haunting story of illicit passion and political manipulation: *The Ruby Ring.*

1. Like Margherita, Raphael idealizes his dead mother, "whose loss had forever changed his life." How is his obsession with the Madonna image linked to this tragedy? Does his sense of abandonment abate once he is involved with Margherita?

2. As the story opens, Raphael has lost the "heated passion toward creation" that once fueled his painting. His artistic block is already well known to his increasingly impatient patrons. Why, then, does he attempt to keep it a secret from his assistants? Is he motivated by pride, or by kindness?

3. Francesco Luti urges his daughter to take the plunge and accept Raphael's extraordinary invitation to model for him. "Look beyond your nose," he argues. "There is a whole wide world out there, and none of us has ever had the chance to see any of it." How does his advice echo the advice pressed upon Raphael by his own father? What are both fathers trying to protect their children from, and what counterargument do both Margherita and Raphael offer in response?

4. Margherita's stubborn refusal to succumb to Raphael's advances stems from a deep cynicism about the entrenched social hierarchy in Rome: "A man who breaks bread with dukes, kings, and the Holy Father himself does not make a wife of the woman who bakes that bread!" she insists. Does she ever fully transcend this sense of social inferiority beside Raphael?

5. Raphael is surprisingly compassionate toward his enemies. Even when Sebastiano Luciani hires thugs to break Raphael's hand, Raphael rationalizes, "He is desperate, and desperation can all

too easily cloud the mind of wisdom." Is Raphael too soft for his own good?

6. It is common Vatican knowledge that Cardinal Bibbiena cares deeply about the happiness of his niece, Maria. Yet when she begs to be allowed to call off her agonizing and embarrassing engagement to the unfeeling Raphael, the cardinal refuses her this relief. Why?

7. What does Antonio stand to gain by telling Agostino Chigi that Margherita is the cause of Raphael's deteriorating work pace? Does he achieve it?

8. With his dedication to his commissions flagging, his distaste for the hypocrisies of the Vatican growing, plenty of wealth amassed, an interested clientele in France, and Margherita with whom to build a new life—why doesn't Raphael simply throw in the towel and set himself free from the constant pressure that plagues him in Rome?

9. At the beginning of the novel, Margherita makes it very clear that she is too savvy to be bamboozled by the likes of Raphael. Why, then, does she allow herself to be charmed by the sleazy Sebastiano Luciani, even going so far as to dismiss Raphael's warnings about him: "Raphael must be wrong about him . . . Sebastiano simply could not be guilty of those . . . awful things." Why does she sit with him, unchaperoned, at the pope's party?

10. When it becomes clear that the kidnapping plan has backfired and Raphael has not resumed his prolific work pace, Agostino Chigi suggests to Pope Leo that it's time to confess the plot to Raphael. Is Chigi motivated by compassion here, or by the same self-interest that motivates Leo and Bibbiena? Why does the pope agree to do it?

11. Only when Raphael lies dying and Margherita is in dire straits do we discover that her relations with her family have deteriorated to the point where "They did not want her back now . . . she could never go home to the bakery or the life she once had lived there." Why do you think the author skips over the potentially juicy story of the Luti family's disintegration?

12. Margherita's motivation for destroying Raphael's new will—which leaves everything to her—and replacing it with the old one, which bequeaths Raphael's estate to Giulio Romano, is left a mystery. Can you decipher a meaning behind Margherita's self-punishing decision?

13. How does Donato gently reveal to Margherita both Antonio's duplicity and Raphael's genius? Why does he betray his brother's secret?

14. Why does Raphael blame the supposed celibacy of the clergy for some of his troubles?

15. Why do you think the author includes the subplot involving Maria Bibbiena and her chief guard? Does the guard's attention and tenderness humanize Maria in your view? What point is the author making about unexpressed attraction?

16. What parting advice does Leonardo da Vinci offer Raphael about how to handle his relationship with Margherita? Is it wise?

17. Does Raphael's pervasive self-doubt and the episodes of self-pity that verge on wallowing—bemoaning his life "with no family, no love, no reason even to exist, but only to paint and work to the point of exhaustion and blindness! To create only for the desire of others, on and on . . . day after day, then return home completely alone!", for example—make him a more accessible character? Why or why not?